MW01123623

Split Embers

by Christopher J. Ridgeway

Cover by: Zach Raw

Dedicated to **Mac Turnage** and JK Rowling, **authors
who both inspired me greatly to write this book.**

**Special thanks to Bryan, Nixon, Nick, Taylor and Bo whom
all helped me at times when I was stuck while writing.
Also thanks anyone who read this story during its early
days on the internet!**

**Also thanks Adam Dwyer, for being the editor of the first
five chapters. Here's to you man!**

**Also, I'm dedicating this to anyone who's dealing with
lonely times, or who has lost contact with some of their
friends- may you press onwards and stay strong!**

Revised edition:
Edits by Nick King.
Minor additions by Chris Ridgeway

Split Embers
Table of Contents

Prologue ----------------Page 5

Part I-Sparks of the Mystical Flame
Arc I
Chapter 1 ----------------Page 18
Chapter 2 ----------------Page 48
Chapter 3 ----------------Page 76
Chapter 4 ----------------Page 98
Chapter 5 ----------------Page 116
Arc II
Chapter 6 ----------------Page 129
Chapter 7 ----------------Page 142
Chapter 8 ----------------Page 163
Chapter 9 ----------------Page 178
Chapter 10----------------Page 199
Chapter 11----------------Page 217
Chapter 12----------------Page 238
Chapter 13----------------Page 253
Chapter 14----------------Page 267
Chapter 15----------------Page 274
Arc III
Chapter 16----------------Page 281
Chapter 17----------------Page 300
Chapter 18----------------Page 313
Part II- Dark World
Arc IV
Chapter 19----------------Page 328
Chapter 20----------------Page 343
Chapter 21----------------Page 355
Chapter 22----------------Page 373
Arc V
Chapter 23----------------Page 401
Chapter 24----------------Page 420
Chapter 25----------------Page 439
Chapter 26----------------Page 457

4
Arc VI

Chapter 27-----------------Page 477
Chapter 28-----------------Page 497
Chapter 29-----------------Page 518
Chapter 30-----------------Page 536
Epilogue   -----------------Page 556

<u>Prologue</u>

May 8th, 1776

Allanon Remus may have been in a self-imposed exile, but that didn't mean he was unaware of what was going on around him. Across the ocean, the Thirteen Colonies were rebelling from the Crown of the British Empire, but that was the least of his worries. Allanon was an old man who was much older than he looked. He was around long before those colonies were even formed, but this was due to his sheer amount of power in the art of Magic. The few other wizards still alive after the Great Purge never admitted it, but Allanon was more powerful than at least half of them. That is why they came to him last week.

They needed him and he still denied them as he had done before. He refused to take part in this war, for Alexander was a great man. Sure, he'd done some terrible things, however he was not evil. Allanon openly refused to take part in the war and that is why he exiled himself from all other people. He knew Alexander had grown too powerful and had unwittingly done unforgivable things.

Still, Alexander was Allanon's friend. Allanon could strike down the man no more than if Alexander were his own son, one who'd many times over proven himself to be a man. Alexander himself used to be thought of as the savior of all Wizards. Now, he was considered a threat to all of them.

Rumors spread like wildfire of his exploits among those permitted to know of sorcery's secret world. The point is that it was hard to separate fact or fiction anymore. He was certainly powerful enough for any of them, but things weren't black and white. Allanon could not blame Alexander for his discontent with the way things were, nor when he openly opposed the other wizards.

There was certainly abuse of power among the council, though the details were the sorts of things no one could prove; they ranged from small things like gambling and using magic to effects odds to things as big as rumors that one of the council members brainwashed his wife into marrying him. Herein lay constant dilemma.

Alexander was breaking many wizard laws and if things continued the whole world would soon know of wizards. If the world at large knew of them there would surely be instability and wars to follow. The rest of the world was not ready for them, something the wizard Council could agree on.

Alexander didn't, however; he believed the world had a right to know of the Wizards and openly opposed the Wizard Council without regard for any of their laws or attempts to keep them secret. Even more disconcerting was that every time they managed to finally succeed in killing Alexander, he did the biggest taboo of all: He rose again from the dead.

Somehow, Alexander had achieved immortality through reincarnation. When he "died" he simply reincarnated as a child under new parents each time, also retaining all of his memories of his past lives and their power and spells. Thus, none could figure out how to permanently kill him.

Admar walked into the council chamber, prompting Allanon to sigh, "I've told you before. I will not participate in this war." Allanon was firm on his beliefs, nothing they said capable of moving him from his position. Admar then did something surprising, kneeling before Allanon and saying,"Allanon. As head of the Council, I ask you one final request."

Allanon was intrigued. "You needn't kneel before me, old friend," he said, "I still emphasize my neutrality. What do you wish of me?"

Admar nodded and replied, "We've found a way to hopefully end Alexander once and for all."

He paused for what felt like a long time, gesturing that it was hard for him to say anything until he continued,

"However, this will come at the cost of our own lives."

Allanon stood immediately, realizing

the severity of these words. If the Council were to die, Allanon would be one of the last living wizards in the world. Many of the remaining wizards had died in the purge many years ago or died fighting Alexander in recent years: losing the Council would be a huge blow to already dwindling numbers.

Admar sighingly continued, "We've found a spell that will split his life force into five, upon death. Thus, he will reincarnate as five children instead of one. He will retain none of his old memories; furthermore, his power will remain dormant for a time. We also even managed to delay the time of his reincarnation, though for how long we are not sure.

"We believe when his power is no longer dormant within the five children, they will be easily recognizable as his re-incarnations. You well know Alexander's greatest gift to be of summoning, so we believe it highly likely their first spell will constitute that."

This surprised Allanon greatly since never in the history of Wizards did anyone have summoning as their first spell, as it was far too advanced.

Admar resumed his proposition, saying, "The Council asks that, upon the day you find them, you become their mentor so that they hopefully won't be as misguided as Alexander. These are our last wishes: you may train them as you wish."

Admar seemed to fall silent after this, Allanon knowing exactly what he thought. Even the head of the Council knew things had grown far out of his control, both against Alexander and among the Council Members. There were no other options, as this was their last resort. Allanon noddingly replied, "I accept your request."

Admar stood up and bowed proclaiming, "May the Magics bless you for years to come", then proceeding with that to leave the room.

River Avon

At any other time this would've been the perfect night for a stroll, but in Alexander's case he could not enjoy even the glow of the moon on the water's surface. All he could do was run and kill to survive the night.

"After him!" Frustration and anxiety hung heavy in the words of pursuers as Alexander ran, a cavalry of battle-hardened Wizards nipping at his heels. With a swing of his ornate ten-foot Zweihander, he cut through more than just the night air; blood painted the road in front and behind him as he slew every enemy– every former comrade.

Several Wizards came for his life but none would succeed, let alone survive. Wizards attacked him from throughout the land, England, Scotland, Ireland, Germany, Poland and other like nations being pursuant of him. No matter the part of Europe they came from, they always met the same fate: death at the hands of Alexander.

A wizard from Germany named Gerald had managed to kill him, momentarily spawning Jessica from Alexander. She retained all the memories of being Alexander, but had to learn once again all the spells that lay dormant to her in memory. She killed Gerald, only to be slain herself by Alexander's former pupil Ciri. It was always an interesting idea that the British-born Alexander had taken Ciri in from a place that would someday come to be known as Poland. Apparently mistaken, he thought he had killed her during one of his previous lives.

After Jessica was slain, Alexander's next life was once again as male looking oddly the same as his original first life. He took it as a sign of tonight, the night of ten thousand corpses.

Wizards, their numbers overwhelming, dropped left and right. For Alexander there stood only one motivation: ideals ignored and positions bought... corruption.

He was no better and as the self-taught wielder of all spells, even he was seen as a problem. The Council had decided his fate from the moment he set foot with drawn sword upon the steps of the great Council hall– it was everyone against a single man.

Alexander remembered what he had done in his first life. The year was 1100 AD;

he warned the council that he'd noticed their corruption and knowing he couldn't prove it, he revealed his plans instead- to reveal the world of Wizards to all outsiders. The Council forbade it.

He simply said that day, "In that case, I'm looking at a bunch of dead men right now" and left the council chambers, that being his only warning. It was now 1776 and so much had happened since.

"Take my life, should it please you. I will still rise again to face the lot of you blinded old fools!"

He stopped, turning and running his hand along the runes on his sword then stabbing into the air in front of him, impaling a female Mage. Her tortured expression didn't fit her youthful face. In truth she was far older than she appeared, having learned a frowned-upon spell that could prolong her youth.

It was none other than Ciri herself who he stabbed. When Alexander first met her she was but a docile child at fourteen years of life. It saddened him to know he had been forced to take her life, even now not immune to the resultant emotions... not that he'd choose otherwise.

"You... idiot...", she weakly whispered as he slid the blade out of her gut. He would then slash at the field beyond her, her blood soon to feed the soil as it ran down each blade of grass.

Several battle-ready men and women, all too young to die in this stupid war, writhed in agony as the flames from his blade set the field ablaze.

"None of you shall fight me as true Wizards?", he askingly raised his voice to the heavens. "Have you all lost your nerve or do you plan to keep hiding, that the world may be ignorant of your powers or their own potential?"

An older male Wizard rose from the ground, his own earth spells grabbing Alexander and pulling him down as he rose above the enraged swordsman. Alexander would have none of it, stabbing the ground beneath him in self-defense and causing the old Wizard to double over. When the illusion broke, Alexander gripped and pulled up his sword from his foe's chest, him already dying while spitting blood.

"You only know trickery, deceit, and lies! What good are you to your cause?"

He wrenched back his sword, the skull-shaped pummel forged in the image of his first foe ramming into the face of an enemy who had appeared from behind shrouded in darkness- he then pushed the Wizard into his own void. As the dark abyss morphed and twisted around them, Alexander slashed his assailant in the neck and left him to bleed out in the darkness.

He ran for the Council chambers and kicked open the doors, then seeing himself was standing on a magic seal on the chamber floor. This talisman in particular was one he didn't recognize, even as Alexander knew nearly every spell in existence. All of a sudden he could not move, out of the shadows arriving four council members and Admar himself.

They began chanting a spell in Latin. Alexander screamed, yet somehow any noise he attempted was drowned out by the loud noise coming from beneath his feet as a red light shined throughout the room. Alexander could feel the strength being ripped out of him bit by bit and just as quickly as the lights shined, his body completely vanished. In the radius surrounding where he once stood the Council members all fell as dead.

At last, the spell had been completed.

September 1st, 1976

Allanon stood his ground holding his magical staff as his hand bled down. A cold sweat beat his brow, yet he dared not blink nor move. To his right was his second apprentice, "John Smith"; an overly common name for such an uncommon man, to be sure. John specialized in healing spells, but that made him far from a pushover; he could cut the hamstrings of a man with the same magic he'd use for medical techniques. He could poison someone in the exact same manner. John had short, blonde hair and brown eyes, his white skin possessing freckles on his face and arms.

Of course, it wasn't John that Allanon was worried about. The two of them had fought long and hard, but they were finally down to the last man before them, the evil magical user Zachariah Gordon. He wore red and black armor and had short brown hair, the magical army having revolvers much like other humans. The difference was that they gave off magical energy.

Allanon and John didn't use any kind of guns, the former preferring his magical staff to aid him in spell casting and the latter using his wand for assistance. John's wand was smaller in size than a staff, but just as powerful. Ever the old-fashioned Allanon preferred his armament, perhaps simply a creature of habit.

Right now that hardly mattered, as both of them were forced to use everything within them to go up against these enchanted guns. Zachariah destroyed the guns and the bodies of his fallen, no evidence left behind and his men's weapons futile against him. John shouted to the vile mage, "Well? We've killed your men! Now it's just you and the two of us, scum! Prepare yourself!"

Zack allowed an evil smirk over his face as he darkly intoned, "You have already fallen under my spell."

Allanon raised his staff and dispelled

the illusion Zack had cast over them to reveal Zack already behind them, the figure before them disappearing. Allanon turned and cast pure divine energy at Zack, the latter deflecting it with a rune-carved sword. Zack was using a sword as his own sort of wand.

Zachariah summoned, "Projectile magic is of little use on me; you'll have to be cleverer than that!"

John replied, "How's this for clever... I'm willing to bet you have no other magic except illusions and that is why you've not used anything else on us so far... even as far back as when we had to fight your men!"

Zack evilly grinned as he said, "In my homeland, they call me Zachariah the Million Butcher. Do you really think illusions alone got me that title?"

This truly surprised Allanon: if Zack had truly committed genocide on such a mass scale, why hadn't he heard of this man before?

Zack sent a massive wave of dark magic at both of them. Allanon stepped in front of John and deflected it with a powerful divine shield! When the dark magic dispersed, John sent a blast of his healing magic at the opponent in its poison form. Such a dose was enough to kill an elephant, Zack allowing it to hit him for some reason.
John responded to Zack's earlier proclamation, "I'm glad you're such a fool.

16

You won't be any further trouble to us!"

Zack laughed as his body flickered for a moment and once more turned solid, his body unaffected. Enraged, John sent the spell a few more times and Zack smiled as he ran right for them. Allanon could not allow this to go on, for he'd have to cast it. Allanon quietly uttered but one word: "Wish."

With that Zack lay beaten, entangled in some sort of magical trap binding him together.

John smacked the man in the face and spat on him yelling, "Where do you come from! What lands would dare attack us?"

Zack laughed as he return spit right onto John's face, cackling, "It's no place you could ever possibly reach. Let me guess, you call this land Earth, do you not?"

Allanon replied, "What is it you are implying?"

Zack laughed, "It's so funny that you think yours is the only Earth out there... there's another. You could call it... 'Dark World', if you like."

Noticing his apprentice's growing determination Allanon ordered to John, "I see that look in your eyes. Don't do it. We need him alive- he knows something."

Zack laughed and bluffed, "You know

what I find hilarious? You two weren't the first ones I saw in this land. Do either of you know a man by the name of Garth? Funny name, really; for someone with no magic, anyways. I'm sure he's still screaming out there, somewhere.

"The spell I cast on him will see to that; his death will be long and agonizing. It sends chills down my spine to know how long it'll take for his misery to finally come to an end."

John became enraged and grabbed Zack's sword, impaling its' owner with it. The butcher began gasping, before his body went limp and finally perished.

Allanon was taken aback by this all happening at once, yelling in kind, "What did you do!"

Enraged, John turned, "Did you know?"

Allanon remained silent; little did he know Garth was John's brother.

John responded, "Yes or no! Did you know?"

Allanon nodded slowly, "I performed a spell to make the death quicker... his suffering is over."

John began casting his poison spell at Allanon, who deflected it. Their battle began for an unknown time thus.

****

On another Earth a ghost fell into a castle room. The apparition took form, flesh encircling his body as he became. It was Zack Gordon, who said to something unknown, "Your majesty. I suggest a better force be sent this time- we were met with more resistance than expected."

The King before him nodded and said, "I will do as you suggest. Soon, this invasion will be but a distant memory and their lands will be ours."

Part I- Sparks of the Mystical Flame

Chapter 1 – Rivalries and Friendships

2012

For Maxwell Schneider, life wasn't easy; he was bullied a lot as a kid and after he graduated high school didn't do much with his life. Max stood at 6'1" tall, wearing long brown hair and a short goatee on his face, having blue eyes and pale skin. He was slim only because of genetics, meaning building muscle was difficult for him. Right now it wasn't his lack of physique that mattered- it was the fact he couldn't think of any good story inspiration of any kind.

He decided to watch some sci-fi movie reviews, as he was bored and figured he'd listen to peoples' opinions on recent cinema. He spent a lot of time on the internet looking up songs and watching movies, the undercurrent somewhat like he'd been wasting his life away. He'd nonetheless been writing things on the side as a hobby. He loved writing new ideas down and fleshing them out into stories, but he never finished any of them.

Maybe he just lost interest too quickly. For a long time it was merely of interest until one day it hit him. He was inspired by hearing of an author who'd become famous overnight for her story about a robot who felt the need to fit into a world full of humans who despised him. Max knew right then what he wanted to do: to finish one of his stories.

Max looked through his old works and found the perfect one, a story about a fictional Wizard who defeated a powerful dragon. This Wizard became famous, but realized it came at a cost: people became dependent on him to the extent that he didn't have time for his ailing son, which lead to the son's death. He therefore blamed the people for it, becoming an evil Wizard who sought vengeance on the humans who took advantage of him. In the end it was his best friend who had to redeem him at the cost of his own life. It was a somewhat tragic story, but was very heartfelt. The story was a huge hit, quickly becoming a best-seller and winning many awards. Having accomplished that, Max was quite proud of himself. He was now sitting away at his computer suffering writer's block, his brother then knocking on the door.

"Open up," he called.

Max sighed, "Gimme a minute, I'm watching a video."

His brother sighed, "It'll only take a minute; just hurry up."

Max finished the video and got up to open the door, his younger brother only slightly shorter than him with short brown hair. He handed Max a piece of mail, the latter asking,

"This came in the mail. What is it?"

Max shrugged and said, "I dunno. I'm expecting a video game fight-pad soon but that doesn't look like what this is, unless it's really flat and paper shaped."

He chuckled. He opened the letter and read it:*"Dear Maxwell Schneider,*

We are pleased to inform you that you have been offered a scholarship for Allan's University for the gifted. Should you wish to receive said scholarship, the location of the university is available on our website.

Term begins March 1st. We accept a response by no later than February 23rd. Enclosed is a list of materials you should bring with you upon arrival and induction.

Yours sincerely,

Allan Remus,

Headmaster"

Max was a little surprised. "I didn't ask to join any kind of college."

His younger brother scoffed a bit, "Probably junk mail" said dismissively.

Max shrugged in reply, "It's possible. But, we just moved here to Florida from Oklahoma, so it's odd they'd know we live here already."

His brother laughed, "Not really, you wrote that book. Maybe you have some creepy stalkers or something."

Max pushed his brother a little before replying, "Don't joke. Anyways, thanks." Max closed the door on his brother and locked it, sitting down on his bed.

"How interesting", he thought.

He decided not to think too much of it, but then when he got online his friend sent him a message: "Dude, I just got invited to some weird school."

Max put the palm of his hand over his face for a moment, then replied, "Was it called 'Allan's School for the Gifted' or something like that?"

His friend Knoll replied, "Yep. That's the one." The funny story of their friendship was that Max was surfing on the net when he decided to try a voice acting role for a minor production. Knoll did too, and they both made it in through the accessibility of the production company's internet audition. The cartoon was eventually canceled, but Max and Knoll had been internet buddies ever since. Max remembers the first time he met Knoll online, his first comment being on his weird first name.

Knoll shrugged it off because you can't really choose what your parents name you; he liked being unique anyways, which was fair enough. They entered into a voice chat on the computer. They'd never seen what each other looked like even with all this time, but it didn't matter since they were just online buddies anyways.

Knoll was the first to speak. "How'd you get in?", he asked.

Max replied, "Oh yeah, good question; It probably does list a reason somewhere on here."

Max looked through the letter, itself specifying that his 'High Achievement in Literature' earned him the scholarship.

Max sighed, "I bet it's a scam or something. So, what about you?"

Knoll replied, "Because of my historical fiction series I wrote."

Amused, Max replied, "Oh you mean 'Grove of Silence?' That was a good read, though I prefer to write fantasy type stuff myself. But no worries; I know how your folks are."

Knoll replied, "Fiction and fairytales leave nothing to the sense of history: in my opinion the best story is the history of our world"

Max laughed, "Such a boring answer, but that is so you!"

Knoll replied, "Actually, my sister visited the campus once."

Max inquired, "Really? Well, I guess it does list a website here. I guess it can't hurt for me to look it up."

After a little bit of reading and doing research, Max sighed. "Well I'll be damned, looks pretty legit to me. Says here's it's a boarding school-based university, with a school uniform and everything."

Suddenly Knoll's mother started calling for him to eat, Knoll sighing, "I gotta go."

Max replied, "No problem, see ya later dude."

Max opened his door and told his mother about what had happened.

She was quite surprised and said, "You're sure this isn't a scam?"

Max showed her the website and told about his online friend's sister having been to the campus. The school was apparently for those with a high IQ, some sort of talent in the arts, etc. It was also all-expenses paid in its' scholarship.

Max's mom heaved, "Well, whatever you wanna do is fine Max. If you really are as tired of staying at home all the time as you've said, maybe give this a shot. But it's up to you; I can't think for you."

Max nodded, "I'll have to think about it."

It did take a few days, but he decided to go. It wasn't like he had any real life friends to begin with since he'd only moved to Florida about six months ago, so it couldn't hurt. Knoll was going too, so he'd at least know somebody on the campus even if this would be his first time meeting him in real life. They exchanged pictures so they'd know what each other looked like. Knoll was average in build- not skinny but not fat either- with somewhat short brown hair and brown eyes.

When he arrived at the Massachusetts school the first thing he noticed was the size of the campus. There was a lot of room to walk from large building to large building, with the biggest being what he could only assume was the main one. He also noticed the dorms, the males' dark blue and the females' light blue. Both of these were located on the west side of the campus.

He was in his school uniform, which for males was a dark blue suit with a blue tie. For females the top was the same as the males, but for the bottom would be a light blue plaid-skirt and black knee-high socks. Both were required to wear the same black, business-style shoes that looked the same on both genders. He also noticed most students didn't look any older than their thirties.

His mom wished him luck and he hugged her as he got off of the bus. He'd told her he wanted to go inside by himself and she respected that, but he was very nervous. Just sitting there wondering wasn't going to change anything regarding the mystery of this place, so him buzzing the gates to open allowed him to walk successfully on campus.Max walked throughout and saw people talking and socializing, deciding it was best to head for his dorm first so he could get to his room to unpack. He headed into the doorway to the dorm, but suddenly bumped into another student.

His peer began to apologize, "Oh sorry, I didn't mean", then recognizing Max said in a sarcastic tone, "Oh well if it isn't Maxwell, gracing us with his almighty presence!"

Max looked at the student and replied wearily, "Oh, brother. Give it a rest."

The student in front of Max was Zachariah Gordon, who possessed platinum blonde hair with hazel eyes. In full uniform he also wore glasses and had a lean yet average build. This student was something of a rival to Max, for around the same time Max released his book Zack released his as well. Since then they would often contact each other online, having a friendly competition over whose book would get the most sales since both books were best-sellers that year. In the end Max won awards for his book, but Zack didn't. Max considered it might make sense that Zack might resent that some. He laughed a little and said, "Relax, I'm just kidding with you."

Max relievedly sighed and said, "Well I hadn't heard from you since I won those awards, so I thought you were mad at me."

Zackk remarked, "Well I have to admit... I was a little sore on the subject. But that's all in the past now!"

Max smiled and said, "That's good. I look forward to competing with you in my writing again soon! But I'd like to have a friend or two around here. Since I know you, this is rather convenient for me. Also, one of my other friends who I haven't met in real life yet, Knoll, is around here too. Maybe the three of us can hang out sometime."

Zack nodded and replied coolly, "Perhaps so, but I can't exactly promise you anything. Anyways, I gotta go, but it was nice seeing you."

Max nodded and replied easily, "Same, same."They shook hands and Zack walked away. Max again sighed, thinking on how he couldn't help but feel he dodged a bullet.

He continued head upstairs with his stuff until he reached the fourth floor, where he saw his room.

"Room 409. Looks just like every room in this hall… Guess that kinda makes sense, since it is a dorm; not like they'd look any different from each other from the hallway."

He opened the door to the room, where inside was a bunk bed on left and on right a TV next to a cello. Viewable from the second you opened the door was a window on the back wall that had the blinds open, where one could see the campus below. This room faced the front, so you could see anyone coming inside to the building from the entrance.

It was certainly beautiful outside and thankfully the sun wasn't glaring into the window too much. In the center of the room sat a very lean young man with long black hair and brown eyes. He was about 5'6" with pale skin wearing school uniform, even though it was being worn kind of sloppily. He was sitting on a black desk chair that faced the window, where on the desk lay tons of sheet music.

The young man lightly strummed an electric guitar a few times, seeming not to notice what was going on around him. He then performed a few guitar riffs, while his amp was carefully made to be not too loud so as not to disrupt the rest of the dorm. At this excellence

Max grinned," Awesome playing man".

The young man, surprised, looked up at Max and said, "Oh. So, you're my new roommate. Thanks, man. Name's Leonard, but everyone calls me Leon."

Max nodded and replied, "Maxwell, but everyone calls me Max."

Leon grinned, "Not to sound awkward or anything, but I can already tell we're going to be good friends."

Max glanced outside as he set his stuff next to the bunkbed. He could see a girl with pink hair talking to a guy with blue hair down below. He found it funny but didn't pay it much bother, then grinning back at Leon and replying amicably, "Thanks. I'm always up for making new friends... So, you in a band or something?"

Leon nodded, "Was, but we split up not too long ago. It was on good terms though, I just had to get on with my life and we just decided to head different directions creatively."

Max replied, "Well, I've always wanted to be in a band. That would be really cool."

Leon was intrigued. "Oh yeah?", he asked, "What do you play?" "I don't play anything but I can sing."

Leon smiled, "Lay it on me."

Max began singing one of his favorite songs, "Child of Sweet."

Leon whistled and said, "That wasn't bad. Sure, why not? We'll come up with something really good, sometime. I've got to go to class in a little bit though, I was just playing some while I'm waiting. What's your first class today? Since we're roommates, we might as well get to know each other a little bit. Oh, I don't care which bunk you want by the way."

Max laughed, "Well, bottom bunk is fine, so if I roll out of bed the fall won't hurt. Anyways, my first class is going to be fencing apparently." He'd only attended that class twice in the past; he wasn't necessarily a natural at it, but found it fun perhaps on the notion of his favorite entertainment hosting sword fights.

Leon laughed, "Wow, so is mine. I'm actually on the fencing team, you know."

Max replied, "No fooling? Well, I've had a little bit of fencing lessons but I'm not that good yet. I'd like to be though. Sounds like a lot of fun. Oh, that reminds me, what did you get into this college for anyways?"

Leon smiled, "Won a Grammy for Hard Rock and Heavy Metal as a solo performer a while ago and also played the cello at a concert for the Queen of England."

Max laughed, "Funny joke on that last part."

Leon smiled, "Who's joking? I got the photographs to prove it." He pulled out the picture and there was Elizabeth. Max sat down on the bed. "Holy crap! Dude... that's... freakin' amazing!"

Leon laughed, "You think so? Well, a lot of people here are pretty talented or smart. That's just the kind of college you're going to. What about you, huh?"

Max told him the whole story of how he got in.

Leon smiled, "Not bad. I'd love to read your book sometime, but it won't be for a while though, cuz I'm kinda busy with well... you know. This place. College life does that to a guy."

Max shrugged, "I wouldn't know. After I graduated high school, I kinda just sat around at home a lot. Embarrassing, really. I mean, I did some writing and voice acting but yeah."

Leon replied," Well, I'm a sophomore here actually. I was one of the first students to join when they changed their policies to allow students of the 'arts,' as they call 'em. They've only been doing that for about a year. Before that, it was just students with high IQs. Not sure why they changed their minds though, but I hear it was just to get more students." "Yeah, kinda odd though, since this place seems so high-class. Whatever, guess it doesn't matter too much."

Leon smiled, "Nope, I guess not. Looks like it's almost time for fencing class. Let's start heading out huh?"

Max nodded, "After you, dude. Lead the way."

When they arrived to fencing class the room was very nice. Apparently fencing team members were also required to attend the class in order to help those who were attending the class for lessons. There was also only one fencing class, so naturally the class was relatively big. The room was long and wide with plain gray concrete floors and the walls were plain white, but with various flags adorned on their upper walls. There was also a closet door on the opposite side of the room to the entrance.

Leon walked to a young man with short brown hair, a brown goatee and dark blue eyes. He was somewhat rounder in build but looked like had a bit of muscle to him as well. "Oh hey, Leon. What's up?" Connor seemed to have an Irish accent. It was subtle, but it existed.

Leon replied, "Not much, Connor. You'll be happy to know you aren't the newest student in this class anymore, this here is Max."

Connor nodded, "Hey, Max." he extended his hand out and Max shook it.

Then there was a brief moment of awkward silence and Leon said, "I guess we should introduce Max to a few of the people here, huh?"

Connor nodded, "Sure, I guess so. Max, that girl over there is Syanne. I don't talk to her much, but...", he paused and caught himself a little bit.

Leon finished for him, adding, "What Connor is too nice to say is... Syanne is more than a little bit of a bitch. I would avoid her if you can. I can't because she's the second-in-command of the fencing team and I'm on the team, too. It doesn't help that she sticks with the team captain when we decide to split the team into two groups for training matches against each other, because that means I get put in charge of the other Team since I'm third-in-charge of the team. Makes the two teams a bit unbalanced, I think."

Syanne was curvy but slender with dense physical proportions, endowment-wise. She had long, curly brown hair, was really pale and had blue eyes. Right away Max noticed a guy talking to a lot of the students, a guy who looked roughly his own age. He was 5'10", heavy and athletic as well as muscular. He had blue eyes, light skin, dark brownish red hair, a scar on both lips but on opposite sides and scar a under his left eye. Max immediately pointed him out to ask Leon who he was. "That guy is Jericho. He's proud of his Irish heritage and likes to drink sometimes, so we always have to make sure he's sober before the big matches. He's the team captain. I'd be careful of him, he's got a huge temper and it's not always fun to deal with. But his leadership skills are quite good."

They walked to the closet to get their sparring gear. "We usually start out with a light spar to see what skill-set we're all at. I can assume you bought your gear, right?"

Max smacked his own forehead, "I completely forgot!"

Leon laughed, "It's okay we got a few spares, just in case."

Max nodded, "I'm worried about this Jericho guy. He sounds like a dick and if I'm not too careful I could see myself getting in a fight with that guy." "If you don't pay him much bother you should be fine. Besides, he can think he's a badass and all that, but if he tries anything on me or my friends he's in trouble." A voice behind him suddenly smirked in utterance, "Really... I'd like to see you try, boy."

They turned around and right behind them was Jericho laughing, "Really. If you're up to it you can spar with me anytime. I'm the Captain for a reason and you know it."

Leon sighed, "Look, I'm kinda in a bad mood, so can we just cut the crap right now?" "Okay, whatever, dude."

He walked off smiling, but you could see his eyes were like looking into fiery pools. Max was quickly nervous of the guy. He was very intimidating to say the least, but it was odd how he backed off so quickly. He didn't seem intimidated by Leon in any way, and yet strangely backed off from the confrontation without a second thought.

Max noticed Leon was remaining quiet as he walked off to join the others, leaving himself and Connor at the closet area. Max turned to Connor and asked, "What was that all about?" "Hey, it's not really my place to say. I don't really wanna get mixed up in that. You want my advice?" "Uh, yeah. Wouldn't hurt." "It's probably best if we both stayed out of it." With that Connor rejoined the others and Max sighed as also did. Knoll walked in saying, "Sorry I'm late guys."

Nobody seemed to notice him even talking, so Max walked up to him and laughed, "You're not. You just barely made it in time."

Knoll smiled, "Oh, hey Max! Nice to finally meet you in real life."

Max was surprised, "So you're taking fencing classes too?"

Knoll nodded, "Yes, I am." Before anything else could be said on the matter, the instructor came inside, saying, "Alright, quiet everyone. Opening spars will now begin. I've chosen whom you'll be sparring for today, so everyone align in this order."

Max began to realize how many people were in the class by how long the list went on, until he heard one that stood out. "Max will be sparring Jericho."

Max thought this was a joke and his gut dropped as the Instructor said, "These matches will be a 5-point match each. Salute."

Everyone brought the blade up to their mask at attention and sliced downwards and point the blade downward in salute.

After a while it reached time for Max's match, so he stood in front of Jericho. "You kidding me?" Jericho smirked, "Try and keep up." Max laughed nervously in reply, "I will." Jericho smirked again, "Don't blink or you'll miss it."

Max was nervous but didn't want to seem like a coward, so he taunted, "I'll try not to trip on your ego."

Suddenly the instructor barked, "Play. Elé"! Jericho moved forward quickly and then gradually moves forward slowly. "Hmph, at least your footing is right."He began tapping Max's foil repeatedly with his own, which naturally created a very annoying-sounding tink. Max was concentrating deeply because he was too scared and nervous to talk at all at this point.

He attempted to knock Jericho's blade out of the way, but Jericho smacked him on the wrist with his foil. "Point!"

Then they went again. The exact same thing occurred. "Point!"

The third time, Jericho was doing it again. This time, the same thing occurred, but Max tried to power through it to attempt a sideswipe and Jericho lowered his blade, bringing it back up and doing the chin nod by smacking him there. Before they knew it the five points occurred, so Max asked for a rematch.

"Sure, I'll rematch anytime."

They went again. The other people were still doing their matches throughout the room at the same time anyway, so this was fine. After the next five points Max was very winded, so he sat for a moment, took a deep breath and got back up responding, "I want another rematch."

The instructor questioned it but Jericho invited, "I'll accept any rematch."

Before they knew it, people were watching the hard-headed Max lose and demand rematches repeatedly. Sometimes he'd get winded but after short breathers ask for another rematch. The hour ended with nothing else happening on that day and Max lost every time.

The instructor looked at the time and said, "Next time, Max, you will be limited on matters such as this. We can't allow this to occur again."

Jericho smirked, "It won't. This kid is pathetic."

Knoll defended him, "He's got more backbone then I'll bet you will ever have."

Jericho gave Knoll an evil look, but did nothing. Max sighed and got up, put his stuff in the closet and headed for the dorm.

Leon walked with him outside. "You alright man?"

Max sighed, "Losing sucks. A lot. Guess I'm just really bummed that I lost."

Leon replied, "Don't sweat it, man, you're still new and he's the team captain, what else did you expect to happen?"

Max shrugged, "I just thought that after that many matches I could at least win one time... One time would be enough to make me happy this time. But I lost. Every. Single. Time."

Leon sighed, frustrated, "I've been having a bad day too. It's been hard dealing with the fact my girlfriend is back home while I'm here, and I also had some punk trying to start shit earlier this morning before you arrived. But I'm not going to let it ruin my whole day."

Max sighed, "You're right. I'll just have to get it off my mind.""So what's your next class?"

Max looked at his syllabus, saying, "Theater apparently."

Leon replied, "Mine's Biology. See ya around, man. Just don't let the day get to ya." "Same to you dude. See ya."

**************Today was the best day of Shakira's life, so she woke up with a smile early in the day. This was the first day that new students would be joining , so she couldn't wait to see what kind of new people would arrive. Shakira got into her school uniform which was tight-fitting due to her build. She was built curvy with a little extra weight, but by no means was she fat.

She had pale skin, large breasts and slightly wide hips. Her pink hair was long and curly, but kept her bangs with abnormally big curls that were very round. She was very attractive in the eyes of a lot of the males there, but few guys could ever keep up with her because of how much energy she always had. She didn't mind it, because she was known for hosting really fun parties.

As Shakira walked down to the bottom floor of the dorm a girl bumped into her.

Shakira quickly smiled and said, "Oh, hi there! My name is Shakira and I made some cupcakes for the new students. If you'd like any, please help yourself."

The girl smiled, having just walked in and not even in uniform. She was wearing blue jeans and a light blue jacket with patch on the left sleeve of a cloud with a lightning bolt coming out of it. She had black hair with dark blue highlights and was slender in build with small breasts.

The girl replied, "Hey wassup. I'm Rally Valentine." "I'm Shakira Nomura! You want some cupcakes?" "Sure, I guess so, they do look pretty good."

She ate the cupcake and Shakira smiled, replying, "I made them myself and everybody loves my cooking. I also am great at throwing parties! You should come to one sometime!" "Sounds like a lot of fun. I got into this College because I made the Billboard list a few times for my singing. What about you?" "Really? I can sing too! I made it in here for my IQ of 170!"

Rally dropped the cupcake on the floor as she exclaimed, "One.. one-seventy?"

Shakira smiled, "I get that a lot, I don't have the foggiest why!"

She giggled as her bubbly attitude continued.

Rally rolled her eyes while trying to be as polite as she could and replied, "Well it was nice meeting you but I gotta go and all... Big day since it's my first day of school here, so see ya!"

Shakira nodded and waved at Rally as she walked away, undaunted by the fact Rally was obviously nervous. Shakira just pretended not to notice, certain they'd meet again anyways. She suddenly remembered that she left her keys in the room. She ran upstairs and went in, only to see Rally putting her stuff on the floor. Rally looked surprised and startled as she saw Shakira. "No way! You're my new roommate? Awesome!"

Rally laughed nervously, "Apparently I am. I had wondered why the door was unlocked... So you been here long?"

Shakira nodded,"Kinda. I'm a junior here!"

Shakira closed the door as Rally started dressing into her school uniform. As Rally was getting changed she decided to keep conversation with Shakira, asking,

"So what classes you taking here Shakira?"

Shakira laughed, "Well, mostly biology, physics, calculus and things like that. But that's for side hobbies to keep my Daddy happy. I actually want to be an event planner for parties and weddings and stuff!"

Rally sheepishly grinned a little, "You really are smart, huh? I'm just taking the Theater major and the required stuff. I was really popular in my hometown, you know. Popular in school, too."

Shakira smiled, "You'll fit right in, then, because everybody knows me here!"

Rally smiled very happily.

"And matter-of-fact," Shakira added, "Everybody around here likes to go to my parties and everything, but most of the people I know just talk to me sometimes, so I only have a few close friends and they're all guys."

Rally shrugged, "I seem to get along better with guys anyways so that'll be just fine. People tell me I'm a tomboy anyways and I guess I kinda am."

She'd just finished changing her clothes into the school uniform when Shakira tugged on her arm and opened the door.

"I gotta introduce you to my friends, Rally!"

Rally sighed, "Hold on, I haven't put on my dress shoes yet!"

Amused, Shakira smiled and replied, "Okay! Hurry up! Hurry up!"

As soon as Rally finished getting dressed they were already out the door heading for their usual meeting place, which was at a fountain in front of the boys' dorm.

Shakira noticed a young man walk by and didn't realize it, but it was actually Max. She saw him bump into another student at the entrance to the boys' dorm and was about to help them out when she heard her friend behind her.

"Konichiwa Shakira-chan. Genki desu ka?"

Shakira turned around, "Joey-kun! Anata o mite watashi wa totemo ureshīdesu! Oya~tsu watashi no ā anata no kami o ao ni someta! Sore wa kawaīdesu! Watashi wa atarashī seito ni atta ā, kanojo no namaedesu Rally!"

Rally stood there completely confused, so

Shakira turned to her and clarified, "Oh sorry! Hee-hee. I'm so used to talking to Joey in Japanese I forgot you don't speak it. I learned it originally to honor my Japanese mother who died giving birth to me! That's also why I have her last name since my Dad is actually Cuban, which is why my first language is actually Spanish and well..."

Shakira smiled widely, continuing, "Obviously I know English as well! This is Joey! He's my best friend! He's half Japanese too, but he's also half British! He looks so young but he's actually eighteen! He's a sophomore, but he got in when he was only seventeen. I'm twenty-three, by the way, because I was born on New Year's, so I have an awesome birthday party every year! Anyways, yes this is Joey!"

She was referring to the boy she'd been speaking Japanese to. The boy had blue hair and blue-green eyes with a slight baby face.

Joey bowed a little and replied, "It's as she said. I got into this place because of my work on a popular British animation I did when I was 12, even though my manga one-shot I did when I had to move to Japan to live with my mother didn't do that well."

Shakira hugged Joey. "It's okay Joey. You're still awesome!"

Joey smiled a little, "Thanks, Shakira-san. Anyways, when's your next party? Can't wait to go!"

Shakira seemed like she was about to jump into the sky, cheering, "Oh my gosh! Which one? I have one coming up next week, but there also might be my half-party coming up tomorrow! But I have no idea what to do for tomorrow's party yet! Crazy, huh?"

Joey laughed, "I'm sure you can figure it out."

"Mhm!" "Well its cool to meet you, Joey. I'm Rally Valentine. I got in here from my singing. I'm a top seller!"

Smiling coyly, Joey whistled, "Impressive. Lots of people here got reasons like that though."

Rally sneered, asking darkly, "Are you tryin to start some kinda fight or something?"

Shakira interjected, "He didn't mean nothin' by it Rally, it's okay! Oh look, my other friend!"

She seemingly bounced for joy at changing the topic as she headed for two boys at the door entrance who were talking to each other. The first one was short and skinny with pale skin, green eyes and black hair.

The short one remarked, "Oh hi, Shakira. I was just talking to my brother."

The brother he spoke of was tall and skinny with short brown hair and blue eyes.

Shakira quickly introduced the two boys to Rally, saying, "These two are fraternal twins. The shorter one is Simon and the taller one is Ikuto! They're part Scottish, part Japanese, but ironically, they aren't fluent in Japanese because they are adopted. They were raised by different adoptive parents, so they never met until they went here! Isn't that crazy? It's so funny because it's not like we have a lot of Japanese students or anything, so it's funny we know each other so well!" "Well, see ya, Simon. I gotta go to class." Simon nodded as his older twin left.

Shakira laughed, "He only does that because he thinks I'm annoying! Can you believe it? Me? Annoying?"

Rally tried not to smirk about the comment as she thought to herself, *"Couldn't imagine why people would find you annoying."* She instead replied with the truth,

"Some people might find you that way, but you're alright with me Shakira."

Shakira smiled, "Thanks so much!"

Joey said, "Hey Shakira, we're going to be late for choir if we don't hurry up."

Shakira replied, "Oh, you're totally right! Sorry guys gotta go! See ya, Simon!"

Simon answered, "Oh. Ok. Bye."

He seemed a little annoyed that they had to go already, but at the same time seemed too sleepy to care as he yawned and walked off. "That's Simon, he seems to always be sleepy! Well, let's go to Choir!" "I have Choir as my first class, too! I forgot to bring it up earlier!", Rally said.

She seemed slightly embarrassed she'd forgotten to mention it, but also eager to get to the class as soon as possible. "Oh awesome! Let's go!"

When they reached inside to the choir room the teacher was a girl with short blond hair and was in her thirties. She was smiling happily and welcomed everybody the warmth of her expression.

Shakira walked in and the teacher greeted her cheerfully, "Hi Shakira! Hi Joey! Oh, it's a new student!"

Rally smiled and said, "Yes, I'm Rally."

The teacher smiled, "Welcome to my class Rally! I've heard such wonderful things about your singing! I even bought one of your CD's!"

Everybody sat down as roll call was performed one by one. It was a big class because choir was all done in one session, since everybody there would be at competitions in the future.They started out afterwards with the basic 'Do Rei Mi' and tongue-twisters to get their mouths clear. They then warmed up with singing a very catchy old Southern song that had everybody smiling at the goofy lyrics. After they got that out of their system the teacher had the students change positions a little bit to better suit their vocals, handing them their sheet music.

"This is the song I had you all work on over the break", she said.

Rally was so nervous she whispered to Shakira, "I forgot to read it!"

Shakira smiled and whispered back, "Don't worry about it, just mimic what we do and you'll be fine. We're also allowed to look at our papers right now anyways, since new people just joined. If all else fails, watermelon or cantaloupe it!"

Shakira was referring to an exercise where one says the words 'watermelon/cantaloupe' to the tune of everyone surrounding the user in order to not look silly. It was a practice newer people used to get by. Rally would rather not, naturally, so she just simply had to look at the lyrics a lot.

It didn't help that they were in Indian. It was an epic orchestra piece that had a massive epic battle sequence feel to it and required full chorus. It was simultaneously something all the guys in the choir found awesome, while the women found to be beautiful. The orchestra music was pre-recorded, written by the orchestra team of the school itself for an upcoming movie that the film team was making. It was apparently a war-based movie involving knights and swordsmen mixed with a steampunk feel, sure to be violent; the song itself was for the final battle. The song started out soft and was doing a lot of build up, then got faster with loud thumps as the chorus sang with a somewhat operatic feel. The song progressively became more intense as they sang in Hindi. The song slowed down as it played violins and got melancholy, the group singing more softly.A sudden loud thumping got bigger as the chorus held a long note. The song got more and more intense and then finally the song entered grand finale.*"No pressure or anything"*, Rally was thinking as the song finished. She luckily blended in enough to where hopefully she wasn't noticed. The teacher did, but waited until most of the students left to stop Rally and say, "I want you to read the material more, next time. I heard you slowing down some at parts and having trouble. I'm sure Shakira can help you out."

Shakira smiled, "Of course I will!"

Rally blushed and got angry and embarrassed as she stormed off.

"Do you think she'll be alright?", Joey asked worriedly, prompting Shakira to reply, "I think we should just give Rally her space, for now. She's embarrassed about the whole situation, but once she's calmed down I'll make her a cake just for her! Besides, I was right next to her and her singing was great! She just needs to cool off and have a friend to be there for her and that's what we are for, Joey!"

Joey nodded, "I guess we are!"

Shakira giggled, "Of course! Friends have to help each other out in their time of need and be there for the good and the bad."

Joey laughed, "Yeah,you're right!"

With that, it seemed things were going to soar sky-high for the future of the school, this at least the sort of impression Shakira exuded through her joy.

Chapter 2 – Theater and the Party

Max sighed: he was still in a bit of a bad mood, but he wasn't going to let it ruin his day. He smiled and walked inside the building his class would be in, one different from where his fencing classes were being held. He was considering doing actual acting for a class, or even voice acting. Theater was nonetheless the most definite way to help him. He'd already taken basic theater classes in high school and whatnot, so this wouldn't be totally unfamiliar in the slightest.

The room was quite large, itself host to blue carpet floors and white walls. The setup of the room reminded Max strangely of his former high school drama classrooms, with the entry door at the top of the room with three steps following. These steps were extremely spread apart and could fit multiple rows of chairs on each step to make neater the room. It was also a round shaped room. The teacher walked in looking like he was in his forties, with short black hair on his head and face.

He said, "I'm Mr. Goodman. Before we begin I want you to know I'm not like other teachers: we can have fun sometimes, we'll be casual. You can have sodas, food and whatever at any given time, doesn't bother me any. We can be as if pals and friends and whatnot. But when it comes time to get stuff done, all I ask is you don't give me any bullshit. You don't feed me shit, I won't feed you shit. We all on the same page?"

The students nodded,

Mr. Goodman continuing, "Alright good. We should get along just fine. If anybody disagrees you can leave right now, anyways: there's the door. Moving right along, I have a project for you guys to work on. If you look under your seats you'll see 1 of 7 different scripts.

"The one you have determines what group you are in. Get into separate groups and begin practicing how you are going to do the scene for when I call time and walk back out here from my office", he said pointing to a door that was a few feet from the front.

"I want your group to perform the scene. This is your first day, so you'll be allowed to hold your scripts and look at them at moments as you perform so long as you don't depend on them too much. Starting… now." He set his stopwatch and added, "Alright guys, see ya later."

He walked into his office and shut the door. There was a window to the office that allowed one to see him on its' computer editing some sort of movie.

Max met with his group, the first thing he noticed being a young lady obviously in a bad mood.

Max kindly welcomed, "Hey. Name's Max." Quiet for a moment, the girl said, "Rally."

She was sitting on the floor with her face downturned,

Max asking, "Bad day, huh?"

"It's obvious, but how else would I start this conversation, right?", he thought to himself.

Rally seemed very hesitant to speak at all but after a few moments managed to speak, not even bothering to look at him as she said,"... Yeah."

Max replied, "I know the feeling. I had a bad time this morning myself, but I've decided I just can't let it ruin my day, you know?"

Rally sighed, "You wouldn't understand."

The next person to join the group was a man of Arabic descent, skinny in build with short black hair. "My name is TJ. Got in for my abilities in sculpting. You?"

Max replied, "Max. I wrote an award-winning book series."

TJ was obviously trying to appear nice, but not that hard. He didn't actually care at all what Max had or hadn't done,

nodding kindly, "Cool, cool."

A woman walked up to them and replied, "I'm Kathy."

All their introductions complete,

TJ asked, "Anybody mind if I take the lead male role?"

"As long as I get the lead female role", came a voice from behind TJ.

Her name was Syanne. She had been standing there listening while leaning against the wall. Rally sat down beside another girl as she just closed her eyes.

While TJ and the others were talking, Max noticed the girl beside Rally and asked her for her name.

"Colleen," she replied.

Her voice was quiet and seemed quite withdrawn, which was kind of saddening.

Max replied, "Ah. That's a nice name. So why are you sitting over here?"

He hoped to help her if he could. It broke his heart to think someone was all alone with no one talking to them.

Colleen replied, "Just... nothing to say."

Max replied, "Don't talk much, huh?"

Colleen nodded, "People think I'm shy, but I'm just quiet. I mean, I used to be shy though."

Max nodded, "I see. Well, you can always talk to me if you want."

Colleen smiled, but paused before saying, "It's not that really. I just... I-I don't really wanna talk about it." That ended the conversation there; she seemed to want to retreat from everything entirely already, as her eyes seemed distant and scared. Max realized he wasn't going to get anywhere with her.

Max sighed, "Fair enough." Colleen scooted further away from everyone else.

This bothered Max but he knew he couldn't do anything about it so he turned his attention to Rally.

"So... everyone gonna be letting stuff get to them? Couldn't we just... you know... talk casually or something?"

Annoyed by his demeanor, Rally turned and walked away from him as well.

Max sighed, "Sheesh, was it something I said? Jeez, everybody is so emo today." Thinking to himself, he said aloud, "Great Max, just great. Try to make a couple of new friends and screw it all up again, as usual."

He wondered if maybe he was being too harsh on himself. He joined the others and asked, "So what's going on over here?"

Kathy smiled, "I get to be the mother of the main character. Makes sense really if you think about it."

TJ nodded, "Yep. I decided it'd be perfect for her. Meanwhile, I'll be the lead male and Syanne gets be the beautiful lead female."

Syanne giggled a little and replied,"C'est très bon...c'est magnifique!"

She seemed less like she was happy, and more like she was just trying to show off her French, as if to think immaturely that she was better than people or something.

This annoyed Max a bit, but he tried to match it by showing that he recognized the language she was speaking.

Max replied," French huh?"

Syanne seemed greatly annoyed that her attention was being drawn away by his comment. She looked coldly at Max; the kind of look that could make you shiver with the amount of contempt in her eyes.

She then put on a legibly fake smile as she said, "Ouí." Annoyed, Max noticed the coldness, deciding to respond to her sarcastically, "Speak English?"

Syanne coldly replied, "Of course, but for you I simply have to say 'Vous êtes un parfait idiot'", this seeming a satisfying insult for her to give. Max sighed at how unpleasant this girl seemed, at least recognizing the word 'idiot.' Connor and Leon were right about her demeanor's bitchiness. She was probably annoyed with how long he held up fencing class, last period. He still didn't like her and he dared not look away from each other's stare, as if for impending standoff.

After a brief moment of awkward silence TJ interjected, "Okay, then. So anyways, that leaves the two ladies you were talking to playing the roles of the twin sisters and Max as the goofy uncle. I think we should start practicing our lines; everything will be great! My being the lead is only natural, since my family descends from the badasses that are the Persians, of course."

Nobody truly understood he was so proud of that particular of his heritage, but neither would they comment on it. He was probably just being goofy. TJ, Kathy and Syanne practiced the lines together, the three of them seeming to get along really well. Max tried to work with them a little at first but found it awkward, so he ended up sitting by himself and just reading his lines. Rally and Colleen each read their scripts by themselves.

Suddenly the teacher came in and called time before he commented, "Now remember, you can keep your scripts with you, but only as long as you don't overly rely on it or look at it too often. I have to be convinced you are acting."

There was nothing noteworthy to say about the first two skits, but when the moment came for the group Max was in, it was time to show their worth. The teacher waited patiently as Max and his group moved to the front of the room, organizing themselves in a way that would be befitting the scene. They began rehearsing their lines as though they meant it,

TJ first saying, "Alas, this morning is cruel. Why is the light so bright?"

He did his lines in a style that rather over the top and hammy, but the girls giggled so he kept it as such.

"Mother, is breakfast ready?"

Kathy looked at her lines on the paper for a moment and said, "Yes son, breakfast is ready. I made pancakes with bacon and eggs."

Her acting wasn't terrible, but not great, either.

TJ continued his hamming up as he said, "Mmm! Sounds great!"

The girls in the class watching giggled again, while

Syanne knocked on the wall and Kathy said, "Come in!"

Syanne walked up to Kathy, who remarked, "Why, if it isn't your dear friend Syanne here with her Uncle John!"

Max was nervous, but still managed to do a passable job saying his lines. "Yes. You know me! Oh, say, what's that on your shirt?"

He pointed at Kathy's chest, her deciding to look down only to be lightly hit in the nose with his finger. From here, he teasingly followed, "Made ya look!"

Kathy did an unconvincing fake laugh as she said, "Oh, John, you never cease to amuse!"

Rolling her eyes, Syanne remarked, "I don't know why people love my uncle so much, he is such a bother." For obscuring the French in her accent her acting rewarded itself to be perfect, like she'd been performing her whole life.

Syanne said, "We'll be late for school if you don't hurry, Josh!"

TJ replied, "Don't worry, I'm coming! I just need to", in the interim making a fake sneeze, "… Blow my nose." The humor here couldn't be more integrating, as

Max remarked, "You know how you make a tissue dance?"

Confused at the question TJ replied, "Not really." "Put a little boogie in it!", Max comically replied.

TJ did another fake laugh, turned to face Kathy and said, "I'm going to school now, Mom!"

"Have fun, son!" Kathy and Max walked off stage to sit down with the rest of the class as the scene changed.

As Rally and Colleen approached Syanne Rally looked at TJ and asked, "How are you, Josh?", with merely satisfactory acting.

TJ replied in his usual hammy manner, saying, "Oh, not too bad. Just kinda heading for class; you know, the usual."

Rally tried not to roll her eyes as Colleen came up and said, "We're gonna be late for class!"

Her acting was a bit wooden but was as good as necessary, so

TJ replied, "So which one of you ladies wants to join me for the fair after school?"

Colleen replied, "I can't, I have ballet practice." Her acting still sounded wooden, while

Rally remarked, "I would, but I have soccer practice."

Syanne replied, "I'm sure we can work something out, but I have to take band practice. So, I'll be late, but I can go."

The scene ended and the teacher wrote in his book, he remaining seven each performing their scenes. Some were doing really well and some demonstrated that they still needed a little work, but by the end of class the diversity couldn't be clearer.

Class ended and Max decided to talk to Rally, saying, "I'm sorry if I offended you. I wasn't sure what to do because I've had a bad day, too."

Rally sighed, "Whatever. It's fine."

Max breathed a sigh of relief. He hoped this meant they had made peace, but part of him couldn't help but wonder if this was 'woman code' for 'Go away, I'm still mad.'"Well, gotta go. See ya."

As she walked off, Max sighed. That was an awkward day for sure, but it was already getting to be late at night. His required classes after Theater were stressful, especially math, something he was never strong in. He had a huge headache from it all and though Leon helped him out where he could, it really was just giving him more of the same.

They later shared a pizza they ordered, when

Leon looked like he remembered something. "Oh! This came by; I think you'll like it."

He gave a note to Max, who opened it and began reading to the extent of pleasant surprise.

"It's a party, tomorrow," he said. "I'm surprised to be receiving an invitation to a party this soon." "Technically the host Shakira normally lets anyone come to her parties, but this one is special. She always does it the day after new students come in to celebrate new friends she's made. Thus, she only lets friends attend, along with one guest of their choice. I got an invitation too; I'm bringing Connor as my guest."

Max was surprised, "I never met her, so why am I invited?"

Leon laughed, "That's the funny thing: rumor has it someone named Rally asked to have you come as her guest. Apparently, Rally is Shakira's new friend, but Rally didn't want you to know that she was the one who invited you so she asked Shakira to write a normal invitation for you instead. It was a secret, but somebody overheard it. So, naturally, everyone going to the party knew about it. You'll find rumors spread around here like wildfire. Of course, it's still just a rumor, so no guarantee it's true. Funny, really. Shakira's a nice person, but sometimes she can be annoying. Don't tell her I said that, though."

***

The next day went by very uneventfully. Max mostly avoided Jericho for the day, not wanting to be beaten in fencing classes again. He definitely learned some useful lessons, though, and he hoped that someday he could beat Jericho. Theater class wasn't very eventful, either; they started doing book lessons on Shakespeare and the teacher had them write notes about his various plays and the like.

It was a really boring day in class. He barely got by today in his required sessions, but what he was looking forward to tonight was the party; it couldn't come soon enough. He'd also gathered that Syanne was apparently a huge flirt. During theater she passed notes to the males a lot and would occasionally giggle while doing so. Max found it annoying, but merely ignored it. The instructor seemed to not notice; either that or he simply didn't care, which was funny because the instructor seemed the no-nonsense type.

Maybe it was that he was as bored with today's lesson as the students were. Nobody would be wearing their school uniforms for the party, naturally; it was being held in a ballroom that Shakira had had her father pay to use. Apparently, her father was very rich.

Max was pretty well-off after his book sold so well, but money quickly disappears with living expenses, especially when he had to pay rent to live with his parents while jobless. Here he was wearing a dark blue T-shirt and blue jeans. He wore black skater shoes with white laces for comfort, as they shared being from home with the rest of his attire. Some liked those shoes lace-less, but Max liked to have laces even though he'd tie them just loose and tight enough. This ensured that they'd stay on so he could slip them on and off anytime he wanted without have to ever re-tie. Leon himself wore dark black baggy jeans and a black t-shirt, as well as black shoes with black laces.

Max realized something, asking his roommate, "Yo, Leon. How old are you, anyways? I never thought to ask, until now."

Leon laughed, "Twenty-three. You?"

Max replied, "Really? Twenty-two. When's your birthday?" "January 5th. Yours?"

Max replied, "June 21st. Guess we were born in the same year."

He chuckled, Leon having a very surprised look on his face.

Max replied, "What? Something on my face?"

Leon shook his head, "No... it's just... you were born on the exact same day as Jericho; same month, day, and year."

It was Max's turn to look surprised, as he said, "No way! You're pulling my leg, right?"

Leon shook his head, "Uh-uh. I shit you not."

Max couldn't believe it, strange the fate of their shared births. "That's freaky!

Really, really freaky." "Maybe you're twins separated at birth or somethin'."

Max smirked, "Pfft, more like we were fated to be rivals or something."

Leon laughed, "Maybe." "Yeah, now if only I could stop sucking at fencing."

Leon did a hand gesture signaling not to worry. "You're new; nobody's that good when they're still new at fencing." "Anyways, we better head to the party before we're late."

Leon nodded, "Agreed. We'll have to swing by Connor's room to get him first though." "Lead the way."

Their venture took them; as they walked in, Max turned to Connor and remarked, "So I never really got to talk to you much; you were so quiet before."

Connor chuckled nervously, "Guess I just didn't have much to say. Sorry about that. I guess it didn't help what happened, that day."

Max assumed Connor was the quiet type, so it made sense. With their first meeting it was hard to tell much of anything about him. He himself noticed something this time h.

Max laughed, asking, "Is that a slight Irish accent I detect?"

Connor nodded, "Yep. I'm known as the fastest guitarist in Ireland; at least that's what people say."

Leon and Max made eye contact before looking back at Connor. This piqued

Leon's curiosity as he said, "I never heard that before. Connor, would you be interested in joining a band?"

Max found it funny they hadn't known Connor's talents sooner. Hopefully this would be an easy transition, even if Max wondered it too good to be true.

Connor grinned, saying, "I don't see why not; could be fun, as long as you don't push me too hard or anything."

Leon laughed, "It'll be a lot of work for sure, but it'll be fun too, and well worth it." "I guess most good music is that way. Sure, you got yourself a band member!"

A voice behind them startled them in question, "Really? You're a band? Oh, my gosh, you gotta play something for the party! It's so dead right now!"

Max turned to see the voice belonged to a pink-haired Shakira, startled in her beauty. For some reason he didn't expect her to be so attractive looking, causing him quickly to blush then compose.Nobody seemed to notice, or at least they didn't say anything. He played it off by looking around and realizing she was right. There was a beer-pong table and rave music, but the party was quite dead regardless of the latter; people didn't seem to be having fun.

Shakira nodded, "I'll also have to be less selective in my people."

She turned to a kid with blue hair, asking, "Joey, can you spread the word about the party? Tell them anyone is invited! Let's heat things up!"

Joey nodded and started heading outside.

Shakira then tugged on Connor and Leon's arms so as to place them onstage. Max stayed near the steps but Shakira dragged him on as well. She handed Connor and Leon plugged-in electric guitars, so

Leon looked at Max and said, "Now's our time to give a shot at our first gig… Why not?"

Max sighed, "'Child of Sweet', then?"

He'd sung the song to Leon earlier, so the choice was obvious in its' fun.

Connor smiled, "Sounds good."

It started with a guitar opening done by Leon and Connor quickly matched his tune. Max started singing and people got excited, so they knew it was actually working. People were certainly into the music, regardless of the cover. Cover or not, they were pretty decent.

After their first song

Leon asked, "Do you guys know 'Hand of Blood?'"

Connor and Max nodded, playing as Max sang. People came in and began headbanging to the metal while drinking beer and having a good time.

The music continued for two more songs; these ones called "Boom Click" and "No More Sorrow." Soon the party was quite lively, but all were getting tired. Thankfully Joey secured a member of the school who was a DJ, who began playing techno/rave mixes while some members of the school's stagecraft handled strobe lights, etc. "Joey, you're the greatest!", Shakira shouted.

Joey laughed, "You kidding? They came here because I said you were the one throwing the party!"

Shakira laughed and kissed Joey's cheek. As Max headed their way he tried his best not to appear jealous. "Thanks for that Shakira...it was just what we needed."

Smiling understandingly with her eyes bright and beautiful as ever, Shakira giggled, "No, thank you! You guys helped set this party up!"

Max smiled, "So who do I have to thank for being here, anyways?"

Shakira smiled again as she put her fingers over her mouth as if to zip it closed. Apparently, she wasn't going to reveal her little secret any time soon.

Max replied, "Can't blame a guy for tryin'."

Suddenly Rally approached the group. She was apparently having a good time as well, but seemed to be avoiding being near Max up until now for some reason. Max simply assumed she was just being shy.

Shakira smiled, "Oh hi, Rally! I baked a cake just for you! It got me in such a baking mood; I've made tons of cake for the party!" One could not deny that there were some beautiful cakes at the refreshment table; one white cake had pink frosting, a chocolate cake white frosting and even a pink cake with vanilla frosting.

Their exquisiteness could not be denied. "Thanks. That's awesome."

That particular smile was the first time Max had seen it from her. She was so upset in Theater that it was nice to see her feeling better. He probably cared too much, but it made for a nice moment. "So you can smile, after all."

Rally tried not to acknowledge what happened earlier, but still wished for a smart reply. She then shrugged, "Of course I can. I just wasn't in a good mood."

Max figured the statement to be fair; being at a party is likely to improve just about anybody's mood, so trying to expand it he asked, "So acting, huh? What got you interested in that?"

This caused a brief silence as she started to think of an answer, then replying, "I guess I've always had an interest in it. I just ended up doing singing instead, for a while. That's why I'm here actually; just figured acting was my true passion."

She seemed quite pleased with her answer, so he replied, "Sounds like the same as me. I've always had an interest, but guess

I mostly went with writing up until now." He didn't even bother to bring up the fact he'd only ever finished one book, ironically his bestseller. That'd be too embarrassing to admit right now, especially since he barely knew anybody around here.

This time Joey chimed in, "Writing, huh? I write, myself. What kind of stuff have you written?"

Max was relieved Joey spoke up, because he wasn't sure what to add. Joey showed a genuine interest though, and it wouldn't hurt to mention the things he'd written notwithstanding they were unfinished. It was nice to see someone else join the conversation, so Max had no problem with replying.

"Well, usually fantasy or sci-fi, really. I've done horror once, though. Was a pretty dark book, though. What about you?"

Joey laughed, "Well, I wrote my own manga once, a one-off bit while I was living in Japan."

That was definitely a surprise because Joey seemed so young. Manga is something Max had a particular interest in, so this made the conversation really easy for him.

Max laughed, "Really? I read a lot of manga myself. What was the name of it?"

Joey replied,"Akatsuka No Henge. Was a ninja-based manga." "Haven't heard of that one before."

He'd read ninja manga and even some pretty decent pirate manga, but this one didn't ring a bell. "Not a surprise, not many have. Never had a stateside release, either."

Joey seemed almost a little saddened by that, causing Max to fumble on words while attempting to brighten the mood. Then, Knoll and Zackk came up to Max with friends of their own.

Knoll said, "Hey Max, this is Charles Rojas. He's a friend of mine from back home. I just realized he was here while at the party, so I figured I'd introduce him to you!"

Charles seemed of Latin descent, having long black hair and slender build.

Zack was politely waiting, so Max asked him, "And who might this be?", pointing to the person Zack was with, a man with short brown hair and an average build.

The man offered out his hand and said, "Shaun Balthier. I'm a friend of Zack's from back home. I gotta say Max, you're one of the better-looking guys I've seen around here."

Max was a little embarrassed as he scratched the back of his head, so

Shaun laughed, "Don't worry, Zack told me you weren't interested in men, so I won't be hitting on you, any. Just figured I'd pay you a compliment."

Shakira interrupted for a moment however, asking, "Well you guys look like lots of fun! How's the party?"

The music had beenloud for so long Max didn't even realize it. It's like his ears had adjusted to it, but as she spoke with Shaun and Charles his mind wandered to the sound of music.

He managed to rejoin the conversation at a moment where they seemed to be talking less as he asked Charles, "So what kind of things you into?"

Charles smiled, "Well, lots of things. I usually play lots of MMOs and watch my fair share of anime."

Max nodded, "Cool, cool. What got you in the college?"

Charles grinned, "Graphic designer. I worked on a game with another student here actually, Vincent. He might be here in the party somewhere, actually. Hope you don't mind if I go looking for him, guys?"

Shakira giggled, "Not at all! Have fun!"

Suddenly, the group heard a woman's voice. "Well if it isn't Shakira."

The young girl was roughly their age but was Filipino,

Shakira sighing, "Hi Sarah."

Sarah growled, "I can't believe parties like these! It's just so atrocious! Do you know how drunk people get at places like this? It's irresponsible!"

Shakira shrugged it off and smiled, "Trust me, I got friends like Joey making sure this place doesn't get too out of control!"

Sarah huffed and walked off. Max was left at a loss for words. His head was starting to hurt from all the people he was meeting in such a short while, so he didn't even know what to say to the others.

Shakira saved the situation by exclaiming, "Enough talking, let's all just dance!" The music was a lot of fun. Max danced with Rally a couple times, but anytime he tried dancing with Shakira he couldn't keep up with her. She was bouncing off the walls with energy, but Shakira found cute that Max kept trying to keep up with her. Max was left panting often, but even though he was no good at dancing he wanted simply to keep up with her as the lights shined back and forth.

The song next changed briefly to a slower song by Jest Rayford the R&B artist. Max blushed a little but went with it as Shakira put his arm around her waist and they waltzed, Shakira smiling with the question,

"So, what did you do with your free time before you got here?"

For some reason Max was suddenly nervous. It was because he was realizing how really attractive she was, so he thought it might sound geeky to mention anime or his love for comics.

He nonetheless sighed, "Well, back at home I mostly played video games, watched anime, and wrote; not much, really. You?"

Shakira smiled sweetly as she said, "I enjoy anime as well. It helps I speak

Japanese, though. I'm part-Japanese part-Cuban, actually. My daddy often makes me switch to various boarding schools in America, however."

At least that explained why she was so beautiful to Max; he had a thing for Hispanics and Asians but he also had something else on his mind about what she said. "That must really suck."

He could only imagine how terrible it must've been having to change friends all the time and then moving around like that. It was certainly difficult enough when he had to move to Florida.

Shakira smiled, "It was alright, because I made tons of new friends every time and I make friends really easy." Max could tell she had a certain air about her that was beaming with friendliness, so this didn't surprise him. "I wish I could say the same. I'm an outgoing person and friendly enough, but I guess I've got a double-edged sword. When people actually notice me, I tend to make both friends and enemies easily... Well, more like acquaintances. Lasting friends have mostly been online ones prior to here."

Shakira gave a caring look as she looked Max in the eyes and replied, "That sounds just awful. Well, don't you worry a thing. You and I are friends as of now and when you're friends with Shakira, everybody knows you! You'll be filled with people to talk to before you know it!"

Max was relieved to hear her reassurances, even though he was already making good progress as he replied, "Well, actually, I've already apparently made friends with Leon, and a couple people I've known before are around this place somewhere... Knoll and Zack. But I always welcome more friends."

Shakira smiled, "Well, that's good!"

As the song came to an end she turned to the refreshments, "You want some alcohol?"

She gave a slightly seductive look to Max this time which made him really nervous, but he still was enjoying the moment and wasn't about to show it. "I don't drink. Soda is fine."

He never liked alcohol. He had a somewhat addictive personality, so he figured it would only make him a drunk if he ever had an attraction. He actually preferred to call his second option 'pop,' but for some reason people never seemed to get what he meant, so he'd gotten used to the word 'soda.' He still hated it, for it would always be 'pop.'

Shakira was still smiling her usual as she replied, "Me too! I just keep them here for the parties, because people like it so much. I hate the stuff, personally."

Max then turned around after grabbing the drink from Shakira. She tried to warn him, but he'd already bumped into someone. Fortunately soda only spilled on the floor and not on the person he'd bumped into.

Max said, "Oh, sorry... Holy crap... Ikuto, is that you?"

Standing in front of Max was a skinny young man around with short brown hair and an old friend of his. He could recognize him right away.

"Max! It's been a while. Haven't seen you in years!" Ikuto seemed relieved that he bumped into max after years not having talked to one another.

Having overheard their conversation, Leon asked, "You know each other?"

Max nodded, adding, "Used to go to high school together, before he moved."

Shakira was already quick to jump in, laughing, "Really? You knew Simon's twin brother?"

This somewhat surprised Max, for he never knew Ikuto had any siblings, let alone he was a twin. Max had a younger brother himself, but the guy was an annoying teenager at the moment.

Max looked at Ikuto, asking, "Twin?" "Turns out I'm a twin and didn't know it. He and I are nothing alike, though."

Max nodded, "Makes sense, it's not like you're clones or something."

He added, "Hey Leon, you mind if I go hang with Ikuto for a while?"

Leon smiled, "No, not at all. Have fun. We'll catch up later."

Max nodded as he walked with Ikuto into another room next door, one just like the first big dance room but mostly empty.

Ikuto smiled, "Been a long time sense we've talked, huh dude? How's life?"

Max sighed, "Boring, dude. Up until I came here I didn't do much of anything with my life. You?"

Ikuto nodded in understanding, but also seemed annoyed when it was his turn to speak. It was probably wasn't at Max himself and more at what Ikuto's life had been like since they talked last.

Ikuto rolled his eyes as he began to say, "The usual. I try to find a worthwhile girlfriend and naturally they've all been sluts. Go figure. I just want one girl who doesn't do drugs and isn't a whore."

Max had had quite a few online relationships himself, but nothing ever serious in real life. Still, he'd had his share of ups and downs, himself laughing, "I know that feeling bro."

Suddenly Ikuto asked, "So what do you think of Shakira? Nice rack, huh?"

His grin was innocent even if the question wasn't, like the hidden meaning of an early Beatles song. That Max remembered Ikuto's oft-perverseness struck him by surprise at first until he giggled, "I, uh, well uh... Yeah she does. Very nice." "Yeah. Don't tell her I said that though, she might slap me or something."

Max laughed, "Yeah. She seems like the life of the party." Shakira was a very fun person to be around, even though he assumed people often found her tiring with the amount of energy she seemed to have.

Ikuto nodded, "She's not my type, really. I want a girl who is sweet and innocent. Shakira is too hyper and stuff for me. She kinda reminds me of you."

He laughed. Max laughed as well. Then he said, "Well I'm not as hyper as I used to be."

As a kid he seemed to have near infinite energy himself, but as Max had gotten older he got more often winded from over-exertion. Nonetheless, that never stopped him from trying anything he set his mind to on a repeated basis. Besides, he usually only needed short breaks, as fencing class had proven.

Max saw Ikuto's nose tingle a little so he took a step back, as he noticed Ikuto acted like he was about to sneeze.

Just as this was happening, Connor walked in with his instrument and said, "Hey Max, they let us keep the guitars-"

Ikuto sneezed and suddenly flames shot out of his mouth and headed straight for Connor! Max quickly jumped out of the way to avoid getting burned alive, Connor reflexively holding up his arm in terror. As he did, arcs of electricity briefly formed a shield around his arm as he deflected the flames.

The ceiling sprinklers went off in the whole building, people next door seeming not to mind it while thinking it was a part of the party. That was until the DJ equipment started electrocuting, causing everyone to scream andhead outside. Max, on the other hand, was left standing there in awe of what just happened.

"What am I going to do now? And more to the point… How the hell did these two do that!"

Chapter 3 - Life or Death

Max was definitely taken aback by what had happened a couple nights ago. It all happened so fast, but they'd at least decided on an agreement: Connor and Ikuto would keep their new found powers secret and in exchange could practice their powers as long as nobody was around to see them; except for Max of course. Max had to admit... he did feel jealous.

At the same time, one had to wonder how something like that even was possible. Still, Connor was taking to this rather well, following Max's advice decently. They practiced near the scrap yard where welders and the like would acquire material. Few people were ever around when classes weren't going on, so no one really saw them. Connor stayed out of sight and Max enjoyed watching his gift.

At first Max thought this would be his favorite thing to watch, but sometimes he questioned if it was. It was something about Ikuto's flame abilities that really got his attention- the beautiful fires that would form out of Ikuto's hands and then launch into the air, something he was actually getting proficient at.

Ikuto had gotten to where he'd mimic a kung-fu style while launching flames from his hands and feet. Sure, he didn't actually know any kind of martial arts or anything, but what it looked like when put together with the flames was quite spellbinding upon examination. At the same time though, something about it made Max uneasy: perhaps he feared the flames, which is why he kept switching back to finding the lightning and electricity to be more interesting.

Connor could cause his arms to be covered in it without even feeling an ounce of any kind of resultant pain, which in itself was really cool looking... especially if done in the shade so you could see it more clearly. At the same time he could send attacks at pieces of scrap as if there were lightning bolts coming out of his fingertips.

They seemed to be catching onto this rather fast, but there was one issue with it. While it'd only been a couple nights since they'd gotten their gifts, they still got very tired from it. It in fact exhausted them often and they'd be tired the rest of the day. It'd perhaps take time the same way one of those RPGs or something would, until they 'leveled up' or something to be less tired.

Max had just ended his classes for the day. That was good, since he was eager to see more of the gifts his friends could do. He wished he had powers of his own, perhaps of wind: he'd fly into the air and send gusts of wind at people, as an example. As he headed outside of the building all he could think about now was if he could fly, which was something he'd often dreamed of doing. Maybe if he was lucky he'd also get powers, but he didn't have long to think about this when something that made him want to faint was before his eyes.

There in the air was Ikuto wearing a tinted motorcycle helmet to obscure his face, shooting flames into the air while showing off in front of the ladies in plain sight.

"What the hell is he thinking? I told him if somebody saw him this could not go over well! They might lock him up in some science experiment or some shit! Especially with as many geniuses as they have at this school!", Max thought to himself.

Max panicked straight for his dresser at the dorm. Thankfully nobody was in his room and the dorm wasn't very packed. He grabbed his cosplay out of the closet. It was a weapons dealer costume who had trench coat with a hood and a bandana: this could cover his own appearance.

As soon as he left the dorm he ducked in a hiding spot next to the building and put the outfit on, running for Ikuto. He hoped that by the time he got there, things wouldn't have gotten ugly. When he reached the place Ikuto last was however, Max realized to his horror that Ikuto was gone.

"Now where the hell is he?", Max thought worriedly as he buried his face in his hands for a moment and sighed. Suddenly, he felt someone tug at him and he was being pulled into his old hiding spot. Before he knew it he was already in location, a young man's voice speaking to him without apperance.

"Are you the one who was putting on that little fire performance earlier?" Obviously he meant Ikuto, but Max wasn't about to say anything too quickly; he wanted information.

"Who wants to know?" The trashcan next to Max floated suddenly into the air and slowly individual objects came out, floating well alongside it.

"Someone who also is special." The apparatus and its objects hit the ground with a thud,

Max replying in kind, "Can I see your face?" Maybe he was pushing his luck but he had to try, the stranger saying,

"Are you him or not?"

Max wasn't about to lie- it was the thing he hated most from people. Lying was something he just could not do. *"Guess the jig is up",* he thought. He then said aloud, "No. He's my friend though. If you show yourself however, I can show to you proof that I already know the two of you are not alone."

The individual came out from behind the building, appearing to be in his early twenties with medium-length brown hair that went almost to his shoulders and brown eyes. He was slender in build, with his school uniform being worn neatly.

"So..?"

Max took off his hood and lowered the bandana as he sighed, "My other friend has lightning abilities. If you'd like I can introduce you to both of them. I'm Max... Max Schneider. What is your name?"

The individual hesitated before replying, following, "...Maverick Williams."A bit surprised, Max said, "The Maverick Williams? I heard you were one of the smartest students in the school. An IQ of what... 190, or something like that?"

Maverick corrected him, stating, "200, actually."

Max nodded, "Yeah, that. Seriously, you must be smarter than Shakira. I hear her IQ is at 170."

Maverick nonetheless shrugged as he paused and said, "An IQ test isn't an exact science. It doesn't necessarily mean your smarter than someone, or not."

Max sighed, "Anyways, let me introduce you to my friends I'm talking about", thinking to himself, *"Luckily, I've already spent plenty of time today hanging out with my other friends Knoll and Leon during fencing classes today, so they won't be suspicious."*

Max found Connor in the guys' dorm, something easy enough but still failing to find Ikuto anywhere. Some progress was better than none.

Max decided to get the introductions underway, introducing, "Maverick, Connor; Connor, Maverick." They shook hands, Max continuing, "Show him your gift Connor."

Connor looked at Max to the latter's nod, the former smiling and snapping his fingers. Electricity danced between his fingertips as he snapped a couple times, allowing a touch of lightning to briefly surround his hand.

Maverick nodded, "Cool. Guess I should show you mine huh?" He went to a soda machine and bought a drink, then levitating it out of the machine's grabbing slot to float it over. "Not skilled enough yet to do more precise things, like opening the can."

Max smiled, "That's alright. As I've seen with Connor and the other guy, Ikuto, it takes time to train in your gift. I only wish I could have some sort of gift myself."

He thought back earlier on his daydreaming of flying then quickly remembered. "Oh, crap! Connor, we gotta find Ikuto! He revealed his gift to a bunch of women!"

Connor shot a look back at him, asking, "Really? Crap." He seemed genuinely concerned, but mostly like he was annoyed because he was enjoying meeting another person with special powers.

Max turned and bumped into the headmaster, thinking, *What the-?... The headmaster?* He then said aloud, "Uh... Sorry sir."

Allan was tall, with medium-length grey hair and a small goatee. He was dressed in a blue suit, but was still clearly the headmaster.

"It's quite alright. Looking for someone?"

Max was very hesitant to speak, *What should I say?*, he thought worriedly. "Ikuto Azure, I believe, is who you're looking for. It's alright... I know his secret. I know all of your secrets."

Allanon looked at Maverick as his soda can opened itself.

Max looked back at Maverick, "Uh... Tell me you did that, dude."

Maverick looked down at the can and back at Max, saying, "I don't think I did, man."

At this Allan chuckled, "You aren't the only ones with the ability to use magic."

Max looked at the headmaster and came to the first conclusion he could think of, asking tremulously, he said, "Oh my god. Are you going to wipe my memory or something, since I don't have magic? Please, I swear I won't tell anybody, sir."

Allan chuckled, "Wipe your memory? Heaven's no! I trust you Maxwell. I know our secret is safe with you." As Max breathed a sigh of relief, Allan continued, "However, you will need a more proper way to have these talents honed.

"To that end I would like both of your friends here to come train with me every Saturday. I've already had a talk with Ikuto and worked things out; he will be joining us for these training sessions. Of course, you are invited to observe as well, Max. Call it a gift for keeping this whole thing a secret."

Allan smiled a sweet, calming line across his face. It was made manifest that Allan was a very kind hearted old man from

83

mere conversation. As everyone walked with him he explained that the training would take quite a while, but he was actually looking for apprentices. He also stated himself to be the last living Wizard, but preferred not to explain why. This made Max slightly uncomfortable, but he and the others decided not to push the matter.

For the next couple of Saturdays after his own classes were over each time, Max observed the others as Allanon guided them through their training. It was interesting, but it made him want to become stronger more than anything. Hopefully for him his day would come, sooner or later.

***

Her classes finished for the day, Shakira wanted to spend a little time with her friends. Her requirements were easy anyway, at least for her; she decided this might be good to have a little girl time with Rally. They headed for a nearby restaurant to eat and talk about whatever came to mind. After getting themselves some cheeseburgers and fries, they sat down.

Shakira asked, "So...had any boyfriends or anything?"

Rally almost spat her soda a little, but stopped. "Well uh... Yeah I guess. You?"

Shakira continued her smiling as she said, "Yep. I've had a few boyfriends and girlfriends. I don't really like one gender more than the other, honestly! Everybody is just so much fun to talk to!"

Rally laughed a little, "I guess that makes sense. My turn to ask something: you like any sports?"

Shakira thought about it for a moment and looked upwards, lost in thought as she placed her fingers to her lips to think. "I guess volleyball is fun. I never really thought about it that much."

Rally nodded, "I like soccer, myself. Basketball is cool, too.""Awesome!", Shakira said as she began eating her food. There was a slight humor to how she ate her food relatively quickly, which didn't necessarily endear poor table manners. It looked more like she was taught table manners, from the dignified air that came with them; the plastic silverware was all placed in precise locations and the napkins tucked neatly in her lap, for example.

Rally couldn't help but comment on it, asking, "So what's with the fancy setup for your food? It's just a cheeseburger."

It was of another humor, because Shakira was even cutting her food carefully into bites each time, except the usual French fry mode one would expect.

Shakira giggled a little before coyly replying, "Force of habit. I'm used to being around people who expect this sort of thing out of me, I guess. I'm so used to it, I don't even really think about it."

Rally seemed to find this rich girl thing a bit annoying, but tried to not pay it much heed; Shakira was pleasant enough and she

85

liked having friends. She then looked down at her burger and realized it had become frozen.

"Oh, my gosh, what happened to your burger?"

Rally looked at her burger, then back up at Shakira with a scared look on her face. "I don't know! I honestly have no idea!" Rally then tried to take it off her plate, but as soon as she touched the plate it was also frozen."Yikes! Whatever you do, don't touch me with your hands!"

Needless to say, Rally was very scared and confused, but today she wouldn't be the only one.

***

Miles sat at his workshop, carefully working on his next puppet. Ventriloquism was an art he had great interest in, regardless of the sometimes mystified demeanor of his peers toward his hobby.

"Well Bob, you are coming along nicely aren't you?" He held his ear to the puppets mouth and then Miles said, "Really? No, I don't think people are that mean. I'm sure they're just as scared of me as anyone else here, but I'll keep what you said in mind."

Tim walked up to him hanging onto a piece of scrap metal; he was welding something together. "You ain't too smart are ya?" Tim Mason was a hick: from the South and proud of it, engrossed in his metalwork. Miles told Tim he seemed a tad obsessed, but to end the conversation quickly would simply reply that it was the pot calling the kettle black.

Tim usually talked to Jared more anyway, since Miles wasn't exactly social and he didn't care.

Tim paused for a moment, since he had finished the meproject he'd been working on for a long time. He decided to get input, asking, "So Jared, what'cha think of my purdy sculpture?"

It was very nice-looking, something he'd fashioned well in the guise of a beautiful woman.

Jared shrugged in his usual very mellow voice, answering, "Wow. It's pretty cool actually. I've made something like that before, but I think yours is better."

Tim grinned, "Hell yeah, its better. You kidding me?"

Suddenly he saw one of Miles puppets get up and walk up to him, causing him to jump backwards yelling, "The fuck is this shit? Kill it!"

He pulled out a shovel and was prepared to smash the thing, when suddenly he heard an authoritative voice. He looked up to see a pale spectre directly in front of him.

"You shouldn't hurt others gifts you know."With the first thing that came to mind Tim yelled, "I don't give a fuck! It's freaky, and I'm smashin' it!" It was then Tim realized nobody else in the room could see what he

was looking at. Right in front of his own eyes
was a ghost.

***

It was a month since Max had joined
the school, it now being April Fools' Day. It
was a holiday he usually hated due to the
often mean-spirited nature of peoples' jokes,
but the last observable couple of them were
funny enough based on his criteria online.
This year would probably be different since he
was having more actual human interaction
this time. He laughed nervously a little at the
thought it could even be fun. Leon was
already out and about that day, so Max was
by himself in the apartment waiting for
fencing classes.

There was a knock at Max's door, so
he answered it and saw that it was Knoll. *"Aw
crap. I've been very distant with him the past
few weeks, or so. I've just had so much on
my mind, what with what's been going on
with Ikuto and Connor. Hell, I only hang with
Leon that much because he's my roommate.
Note to self: 'Make more time for all of my
friends.' It's not all about just Ikuto, Connor
and Leon."*

Knoll spoke first, "Hey Max. It's
Blueberry Waffle Day at the Waffle House
down the street, you wanna go with me?"

Max grinned, "Sure. Oh! Can I invite
one other friend with us?"

Knoll shook his head earnestly, "No!
Never!", prompting from Max a nervous and

unsure look until Knoll grinned saying, "April Fools! Yeah, sure, I guess. Who is it?"

Max smiled, "Oh, it's a writing buddy of mine; his name is Zack. He lives down the hall from us, but I've only ever spoken to him once since I've been here. I figure the three of us could hang at the Waffle House together.""Sure. The more the merrier." Knoll seemed to be in a friendly enough mood, even though Max was sure Knoll noticed how distant he recently was. Max noticed that Knoll was wearing a jacket, so he also decided to put one on for the possible chill.

Max nodded, "Yeah. It'll just be Zack, plus us. I don't want it to get too crowded."

With that they headed over for Zack's door and knocked. Luckily he was at his door, when he yawned out, "Oh, hello there. What brings you to my room?"

As usual, Zack was polite with his mannerisms notwithstanding the earliness cutting his wake in half.

Max decided to be the one to offer, since it was originally his idea. "Knoll and I decided we wanted to go eat breakfast at the Waffle House and I figured I'd invite you to go with us.""Sure, just give me a minute to make myself decent." After Zack got ready, they headed down to the Waffle House.

After ordering their waffles Knoll was the first to speak. "So Max, you've been kinda distant lately, what's been on your mind?"

Max grimaced the thought,

"Straight to the point eh? Meh, it makes sense he'd wonder about it." He then said aloud, "Oh, I've just been hanging with Ikuto and Connor. I guess with the busy days my mind has been elsewhere."

Max slightly felt a squirm in him; he didn't have to tell the whole truth, but it would be difficult to transmit even partially what was going on, hoping it would suffice.

Knoll could infer the discomfort of his friend so he changed the subject, asking, "So Zack, how do you and Max know each other?""Well actually, we both wrote a best-selling book and met online, so we decided to compete with each other over our respective books. We've only ever met in real life once, which was here. What about you?""Max and I are internet buddies too, actually, though not over anything like a writing competition. Actually, we were both working together on an online voice-acting production. It was cancelled, but we've been friends ever since."

Zack nodded in understanding, but before he could speak Max noticed something. "Knoll, is that a manga in your jacket pocket?"

Knoll pursed his lips for a moment, then hesitantly replied, "... Yes."

Max was hysterical in his laughter. "Oh, man! You gotta be kidding me! You always say how much 'history matters most' and how 'the world of fiction is a waste of time and blah, blah, blah.' I thought it funny you wanted to voice act with me, but it turns out you read manga, too?"

Knoll sighed, "...Yes. Truth is, I love manga and anime. It's just a bit of a guilty pleasure because my parents don't like it. They think it's a waste of time and last time they caught me with a manga they made me throw it in the trash. They don't even let me have science fiction, or fantasy novels.""Sheesh. That is harsh, dude. I don't know where I would be without the world of fiction and fantasy. I grew up loving superheroes, giant robots, space battles, elves and wizards."

Knoll nodded, "But on the bright side, I've always had a knack for history and historical battles! I mean, you know that from my book *Grove of Silence*!"

Max nodded, "True, true. So I guess we've all been book authors."

Zack himself added, "I guess so. I never would've thought that I'd be making two author friends here."

Time seemed to fly by as the 3 talked and enjoyed their meal. Max loved waffles; for him they weren't quite the same as pancakes, but it was Blueberry Day, so he couldn't complain. Syrup always had this sweet taste to it that made it addictive to him, so naturally he always put too much on. Max then looked at his cell phone and saw what time it was. "Oh, shit! Look at the time! We gotta get back to class, or we'll be late for Fencing! Sorry Zack, Knoll and I gotta go! I'm sure we'll see you again sometime soon!"

Zack waved politely as they started hurrying for the door saying "Sure thing. See you again soon", though they didn't hear him out the door by the time he spoke.

As they were heading through the halls most of the people were already in their classrooms, so the hallways were relatively empty. As they ran, however, Knoll suddenly was floating in mid-air.

"Uh... Knoll... You're floating!", Max said agape.

Knoll promptly started freaking out, yelling, "How do I get down?" He started flailing as he continued forward, until he realized he started at a fast pace. "Max, how do I stop?"

Max shouted across to him, "I don't know, dude! It's you who's flying, here!"

To make matters even worse, Knoll inadvertently flew into the door of the girls' locker room. Max sighed, unable to leave his friend and pursuant of him through the opening door and screaming women. By the time he opened it most of them were running out the other way.

Running over to him Max saw Knoll with his head bleeding and a dent in a locker door, where his head clearly made impact.

Frustrated, Max asked, "You alright, buddy?" A girl was already sitting beside Knoll, but Max didn't pay much attention to her, as she rubbed Knoll's forehead with slight futility. It was then he noticed her hands turning green as she touched his chest.

After a few moments the bleeding had stopped and the wound on Knolls head closed.

Max suddenly recognized the girl as none other than Colleen, so he bewilderedly asked her, "How'd you do that!"

Colleen looked at her hands, exclaiming, "I-I don't know!"

Max muttered, "Dammit. I can already tell I'm going to be late for fencing, but I can't just leave my friend like this!"

Knoll stuttered, "Y-you'll get in trouble for being in here. All the girls saw me, but only Colleen and I saw you. If you head to fencing class nobody will know you were here, so you won't get in trouble."

Max sighed, because he knew Knoll was right, but... "Dude, I can't just leave you here!"

Knoll chuckled lightly, "It's okay dude. Colleen here can help me. I've met her before and I'll be fine."

Max sighed, as there wasn't much more time to argue because a teacher would be here soon, thus darting him to class. He was late, but the instructor let him in regardless.

As a couple of transfer students were being told the basics Max thought to himself, "*Seems Knoll has gained flying powers of some sort. I gotta admit, I'm jealous; very jealous, since that's the power I want most. Well, more like wind powers that make me fly, but that could be what he has, anyway. At least it'll be easier to explain to him what's going on with Connor and Ikuto now. But I wonder…"*, the instructor's calling concluding his ability to think. "Yes?"

The instructor smiled, "I'd like you and Jericho to give a demonstration for the transfer students. Ten-point match, no rematches. As for the rest of the class, you will all do your usual lessons for the day."

Max was nervous, but felt more confident today than before. He'd been paying for additional lessons on top of the regular fencing classes, which was part of why he'd not socialized with people as much. Jericho had a slight sleepiness in his eyes as well, something Max couldn't wait to take advantage of.

"Play, Ele!", the instructor suddenly barked. This wouldn't be like their previous matches on the first day, as Max took the offensive. He'd previously avoided fighting Jericho for the most part, so he'd wait until he was ready. Jericho parried and went for a stab, but Max parried in return. Jericho smirked, "You're getting better, boy."

Max smirked back with cool reply, "I'm the same age you are, `boy.'"

Jericho gave a dirty look that one could see from behind the mask as he said, "Today I'll show you what separates the men from the boys, kid."

Jericho thrust toward Max, the latter parrying in kind and quipping, "What was it you said about men and boys?"

Jericho growled alongside a deepening aggression evident in his moves. Max was barely managing to dodge and parry each attack, but wasn't able to get a single hit on Jericho. It was like watching a game that he and his old friend in high school played before moving to Florida. It was sometimes referred to as "Dodge!," where the point was simply to block and dodge punch-based attacks.

Jericho grew more furious as they separated and re-entered the fray with no result. Max couldn't land any attacks on Jericho, but he didn't need to. He was simply amused by how increasingly angry Jericho was becoming by being unable to hit him. The latter sighed and they separated for one more moment, Jericho swerving slightly and hitting Max with a satisfactory unprecedented blow."Told you."

Max laughed, "One hit; whoopee. Try it again."

Jericho tried the same move again, but Max saw it coming and parried as such. Yet again Max was stuck on the defensive throughout this part of the match and Jericho couldn't land a single hit. This caused him to snarl, "If you know you're not going to hit me, why don't you just give up?"

Max grinned as he roared, "Who the hell do you think I am? I never give up!"

Jericho growled as the match continued, yet as their foils collided they didn't notice that portals were forming above each of their heads. A swirl of purple and black smoke belched forth as the portals formed, then a disturbing sound shook the room.

From somewhere the call of a bird continued this quake, everyone in the room stopping to remark the noise. Everyone noticed except for Max and Jericho, who continued to fight as if they weren't noticing anythingelse.

A red feathered bird that resembled an eagle with flames lightly forming around its head came out of the portal and landed beside Max. A crimson lizard-like head with flames flaring from its nostrils came out of the portal beside Jericho, as well. Beside Jericho was a dragon and Max a phoenix. The phoenix made angry sounds at the dragon, the dragon snarling in return. Suddenly, Max and Jericho collapsed from exhaustion.

The dragon looked down at Jericho and then spoke, "You summoned me? How pitiful. Such a weakling as to heed me at half-strength. It's insulting. I should kill you now for bringing me here."

The phoenix looked down at Max and also spoke, "The fact you summoned me at half-strength in itself is a miracle; it's never happened before. It should be impossible. You should have to be a great wizard and then summon me at a later date at full strength. However, though I respect the kind of aura I sense from you to summon one such as myself, you are too weak for my tastes. I therefore take my leave."

The phoenix then flew as it vanished into the portal from whence it came, the portal closing shortly thereafter.

The dragon huffed, "This is a waste of my time. I'm going home."

The dragon flew into the portal from whence it came, thus closing the gateway

Max and Jericho slowly sat up as they noticed everyone in the room seemed frozen with fear. That's what it looked like at first, but after a few moments they realized the students physically could not move. They didn't even blink.

Allanon suddenly appeared beside them. "When the rest of them awaken, they will remember none of what has transpired here. But you two... You will. I highly recommend you come with me if you do not want to die."

Max and Jericho could both barely move and Allanon knew it. He acted as if he'd just noticed as he spoke again, "I will take both of you with me myself, with the aid of my magic, but first you must accept it. Know that if you do not come with me, you will surely be killed in the days that come. What say you?"

Jericho smirked, "Do I have much of a choice? I accept."

Max huffed, "What he said. But this sounds fun anyway... I accept."

And with that they felt themselves vanish into a void of darkness before appearing in Allanon's private study. Only time would tell what await them in the coming days of their scholastic life, now that all was revealed.

Chapter 4 - Everyone Gets Acquainted

Jericho slowly opened his eyes. His head hurt, but he wasn't the type to verbally state his complaints, so he just dealt with it as his blurred vision came into focus. The headmaster wasn't yet in the room and lying on the floor across from him was Max.

Max... He had really surprised Jericho, today. The latter thought of him as nothing more than an annoying kid, but today he proved he had a lot of moxie. He had also proven that he was a deserving adversary, to say the least. Jericho couldn't help but respect him a little bit now, though he wasn't ready to say it just yet.

Jericho wasn't your typical collegiate; he grew up in a rough neighborhood, so he was expected to act tough on a daily basis. Some would call that bad, but he was used to it. He wasn't wealthy or anything either, he got in under a scholarship for sculpting. If his buddy Sho could see him now Jericho wouldn't feel as tough. It was good that he didn't then, since Jericho didn't like showing weakness to anyone.

Jericho saw Max sitting up and looking at him. Jericho sighed, "What?", asking mildly.

Max, a little startled, responded, "Nothing... er... did you notice what we did back there?"

Jericho felt like he was talking to a child again, but decided to humor him anyways: "Of course I did."

Max nodded, looking around and turning back to Jericho. It as if he'd known what he wanted to say but had paused anyways, Max finally saying, "I gotta admit, that was pretty cool."

Jericho shrugged, "I guess it was." To himself, he thought, *"If almost getting eaten by a dragon is your idea of cool... though I guess it was really cool to see a real, actual dragon. Phoenix wasn't bad either. Always been a fan of fantasy stories."*

Max suddenly grinned. Jericho sighed, "You find somethin' funny?"

Max shrugged,"Nothin'."

Jericho smirked, "That's what I thought."

Max sighed, "Would you stop trying to be a badass all the time? It gets old, dude."

Jericho shrugged, "I can't help it. It's how I am." Jericho was actually serious that it was his nature, no malice intended. He had a temper, which is why outside of fencing he kept to himself, bar his personal friends.

He did that to avoid hurting anybody. He knew all too well he had a bad temper, so he did his best to keep his distance from most people and then let out his frustrations while fencing. The fact he made fencing Team Captain was just a bonus, though today hurt his pride quite a bit.

Suddenly the headmaster appeared atop his chair as if from thin air. "My actual name is Allanon Remus, though everyone knows me as Allan. And as Max has somewhat come aware of, and you Jericho might have guessed... I am actually, a wizard."

Jericho smirked. "*Gee, wouldn't've guessed that one Sherlock",* he thought to himself.

Allanon continued. "The story I am about to tell you is a difficult one, but you must know it... for it involves you greatly."

Allanon spoke of his first apprentice, a man named Alexander. He grew to become the strongest wizard of his age group, and arguably the strongest wizard that ever lived. One day a large war came about between Alexander. The few remaining wizards who were all members of the Wizarding Council, all except for Allanon– who refused to get involved– left.

Alexander had various myths and legends around him, thus leaving unclear if the individual was evil, good or simply a threat. Allanon made it unclear which was true, but stood by that Alexander was in his own eyes his friend to the end.

Either way, they couldn't ever permanently kill Alexander, as when he "died" he simply reincarnated each time as a child under new parents. Not only that, but he retained all his memories of his past lives and all of his power and spells. They thus couldn't figure out how to permanently kill him. The solution the wizards ultimately decided on was to create a new kind of spell: one causing him to die and thus reincarnate, but as five children instead of one. Therefore his power was split equally between five different people.

In addition they had no memory of his past lives, hopefully giving them a clean slate. The Wizards asked Allanon, should they succeed, if he could someday seek out the children and train them. They said this as their last request, so he accepted. The spell was cast at the cost of the casters' lives, leaving him as the last living Wizard in the world.

Allanon was informed that the way he'd know who these children would be was that they would have a Summon as their first spell. Summoning was supposed to be far too advanced for people to have as their first spell, so this was a clear way to know.

Max was the first to speak. "So you're saying Jericho and I-"

Allanon immediately replied, "Yes. You are two of the five children. Normally when a Summon is performed, the biggest trait of yours reflects that whom you summon. That trait, I believe, is one trait you each inherited from your previous lives as Alexander, a different trait for each of you.

"Max, you inherited Alexander's determination. Alexander was the kind of man anyone would follow into the fires of the Underworld if he asked them to. He was also the kind of man who if struck him down would never stay down. He would get up and fight again every time. You have inherited this will to never give up, making your Summon is a Phoenix."

He then turned to Jericho, saying, "Jericho. You inherited his fiery temper, something thing for which Alexander was known. But it wasn't just blind rage, though many thought it was. He was angry at the way our world was. Ergo, part of his temper was also largely due to protectiveness over his friends. He was, above all else, a passionate person. He had a passion towards all things he liked and things he wished to protect. You've inherited this. I've witnessed it myself: you defend people whom are bullied and use your temper against those whom would bully others. In fact, it's nearly gotten you expelled on multiple occasions. This temper is the reason for your Summon... the Dragon."

Jericho tried his best not to smile at hearing that part. To say he was proud of it was an understatement, but he didn't want to push his luck either.

Then he heard Max speak up. "How am I supposed to believe something like that? I mean, don't get me wrong, having a Phoenix is awesome and all... but reincarnation? That sounds like bullshit to me, dude. Plus, I don't like thinking of myself as having been anyone else but myself, even if it were true! I'm my own person, an individual! Maxwell Schnieder! Not part of some stupid juju magic wizard from the Stone Age named Alexander!"

Jericho was about to make a sarcastic remark when he suddenly saw Allanon's face change its expression. He saw Allanon's eyes seemingly catch fire, so to speak. *"Oh shit...this doesn't look good",* he worriedly thought to himself.

Allanon's anger rose, to the extent he yelled, "How dare you insult Alexander like that! I have a mind to expel you right now, boy! He's more than half the man you are, both literally and figuratively! You will have to pray that someday you will be as good as he is! I don't want to ever hear you insult that man's name again! Do you hear me!"

To state the obvious intimidation emanating from the headmaster's voice would've been ill-advised. Even Jericho intimidated by it as a mere bystander, as he watched

Max stutter out, "I'm sorry I insulted your friend... It's just that I also want to prove that I'm a good person because of who I am, not because of who I might've been in some sort of past life... I don't even believe in past lives."

Jericho decided to speak up for Max as well. "I'm sure he didn't mean much by it, Headmaster. I can understand wanting to blow off your own steam. My mom is a single parent and I had to be the man of the house back home. I know how hard it is to try to prove yourself around people. *"This makes us even, Max",* he thought.

Allanon nodded slowly, his face softening as he replied, "True, true. I'm sorry as well... I just don't like people speaking ill of my dear friend. Since he retained all his memories each life, it was like he'd never died, until that last time. In all truthfulness, I just miss my old friend. I miss a lot of what my life once was like."

Allanon quickly regained his composure and continued, "But, more to the point: you are individuals. Don't think any differently. Likely, you were born as the personifications of his Determination and his Rage respectively, but as you grew up you became your own individual people based off of life experiences. Anything after your pampers was based on your own decisions in life and who you are as individuals, not my friend from many years ago."

Jericho would admit this calmed him, such as seemed to have the same effect on Max. "*Good*", he thought to himself. "*The last thing we need is a fight between the Headmaster and Max. I doubt that would end well.*"

Allanon nodded, "Now. I will be your mentor from now on. Every day you have classes, I will have you come down here after you've completed them to train in your magic. There is a coming threat that will come and you must be ready for it." Such announcement was provocation for Jericho to say, "Excuse me? Coming threat?"

Jericho thought it peculiar that Allanon disclosed a matter of life and death so casually for the while, since the description was beginning to transcend his comfort.

Allanon sighed, "I'm not ready to speak with you about that just yet…you will just have to trust me. We need each other, I assure you."

**

Max was nervous about it all and decided to immediately accept Allanon's proposal. He unquestionably had his suspicions, but what choice did they really have? This threat was going to come whether they knew about it or not and they needed preparation, so it was best to go along with Allanon nicely. He hadn't exactly scored points with the Headmaster a few mere moments ago.

"I kinda gotta make up for that as much as I can," Max thought to himself.

Allanon stopped at the place Connor and Ikuto trained at, the same where Max also saw Mavrick. *"Oh yeah, I forgot Maverick was training there as well…guess I just didn't really notice him there most of the time. Quiet guy I guess."*

Allanon spoke, "People, please all gather here and listen closely."

Max jumped, seeing people he'd not noticed were there. He noticed a young man that kept to himself holding an eerie puppet while talking to it. Even Knoll, Colleen and

Rally were appeared, but what surprised him the most was that he also saw Shakira.

There were a few other people there he didn't quite recognize, as well; there was a redneck with short brown hair and a messy school uniform, but one could tell by his speech mannerisms as he talked to the person next to him that he was Southern. There was also a kid with nerdy glasses, short brown hair and a scar through his left eye.

Next to both of them was a guy with darker brown skin with a mellow expression on his face, none other than his old friend Jared! He'd have to catch up with him later, since Allanon began orating, "I know most of you just arrived today, so I will need help with training you all. I have two students here who have been quick learners. They will be helping me to teach you. Ikuto and Connor... Congratulations on your new responsibilities!"A brief awkward applause commenced, then Allanon continued, "Ikuto, you will be aiding the training for your brother Simon as well as Nero, Miles, Maverick, and Jared. Connor, you will be aiding Rally, Colleen, Tim and Knoll. While I will be providing the training for all of you I will have Max, Jericho and Shakira directly under my wing. Please split off into your groups, I will be talking to the rest of you shortly."

As they did so Max and Jericho were joined by Shakira, the former's mind drifting briefly to Maverick. "*Poor guy is the odd man out, being the only person who's been around as long as Connor and Ikuto but is among the newbies. Heh, look at me talk. I'm basically a newbie myself,"* he thought.

The silence was uncomfortable, so Max decided to open with, "Hi, Shakira! It's awesome to see you again."

Shakira hugged him immediately, cheering, "It's good to see you too! I wish I could've been in the group with Rally, but we're different so I understand."

Shakira releasing her hug left Max to his surprise at what she said, an emotion he couldn't understand, himself.

"You mean, you're?"

Shakira giggled and nodded, "Mhmm!""So what's your-"

Shakira smiled, "A monkey! Headmaster Allany said it's because of my energy and stamina of Alexander!"

Max started asking, "So how'd you summon-"

Shakira silenced him with a look. Her face suddenly solemn with dread, she replied, "I don't want to talk about it."

Max felt the hairs on the back of his neck stand up on end, so he quickly tried to come up with a new topic. "So! Why's Rally here?"

Shakira's expression reverted to a smile just as quickly as it had gotten serious. "Oh, she froze her cheeseburger. Apparently, she has ice-powers or something! What about your friend Knoll?""Apparently he can fly because he accidentally flew into the girls' locker room. I'm thinking it might be some sort of Wind powers though. Colleen healed him with some sort of green energy, so that must be her gift."

Shakira smiled as he grinned a little, "Neat-o. So, what an April Fools' Day we're having, right?"

Her demeanor was still chipper, but calmer than she'd previously been; this was something that Max was pleased by, since if she was always as hyper as people said she was it might get old. This allowed him to recognize the depth of her beauty, her hair and breasts adored. Even if pink was an odd color in Max's opinion, he felt it looked good on her. He blushed a little for realizing he was staring too much, something luckily breaking silence.

"How dare you!" It was the nerdy looking kid, Nero. Ikuto laughed, "I'm sorry, Nero, but you do look like him. You got the short hair, nerdy glasses and the scar on your head, and you're a wizard now too."

Nero shouted, "My last name doesn't even resemble pots and pans, and I just found out I'm a wizard today!"

He then noticed Jared laughing and looked back at him, "What's so funny huh?! I'll have you know I have Earth Elemental abilities!"

Jared smiled calmly, noticeably restraining himself in reply, "I got lava."

Nero was taken aback by this as he dramatically jumped backwards, like a cartoon character of some sort displaying dramatic shock. He then celebrated, "Oh yeah, well with my earth skills I can dig underground and attack you from below!"

Jared maintained his calm smile as he interjected, "But, I got lava."

Nero shouted briefly, making random wild sounds before continuing, "Oh, yeah? I'm not going to lose this just yet! What about this, then: I can send giant stone pillars at you if I train enough. What say you to that!"

Jared laughed lightly and responded, "I still got lava", then caused lava to form around his hand for a spell without singing his being. After a brief few moments the lava turned into a bunch of ash as it fell to the ground. At this

Nero simply pouted and folded his arms, then noticed everyone staring at him. He began blushing as he adjusted his glasses, saying, "I have other talents anyways. Like I know how the US government started all the world's biggest conspiracies and-"

Before he could finish, nobody was paying attention to him any longer. The talking in the earlier procession resumed, Nero defiantly scoffing, "Well then, your loss!"

Allanon was talking to Connor and his group, so Max decided to take the advantage and head on over to Jared and greet him. Shakira was already headed to talk to Rally and he didn't care what Jericho wanted to do, so he just left him behind. Hewalked over to Jared and said, "Hey, dude! It's been too long!"

Jared smiled and said, "Wow, it's been a long time Max; I haven't seen you in years." Jared's speech patterns were usually mellow and calm, but Max knew better that he could be really funny sometimes when he was willing to open up; he also had somewhat of the occasional temper, which must have been the origin for his Lava powers.

Max smiled, "I know, dude! So how you been?""Eh, same ol' same ol'. The usual, I guess; at college now, as you can see."

He smiled while scratching the back of his head, unsure what to say. For the most part Jared was a friendly person, even if he was pretty quiet and got along with most people fairly well. That was probably what made it so easy to talk to him, after all this time."Yeah, apparently. Same here, as you can see." He was being sarcastic this time so as to kindly tease Jared. It was something he liked to do from time to time and his old habits of friendly picking with Jared just came naturally.

Jared paused to think, following, "Well I'm in welding, nowadays. I made a statue in Tulsa, Oklahoma. It's pretty popular; they like to show it off at the fair every year and stuff.""Yeah? Sounds pretty cool. Actually, a statue would be really neat to see, something big like that. I made a best-selling book, but you've probably heard of it before. I guess we both did our own amazing stuff in our own way."

Jared nodded, "Yep. I read your book too. It was pretty good", maintaining his mellow, friendly demeanor. Maybe a little familiarity could calm Max down after the crazy day he'd had.

Max sighed, "So what an April Fools' Day, huh? I mean, a whole bunch of people are here!"

Jared laughed a little as he said, "Yeah, I know, right? It's pretty crazy!"

He was still quiet when in entered emphasis to his voice, but that was regular.

Still, talking to Jared sometimes got boring, so Max was fortunate sometime else entered the conversation. It was the Southern guy Max had noticed earlier, who seemed to prefer hanging with Jared over being with his group.

Tim said, "Shut up, I'm askin' 'em, I'm askin' 'em."

He appeared to be speaking to someone next to him, but as far as Max could tell there was no one there. Tim continued, "So… What's wrong with y'all, to be asked to join this club of freaks and wierdos?"

Max smirked, "Aren't you the pot calling the kettle 'black?'"

Tim replied, "Well, aren't you a wordy little bastard? I was askin' why y'all are freaks, not your input 'bout me."

Max shrugged, "I can summon a Phoenix, and as for Jared... Well, you saw that lava in his hand, earlier..."

Tim replied, "Bird Boy and Human Torch? Oh, we gonna save the world, alright! Don't forget, we got the Southern man who can see dead people!"

Max smirked and replied, "Actually, the guy with fire is someone else here, but you know that."

Tim nodded, "True that. We got two people with the same power here; I think there can only be one. Hey Jared, you should go duke it out with Wonder Boy over there. There can only be one."

Jared looked nervous and said, "I just got my lava today, I ain't that good with it yet."

Tim smirked, "Well I'll be, you do speak.""I've talked before, smartass. You just don't shut up.""Awe I love you too", making kissing noises sarcastically at Jared.

Max decided this was getting too awkward and responded, "I'll talk to you guys, later."

Jared replied, "Okay. See ya later, Max."

As Max walked off he heard Tim behind him saying, "This is why we don't have many friends: you always scare off the new guys."

Jared disagreed, saying, "No, I think just you did."

Max knew who he wanted to talk to; it had been on his mind earlier.

"Maverick... I'd forgotten about you completely. You doing alright?"

Maverick was sitting on a bench only a couple feet away, quietly piddling with a piece of metal. "Oh yeah, I'm fine."

The way he said it made Max a little worried so he walked over to him.

"Dude, any idea why Ikuto and Connor got to be leaders and you didn't?"

Maverick seemed to retreat a little, when he said that. *Great Max. You and your big mouth,"* he thought to himself, irritably.

Maverick defensively opined, "I'm just... having trouble getting the hang of my abilities, I guess. Ikuto and Connor were fast learners, so I guess it's just kind of discouraging", prompting

Max to sit next to him.

"Don't worry about it too much, I'm sure it's different with everybody. Some just take longer to understand things than others, you know? Look, I had trouble with fencing. On my first day, I got my ass whooped. But you know what I did? I kept practicing and now the same guy can't even touch me!"

"Yeah, fair enough. Just can be difficult to deal with I guess. Thanks, though."

Maverick got up and started practicing his abilities by lifting a trash can, signaling to each of them that there was hope for him, yet.

***

Shakira split off from her incarnate peers Max and Jericho relatively fast. It was too quiet and she was getting bored, so she headed over to talk to Rally. She noticed not long after she left that Max was going to meet someone, so

Shakira smiled and asked Rally, "Hey, so are things getting any better?"

Rally nodded slowly, "At least now I can touch things without freezing them. Headmaster Allanon helped me with that.""Well, that's good!""So, what brought you here? I remember Allanon taking me to the infirmary and assuring you that everything would be okay, but I didn't see you at all, until now."

Shakira smiled, "I can summon a Monkey."

Rally had a very surprised expression on her face. "Well, that's... different. How'd you manage that?"

Shakira's face again turned stony as she thought to herself, *I'm not about to talk about that.* Her frightening expression announced well, so Rally changed the subject, nervously saying, "S-so you noticed Simon's here?" Once again smiling, Shakira said, "Yeah I saw that! That's totally neat!"

She then turned to listen to Allanon speaking to the others, himself speaking from a gently audible volume, "For today, I just want you to see what you are comfortable with. Don't do anything too dangerous... Try and practice meditation where you think it best. You have to learn to calm yourselves and keep yourself at peace, because the last thing you want to do is let your powers run amok without your permission."

In the background Tim and Miles were talking, Tim replying, "Oh! 'Gay Chicken', is it? Pucker up, bitch!"

Miles got ready to kiss Tim, when he backed up and says, "Ah, shit! Damn, you win!"

While there was definitely awkwardness that day, it seemed to be that was all that was happening. In the end it was more about socializing than anything else, but that's what any of them needed that day: to calm themselves from the craziness of its' circumstances and to know that they weren't alone in them. Nobody outside of those present would remember any of the various magic incidents that had occurred, so it was almost like their own secret little club. In the end this day was definitely going to be the most memorable April Fools' Day any of them had ever had so far, perhaps more than they'd ever have.

Chapter 5 – Leon's Loyalty

Leon smiled, for today there was a good start to his day. He woke up bright and early and even though he wasn't usually a morning person, he woke up as if he was, full of energy and in a good mood. He ate a very light breakfast because he typically didn't eat as much as one averagely would. He just didn't need it.

After all of that was done he proceeded towards class, on the way meeting up with Connor. The two of them ended up in conversation about heavy metal bands. April 1st was an odd day in that he somehow couldn't remember much of anything worth noting. Today, however, was the next day and things were going smoother.

It was now time for fencing classes to begin and when everyone was paired off for the dueling portion Max was against Jericho as usual. At this point it was like the instructor kept them fighting each other on purpose to develop their rivalry. Meanwhile, Leon fought Syanne, which was somewhat typical. Sometimes he went up against Connor, but in recent times it wasn't the case because of the skill gap between Leon and Connor; Connor was a decent fencer but was not a member of the fencing team.

Meanwhile, Leon was third-in-command of the team, effectively a figurehead in primary. Jericho made most of the decisions for the fencing team and Saynne helped him reach those decisions. Leon was rarely involved unless they asked

117

for it, which they rarely did. Other than that Leon's role was essentially just to sit and wait as backup if Jericho or Syanne ever had a sick day and if they ever wanted to leave the team, he could take their place. The Team actually hadn't even begun competition this year. The previous year they had gone against some of the local universities and were actually among the top three, a role they tended to hold consistently. Time would tell how this year would go.

For this moment, Leon would be fighting Syanne. She was a bitch and Leon said this openly in the past, so it was needless to say they did not get along.

Syanne replied, "Ready to hit the mat, today?"

Leon responded, "You seem pretty sure of yourself."

Syanne respond by speaking in French, expecting Leon to not know what she was saying. On the contrary, Leon had taken French classes before and he knew that what she said in French translated to, "I'm far better than you, idiot."

Leon smirked, "Essen sie eine tüte du dicks." His German in this case translated to "Eat a bag of dicks."The phallic reference completely obvious in the phrase gathered her blush in fury to swing down her high overhead strike. Leon redirected the strike by raising his left hand straight up and his tip pointed to the right. As it angled downward her blade glanced off of Leon's, missing him harmlessly. This was because Leon was left-handed. Syanne brought her blade up and tried to slice his stomach, but managed to get out of the way. This was notwithstanding that the padding would've protected his stomach regardless.

After a while Leon began to get tired, so Syanne took advantage of that and went for a leg sweep. This cheap move left Leon on his back with his left leg underneath him. He shouted in agony as Max ran away from his fight with Jericho asking, "Leon, what's wrong?"

Leon, was in pain and not in a patient mood, shouting,"Look at me! What the fuck do you think happened!"

Connor muttered under his breath, "Syanne is more of a bitch than even I realized."

With that Connor and Max walked Leon to the nurse and therapist Ms. Smith.

"Good lord, y'alright?", remarked a beautiful woman with blonde hair and green eyes. She had freckles on her cheeks and wore a brown cowgirl hat, black cowgirl boots at all times. Hardly professional, but the rest of her attire made up for it. This included a white labcoat over a white button-up shirt and black dress pants. Her name tag said

'Anna Smith,' though obviously she preferred everyone call her 'Miss Smith.'

Max responded, "Leon twisted his ankle really badly in fencing class."

Connor replied, "So in other words, Syanne is a bitch. Nothing new there."

Bumping her fists to her waist Ms. Smith responded, "Well shucks, ah better help the poor feller out! Bring him in!"

Max and Connor helped him to the bed as Smith removed his shoe and placed a splint on his leg.

Miss Smith responded, "I don't recommend walkin' on it too much, but I know Leon usually isn't one fer listenin' to medical advice. Oh, and 'Max,' is it?"

Max replied, "Yeah?"

Miss Smith responds, "If ya see Saynne around, tell her she's due fer a session with me for this."

Max chuckled, "I'll let her know next time I see her in class."

As they left the nurse office Max and Connor were striking up a conversation about a movie involving two Irish immigrant vigilantes, one they both loved seeing. Max and Connor seemed to be getting along better each day. Connor was presently headed for orchestra practice and as he walked into class there stood a slightly overweight large man with short brown hair, a slight sunburn and kind-hearted blue eyes. For some reason Mr. Darren preferred they use his first name alongside the 'Mr.' Perhaps it was his way of effacing simultaneous formal and casual. He was a kind man, but also strict and direct about things.

Leon smiled, "Good morning, Mr. Darren. Are we going to be doing the same song today?"

Mr. Darren smiled, "Yes we are, actually. Don't worry, we're still taking it slow on this song for today since it's a more complicated piece."

Not long after VIncent and Roger came inside, Vincent somewhat muscular in build, 6'5" with blonde hair and beard. As a cat he possessed one red eye and one blue eye, while Roger was tall and thin with round glasses and dark brown hair.

Vincent was multi-talented, an expert in computer graphics design and the like. He made a bunch of 3D models based on various types of architecture such as statues, having won an award on making a realistic depiction of a probable Atlantis. He'd also hacked into several government websites and consequently went to prison twice for it.Nonetheless, Vincent also had a passion for the drums, be it in orchestra as well as in rock and metal music. This is why Leon asked him to join the band; Vincent agreed but was too busy to meet Max yet.

Roger had a similar story, though perhaps less extreme. Roger had an IQ of 145 and had an interest in theater and acting, but also had a passion for bass guitar. He also enjoyed playing the violin; depending on where you came from, 'the fiddle.' He felt people often underestimated the nice melody one could create with the instruments. Not that people would believe him since people often found Roger annoying, but Leon didn't mind it.

As class started the song began for the day. It started out as a simple melody with an acoustic guitar being played, followed by Leon and a few others on the cellos. The song was soft and melodic at first, with beautiful singing being done by an echoing female over a recording. The song was soothing and calming at first, with a gradually speedy procession of Vincent and the drummers along with the strings. All went silent as Roger and others softly played the violin, displaying the piece's melancholy that followed up with the strings displaying tension. Then the other instruments starting increasing in speed as the strings and drums built anticipation. Afterwards, the piano joined in calmly while the instructor spun the conductor wand carefully to each member of the orchestra.

He had them stop to rest for a few moments and they resumed where they left off. The song seemed to hint at a journey as the strings moved slowly and gained speed. The song became almost playful, yet adventurous. Then, the drums and cymbals' intensity suggested a darkness, like an approaching calamity.

It followed with silence and the drums' thumping. Thump-thump-thump. Thump. Thump. Thump. Thump-thump-thump. Thump. Thump. Thump. Thump-thump-thump. The song became loud and frantic as the pace grew, referencing the climax's great payload. Then, the finale ended with a loud BUH-BUM! The piece was a fun song for Leon and the others who enjoyed it, even if it was more technical. The teacher noticed a few minor hiccups, causing them to repeat with the same break in the middle as before so that they didn't have to do the whole song in one go.

When finally the class ended, the rest of the day was less eventful.

A few days later Leon had Vincent and Roger meet up at the dorm to introduce themselves to Max, who seemed surprised when he first saw them. Leon was a little nervous about scaring Max off, but thankfully Max seemed more surprised than scared.

"Guess I should handle the introductions", Leon thought as he smiled and said, "Max, I'd like you to meet Vincent and Roger. We're going to try them out for our bassist and drummer; I'll also be helping with background screams, since as we've discussed before you prefer mostly singing. That's why you'll be the main vocals. That leaves myself as guitarist, along with the other guitarist being Connor, of course. Sound cool?"

Max nodded, "Of course, I guess. I mean, it's a little weird to be meeting them all at once, but I'm not the music expert here really; so, it's whatever."

Leon nodded to himself. *"Guess that's as good an answer as I'm going to get really. At least Max isn't mad or anything."*

They ended up deciding to go to Leon and Max's room to plan, Max saying, "Well for lyrics I was thinking of this", showing lyric papers to him.

Leon smiled, "Pretty impressive, I've got to say", thinking to himself, *"Reminds me a lot of my own lyrics... really dark, like the songs I wrote after my mom passed away when I was little.*

Max smiled, "By the way, I think I remember hearing you were German? I looked up some translations and was thinking we might have one part be in German, since I've always found the language cool anyways."

Leon nodded, "It's funny, really. I ended up learning a lot of it from Dad actually, but yeah, German sounds awesome."

Leon pulled out his guitar and began riffing. Max nodded and said, "I think it should go a little slower, making the song feel a bit more... foreboding, ya know?"

Leon nodded, "Got it... like this?" He slowed his playing down somewhat, with a bit of deeper tuning to it.

Max nodded in response, "Yeah, that's it!"

Vincent nodded, "And for the drumming, what would you think of this...?", hitting the side of the bed in a certain manner that gradually increased in speed, making an apt drumming beat.

Max grinned, "Yeah! That's great!"

As they day continued they were already starting work on their first song, Leon smiling, "Oh! I forgot to tell you all, but I got us a gig at the Waffle House near here. You guys know the place?"

Max nodded, "Yes, actually. I ate their once recently with my buddies Knoll and Zack."

Leon nodded, "Yep. We'll just be covering some songs for now, but a gig is a gig!"

Max grinned, "Wow. That *is* fast! I can't wait!"

Leon smiled, "Glad to hear it, man! I'm looking forward to it!"

That night, they rocked the house, Leon laughing as he thought, *"Definitely an unorthodox place for a metal concert, but, why the hell not?"*

They started with covering 'Child of Sweet' again, following it up with 'The Beast and the Harlot.' The guitars were in perfect sync from earlier practice, so things were proceeding as planned; people even liked the music, one of the people in the audience even said "This makes eating Waffles seem epic!" As Connor began shredding, Leon began screaming until the solo let up and it was Max's turn to sing again. The guitars created melodies as Max continued singing, Leon backing up in synchronicity. The drums went rapid as the guitars and bass built up to the next section. Leon's guitar started strumming the next part, while the drums messaged the background for the singing up front.

The whole band reached the end perfectly, concluding the availability of the minimum two-song set. They stayed and ate some waffles and chatted it up for a while. Then when they decided it was time to leave, Max and others heading for a bathroom break while Leon stepped out to the fresh air.

He looked up at the sky, how beautiful it was; it was cold and dark out, but the night sky ascended its' glamor. It felt almost welcoming to him, a feeling he didn't get to enjoy for very long with drunkards approaching. One of them stopped at Leon, yelling,

"Hey! I remember you! You were one of them singers at the Waffle House, earlier!"

Leon thought to himself, "*Oh great. I've got a bad feeling about this,*", nodding patiently and asking, "Yes, I am. Why?"

"Hey, you should join our band or somethin', man. Leave the newbies behind. We've already got a record label and everything, but our old singer just quit on us. What do you say... give us a try?"

Leon smiled but shook his head, "No thanks. I'm happy with my friends, but thanks, anyway."

The guy gave him a dirty look, saying, "You'll regret that, you know."

Leon ignored the guy as he went back inside, not noticing Connor had gone outside as well. After a few moments Max came out of the bathroom, Vincent and Roger also already out by then.

Leon laughed, "Did you fall in?"

"Oh, ha-ha. No. I just ate too much I guess. Was afraid I'd never leave that toilet," Max responded sarcastically.They then heard a bunch of noise outside, as if something were breaking; Leon ran outside and saw Connor, beaten up with his head through Leon's car window. He looked at Connor and spoke urgently to him, "Can you hear me Connor? Who did this to you?"

A dark, drunk-sounding voice behind him said, "I did."

Leon turned around and dodged a punch from the drunk guy from earlier. He brought friends and soon everyone was fighting in the street, provoking Leon to yell furiously,

"How dare you do this to my friends! I told you I wouldn't leave my friends behind for your band! What more do you need?"

The drunk guy swung at Leon again, but he instinctively dodged as he punched him back. This time the lush went flying, Leon looked at his fist and asking himself, "I didn't hit him *that* hard...did I?"

He then felt like something was behind him and turned to see a wolf walking on its hind legs like a human, almost werewolf-like. It stood taller than him with calm, yellow eyes. It smiled at him with its sharp teeth, yet somehow effacing beauty with its white and black fur.

Suddenly the Werewolf asked, "*You* summoned *me*? I'm impressed. Only one with great loyalty to their friends could do that, even at half strength as I am now... I take my leave for now, but you have earned my respect, Human."

The wolf seemingly vanished into the night, leaving Leon and the others completely stunned by what had occurred.

Suddenly he felt nothing but black surrounding himself before he appeared in Allanon's study, who would explain all the things he'd told Jericho and Max.

"You, my friend, are showing one of my favorite of Alexander's features. You see, Alexander was the type of man to never abandon his friends, no matter the cost. He was brave, and strong... but most of all, his friends knew they could depend on him for anything they needed. You have inherited his Loyalty", Allanon chuckled.

Leon nodded, "Though I believe you, it's a lot to take in. However, reincarnation is in fact a part of my beliefs anyways, so this is rather easy to follow. It's just really crazy to think that Max, Jericho, Shakira and I all reincarnated from the same man... especially since we're all so different."

Allanon nodded, "Yes... And there's still one more of you out there, somewhere."

End of Arc I

Arc II

Chapter 6- Killjoy

Brokk looked at the dark skies, where not even an ounce of light had ever shown through once in the 23 years he'd been alive. People say there was a time when it did, though only the elderly ever said so and their days were numbered; too weak; easier to kill. The world Brokk lived in was quite like ours, but different.

In his world technology was much more primitive than ours and magic already reigned supreme.

Brokk had short blonde hair with some brown streaks in it, a black cowboy hat and wore a dark blue trench coat over all black clothing. He was tall and skinny while having a very threatening appearance, wearing black boots without heel spurs per the lack of horse.

This environment was much like our American Old West, except magic came along and made it to where there was little need for technology to go any further. It became quite common for even middle-class citizens to have some level of magic. The force that was discovered in general drew from darkness itself and corrupted the planet's life force, causing the world to be encased in both literal and figurative darkness.

What they still used of technology's pollution didn't help, though most of the sky's black was from the dark magic. It was so strong within the world it actually made people hostile towards one another, regardless of intention. Representative of their technology were things such as trains, which caused a lot of pollution but were mostly used by the wealthy.Then there were Jade lights. They were made by a mix of technology and magic rune inscriptions put onto Jade; this blend meant that magic powered the lights and technology sustained them. If it weren't for these lights there would not be light. In addition these lights weren't the only form available, as sometimes Jade was not accessible and other utility rune types varied from city to city.It was also not recommended to travel alone from city to city, as very dangerous animals thrived outside them and were often strong enough that those who weren't experienced magical users would find themselves quickly devoured.

They had a weakness in that they were afraid of the Jade lights, but these were not very portable, meaning that treks between city were dangerous. Brokk was lucky in that he happened to be strong enough to do it by himself, though just barely.

In any case corruptions throughout caused many wars pre-present day and some still occurred around. It was common for not even a country to maintain unity, so the world was separated by cities whose harmony certainly kept impressively.

The 'ruler' of this world was simply the strongest and wealthiest man on the planet. Other than his own military, the city he ran and the fact all other people were afraid of him he controlled very little of what happened in the world. Despite this, people still referred to him as the 'Leader' of Earth.

Most of the wars that happened were in a sense merely excuses to let out pent up aggression from residing on this plane. Either way, this was a land commonly referred to as the "Dark World."

Brokk hadn't interacted with many people, which perhaps led that this city felt so uncomfortable for him. As he walked along the city he saw the size of the buildings, themselves much taller than back home. They were made from harder materials, for one, though he wasn't sure what the material was. They had a clean glossy feel... this place had to be of status.

Not like his old hometown... the place was by now a hollow shell destroyed in a previous war. Even before that it was more of a small town than a city, with wooden buildings and very little plant life, meaning they had to rely on stealing resources from other cities. This was likely why it was marked for destruction.

All that could be said was that he was another victim of one of the many wars. He often tried to avoid everybody. Everybody that is, except for 'her.' 'She' was Morrigan, his only companion over the years. She was untainted by this world, a sweet, naïvely innocent girl.Merely days ago she vanished from the city, however. He looked high and low for her but could not find her anywhere. He ultimately decided she wasn't anywhere in the city at all: she had to be outside of it. Thus it was on this day March 1st he'd be searching for her. He had to find her. She was all he had, and he loved her.

He had his hand on his revolver, the gun modified with magical runes and could fire rounds to pierce armor. People that used magic weren't uncommon, so it was a small comfort to him to even have the weapon. Better than nothing, though. He walked along the beautiful city, "Jariahville" they called it. Its' difference from his home made it feel claustrophobic.

He found a nearby saloon to be familiar, so he walked in and ordered a whiskey. It was the last of his money, but he didn't want to feel out of place, even if he sat at the bar with his gun. Suddenly he heard a voice behind him.

"Turn around slowly. You're under arrest." While searching for Morrigan he'd become a wanted man. His legendary temper had gotten him into a lot of trouble while looking for her.

Brokk did as asked as he said, "I didn't mean any harm." The words could barely escape his lips. He'd been depressed and lonely this whole time, almost defeated.

The woman looked at him with fierce eyes. "I don't give a shit what you meant, you are going to jail all the same!"He was tempted to kill her right now, but was exhausted, broke and hungry; jail food was better than an empty stomach. He decided to surrender peacefully almost immediately. She picked him up, removing his firearm and placed it in the back of her pants as she manned handcuffs of the strongest magical repression on him.

She continued, "You have the right to remain silent. Anything you say will be used against you in the court of the city law. You are guilty until proven innocent. You have the right to an attorney: if you cannot afford one you will have to represent yourself or face immediate execution. If you attempt to escape from jail you will also be executed. If any magic is performed in jail, you will be immediately executed. If you wish to pay a fine and be set free at this time, please state as much."

Brokk shrugged, "I'm broke." This provoked a few patrons to sneer. Rich people often held contempt for the poor as useless wastes to society, nothing of surprise to this captive.

She nodded at his remark and kicked him in the legs. "Filthy bum! I was looking forward to another fine payment today for my new shoes! Your ass is going to jail!"

The serious woman had long pink hair in a braided ponytail, an officer's uniform and looked to be not much older than Brokk himself. As they arrived at the jail she went past a security guard to the large number of cells. They passed them, the prisoners in jail all seeming tired and exhausted. Most of them, however, also looked intimidating and like they didn't want to be spoken to.

He was thrown into a cell with a man with medium-length black hair, unkempt as a rug. He wore a gray-denim jacket, a basic white shirt, and black pants. Brokk was thrown into the cell seeing the man sitting on a bed while cuffed, himself looking at the ground refusing to do much.

The man looked at him and spoke, "So I guess you're my new roomie?"

Brokk was silent for several seconds and then said, "Yes", returning to silence.

The man smirked, "Hmph, don't talk much do ya?", seeming to emanate arrogance to the extent of Brokk's straight-eyed annoyance.

"I don't talk to people who are going to be executed, anyways."

The man smirked, "Like you are much different", prompting his target to ignore him.

"If you're on death row, might as well get your life out there. Who knows? I might be able to tell your story, one day."

Brokk stared off into space as he replied, "Nobody would care."

The statement held truth, but Brokk had mixed emotions; he couldn't really help it. He never had much of a social life or any frame of reference, which often made him unsure of the right words to use when speaking.

The man replied, "Hmph, maybe nobody would, but fate can be really funny sometimes. Name's Cael."

Brokk nodded and said,"Brokk", retreating to his thoughts."... 'Brokk.' Simple, kinda like it. Honestly, they were lucky they even caught me. I was ready to give them a nice piece of my mind. Wouldn't you know it, though... they caught me!"

Brokk grunted as

Cael continued, "I'm a pretty good shot you know! One time, there was this lizard and-""... Do you ever shut up?", clearly indicating a case of heated nerves.

Cael grinned, "Why does it bother you?"

Brokk looked at the floor and replied, "Does it matter?"

Cael replied, "Maybe not. But if so, it'll be the longest hours of your life", marking the verbosity of a demeanor that was likely to be anticipated.

Brokk walked up to Cael and grabbed him by the collar, booming, "Shut up." Given the handcuffs were on their front, Brokk could easily still grab him by the collar.

Cael smiled," Hmm. Looking pretty angry there, is that a challenge?"

Brokk's seemingly deathly stare sat alongside him saying, "No. It's a promise that if we live through this, I will kick your ass", his impatience the never ending and a mind on the trigger. "Sounds pretty fun. I'd like to see if you could live to up to your words", Cael said as

Brokk let go to to continue his brood. He then muttered, "Hpmh. Killjoy."Many of the several passing hours were made up of Cael attempting to speak to Brokk, the latter acting like Cael wasn't even there; finally the prison cell opened and the woman who handcuffed him spoke,

"If you try anything funny, I'll have you know I'm the Sheriff and high in magic rank, so I don't recommend it. I will now be un-cuffing you both and re-cuffing you two for the Courtroom."

Cael looked at her with incredulity, asking, "What? Mr. Emo here?"

The woman gave him a dirty look, but otherwise ignored him. As they were in the stage coach heading for the courthouse, Brokk asked after a while,

"What did you do to get in Jail?", his curiosity meant to delay the inevitable."Why so curious?"

Brokk huffed eagerly, "If we're going to die anyway, why not? I'll tell you mine, if you tell me yours."The Cheshire smile occurred, Cael saying, "Ah, thinking like me for a change. Nothing much, causing havoc around town, getting in some fights. Nothing much."

Brokk nodded, "I have a bit of a temper. The last few towns I went to, I beat up people at each of them and had to run off before they could shoot me."

Cael smirked, "Hmph. We're more alike than I thought."

Brokk allowed a small chuckle as he said, "I doubt it."

The man was obviously arrogant and liked to pick fights. Brokk tended the same due to his temper, not usually one to look for trouble. "Whatever, bigguy."

Cael seemed rather relaxed about the whole situation, which was almost unnerving to Brokk since they were probably going to be killed with the system's corruption.

As they reached the courthouse the building was massive in white exterior and well-secured. The design clashed with the other buildings' blue, the logo on the courthouse in all black and the symbol of a gavel.

As they were let out of the carriage there were gunshots with the cop returning fire;

one of the people firing angrily shouted, "My brother was innocent! Me and my boys are out for a little revenge!"

The sheriff was walking off and all of the security was caught in the firefight. Their distraction seemed a good foil,

Brokk turning to Cael and saying, "We should leave. This is a good opportunity."

Cael smirked, "Hope you can keep up."

Brokk smirked back, "That's my line."

Cael laughed, "Alright, 'bigguy', let's see what you got."

As they were heading out Brokk motioned for Cael to stop, then speaking, "I was hoping to find an opening to get away. Just for this."

Brokk grunted, then stopped. He then attempted again and remarked, "... These aren't like the last cuffs I was in. They're more potent. Otherwise, I could've broken us out of these cuffs with my magic alone."

Cael grinned, "Oh a magic user, are ya? No offense, you don't exactly look like someone who could do so."

Brokk ignored him, though if he had replied he would've thought the remark was rather ignorant; these days it was unusual and yet unremarkable for someone to not have magic. It actually hurt what little pride he had, but he wasn't going to announce it. He did have a backup plan, nonetheless. "I don't think we can stay, since too many people here would try to catch us. I kept two extra six-shooters under some stones right outside of town. They are rune powered, meaning they are supposed to use magic. But they are modified to be able to fire normal rounds, which is what we'll need since we can't get these cuffs off, apparently."

Cael smirked, "Really? Well, if you were able to buy those, why didn't you bribe yourself in the first place?"

It was Brokk's turn to smirk, as he said, "Who says I bought them?"

Brokk thought to himself about how he made a fuss in order to get in a fight with someone in the last town, managing to kill the man and procure what were now their current pair of revolvers.

Cael replied, "That makes more sense, but it's almost that you knew we'd escape. Well, more like you knew you would, but still."

Brokk replied, "I let myself get caught on purpose. I didn't have any money and needed it for food. However, I expected to be able to get out of these cuffs on my own. That didn't really go like I planned."

Cael replied, "What, didn't you know? Jariahville is one of the wealthier cities around here.""Apparently, but we're spending too long standing around talking, so let's get outta here!""Well, I guess. Don't bite off more than you can chew... Fair enough, let's go."

They ran out of the city as fast as they could, though as they reached for their guns they heard growls all around them,

Brokk responding,"Jakaloves."

Jakaloves were a hybrid of Jackals and wolves, referred to as such somewhat sarcastically since they were mean and originally bred for war. Unfortunately, they proved not obedient to humans and bred relatively quickly, leading to them being very common. Their magic origins helped them outweigh their parent creatures through the genetic mix, so

Cael brought a certain culture to the sigh, "I hate these things."

Brokk nodded, agreeing, "Me too. It'd be easier if I had my magic, but these guns will have to do", throwing one into Cael's hands and remarking, "If you were dead I'd have to drag your body along with me. It would only slow me down and get me eaten, so I guess we're allies, now."

Cael nodded, "Guess so", seeming Cael reasonably determined to survive. As they fired on the Jackloves they were in luck as to their small droves; these normally hunted in packs and have a taste for flesh, sometimes attacking humans more often.

As they shot them down Brokk turned to Cael and said, "We better get moving. There will be more of them where that came from, I'm sure. Just be glad it was only Jackaloves."

Cael sighed, "Yeah, it could've been worse- it could've been a Bregal", himself shivering at the thought alongside his compatriot. Bregals were a mix of Grizzly Bear and North Sitarian Eagle, the latter known for being human-sized with a massive wingspan. Leaders of cities failed attempting to make them war mounts, trying to mix them with grizzlies to create a more powerful hybrid. What was produced was essentially a grizzly bear with bird-like hind legs and a massive wingspan on its back.

In addition, North Sitarian Eagles were not the friendliest crossbreed, one never discriminating in its' hatred of all. Due to the fact multiple were created at once, it eventually became a race unto itself.

Brokk instinctively nodded, "A Bregal would've sucked. Anyways, let's get outta here."

Chapter 7 – Slice of Life The first two days of April proved revelatory for the students of Allanon's school, making good news in this context of tiding a little strange. He was standing happily in front of his apprentices and from the looks of things something big was to be announced, yet of what Max didn't know. The headmaster nodded and when he spoke his voice boomed confident. Thankfully, there was a spell making the area they always trained in soundproof.

"My dear students, I am happy to announce five more students will be joining you in your magical studies! They are Charles Rojas, Joey Tuckfield, Shaun Balthier, Sarah Mang, and Vincent Kleiner! Show them your talents, everyone, in the order I named you!"

Charles was first as a blue energy shot out of his hands into the air.

Allanon smiled instructively, saying, "Raw Arcane Magic. Something of a rarity actually! What a splendid gift! Next is Joey, I believe?"

The thus named student sent a lightning bolt into the sky, prompting Allanon to say, "Ah, lightning element user! You'll fit right in training under Connor I'm sure! Shaun?"

They sometimes trained inside, but at this time were outside in a hidden area of the school.

Shaun sent gigantic flames at the sky, Allanon quickly using his staff to extinguish the flames so as to pre-empt possible panic of the students.

Allanon greatly grinned. "You certainly have a lot of power, but you lack control. Still, we have Ikuto to teach you that." He paused for to continue," Sarah?"

She nodded as she flew into the air, forming circles before landing. "Wind Element. My, my, I guess Knoll isn't alone in his studies now. Vincent?"

Suddenly, a large dragon appeared all about them, everyone wide-eyed in reaction. Max was looking at Jericho, who shook his head perhaps to brush it off or in even amazement. Was this another summon?

Allanon smiled, "Illusions... splendid. Very impressive, the size is quite amusing. Though as one can see...", the illusion dissolving and Vincent panting while holding his chest.

Allanon continued, "You over-exerted yourself, and an illusion of that magnitude can't stay for long yet. Anyways, continuing onwards... Yes.

"Well, now that we have that out of the way, I have an announcement to make. I've listened to your feedback as well as re-thought whom might be best compatible with whom, and have changed things in the following way... first, a new teacher. Maverick, step forward."

Maverick stepped forward and spoke, "I-I can't even control my powers properly, yet."

Allanon nodded, "This is true, but I've observed you and noticed that when it comes to cognitive intelligence you're the smartest one here. Just because your application needs work doesn't mean you can't teach others the basics through this; I'll be providing you, Ikuto and Connor with old wizarding books that will aid you in teaching understudies... Which brings my next announcement, everyone.

"The new assortment of students is as follows: Ikuto will be teaching Colleen, Knoll, Simon, Sarah, and Shaun. Connor will be teaching Charles, Joey, Rally, Jared and Nero. Last but not least, Maverick will be teaching those like himself who are the more unique of the gifts among us.

"Know that no one power is truly greater than another in the right hands, but sometimes it takes one with similar gifts to your own to help understand what you go through. That said, Maverick will be teaching Tim, Vincent, and Miles.

"The books for your teaching are on that shelf over there, on the east wall. Let's split into our groups and begin; I will occasionally observe your lessons and give aid where I can. Max, Jericho, Shakira, Leon, come with me."

A floorboard opened to a staircase in the floor. A nervous Max knew this was likely important and followed the others down, Allanon leading them through a dark hallway into a large underground room."This is a room intended for emergency purposes. I keep it secret for that reason, as one can never be too cautious. But I am sure I can trust my students. Now... Let us begin. Please, each of you sit down in front of me in a straight line."

As he said this Allanon sat in front of them, saying, "Normally this would be much easier if you had learned any previous spells beforehand, so this will be a long and, sorry to say, rather unentertaining process but the results will be worth it.

"I want you each to close your eyes and think about what you felt the moment you brought forth your summons, last time. I want you to quietly close your eyes and picture that emotion in your heads. Breathe in... and then out."

Max thought to himself, "*Great just great. This is going to boring as hell.*"Several moments of absolute silence confirmed his reservation, as it continued reminding of the quietude's peace. He had a great deal of trouble getting his mind to concentrate on any one thought let alone a feeling, but the silence was calming and pleasant enough, so he remained calm and sat there.

Allanon spoke quietly, "I don't expect any of you to get it this time, so you will spend a half-hour each day down here, where outside distractions and noises won't bother you and you do just as you are doing now. It would be pointless to make you stay down here the full hour or for more than these training sessions with the others will last, so you may use the remaining time to socialize and observe the training of the others up above.

"Also, one word of advice... Don't tell the other students of your training. I set this area with a magical field that only allows us to enter, so none of the other students will come down here.

"I have many valuable items hidden in areas of this room that you will likely never realize are down here, but I don't want to risk anyone getting their hands on them. The things down here are such things too valuable to keep in my study above here. Its best nobody sees them unless I want them to." Ikuto was reading the book he was supplied with up above, saying,

"Alright, so it says here for Knoll to use these."

Ikuto pointed to a setup he'd made of wooden paddles hung onto the tree next to them, saying, "It says you need to learn to walk around and through them without getting hit by them, moving as light as air."

Knoll tried and got knocked down on his ass. Sarah laughed at him, Ikuto barking, "What're you laughing for? You gotta do the same thing."

Sarah sighed as she attempted and had the same result;

Ikuto knew he needed to continue for now, though teaching made him very nervous from both his inexperience teaching and his own continued education with flames.

"Alright. As for Shaun, it says for now you have to hit those targets."

He pointed to a small few targets that were alongside a few other trees, saying, "You need to learn to hit only the centermost point of the targets and do it without destroying the targets, without hitting the rest of the targets at all. You're learning accuracy and control. It also advises us not to stand too close to you.

"Colleen, you're meditating. You'll be sitting down and focusing on the feeling you got when you healed a person and when you feel ready, you will heal a cut on this piece of meat I placed beside you."

Ikuto turned to his brother Simon, saying, "I'll just ask you to mimic my movements. We're both fire, so if we work in good sync we'll be able to figure out the rest, I think… Jared, Nero. Your training is very similar to each other. You're going to learn to place your element carefully at the targets over there.

"For Jared, you must send it at a speed good enough to not let it touch the ground, but only hit the target. It doesn't have to hit the center of the target for now, however. Nero, you will be doing similar, except you must not allow your element to leave the ground until it's right beside the target."

He paused and explained the training method Joey would use, which was essentially the same one being taught for raw Arcane but with the added requirement that it only be in short bursts. Rally would focus on meditation, learning when to allow her hands to be frozen and when to will them to not do so, since she still lacked control over it. Of most primary note about the exercises was that instructors such as Connor and Ikuto had to not only determine training methods from the books, but also note that people learned at different speeds. These students probably needed more basic training before the next step, while others didn't require as much and needed accuracy training instead, etc.

Maverick had his training the strangest, looking at the book and saying to Miles, "You will be learning control over your puppet. You must use it, and not let it use you. Puppet masters have the side effect of sometimes accidentally thinking their puppet is a living thing. You need to focus not only on the fact it is an object, and not a person, but focus on the fact that it is an extension of you, and thus you can control what it does.

"Tim... You need to learn about your ghost who first spoke to you. Speak to him, learn his name, his history... It says you should spend a lot of time doing that for now, before I give later steps. Vincent, yours is down to practice. Start with smaller objects, don't go as big as before. Work on making it more believable and make sure the objects look solid when you want them to; I noticed some transparency to your illusion earlier."

****

Leon sighed. The previous day had been weird, making difficult his meditation session for the sheer indecipherability of its' human content. He certainly felt loyalty, but it was a mixture of emotions since he was also angry and upset at the bar bastards earlier. He guessed it came with loyalty, not providing an easier call to make.

Still, he could hang with Vincent for now. Apparently Vincent and Charles were old buddies, so they were bound to be gaming. Max was out hanging with Zack and Knoll, so Leon wanted to find some friends to hang with, too.

He headed over to Vincent's dorm room and knocked, the door opening to a with a friendly smile. "Hey, Charles is already here, make yourself at home."

Vincent headed over and put a small pizza in the microwave and it was heating up, the appliance cooking and

Charles microphone-shouting in front of the television, "Dammit, cover my six!"

Apparently, he was playing a first-person shooter online and was having trouble with his clan members. He turned to Leon and grinned, "Sorry about that. I swear, it's like these guys have never played this game before! After this match you're welcome to hop in."

Leon had a sarcastic grin, "Sure, why not?", he said sitting on the beanbag next to Charles' chair. The match ended with the other team winning.

Charles threw up his hands and sighed, "Can't win 'em all I guess. I swear, though, these noobs."

He held the plan of his hand on his face. Vincent ate the pizza while grabbing one controller, and the other two had their controllers; it was three-player split-screen affair.

Vincent laughed, "ERH MER GERD UR DURD!"

Typical Vince, goofy as ever. It amused Leon, as he was glad to have a friend like him; one not afraid to be goofy and fun from time to time.

Leon shouted, "Watch out Vince!", shooting an enemy behind Vincent and laughing as Charles shouted. He began flailing his hands, giving an upset face less angry than annoyed.

"Dammit, that was me! You sure you weren't screen looking?"

Leon laughed, "I wasn't, but could you really do anything if I was? Also, you sure flail your hands a lot!"

Charles began dramatically flailing his hands some more as he gave a goofy yet sarcastic look,

Vincent shrugging, "If you don't want screen looking, you should've been on the same team with us."

Charles shrugged, "Where's the fun in that? I wanna own you guys!"

There was a knock on the door, so Leon answered it and it was Connor holding a controller. He grinned like he was going to ask something he already knew the answer to, askign, "Room for one more?"

Leon shrugged, "You'll have to wait after this match, but is that okay with you guys?"

Vincent put his finger to his chin for a moment and shrugged, "Sure, why not? Gives someone to be on Charles team anyways. Just be sure not to electrocute the console", he said smirking.

Connor laughed shrugging, "I'll try not to", afterwards grinning.

Leon smiled at the banter, something relieving and joyful to have from time to time. It took a while, but after the match ended all four were on splitscreen against the online players. By the end of it the controllers were greasy from all the potato chips and pizza consumed, but everyone had brought their own controllers. All in all it was a fun way to waste time a little bit when classes weren't going on, and what more could one ask for?

****

Max just got done playing a fighting game against Knoll and Zack. They'd have whoever lost play the winner each time, Zack the weakest of the bunch and Knoll's skill dependent on the game. It was most entertaining, so now they were just chilling and conversing in Knoll's room.

The room was full of various history books and clothes everywhere, making it hard to tell what were Knoll's possessions and what were his roommates'. It likely didn't matter and Max heard Knoll's roommate was rarely in the room aside from when he was asleep; the clothes were probably mostly his, who was somewhat slovenly.

Max thought to himself, "*Well isn't this just boring as all hell*. So what now, guys?"

Zack shrugged, "I don't know. What do you think, Knoll?"

Knoll put his hand over his face and sighed, "I got no ideas."

Max had an annoyed expression as he said, "Well, this is just boring! We can't sit around doing nothing and I'm tired of playing fighting games all day. This sucks!"

Knoll nodded, "Tell me about it. Guess we should just think of something to say right?"

There was a knock at the door, all of a sudden. Knoll said receptively, "I'll get it."

He looked through the peephole and it was Shakira, so he opened up and asked, "Yes?""I heard from Leon that Max was here. Let me talk to him real quick?"A bit surprised, Knoll nodded, "Sure, why not..."

Max was close enough to hear and went to the door and asked, "So wassup?"

Shakira giggled, "Well, I was thinking about the fun we had at my party and was wondering, would you like to go get some dinner together later?"

Max was taken aback by this, blushing and asking nervously, "Do you mean like a date?"

Shakira laughed, "Not like a date silly, it would be a date!"

Max laughed nervously,"U-uhm... Y-yeah, sure."

He smiled, but was then blushing a lot; Shakira was a beautiful woman and she'd just asked him out on a date. Shallow as the reason might've been, she was a good person nonetheless and he'd been single for a really long time; excitement was nothing but healthy.

Shakira giggled and said, "Awesome! Okay, see you then! Bye bye!"

She then quickly walked away with great enthusiasm, probably overjoyed at the answer;

he closed the door and shouted, "Yes! Oh my god guys, you hear that?"

Zack smiled a big grin and nodded, "Yeah we did. Congratulations."

Knoll laughed as he teased, "Uh-huh. Max has a girlfriend, Max has a girlfriend."

Max knew he meant no harm so he tried not to look annoyed and instead he grinned, "Ah shut up Knoll", he said laughing.

He waited nervously dressed in casual clothes, but with some decent body spray. He was as clean shaven as possible and had taken an additional shower in preparation, wanting his date to be perfect.

He answered the door, hair all straightened except the still-curled bangs. She wore a pleasant scent of cotton candy, hugging him right away. He always liked hugs, so giving one back was easiest.

"So where shall we eat?", she smilingly asked.

Max then thought about it, realizing he didn't have any money. He was basically on a scholarship at school and didn't have a job. Like a telepath, Shakira laughed with Max's fear.

"My Daddy is rich. He sends me money all the time. Don't worry, dinner is on me!"

Max protested, "But isn't it rude for the male in the date not to pay for dinner?"

Shakira smiled, "Don't worry about it! Like I said, Daddy is rich: it really doesn't inconvenience me, at all!"Deciding that having her way was best he sighed, saying, "Okay, then. Where do you want to go? Dinners on you after all."

She smiled, "I know just the place!"

As they walked outside the gates Max turned around and looked back at the school, once again feeling odd when he left campus. This was a reoccurring pulse, like he was needed there. At the same time he was restless, like he'd been at the campus too often recently. As with Waffle House before with Knoll and Zack, it was really nice to frolic about. They walked down the road, him re-realizing that the school was several miles from town. *Normally this would be very tiring. I'm so glad it isn't.* It's a good thing I like going for walks, or this would be exhausting."

Shakira laughed, "I don't really get tired very often, so it's no problem for me."

Max tried not to laugh. "You're telling me. You were full of energy last time I saw you. In fact, you always are, but it's amusing. He shrugged, "So, what do you want to talk about? I've run out of ideas."

Shakira found what Max said as cute, giggling, "That's funny. I heard you talked as much as I do, which is a lot. In fact, I talked to Jared and he says you always have something to say. That's why he used to call you on the phone all the time when he was bored!"

Max laughed, "No, I just made stuff up so there wasn't awkward silence. I hate those!""Me too! So, you like video games right? What's your favorite kind?""Fighting games. You?""I'm mostly into party games like Italian Plumber Party, but I love fighting games too! What's your favorite?"

Max shrugged, "Probably the one with the guy who has a dark side where he turns into this demon thing. He uses Karate and wants to end his bloodline, because his father was possessed by the devil. Iron Fist is the name, but I don't play as him though anymore. I play as that silver-haired guy based on Bruce Lee! I used to play it almost obsessively; I want to get competitive at it, someday!"

Shakira laughed, "Ah I know that one! I don't play it much, though. I play the one where people turn into animals like Wolves, Rabbits, and Bats! It's a really fun fighting game. Roar of Blood, I believe it's called?"

Max smiled, "I love that one! I play as the guy who turns into a wolf! What about you?"

As they continued walking he could already tell they were in for a fun conversation,

Shakira replying, "I like playing as the girl who turns into a Rabbit actually! Her punching is really fast, but her kicks are slow yet strong!"They reached their destination, even if the arrival felt quicker than it really was.

156

"Time sure does fly, when you have a good conversation."

Shakira nodded, "Mhm! It sure does!" Shakira turned her attention to the restaurant they'd arrived at. "I love this place! Daddy owns it! It's called the Carne de Res. My Daddy's Cuban, I think I mentioned that before, though."

Max nodded, "Yep, you have. What kind of foods does it have, though? I'm a picky eater."

Shakira laughed, "Don't worry, I'm sure we'll find something you'll like!"

****

Zack was rearranging things in the dorm room, proving of Shaun that one shouldn't generalize about the neatness of bisexuals; he was a messy roommate despite preferring men, further proof that stereotypes aren't always true. He was nonetheless a good friend and respected Zack's boundaries, even if he liked often to make gay jokes that Zack laughed at with slight discomfort.

In any case he was presently searching for his homework, which explained him and Shaun tidying up. Shaun was helping him, what good friends were for. Anytime Zack needed him Shaun had his back, Zack performing likewise. It was nice to have people you could depend on, even if Shaun was messy and needed to keep his things off the floor.

Shaun laughed, "Guess we'll never find it at this rate, huh?", obviously trying to lighten up the situation. Zack was trying to be polite and patient, but it was just making him nervous because of how bad he needed it.

Zack chuckled, "I hope not, I really need it. You know, it'd be really nice if I had a twin set of my homework. That way if I ever lost it, I could just turn in the extra copy. Kinda like this right here... See this notebook?"

Shaun nodded as Zack pointed to the notebook, saying, "If there was a copy of it right over there-"

Before he could finish, a copy of the notebook appeared in the chair; Zack was taken aback by this, walking over to the chair and opening it up. The first thing he noticed was that it felt lighter, almost like the notebook wasn't even there. He felt he was holding something of some sort, the notes from the original like mirrors to one another. "*Well, that's just weird. What if I stop imagining it?*"

He stopped imagining it the best he could and it vanished.

Shaun grinned and said, "Congratulations, Zack, I think you just learned your first Magic Ability! I think it's time you and I went and saw Allanon!

****

A couple weeks had passed since Shakira's first date with Max. It was now April 15th. Their first was a rather pleasant date,

and they'd gone on a few more since then.
Since then Zack had joined the ranks of
training as well, being good at illusions,
though at present manifesting this in the form
of swapping objects. Shakira preferred not to
try to work out the details, when it came to
hers.

Joey laughed, "So Shakira, how goes
your training?"

Shakira huffed, "The usual. I can't get
the monkey to come out, no matter how hard
I try. What about yours?"Lightning forming in
his fingers, Joey replied, "Quite well, Connor
says I'm making good progress- and don't
look now, but here she comes."

Shakira replied, "Here who comes? –
Oh boy, you mean her."

Sarah Mang. She was angry and fiery
as ever, saying, "Why must I be around such
an environment as this? It's unsanitary!
People really shouldn't allow so many to walk
around so casually. I may not like you
Shakira, but at least your IQ and mine are
the same. We should be handled better than
this."

Shakira sighed, "Why do you act like
you're better than them? It's not like you're
rich or anything! You constantly complain
about everything! Can't you just learn to get
along with people, you big meanie?"

Sarah Mang huffed, "I beg your
pardon! How dare you talk to me like that!
Just because I'm a Filipino immigrant doesn't
make you any greater than me! Do you know

what I had to get through to get here? No! You know why? Because you, little missy, had everything handed to you on a silver platter by your stupid Daddy!"

Shakira typically would've let things go or try to keep the peace, but Sarah had a way of getting under her skin. She was about to curse out Sarah Mang when Sarah McKnight arrived to break it up, saying, "Alright, you two, stop fighting."

Sarah Mang growled, "Who asked you, new girl? Hmm?"

It was this that made Sarah Mang jump at her to begin pulling her hair and scratching her. Sarah McKnight pushed her off and they began hitting each other in fight.

Tim was in the background shouting,"Woowee! Looks like we got ourselves a cat fight!"

Leon was grabbing Sarah McKnight and restrain her while Jericho ran in to do the same with Sarah Mang.

As Leon held Sarah McKnight and Jericho held Sarah Mang they were both trying to force the men to let them go. They clearly wanted a tussle,

Allanon arriving from his study yelling, "Children!"

Sarah Mang shouted, "How dare anyone call me a child!"

Allanon gave a dirty solemn look, scolding "I'll call you whatever you act like! Now both of you knock it off right now, or so help me I'll erase your memories of this place and if you cause any further incident after that, I will have you removed from the premises! Is that clear!"

Both Sarahs stopped in deference to Allanon, the latter nodding, "Good. Leon, Jericho. You may let them go now. Thank you for your assistance."

Leon said, "No problem. Actually, Sarah, we should talk sometime."

Sarah McKnight turned to him and asked curiously, "Oh? Why's that?"

Leon took a deep breath and said, "Well... I heard you were my half-sister."

As Leon and Sarah continued talking Charles had been watching the fight as he turned to Knoll. "Jeez man, looks like they were really going at it, huh?"

Knoll sighed, his face seeming hopeless as he said, "You don't know the half of it. I have to train with the mean one."

Colleen was extra quiet while standing next to them both, Charles turning and looking at her to softly say, "But you are teaching the other one your healing techniques right?"She nodded slowly, returning, "I don't mind it, though. Miss McKnight is actually quite kind to me. She's always saying how amazing I am for learning healing techniques so quickly. She even likes to call me 'sensei,' even though I've only been doing healing a short while, myself.""Well, you are the one teaching her what you know, right?"

Knoll added, "And you are quite good at it."

Colleen shyly muttered, "Yes... I guess so."A large thud was heard in Allanon's office and from out of the doors came Vincent running to him. He said to the headmaster in panic, "Allanon, you've gotta see this!"

Allanon hurried into his study and there on the ground was a dead phoenix, roughly the size of himself. It had a crest on his chest of a magical staff. As Allanon stared at it, he went ghostly pale.

Vincent was quite concerned, asking, "What does it mean?",

Allanon's face countenance fallen with a hush leaving his lips as he said, "... The Mages Guild. They're here."

Chapter 8 – Don't Panic, pretend everything's Normal

Allanon nodded slowly, "Whether I like it or not, you are already a part of this. Gather the summoners and bring them in here. I must inform them and you of what is going on, because it may already be too late."

Vincent went and did as told, bringing all into the room. Max was the first to look at it.

"Is... is it mine?"

Allanon shook his head, "No... Your Phoenix was never involved in this sort of thing. I think I would've known if he was. But then... I'm not sure of anything anymore. I need to tell you all something. Please have a seat."

He waved his hand and chairs went behind them as they all sat down,

Allanon nodding, "Myself and my apprentice Alexander didn't always do things people considered... right. But we did what we always thought we had to. You may or may not know this, but we were a part of a Wizard's Guild. That phoenix there... he's from the Mages Guild."

Max looked puzzled, "The Mage's Guild kept phoenixes?"

Allanon shook his head to reply, "No Max, the Mage's Guild were phoenixes."

They all had a look of surprise as the room began to feel like the world was standing still.

Allanon nodded, "I was the one to discover it... The Journal of Merlin... Yes, that Merlin! He was the one who taught humanity Magic. After a time period where humanity had seemingly lost all ability to use it anymore Merlin came from the shadows. He helped King Arthur rise to power, but most of all he taught humanity Magic. He made each person he taught swear to keep magic a secret, but would not say why. All the same, each person swore. At first the guild he formed, the Wizard's Guild, thought he was human.

"But he was in fact a Phoenix. But still, nobody knew. He wrote many secret things in a journal of his, which by the time I became a member I eventually found. The first person I told, was my apprentice, Alexander. We both agreed I would tell the order after I deciphered some of its codes, for we feared the messages within may've been hidden for a reason. I not only discovered he was a phoenix, I discovered... we weren't the only magic guild. There existed a guild known as the Mages Guild. Many hundreds of years ago, they disguised themselves as humans using shapeshifter magic and posed as a human guild of Magic.

"But in fact, they were all Phoenixes. Some Phoenixes resented humanity for killing them for their healing tears and phoenix feathers that were useful for creating fire arrows. The Mage's Guild wanted revenge; they'd declared war on humanity once before, but ultimately were thought to have died out. But it turned out Merlin found out they had not. He also calculated where they were and when they would next attack. It wasn't long from right then.

"Alexander and I told the Wizard's Guild and we decided to attack the Mage's Guild before they attacked us... so we did. Alexander and I became war heroes as we fought the Mage's Guild. It was a fairly even fight for quite a while, but in the end we had won and as far as we knew, the Mage's Guild had been slaughtered. All of them. Now, I'm not so sure. Do you notice anything about this Phoenix?"

Leon shrugged, "I assume the crest is that of the Guild."

Allanon nodded, "Good, but what else?"

Max remarked, "It's dead. But don't Phoenixes rise again from the ashes?"

Allanon pointed and nodded, "Exactly. Now tell me, why would a phoenix, who is supposed to rise again from the dead, not do so?"

Shakira remarked, "That is a very strange question."

Jericho spoke, "Because he doesn't know how?"

Max remarked, "But how would a phoenix not know how?"

Allanon nodded, "Precisely... And I know the answer to that question: because he didn't know he was a phoenix. He had to have been a sleeper. A spy. Working for the mages guild and hiding among us.

"That's the thing about sleepers, they don't even know they aren't one of us. Fake memories. They can be planted as far back as they choose within our lives... You never know who is a sleeper and who isn't. It could be anyone, even one of us. And we would never even know it. Not even if we were one ourselves."

Max held his head with headache and said, "Then what do we do?"

Jericho sighed, "It sounds like we can't trust anyone. We'll have to-"

Allanon interrupted, "No! That's just what the Mage's Guild would want! To incite panic! We can't let them tear us apart! Not to mention in order for sleepers to work a trigger is often used; in order to use a trigger, that would mean one of the spies will have to know who he is. He could activate them at any time and cause chaos if he knows we are on to him!

"No! What we'll do is simple. Be on the lookout for strange things. But for now, act like nothing has changed. If we continue acting like nothing has changed... but be watchful... at least we'll be more prepared than we would be.

"The spies were probably planted a long time ago, we can't be as prepared as we'd like, but it's the best we can do. I'm sorry, I'm so sorry.... But that is all we can do, right now. But first, Vincent, how did you find this phoenix?"

Vincent said, "Well, it was outside the welding area. I take welding lessons on the side and went down there and found him already dead. I didn't see any kind of wounds showing how he died, but I figured it'd be a bad thing if the whole school saw him so I brought him here via that secret entrance you showed me and Max once."

Allanon nodded, "Good thinking. We don't want all of the students to see this... We don't want to spread panic. As I said, don't danic. Pretend everything's normal. I've also learned the names of your summons; your Phoenix is named Heliopolis and your Dragon is named Goron, at least... if your descriptions you've given me are accurate"

Max sighed, "That's hard to think, that we could avoid panic... but speaking of our summons, what about Heliopolis? Couldn't he help?"

Jericho laughed, "If I could summon Goron I'd bet he helped."

Allanon looked at them both, "No! You'd only be making it worse by summoning Goron! Dragons and Phoenix are age-old enemies, they've always hated each other. As far back as I can remember, they were the bitterest enemies you'd ever seen!

"It'd be a disaster! But, yours IS Goron... He has a history. Only one Phoenix ever was able to put him in his place... Heliopolis. I'll consider it." Allanon changed his attention to Max, "Besides. You guys still both haven't been able to summon your creatures yet... But we probably will need your phoenix's help. He might know something. I think... Tonight I'm going to have to give your summoning spell a pair of jumper cables."

****

******Back in Dark World Brokk found it awkward being hand-cuffed to Cael; in a way, Cael's cocky confidence made Brokk feel he had a glimpse of what he himself might've been, were his life any different. Pitying himself for that would only wax annoying, so he tried to ward off incessantly thinking about it. He still needed to find Morrigan, the woman he loved.

As they traversed the desert for what seemed like miles in the dry heat, they saw what they hoped never to see; two Bregals were growling at them, arriving from what must've been their cave a few feet behind. These were territorial creatures,

Brokk calmly but quietly saying, "Cael, whatever you do, don't do something crazy."

Cael fired at the Bregal,

Brokk cursing, "Damn it, Cael, why did you do something like that!"

Soon they were running with Bregals growling and chasing them, the loud snarls constantly bearing down. They often needed to duck so as to avoid them, which

They kept firing in their defense, but the shots weren't doing much,

Brokk sighing, "We don't have much choice, in this heat... Our safest bet is the caves!"

Cael smirked, "Their homes? How is that safe?""Trust me. It's a lot cooler in the Bregal cave than out here. We'll just die of dehydration, out here!"

Cael sighed, "Caves, it is!"

They searched until they finally reached the caves. As they ran from the sound of bregals all was soon quiet, but it was hard to tell where they were. The cave all looked the same. Still, it was only slightly darker than outside.

Cael sighed, "Great. A cave... How boring. Now what?"

Brokk sighed, "Let me think for a minute, ok? Wait... Hear that?"

Cael nodded as he listened carefully, replying, "Yeah."

They ran towards the sound as they reached a small little grouping of water in the earth. It probably wasn't the healthiest but they drank from it without fail from all their previous desert heat, falling sick from it minutes later.

Cael weakly said, "Who's bright idea was this again? Oh, right, yours."

Brokk groaned as he said, "If I hadn't brought us in here, we'd be bregal chow, right now. How was I supposed to know cave water would make us sick?"

They both decided they switch shifts for sleeping, as there was no use going anywhere and making things worse. The next day drew on through the endlessly indiscriminate darkness of Dark World, the two then hearing a growl. Brokk said, "What was that?", he said shaking Cael.

Cael groaned, "I'm sleeping man… We're both sick cuz of you, what do you want?""I heard something. Might be a bregal. I'd want to be awake if I were you."

Cael snapped awake after hearing Brokk say that, but it wasn't a bregal that walked up to them. It at least looked kind of like a man, except over eight feet and with one eye on its' forehead.

Brokk turned to Cael and said, "I think that's what they call a Cyclops!"

Cael replied sarcastically, "You don't say?""Run!"

They both ran outside and kept running until they couldn't, putting distance between them and the Cyclops to their hope. They eventually reached rocks for vantage point atop of a hill that only went down on all sides. "It's my turn to sleep now."

Cael sighed, "Fine, but don't expect me to move much."

Brokk nodded, "Fair enough."

He drifted off to sleep; they'd been switching shifts to keep watch by the rocks and he wasn't sure how long he slept, but it must've been a long time. The sudden of gunfire again approached,

"What's going on?", Brokk quickly jolted awake with.

Cael was firing at someone and had a serious look on his face. "There's something I might've forgotten to mention."

Brokk groaned, "What is it?" Surprises were the last thing he wanted right now; he was just glad the rocks provided cover, or he might've been shot in his sleep.

"I used to be in a gang, and we kind of robbed the leader of City. We split ways in the gang eventually, but apparently, the guy remembered my face. He kind of wants me dead."

Brokk slapped his own face as he replied, "That's the kind of thing you should've told me beforehand!"

Cael shrugged, "I didn't think it'd come up."

Brokk sighed, "I see you're still going to be as annoying as yesterday." He looked around and saw a fence few yards behind themselves, saying, "We can make a run for that fence, climb over it and go in. That might at least slow them down and get some distance between us!"

Cael smirked, "And here I thought you were nothing but a killjoy! Alright, let's go!"

Cael would occasionally turn around and fire as they headed for the fence, so that the enemies didn't come closer to them from behind the rocks, but after a couple times they ran and made their way to the fence.

Brokk noted mentally that the sign ahead read "Restricted Area",

Cael smirking, "You aren't going to let that stop you are ya?"

Brokk sighed, "We don't have much of a choice, do we?""Nope!"

They climbed while making their way over, hiding within a gigantic brown building. The size was hard to be sure of, but the building was massive and had no windows. As they went inside it was dark even by the standards of places between cities, somewhere without sight to imagine. They heard snoring.

Cael feeling something on the ground and yelling, "A match!"

He struck a match to create a little light, but could see skin scaly and brown; it was somewhat overweight, but seemed like it put its weight into strength if it were to wake up; it had horns on its head that looked like goats', having gigantic wings of a bat; it possessed four muscular legs with claws on each end; smoke came out of its nostrils for a brief moment.

A Dragon.It must've been many feet tall, while laying down; here it was, finally sleeping before them.

****

**Yesterday Max was told that he would have to summon his phoenix. Allanon said the words "jumper cables", as if his summoning would have to be jump-started. He didn't know what to make of it, but he couldn't think of that while swamped in school work involving mathematics. Luckily, Shakira was there to help him.

Shakira was actually quite smart; she pointed out the equations and he managed to get through it well enough, so he wouldn't be anywhere without her.

Max sighed, "Thanks, Shakira, I really appreciate it. Math has always been my weakest subject."

Shakira giggled, "No problem! I've always been just fine with it, but I understand we all have our strengths and weaknesses!"

She kissed Max on the cheek, to his usual blush as she headed outside to hang with Rally and Joey.

Shakira hugged them both, proclaiming, "I told you all he need was school work help! I wasn't going to abandon my friends on our fun day!"

Rally looked off to the side as Joey laughed with Shakira, with her looking at Rally inquisitively and asking, "You okay?"

Rally laughed nervously, "Heh, yeah... Everything's fine..."

Shakira smiled, "Okie dokie lokie, then! So where to?"

Joey nodded, "The coffee shop is fine. I'd love to get some of my favorite candy there."

Rally nodded, "A Frappuccino would be nice."

Shakira smiled, "Okay! Coffee shop it is, then!"

She bounced for joy as they headed for the coffee shop, paying for everything like usual. She was always glad to have Rally and Joey. Everyone else would've taken advantage of her, but with Rally and Joey she only paid for everything because she insisted on it.

As they sat at the table, Rally went to the restroom. Joey seemed to have something on his mind, as his eyes were looking into space from deep thought.

Shakira giggled, "What are you thinking?"

Joey sighed, "I... I don't know how to tell you this. I... Okay. Promise you won't say anything?"

Shakira nodded, "I promise. You know me, once I make a promise, it is never broken! It's a Shakira Promise!"

Joey nodded, "Okay. She won't ever admit it, but I can tell. You just have to look at her reactions every time you and Max go out; Rally is jealous. I think she likes Max, but won't admit it to anyone. I'm willing to bet she doesn't even want to admit it to herself."

Shakira's face turned serious as she calmly said, "I see... Well, he's my boyfriend, so I don't really know what I could do about it. I definitely don't want it to ruin my friendship with Rally, either..."

Joey nodded, "I agree. I don't really know what to say about it myself... I just thought you should know about it."

Shakira nodded, "Thank you, Joey. You've always been an honest and good friend to me."

Joey replied, "No problem."

It remained on botheringly on Shakira's mind the whole day as it reached night for the moment of truth; Max was told to meet Allanon to begin the next summoning.

When he arrived the other summoners were there as well,

Allanon sighing, "I thought long and hard about this and I'm doing what must be done. If we are to be prepared for this, you all will need to be able to defend yourselves and your summons are the way to do it. I warn you though, this will be painful.

"It will allow you to do your summons at will, but every time you do there will always be a possibility it could have negative adverse effects on you, such as you tiring or getting sick. In rare cases, it could quite possibly cause death... But as you grow used to it, the effects will subside and it will be like normal summoning. Are each of you still willing to continue, after being warned of all this?"

Each of them nodded,

Allanon saying, "Then let us begin."

He sat down and began channeling his own magic, as they did the same. Lightning filled the study, seeming not to affect anything around them. Wind from nowhere blew as the room seemingly shook, then all was quiet and portals above their heads opened; out came their summons one by one.

First the monkey came out, wearing a shower cap with a curtain around himself.

"Do you guys have any common decency? Really! It's not like the whole world revolves around you! Now look at me, without any pants on!"As she opened her eyes, Shakira asked, "You wear pants?"

"Oh now you want to know, huh? Sometimes I do. On Thursdays."

Shakira sighed, "But today's a Tuesday!"

"Oh, 'Miss Technical,' are we? Okay, so what? It still begins with 'T!'"

The wolf appeared, saying to Leon, "Ah, 'Leon,' yes? I always find it interesting when you summon me. I have a lot of respect for that. Why did you bring me here?"

Leon nodded, "We'll have need of you soon, but let's wait until the others get here for it to be explained."

Next was the dragon, as he appeared growling, "Who dares summon Goron the destroyer!"

Jericho opened his eyes and returned, "I did. Get used to it."

The Dragon laughed a little, "You got guts, young one. I'll give you that."

Jericho shrugged, "Young, huh?"

The Dragon laughed, "I've lived longer than most of you humans have! Just because you summon me, tiny, doesn't mean I'm a youngin'!"Flames shone brightly when the phoenix appeared; he was starting to speak, then saw Goron and the two began their growls' tether.

"Who dares put a Dragon before me? 'Max,' was it? Do you have any idea what mad thing you have done! Phoenixes and Dragons have hated each other for more than millennia!"

Goron huffed a little bit of flame out of his nose, barking, "The feeling is mutual, bird-brain!"

Chapter 9 – Life goes on

"I'll have you know that my brain is quite decent in size, which is the least I can say for your breath, lizard lips!"

The Dragon huffed as his face became enraged, "My breath is none of your concern, tweety bird! I'll take you on right here and now! Let's fight!"

The werewolf got in between them, calming,

"Heliopolis. Goron. You are both my friends, but you know how these things go. You and Goron would be fighting for hours and nothing ever gets achieved. You're too equally matched."Goron huffed as mad, but this time seemed more willing to listen. "You're just lucky we're friends Lucian or I would kill you for getting in between me and my prey!"

Leon smiled, "So you're all friends then huh?"

The Monkey was certainly annoyed as he shrugged, "Not me. This is my first time meeting them. Thanks for forgetting about me though, wolf-boy!"

Shakira sighed, "Couldn't you be more friendly?"

The Monkey started screeching and cackling as it began hitting her with a wooden spoon it kept unnoticed in its' foot.

Shakira screamed as she ran around the room from her own summon.

Allanon had the palm of his hand covering his face as he sighed, "This... doesn't seem good. Heliopolis, was it? Do you know who I am?"

Heliopolis became very serious once he realized Allanon's presence.

Heliopolis spoke, "Who among phoenixes of this world doesn't? You've killed more of us than anyone in history, save for Alexander himself."

Allanon was silent for a moment and nodded as he said, "They're back."

Heliopolis had a very serious, almost scared expression on his face as he replied, "The Mages Guild has returned?"

Allanon nodded, "I have a... request of you."

Heliopolis nodded, "What do you request of me?"

Allanon spoke, "I want to teach you the shapeshifting spell of the Mages Guild and I want you to enroll in this school as a student. I want you to help protect this school."

Heliopolis stood up straight for a moment and said, "This... isn't something I would normally do you know."

Allanon nodded, "I know. But then... the ending of your name is 'Polis,' isn't it?"

Heliopolis sighed, "I know... You spared my father and I am grateful for that, but I have never met you. What my father owes you isn't the same as what I owe you."

Allanon replied, "I beg of you, this school needs your help. Whom would know a phoenix better than a phoenix? I know you do not accept Max as your summoner yet. I'm not asking you to. If you stay around this school I promise to unbind you from the summoner's pact you now have with Max; you will be temporarily tied to me. In other words, you will be at full strength temporarily. Wouldn't you like to be like you used to be, again?"

Goron growled, "Oh, so little mister gets to be a full strength because he's too weak to depend on his own? Pfft, hardly seems fair."

Allanon sighed, "I'll teach you the spell as well, if you're interested."

Goron ripped at the thought, but also knew what this meant and decided to consider it. "One condition.""You want me to beat you in combat first, am I correct?""You understand dragons well.""Ready when you are, then."

Goron growled, "Ready."

Allanon pointed a single finger towards Goron and suddenly light magic had ensnared him in binds, rendering him unable to move anything but his mouth. "Y-you've earned my respect human. Teach me the spell."

The Werewolf said, "I have a human form already, being that I'm a werewolf. Unlike the mythology says though, I can turn at will, but as you know, the full moon gives me no choice. Still, most nights there is no full moon. I will be stronger during a full moon, but I will lose my sanity... You may need me to help keep a leash on these two, lest they actually kill each other."

Max spoke up, "You're sure it's temporary, right? I don't want to lose what little magic I have! I doubt anyone else here does either! Except for maybe Shakira..."

As he said the last part he looked at Shakira and her summon which, were arguing in the background about something.

Leon nodded, "I definitely don't."

Allanon replied, "Yes. Only temporary, I promise. Anyway, I agree, Lucian. And I know all about the mythology being untrue. Merlin's journal said that most of the world's mythologies were lies fabricated by the Mage's Guild itself, in order to throw off people from the truth."

Lucian nodded, "Luckily anyone who would recognize me is either in Europe or has long since passed on; I'm much older than I look, but that comes with the territory of being an immortal race."

Allanon nodded, "That's another thing. You'll need fake names. We don't want people realizing who you all are, and your names aren't exactly common in this age. I'll let you choose your names after I teach you the shapeshifting spell."

The monkey shrugged, "I'm out of here! I don't have to be a part of this.

181

Toodles!", then opened his portal and jumped in, the doorway itself finally vanishing.

Allanon spoke, "First, I shall do as I said on the contract."

He raised his hands as lightning filled a suddenly growing room,

Allanon yelling, "Don't worry, anyone. I simply made the room bigger on the inside… It will be needed."

Max and Jericho looked at each other and then back at Allanon, full of curiosity as to how large these creatures likely were.

As the spell continued its work they saw the Phoenix and the Dragon continuing to grow until they reached about a hundred feet long, full of wingspan. It was no wonder why they felt insulted by being summoned at half strength, because they also had to have been summoned at less than half their actual size prior.

Allanon placed a protective wall between himself, the summons and the humans and said, "The details of this spell should remain only with myself and these two. I will return when the summon is complete."

Several minutes passed, before the wall lowered and there were three males in front of him.

One had red hair and green eyes, was muscular in build and had on a black tank top and black jeans.

"These clothes suit someone as I just fine; Goron likes the color black."

Jericho smirked, saying, "So that's what you'd look like as a human, Goron."

Goron looked to him and growled like he would in his dragon form , saying, "You don't get to use my name."

Heliopolis had brown short hair with red streaks and was skinny in build, but having some muscles. He had one blue eye and one green eye, wearing a red t-shirt and blue jeans.

Last was Lucian, with short black hair and a muscular build. He wore a black leather jacket over a black-t-shirt and had on black cargo jeans,

Goron remarking, "Figures you'd wear black too, copycat."

Lucian laughed, "I just like the color. I wasn't copying you."

Allanon replied, "So have you come up with your fake human names?"

Lucian nodded, "Lance."

Goron replied, "Draco",

Jericho sneering at the name with comments withheld.

Heliopolis replied, "James."

Allanon nodded, "I suppose those will do. As for your reasons for being in my school we will have to fabricate those, based on any talents you may have... This will be difficult."

Lance nodded, "Not for me; I used to be quite the violinist in my day, we can use that for me."

Draco thought for a moment and suggested, "Why not fencing? Just say I was such a skilled swordsman, the team wanted me here."

Allanon nodded at both and then turned to James, asking, "Well?"

James replied, "My father used his human form within the Mage's Guild to write, from time to time. I suppose that sounds as fun as anything. Say I got in for literature, I suppose."

Allanon sighed, "I wrote a story awhile back that was popular enough: I could fabricate the school into thinking you wrote it recently and use a memory spell to block out folks from potentially remembering otherwise. Just don't try to pass it off as true outside the school grounds, or you might get caught."

He turned to each of them and said, "I will also ask you refrain from turning into your real forms, or using your abilities in your human forms. You will find you are capable of doing both, but I request you do your very best not to. Is that understood?"

They each nodded but Lance added, "I will say one thing, however. I will have to hide in here if we ever face a full moon. I have no choice in the matter during a full moon; I'll be in my wolf form whether I like it or not, and at night I tend to get… Let's call it 'crabby.'""I'll agree to that. I'll take good care

184

of you if that occurs. I promise you'll be safe and I'll make sure you harm no one."

****

*****Yesterday was odd for Jericho, but he wasn't sure how to explain to his buddy Sho how he knew Draco. "I guess he's a fan of mine?"Annoyed, Jericho stated while human-sounding, "You wish, Jericho. I could beat you with my hands tied behind my back."

Jericho smirked, "Wanna try?""Let's do it!"

They fenced later, not to even contest; Draco had won in a single strike, Jericho huffing, "Let's try again!"

This time Jericho tried to parry the strike, but Draco moved easily past that and won another point, leaving Jericho only to his game.

Sho smiled, "I know that face. You're having fun with this aren't ya Jericho?"

Jericho smiled, "You bet your ass I'm having fun! A real challenge!"

As Jericho kept losing Draco realized Jericho was learning very quickly, almost totally respecting that. "That's enough kicking your ass for one day."

"If you say so."

Sho handed him a sweat towel as he said, "Here you go, stinky.""Thanks, bro."

Jericho liked having friends and Sho was a good guy; Jericho witnessed one of Sho's violent outbursts when they first met, because of bullying by three students for supposedly being 'inferior' to them. He then realized that Sho was not in his right mind and knocked him out before he could do anything he'd regret, thus beginning their friendship.

Sho wasn't Jericho's only friend, as Justin could prove. He wasn't into fencing competitions anymore, but would probably be great at it due to strong muscle memory. Justin was Jericho's high school best friend, as they were on the football team together. He'd not seen Justin in a while, until he was enrolled in Allan's for welding.

Jericho sighed, "Well Draco, I'll see you around."

Draco shrugged, "Whatever."

Jericho turned to Sho, saying, "Let's go meet up with Justin."

Sho nodded, "Okay. After you, my friend."

Jericho smirked, "Knock that Asian respectfulness shit out, Sho. I told you, we're casual here. We're all friends."

Sho laughed lightly, saying, "Sorry. Can't help it.""Stop apologizing""Sorry."

Jericho walked up to Justin, each bro-fisting and

Justin sweating. "Welding was a bitch today, but I got through it.""So, how's your wife?"

Justin was barely older than Jericho, already married; it was always a reminder of their adulthood,

Justin nodding, "She's good. I visit her when I can, but she misses me a lot since college is out of state.""I know the feeling. My mom writes me all the time. I still sometimes wish I could've stayed behind to help take care of her, since she stays home so often and I worry about her a lot. But you know my mom, she's too stubborn to accept too much help."

Justin laughed, "Yeah, I know, dude. So what do you say to a spar? I know I'm not on the fencing team, but we can use your swords from your closet, right?"

Jericho said, "If you don't mind that they're sharp.""Don't care."

Jericho turned to Sho, "And you are on the team, so you gotta join us.""Okay."

Justin was the only person around who could beat Jericho in a fight that wasn't Draco, but was one of the people who taught him how. Their high school life was of rough hue and people tended to fight more often than not.

Jericho fought Justin first without the standard fencing rules. They didn't even bother to put on protective gear aside from chest guards, citing their boldness; Sho, on the other hand, didn't see it that way and displayed it well through the regardless utility of his protective equipment. The swords were longswords, edges sharp on all sides and tips likewise.

They fought in the expensive closet Jericho had paid extra for by working part-time; he also occasionally had his friends help pitch in. He kept his swords in there but there was also a little room to fight; tight, but effective.

Their swords clashed and Justin went for a swing at Jericho's arm, but he dodged and went for a swing at Justin's legs. Justin dodged and hit Jericho on the head, using the dull side to do so.

Jericho sighed, "You won that one."

As the fights continued into the evening, they all decided to call it a day. It was certainly a fun day, perhaps where there were to be few of the same.

****

Today was going to be their seventh date and Max was excited; Shakira was really nice and he enjoyed their time together, overall. As he got ready he put on his black jacket for the cold night. He put on cologne this time, hoping she would like it. As he got ready he heard her knock and opened the door.

Shakira was beautiful as always; she had on a blue dress with a V-neck that went to her ankles, also adorned in a bright red jacket over the dress. Her pink hair was kept somewhat pinned up in the back and her face looked simply gorgeous. Her typical goofy self, she wore rainbow socks and regular tennis shoes; these notwithstanding, Max blushed all the same as he said, "H-hi Shakira. You look beautiful, today."

Shakira giggled, "Thanks, Max! I look forward to our seventh date! I can't wait to surprise you with where we are going!"

Max started to leave the apartment and she put her arms around his right; he almost jumped, but went with it as they started heading outside. The night sky was beautiful, the stars' aglow scintillating.

When they finished walking to their location they reached a lake; Max was a little nervous about being over water, for he could swim just fine. For some reason though, he had a fear of drowning. Still, the view was beautiful.

Shakira giggled, "Surprise! I got us a boat!"A small but simple boat; it had a man rowing for them, herself giggling, "He's a friend of my family, don't mind him. Shall we go?"

Max nodded slowly, nervous of getting onto the boat. He was afraid it could wobble and Shakira sensed what was on his mind, since she went onto the boat and offered her hand. I'll help you get on."

Max chuckled a little at the silliness of the request, but thanked her. "I'd appreciate it." He finally sat, countenancing the view beautiful; there were the occasional ducks and fish he saw moving under vessel. For a few moments they both just took in the scenery, complete calmness and silence their companions. She then asked, "So, Max, how was your day?"

Max was distracted for a moment at the view, but then noticed she had spoken. "Hmm?"

She giggled, "How was your day, silly!""Oh, it was okay. Nothing really interesting. Not much to say, really; only things that come to mind is Leon and I had band practice with the guys, I played some video games with Knoll and Zack and that's it. really. You?"

Shakira smiled sweetly at his comments and she shrugged, saying, "Oh, about the same, really. Rally and I had lunch together, then Joey and I played some Italian Plumber Party. It was lots of fun but really, all I could think about was that I wanted to spend it with you."

Max chuckled, "That's sweet. Thanks, Shakira."

Shakira leaned in and kissed Max on the lips. It was just a peck, not a short nor a long one, but it surprised him and he blushed.

Shakira giggled, "Was that your first kiss, or something?"

Max laughed nervously, "Actually, it was. Don't get me wrong... I loved it. I just... You surprised me, is all", ending the sentence with laugh.

She giggled, "You're cute, Max."

They enjoyed the quietude and serenity of the boat ride, when she turned to the driver. He nodded and looked back at Max, saying,

"Hey Max, I have a surprise for you. I had Daddy pay for it."

She pointed to the sky and then a single pink firework hit the sky and lit it up, a couple more red shots then proceeding and hitting the sky."You're kidding! Really?"

Shakira giggled, "I thought it'd be cool to see right about now. Well? Is it awesome, or what?"

Max laughed and nodded, "Very awesome! Um... Can I kiss you, Shakira?"

She giggled, "Of course, silly!"He leaned in and kissed her as the fireworks continued to go up into the sky, Shakira giggling afterward.

He turned to look at the fireworks and saw several small white ones hit the sky, making a sizzle as they exploded. He saw several green, red and blue ones, remarking their extravagance.

"You're amazing Shakira, you really are.""Nah... I just have a rich dad. No biggie!""Well yeah, but still, fireworks on a date is really impressive.""He came up with an excuse involving a sale at a store with fifty percent off on some stuff, or something like that. Makes it look like the fireworks had a reason, or something."

Max laughed, "Only someone related to you would feature fireworks at a store sale."

191

Shakira giggled along with him and after that there was quiet once more, the fireworks coming to a close with his arm around her. Max felt like he had the whole world at that very moment.

As they left the lake and started heading back home to his apartment he unlocked the door and began to open it, but turned and nodded, "I had a good night Shakira... You sure you don't want me to walk you back to your apartment?"

Shakira nodded as she said, "I'm sure!", and began kissing him passionately. Max fell against the door as it swung open, thank God nobody was home. She began feeling the crotch of his pants and he immediately became erect. Shakira's face turned red, herself giggling, "Don't worry about it. Do you... Want to do it?"

Max blushed and nodded, "S-s-s-sounds fun!", Shakira giggling as they entered into Max's room locking the door."Is it your first time?"

If one were outside the door, they'd hear Max say, "Y-yes.""Don't worry! It isn't my first time, I can help you!"

The mounting chorus of 'yes' would proceed from the walls like photosynthesis, an excursion of great and celestial erotic glory, for the next day Max was in a wheelchair out of his bedroom, about to head to fencing with a doctor's note. Leon and Knoll were laughing, Jericho turning and asking, "What happened to Max?"

Knoll was having trouble speaking with laughter, "Ask... Ask him", his voice the hyena's tickle.

Jericho turned to Max, but the latter interrupted, "I heard him!"

Max sighed, his face a mix of embarrassment, amusement, and said, "Well... We had sex. Apparently, she really is the energy and stamina of Alexander, because she seemed to never get tired! She kept going and going and me... Poor me, I just wouldn't give up! And now? Now I have a doctor's note saying I shouldn't try any walking for the next seven days!"

Knoll couldn't not contain it, laughing hysterically to say, "What didn't she do to him, I wonder?"

Max tried to laugh but was too tired, then saying, "Ha-ha. I would give a sincerer laugh, but I think I lost my lungs last night. I'm just glad the shower was successful in washing off the smell."

Max was lucky because Shakira was excused from her first class in order to help keep him entertained. They talked a bit, though Max sometimes got short of breath; he didn't let that stop him, nonetheless pioneering towards his usual talkative self.

Shakira giggled a little, apologizing, "Sorry, I guess I just don't know my own strength."

Max attempted a laugh, failing and saying jocularly, "You're telling me! I think my lungs, my heart and my muscles at some point decided to say 'fuck it' and left me, last night!"

Shakira giggled, "Yeah, I know what you mean", turning serious for a moment and saying, "Actually, I'm kind of glad I could spend my morning with you. I fear Rally might be mad at me; I think she's jealous of us."

Max sighed, "I don't even like her in that way, honestly."

Shakira nodded, "I know! I honestly don't know what to do about it. I mean, I could try talking to her, but I don't know if that would just make it way worse, so I've just been pretending I didn't notice and trying not to rub it in her face."

Max nodded, "Yeah, I know what you mean… but yeah, you probably would hurt her feelings. Still, if you don't talk to her about it sooner or later it could get worse. Don't think it would help if I talked to her about it, either. It should probably come from you."

****

Brokk was taken aback by this dragon, having once thought they were just old fairytales. He'd never thought he'd see one. While he found them exciting in appearance, the worst of it was his own terror. If awoken it could easily devour,

Cael and Brokk nervously backing up and bumping into each other.

This one was mostly blue in color, horns larger than the one on the brown dragon and a yellow belly of armor-seeming scale. It had finlike spikes on its back, neck, and tail and its wings were the same as the brown dragon's massive. While not as giant itself, both were enough to where if one had opened its eyes each pupil would size to human's own.They looked around and saw a Red one that looked almost just like the Blue Dragon, a Green Dragon, a Purple Dragon, a yellow dragon, knowing there wasn't only one for out of the pattern. These were several of each kind, almost the multitude.

Cael noticed a large sign reading, "Warning: Dragons heavily drugged and are not to be awoken under any circumstances. They are to be drugged every two hours to maintain safety for the surrounding cities." They then realized the Dragons were chained to the floor, the bonds not likely to do so well if one were to awake.

Neither one of them even spoke. The just looked at each other and nodded, knowing they were going to leave and take their chances with whoever was outside. That's when it happened. The Blue Dragon from before opened its eyes, and growled.

"Who has dare chained Grath! I am a Dragon of Noble Birth!", it said waking up other dragons with him.

Cael and Brokk ran outside as quickly as they could. They headed out of the building a different direction than they'd come in, assuming the fence would be safe on the other side. As they made their way back over the fence they heard roaring behind them. The building burst into flames as the dragons flew out, roaring flames upon the ground. They saw no less than ten Bregals ahead of them growling up at a Red Dragon, which would itself breathe instantly-killing flames.

Another was the Blue Dragon, breathing flames into the sky in anger but turning to Cael and Brokk's pursuers; these were men in cowboy equipment and black shirts. It fired out of its mouth a high-powered water burst, killing the band while doubtless in its immediacy.Above them a yellow Dragon was growling as bursts of lightning surrounded its body, yellow bolts of what some in our world might refer to as 'electricity.' The Dragon screamed at Cael and Brokk with blood thirst, until a creature with red wings massive and size comparable suddenly appeared. The phoenix yelled, "Leave this place! This is a fight for a Phoenix, not a human!" They ran for a long while, continuing upon realization of even a fatigue. One foot after the other, they were exhausted and tired by the time they turned and reckoned fight long behind them.

Cael was the first to speak, laughing, "What a rush! That has to be one of the most exciting moments I've ever had!"

Brokk punched him across the face, falling alongside Cael afterwards and sitting up. "Are you nuts? We could've died, out there!"

Cael smirked, "But we didn't."

Brokk shouted at him, "And that itself is a miracle!" He was really sick of this man, as he was nothing but trouble. The sooner they separated from each other, the better.

Cael looked back at him and said, "It was your idea to go in there, so I don't know why you're taking it out on me!"

Brokk sighed, "Whatever."

Cael was right, but Brokk didn't want to give him the ego satisfaction of being told that. He then looked around and realized they were in the middle of the desert with nothing in front or beside them; this was notwithstanding the dragons to greet them if they turned back. "Great. Fan-tucking-fastic! We're lost!"

Cael laughed, "Apparently we are", making that the final remark. Brokk ignored anything Cael kept saying along the way as they walked along the desert. The heat was strange, considering the hidden sun. If the two travelers were to run into anyone, they or it were surely of violent breed.

It was of fortune that not creatures were appearing, perhaps from the notion that dragons would swim the world.

Chapter 10 – Paranoia

The seven days had passed by now, so thankfully Max could walk again. Shakira smiled happily because she was talking to her everything. Anxious with joy, she got the weekend off her chest in a loud rally.

"Oh my gosh! Ok, so basically I bumped into my auntie Petunia and we had ice cream and cake and it was amazing! I swear, best ice cream and cake I'd ever had! Then, after that, we went and visited Paris! Can you believe it? I've not been to Paris in a long time! Bonjour!"

She bowed and giggled, Max starting to say something as she continued,

"And then after that, we went to see the Eiffel Tower. Because of course, that's what one does while in Paris, right? But it didn't end there, because we afterwards visited Italy! I love the Italians, they are such silly people! We had all kinds of foods at Paris and Italy, it was amazing!"Her constant chattering was annoying Max, so she switched the conversation over, "How was your weekend, Max?"

Max stopped and seemed like he was thinking it over, then said, "Well… I can't say it was anywhere nearly as amazing as yours. Hung out with Knoll and Zack, as usual; played some fighting games with them. We also played an MMO some, this one being more action oriented, because I hate those Land of Spellcraft games where you have to click and wait for basic attacks. I like the combos and hack-and-slash being mixed alongside the number spells, you know?"

She let Max continue. "Yeah. After that, we went to the coffee shop near here and I played a small gig with Leon and the guys. Knoll and Zack watched us and cheered us on, which was nice. We didn't have that many people really caring honestly. I think it's because coffee shops are usually quieter places. Maybe it was a bad place for us to play? Or, maybe it wasn't that kind of coffee shop. Guess I'll never know for sure, huh?"

He laughed, apparently finding it funny. Shakira didn't get it, but giggled alongside his laughter anyways. Shakira loved to flirt, even when the situation may've been awkward like this one. She still hadn't talked to Rally about the whole thing, because she didn't know what to say. It was a few days ago that the seventh date happened and now it was May and she still didn't know what to say, on the matter! She decided to try to get her mind off of it, because it was just driving her nuts and she needed to de-stress from the whole situation.

Shakira said, "So let me tell you a bit more about myself. As you know, I'm part Cuban, part Japanese. I actually didn't spend that much time with my Dad growing up, but I understand why, because he works a lot and business keeps him busy in Cuba. It can make me frown sometimes, but I just remember all the great gifts he gives me and I do enjoy the time we spend together, you know? Like this one time, we went to Mouse

World in Florida and that was great! I saw so many of my favorite cartoon characters!"

Max started to say something, but Shakira was so excited she had to continue; oh, the cartoon characters of her childhood!

Shakira giggled, "Oh my gosh! Like Mr. Mouse and Doran Duck! Such amazing characters! I watched their cartoons in my childhood! I can even still sing the songs from their Ali Babba cartoon! Like 'A Whole New World!' Beautiful song!"

Max sighed, but realized he could talk and said, "I love that song too! Good times, I know the lyrics still even now! Wanna sing it together?"

Shakira nodded, singing the song together with him; it seemed both were decent singers, though Shakira was much better than Max at this particular song. To Shakira he sounded fine and she loved to duet with him; it pleased her to be spending time with the guy she loved.Their kisses reciprocal, she said, "Well, I gotta go; Joey and I are going to see about his sister's upcoming wedding in a few months! He wants me to help him and his sister with her wedding gown!""Sounds amazing! I hope you guys have fun!""We will! Love you, Max!"

Max hugged her and said, "I love you too Shakira!", her interface a running skip away.

****

Back in Dark World sitting in a small room with wanted posters strung about was Captain Harding, a man with long black hair and a scar across where his left eye used to be. He had on dark blue jeans, black military boots, and a dark blue button-up shirt while cleaning his revolver.

Lieutenant Hackerman walked in; Hackerman had green hair that was short, himself being slender in build and in uniform, unlike Harding.

He told Harding about the release of the Dragons. If if they had the strength to, they would've killed the idiots who woke them up on the spot. The Earth's 'Leader' could, but he refused to do so, thinking they might be useful.

Harding always remarked the futility of such preservation, cleaning his gun as he spoke, "This is a most... unfortunate set of events."

Hackerman was clearly upset as he responded, "Unfortunate? Unfortunate? My ugly, blind, poor cousin is unfortunate. My ingrown toenail is unfortunate. This is a disaster! A disaster!"

"Calm down, Lieutenant."

"Calm down? How can I calm down when there are now dragons everywhere on the loose!", thus prompting

201

Harding to put a couple of bullets into his gun.

"I-I'm sorry. I-I'll calm down. See? I'm calm! There's no need to-", Harding finally shooting Hackerman."Little shit. Making me waste my ammunition."

Another man walked in; this had dark brown hair and a cold expression on his face that was almost emotionless,

Harding saying to him, "You are the Lieutenant now. Prepare our Griffins for battle immediately."

The man replied, "Yes, sir."

Griffins were interesting as one of the Chimera that man had created and successfully made useful, unlike the Bregals or Jackaloves. Instead of mixing the Sitarian Eagle with a Grizzly Bear, this mixed the former with a Lion. They were tasking in the energy it took to tame them, but Harding personally oversaw that operation and the Griffins were deemed the first successful chimera experiments. That was not counting the Jackalopes, which were essentially rabbits with antlers. These were holdovers from when this world was less dark, meant to appease children. Simultaneously, there were only good for food.

As Harding walked outside he got on his Griffin several times bigger than the others. This one was numerous times the size of a lion and left a trail of lightning behind it when it launched into the air.

Harding shouted to his men, "To battle! We shall take down the menace of the Dragons here and now, before they get further out of hand!"

The men all cheered; he held up his hand for silence and pointed forward as the Griffins moved in perfect unison with their riders on each. They were going into battle against creatures that were exceedingly powerful, but Harding and his men were all magical users of varying degrees of experience. This battle wouldn't be as one-sided as it would feel to some, but then Dragons never were easy prey.

****

Captain Nrath heard about the dragons and wasn't about to let those miserable Griffin Riders of the neighboring city receive glory for taking them down.

That's why he had a secret weapon. They too had made Chimera, these different than one would expect in Dark World. They'd successfully taken a Red Dragon in secret and bred it with that of a Kamrat Lizard, a reptile big enough to have a head about the size of a human. The Lizard was dangerous, but not nearly as powerful as a Dragon.

It lacked firebreath or any kind of magic, making it nothing more than a lizard. When merged with a Red Dragon, however, it created a new creature called Wyverns. They were perhaps smaller than real Dragons; a dragon's eye was about six feet, a Wyvern's head the size of a dragon's eye. They didn't have four, but two hind legs and their wings were located where the front legs of a dragon would be, instead of on back.They could still breathe fire, Nrath's own bigger than the other Wyverns. He had kept them secret for a specific purpose; someday he was going to rule this planet, but he had to handle things one step at a time. It was of imperative need to go into battle against these dragons in order to prove his power, hopefully before Captain Harding.

He got onto his own Wyvern 'Longtooth' and rode alongside his other men with theirs. This battle would be for to take on the Dragons and prove their own worth.

The Dragons were presently burning down a city; one long gone, name all but forgotten due to the destruction the Red Dragons in the area were causing. Captain Harding swooped in with his Griffins, his men firing lightning magic at two of them. Then came the Wyverns and the two armies clashed.

Fire rose into the air as an immense battle took place, the battle a bloody drought. The Red Dragons coursed fire at the Wyverns, the Griffins fighting as best they could through an endless supply of terror.

Captain Harding shouted, "Men, settle together! Do not falter your ranks! East Flank focus on the two Red Dragons, the rest of us will focus on the rest of unexpected guests!"

Captain Nrath shouted at his men, "West Flank focus on the two Red Dragons,

Lieutenant Dar, lead them. The rest of us, let us meet Harding in battle!"

Harding fired lightning magic at Nrath, who retaliated by having Longtooth launch fire at them with an infusion of his magical bursts of energy.

Harding banked right and dodged swooping up and firing his rune revolver with magic in it into the Wyvern. It did hurt it, but little; Nrath churned as he pulled out his revolver at the Griffin, something more effective due to its weaker hide. He only got one shot in before it dodged, wounding it the hardly.

The Creatures both dived down to meet each other in battle as Harding and Nrath fired at each other; they then swooped apart right before it looked like they'd hit the ground, both sides reloading their weapons. The wind whipped through their hair as they continued firing at each other, but to no avail as they dodged each other's assaults.

Harding then shouted, "Samatuel Baloga!" Lightning appeared in the clouds, raining hard. "I have the advantage! How much can your fires work, now?"

Nrath knew this was true, but he also knew his enemy relied on electricity. He also couldn't use his Griffin's abilities in the rain, the Wyverns and Dragons making little progress through the thick of it. As it continued to pour Harding's words came to Nrath,

"Retreat!"

Nrath looked around and realized that most of their men on both sides had been killed by the Dragons while the two of them had been busy fighting each other, growling, "Dammit! Retreat men!"

With that the men on both sides retreated from the battlefield riding on their mounts. This day was a bloody mess and nothing was truly achieved except for one thing: Nrath's secret weapons would no longer be a secret.

****

Max held his head. "I... I just don't know how to say this, guys. I like Shakira, I love her even, but... she talks a lot. I mean a whole lot. She goes on and on and... It's just really tiring!"

Zack chuckled, "Sounds like someone else I know."

Max sighed, " Yeah, okay, I talk a lot too, probably as much as she does. Hell, my mom often tells people I 'never spoke a word' until I was '5 years old and never shut up since' so yeah, I'm known for talking a lot, but maybe that's the problem? She and I are too much alike. It's exhausting. I do love her, I'm pretty sure I do.

"I just wonder if, maybe she and I just aren't meant to be. The problem is that I don't know how to break it to her that I just want to be friends. I mean, she spent so much money on our dates, I'd feel guilty about that. Hell, I already do. Plus, I do love her, I just think maybe I love her more like family, not really like a girlfriend. Not as much as I thought I did, anyways."

Knoll sighed, "Well, dude, you just gotta tell her. The longer you wait, the worst it'll be and the more it'll hurt you both.""You're right dude. I know you are. Just... I wish I didn't have to do this. It'll break her heart and I just really do love her, ya know?"   "But if you really love her, that's why you have to be truthful with her. If you really have something, maybe you guys can continue as friends."

Max nodded, "... And to further complicate things, well, can you guys keep a secret?"

Zack and Knoll nodded,

Max sighing, "Apparently, Rally is jealous of Shakira and I. I'm not into Rally that way, but Shakira still hasn't talked to Rally about this. I don't know if this is going to end up causing some sort of huge drama shitstorm or god knows what else. I mean, you guys know how dramatic Rally can be sometimes when she's upset."

Zack nodded, "Fair enough, but you still need to do what's right and accept the consequences."

Max looked at the ground with an almost sad expression, muttering, "Yeah, you're right."

****

Knoll sighed, because Sarah Mang wasn't the most pleasant person to train with;

he'd supposed he would learn to deal with it. She looked like she'd stopped to think for a moment and said, "How about a spar? I may be known for being a bitch, but that just means the chance to fight me would be entertaining, right? I promise I won't complain, if you hurt me."

Knoll was a little puzzled at its' lack of her casual temperament, but he nonetheless nodded, "Sure, why not?"

He dodged her fist as she attempted a speed-increasing wind punch, then kicked downwards at her with gust-induced speed and she jumped over it. She then managed a single punch on his face, to the extent he jumped back a little and held his face. "OW." Wind based-punches packed a wallop, but he shook it off before she could say anything and managed a back-throwing hit onto her forehead.

Students were training everywhere with their magic and occasional spars weren't uncommon, but this nonetheless drew some attention from students who began to spectate. She sat for a spell, as if speculating. "*What is there to think about? What is she playing at?*"

She got up and flew quickly at Knoll, this time with much more speed than he'd ever seen her have. A few students seemed to cheer Knoll on as she began beating on him, but the cheering stopped when they realized Sarah wasn't subsiding in continually punching.

"You! How dare you strike me, human!"

She then stopped and looked around, muttering, "... Fuck. I just regained my memory and I already drew too much attention."

She stopped but then decided one more punch would hurt. Charles got in the way, stricken to a tough he took well. "That's enough, Sarah."

Sarah sighed, "You, huh! This isn't over."

Charles, "Yes, it is... You said something about 'memory.' There's something different about you, isn't there? What is it?""You never were much of a fighter. Just let it go."

She began to walk off, but then Allanon appeared before them to her teeth's own gritting; he here

angrily maximized, cannon-yelling, "What happened, here!"

Sarah bowed, apologizing, "I got carried away. I'm sorry."

Allanon gave evil eye and said, "Sorry? Hear now, rebel, you should be more than just sorry! Someone get Colleen, she needs to come over here and tend to his wounds... I should honestly expel you at this point, but instead we will talk about this later. Understand? Now leave this place at once and go back to your dorm or something. I don't want to see your face for the rest of the day!"

James was in the crowd as well, turning to Allanon and giving him a slow nod. Sarah seemed to notice this, grabbing Knoll and putting a finger to his throat.

Sarah sighed, then laughed, "I didn't want to have to do this, now. We aren't ready for you yet. I'm not the only one here, you know... Rallalion activate #4!"

Charles began holding his head. "W-what? No... This isn't me... I'm a human and my name is Charles Rojas... That... That isn't me!"

Sarah rolled her eyes, moaning, "Get over it, Phalanx! You're #4, which means that if something happens to threaten me you are second to be activated! You know this!"

Charles looked at the ground. Knoll wasn't scared at all and was trying to think of a way to get free, but Sarah's grip was unusually tight. Knoll and Charles went way back, best friends since childhood.

They played video games together, went to high school together, and now the question was whether Charles was in on this or not.

He looked back at Sarah, asking, "Don't you wonder why it's just us who have our memories from back then? Where are the others? Why are we the only ones to know who we are?"

Allanon very seriously intoned, "This fight is between you and I. Leave the boy out of this!"

Sarah laughed, "Surely you jest! You know what I am now! I know fully good and well that I could never beat you, but you know what? I don't care! It's not like any of you stinking humans gave us a chance! Especially you, of all people! You must face your sins: you slaughtered so many of my people, and for what? Some petty war?"

Allanon growled, "Perhaps you were too young to remember, but it was your people who planned to attack us. We just struck before you could!"

This time it was Leon who came out of the crowd holding a sword, winging it at Charles to his jumping dodge; it was from here Charles sent raw arcane to his opponent, Leon somehow glowing as its' magic hit him and reflected Charles' own fall.

Sarah sighed, "Get up, you idiot! We don't have time for this. You! Leon! Stay back unless you want your friend's entrails all over the floor!", Leon himself heeding the demand.

James challenged her. "I'm not a human, either. I'm a phoenix just as you, so let me ask you something... Who's to say I won't attack? Go ahead. Try to kill him. The second you do, you'll be dead as well. I'll see to that!"

Sarah growled but then Charles put his arms around Sarah and pulled her off of Knoll, which left neck scratches behind. These were nail-like in their protrusion, their hurting to the extent that they bled. To some students it somehow made sense that Charles got past her guard, his knowledge of this battle's contents thus obviated; he turned to Knoll and squeamishly whimpered, "You were a good friend, Knoll. I'm sorry for what I was before we met."

Knoll could barely speak due to his injured neck but he responded anyways, "What are you talking about?"

"I just hope someday, when you think back on me… it will be with fondness… Goodbye."Charles grab of Sarah headed into the sky from his airborne ascent; before Knoll could be surprised of that they both reverted into phoenixes now engaged in winged combat,

Sarah shouting, "How can you defend these humans after all they've done to us over the years!"

Charles shouted back, "They are my friends! While being Charles all these years… I've realized that we are wrong for fighting them! I'm sure they'd not be the same way they were years ago, if we gave them the chance!"

Sarah shouted, "Are you mad? Fine! If I have to, I'll go through you to take care of this!"

Allanon seemed prepared to act, but Charles headed straight for Sarah and they both exploded into ash. The ashes fell from the sky slowly, blowing away in the wind while

Knoll passed out. It was there Colleen was finally reaching him.

****

Tears went down Shakira's cheeks, for she'd been told over the phone of all impersonal things possible.

It turned out her father wasn't the upstanding person she'd thought he was for so long; he'd been a Cuban druglord the entire time and the authorities finally had enough evidence to use against him. All the money Shakira had been so proud of was in fact drug cash.

She was sitting on her bed in nothing but a long t-shirt a friend had bought her. She was nude underneath it and refused to put on any other clothes, ashamed of what she'd bought with her father's money.

Her father was now on the lam and one of his men had called to warn her that she should stay where she was; it was the safest place she could be and all of Cuba's people were in hysterics over the whole thing, so her dad didn't want her involved. It was all in Spanish of course, which was funny to once more speak and hear since she'd been speaking English and Japanese for so long.

It was like her world had been turned upside down; Max was hugging her as she continually bawled. Max seemed to be her rock at this moment; she certainly needed it, especially because she wasn't ready to tell Simon, Joey or Rally yet.There was suddenly a knock on the door, Max answered it to see

Connor saying, "Knoll is in critical condition! They say he might not make it through the night!"

Shakira understood well that she couldn't let Max go alone, since this could affect him quite considerably. "Let's go see him… together, Max", she said wiping tears.

Max nodded, his face extremely panicked and one could tell him hurrying. She placed on a pair of jeans she owned and her usual tennis shoes without time to put on any underwear; she didn't have it to let the fact her clothes were bought with her father's money bother.

Max was going to need her more than that. They headed for a private medical area where Colleen and Sarah McKnight, Leon's sister, were both working on healing Knoll.

Max turned to Allanon. "How bad is he?"

Allanon replied, "Well, aside from the bruises he has fractured ribs and his neck was bleeding a lot, which is unsurprising as Phoenixes have tougher nails than we do."

Max upped surprisingly to say, "Phoenix? A phoenix did this?"

Shakira was so worried about Max that she didn't even have words; she was still in shock over what had happened with her, but she had to be strong for his sake.She asked Allanon,"What happened?"

Allanon relayed the whole story of how Knoll was attacked by Sarah Mang the phoenix and how Knoll's childhood friend Charles had turned out to be a phoenix, but sacrificed himself to save the school. Allanon ended up having to explain everything to the magician students as well as cover up what happened from the rest of the school that saw it. The whole thing as he put it was 'a big mess' and there was now paranoia among the students about who was and wasn't a phoenix.

Allanon added, "I think that was the intention. Whoever restored their memories only did it to Sarah Mang and Charles to cause paranoia, knowing that these two could never do much damage as soldiers but could do a lot of damage to us psychologically by letting the remaining students know about them."

It was Max's turn to cry. His face turned into a look that Shakira had not seen before, like everything was taken from him at once. The next hour or so that followed felt like an eternity, holding each other in the room waiting to see if Knoll would recover.

Chapter 11 – Another one bites the dust.

Zack hadn't heard the news until now. He'd been away eating dinner at one of his favorite local places and when he heard about what happened he headed for the medical room as quickly as he could. It didn't have any real doctors or nurses, for fear of revealing the magical world. Despite that he was hooked up to proper medical equipment, but was being healed via Colleen, who'd stayed by his bedside with magic green light coming from her hands into his arm.

Max was sitting on a chair rolled up right next to Knoll's bed. Max's head was lying on the bed and his eyes were still open, but you could tell he'd been crying and exhausted. Shakira was asleep on a chair in the corner across from the room's entrance. As Zack walked in Max looked up at him with fatigued expression making petty the use of words.

Zack bit his lip under eyes carrying a look of deep sorrow, such as couldn't look at Max but to say he was sorry. The latter slowly nodded as he turned and looked back at Knoll. He managed to barely utter the words, "Well… I've cried more than I ever remember crying. Guess I've done enough of that." Max attempted to make light of himself and his sorrow, but he couldn't. It was instead that Max was simply unable to know how to handle the situation.

Zack took a seat in the chair behind Max's to the direct right of the front door. He was doing all he could to keep his emotions in check, but having difficulty.

None of them left Knoll's bedside, well into the night. Then, at about two in the morning his eyes blinked and opened. Max was the immediate first to notice, crying again and never minding the possibility of his own silliness.

These were silent tears as he smiled and asked, "Hey dude, how are you feeling? You gave us a scare."

Zack got up and darted for the bed to look at Knoll. Knoll said, "Wow. I feel like a semi-truck hit me."

Max and Colleen gave a small laugh in response,

Zack chuckling as he said, "If only it were that simple."

Shakira awoke after that and got up and to Knoll's bed. She sighed and said, "I know I don't know you well, but you mean a lot to Max, so therefore, you mean a lot to me as well. It's good to know you're awake."

Now Colleen was crying and she hugged Knoll, holding him very closely as she said, "I was afraid I'd never get to see you open your eyes again. I am so glad to see that I was able to help you. "

Max chuckled a little as he said, "You know Colleen, I don't know you that well even though we are in the same class, but I'll be grateful to you and Sarah McKnight forever. Thank you so much, so very, very much."

Max began to cry a little again, wiping the tear.

Colleen let go of Knoll and nodded slowly in response to Max.

Zack smirked at the scene, but deep inside he couldn't. The extent of emotions traveled through him at the sight of a friend near death. The whole fact he was still alive put him at ease a bit but, he still couldn't get the scenario of what put him in this situation out of his head."To think this whole thing happened because we had Phoenixes among us this whole time and we had no way of knowing who they were. I'm going to talk to James. He's a phoenix, so maybe we can work something out; otherwise, what the hell was the point of making him look human in the first place?"

Zack turned and asked, "What exactly happened? All I knew was that Knoll was in critical condition and where he was. And what do you mean 'Phoenixes?'"

Max sighed and tried to relay the information as best he could. "Well... It's really complicated, but the best way I can explain it is... Allanon and Alexander fought and killed a bunch of Phoenixes because they were planning on killing all the humans. The whole thing was a sort of continuation of a previous battle that had been started because humans slaughtered phoenixes for their fire arrows and healing tears.

"The Mage's Guild was born out of hatred towards this and posed as humans. This time the Mage's Guild was supposed to all be dead after Allanon and Alexander, plus their fellow members at some sort of Wizard's Guild, had killed them all. However, it would appear they've been in disguise as humans among us at this school and even they themselves don't realize they are phoenixes, until it's too late. Charles Rojas was Knoll's best friend since high school, even in his childhood, yet he-"

Knoll interrupted, "He was a hero... He was my best friend until the end. He sacrificed himself to take out Sarah Mang, who was also a phoenix just as he was. If it weren't for him, Sarah might have actually killed me."

Zack tried to sort out everything that was just said, which wasn't easy considering everything else going on inside. That is when he replied, "So, we have a whole bunch of dangerous creatures right under our noses-"

Max interrupted, "I don't like to think of them as creatures. They are too intelligent for that and remember that we still have one of those said creatures on our side, James, who I'm sorry I didn't reveal this to you sooner: he's actually my summon, Heliopolis. Jericho's summon is also in disguise. He's Draco, and Lance is Leon's Werewolf."

Zack shot him an angry look, gruffly scratching, "You're only now bringing this up?"

Max sighed, "Allanon swore summoners like us and Vincent to secrecy. As you already saw, Knoll's own childhood friend was a phoenix, so we had no way of knowing if anyone else was.""You could've still told me about this whole fact about James not being human!""That would also be an issue, because that would arise suspicion. For all we knew, you could've been one of them."

Zack sighed, "Even if I was, don't you think I would've been trustworthy enough?"

Max sighed deeper this time and said, "You don't understand. Once they regain their memories, they might not even be the same person we knew before-"

Knoll cut him off, saying, "But obviously Charles was. He chose to save me anyways."

Max replied, "Well yes, but there's always the possibility that upon regaining their memories, their hatred of humans could override any experiences they had when they thought they were human. It could've easily caused panic and all kinds of espionage."

Zack felt like he was about to explode with anger about the whole ordeal, instead leaving the room and slamming the door.

As he headed the natural direction from the medical area he entered the training facility and heard a few people of the magical lessons talking amongst themselves, guessing they hadn't gone to sleep either with all that was going on.

He'd heard things like "What if you were a phoenix this whole time? What if I am? What about my teachers, or my friends? We could all be among phoenixes that want to chop our brains out, and we wouldn't even know who they are!"

Nero nodded to the person and said, "I know. I mean, for all we know he could be one as well", he said pointing at Zack. This caused the latter to immediately gnarl, "Excuse me?"

Nero shrugged in almost sarcastic tone, murmuring, "I'm just saying, it's possible."

Zack was on the defensive as he said, "So what if I was?"

Nero smiled at his own intelligence as he said, "Well, obviously then you'd have tried to kill us all and we'd have to stop you."

Zack quipped back, "In case you've forgotten, the other Phoenix tried to save everybody! He knew where his loyalties lie, and so do I!"

Nero nodded but then said, "But we have no way of knowing if it'll always work that way. I mean, what if before he was in human form he was some super evil bad dude and it has overridden the friendship he'd made? Then we wouldn't be having this conversation right now, would we?"

Zack smirked and said, "In that case I have a question for you."

Nero gulped a little and said, "Yes?"

Zack replied, "Who do you trust enough to stand by your side, despite what their past was?"

Nero stopped and thought a moment, going a ghostly pale as he said, "No one. I don't have any friends, just people I talk to."

Zack nodded and said, "I see. However, if you're that paranoid about it, just know there are at least a few people you can depend on."

As Zack said this Jared approached them and turned to Zack and asked him, "How's Max? He's an old friend of mine and Ikuto, Connor and I were worried about him, but we kept our distance. Leon visited him a couple times, but it didn't really do much good because Max was in shock, or something."

Zack sighed, "He's still shaken, but he's doing better at this point. Knoll woke up."

Jared nodded, "Well, that's good. We were worried about him. I'll tell the others about it. Thanks, dude.""*I just hope this doesn't tear us all apart*", Zack thought to himself.

****

Anna was cleaning her awards. It was nearly lunchtime, but she'd already eaten one earlier; besides, cleaning these awards was a good way to calm her. She had a master's degree in psychology and a doctorate in medical science, having earned those through hard work alone.

She'd never once used her 'abilities' to get an unfair advantage, adding to her pride in herself. She earned everything she gained, just as she'd had to do with learning her magic. Because of that it had been easy for her to infiltrate the school and become both the school nurse and the school counselor.

It also helped people tended to love her, for she was an honest, and kind woman. She was beautiful and wasn't above using it to her advantage. "*Swell. When the time comes, it'll make my mission easier*", she thought to herself.

Still, she couldn't help but feel confused. She hated Allanon with a burning passion, yet she'd grown to feel something else, something she couldn't explain. Was it admiration for him? She was disgusted by the very notion... but it was probably true.She nonethless couldn't let them be unprepared for the coming threat, so she was the one who killed the phoenix; the body was left where a student eventually found it, which was as much as she needed to know. She suddenly snapped out of her reflection to realize someone had walked in, then putting on her trademark sweet-hearted smile and asking, "Yes? What is it?"

It was Sho, with Allanon behind him as well. "*Ugh. Bein' in Allanon's presence makes me sick. But, it just ain't time for me to take him out. Not yet.*"

Allanon sighed, "A student was expelled for beating up Sho here. Jericho stepped in and attacked the kid for brutalizing

223

him. I nearly expelled Jericho too, but I didn't. "

Anna smiled and politely replied, "I guess you're getting soft, Headmaster Allan."

Allanon chuckled, "Perhaps. In any case, I want you to help Sho here with his wounds, please."

Anna nodded as she smiled very sweetly and said, "Sure. It would be my pleasure."

"It would be an even greater pleasure to knock your face clean off, Allanon."

Allanon smiled and nodded, "I'm glad! Well, I best be off. I have a busy day ahead of me!"

Anna smiled and replied, "Buh bye, then! I look forward to seeing you again! *Sometimes even I wonder if I might actually mean that. I don't understand it."*

After Anna was all done nursing his wounds she decided to go for a stroll in the nearby forest. As she voyaged she noticed that the fencing instructor Klaus Einslaughter was out there as well. She walked up to Klaus, saying, "Good to see ya. What bring you out here?"

Klaus nodded and spoke quietly, "Oh, nothing too much, Miss Smith. Just enjoying this beautiful view. I have a lot of time for that since even though I'm the only fencing instructor here, I only teach one giant class per day. Gives me time just to enjoy this view. "

Anna nodded understandingly and replied, "I agree; mighty purdy, really. To see the trees, the deer... The best part is, not many people around. It's nice to be able to switch off once and awhile and just enjoy some peace and quiet, ya know what I'm sayin?"

Klaus nodded agreeably as he quietly replied, "I'd have to agree with you, Miss Smith."

Just then they spotted a deer a few yards in front of them looking back as its ears lightly twitched in both directions. It was beautiful, eventually hopping off into the distance *and leaving* Anna thinking,

"Maybe I really have grown to love this place. What in tarnation is gettin into me?"

****

"Well, aside from the fact I already got on Zack's bad side... Zack of all people. He, Knoll and I have had a lot of good times together at this school. Knoll means as much to him as he does to me. I should've been more sensitive to his feelings. I just hope he'll forgive me."

Max was in the room with James and Allanon, the former having asked them to meet in his office because something had bothered him. He cleared his throat and looked up at the ceiling, then back at them saying," I have to know... How did we not see this coming? Wasn't the point of having Heliopolis become James that we'd have another phoenix among us, but this one on our side? I mean no offense, James, but will you be able to help us?"

Before James could respond, Allanon spoke up. "He normally could. A phoenix can recognize another one quite easily, even while both are disguised as humans. As you've seen, this was also worse than expected as Sarah displayed that her transformation still granted her physical things, such as her fingernails being as sharp as her real talons.

"They've improved since I last saw them. This is greater than the one I taught James and Draco; it actually hides them from even their own kind. Through study of the body Vincent found, I believe I may have found a way to detect them. In fact, had the fight between Sarah and Knoll not occurred, we might've had the time to test it. My first idea was to test all the magical students, then the staff, then the remaining students.

"The test is simple actually. All that need be done is that I cast the spell on James and he would be able to detect them as well as he would, if the spell on them was of same strength as the older version I taught James and Draco. Things should become easier on us now."

Max nodded, "That's all I needed to hear. How soon can you begin testing the students?""We have to be sensitive about this, but I plan to start today, during training."

Max looked at the ground and heaved, "Well… That's at least some relief. So how is Knoll?"

226

Allanon ran his fingers through his beard, seeming in thought as he replied, "He should be fine. He just needs to rest for a few days. Besides... Isn't today special?"

Max nodded, "How so?"

Allan laughed, "It's Mother's Day, Max. Perhaps you should let your family know how you're doing."

Max smacked his forehead, because with so much going on, it had slipped his mind; he hadn't even spoken to his mother or his seventeen-year-old brother since he'd arrived. He turned and headed out the door saying, "Thanks, Allanon, I will!"It hit him as he was pulling out his cell phone that Shakira didn't have a mom and her Dad was on the run due to being a wanted criminal. Now she was afraid to use her own money knowing where it came from, as well as only having the money in her bank account since her Father's income wouldn't easily extract; that was if she ever decided to touch it again. Max still wanted to be just friends with her, but this wasn't the time to tell her. There was also the fact she still hadn't talked to Rally, who was jealous of Shakira for being with Max but wouldn't admit it: he didn't want to let it get to him and it would be depressing to try to get in the middle of that, so he decided to call his Mom.

She picked up on the third ring, asking, "Hello?"

Max smiled and said, "Happy Mother's Day Mom!"His mom replied laughing, "Thank you, Max, long time no talk! How's school been?"

Max sighed, "Well Mom, it was fun but uh... Can I ask you something?""Go ahead."

Max held his head dreading having to ask his mom about this, but he always used to go to her for problems when he needed her help.

"Well, the thing is... My girlfriend, Shakira. I was about to break up with her, but it turns out her father is on the run from the cops and stuff and so now she's all depressed and realizes all her money was illegally obtained and all that. She's just really hurting right now.

"Now I can't tell her because it'd just make things worse, but I'm afraid if I don't tell her she'll notice something's wrong and it could just make things worse regardless. I really do have romantic feelings for her, but she just kind of gets on my nerves and I'm starting to wonder if maybe I don't feel as strongly for her in that way as I thought... But I don't want to make it worse. What do I do?"Well, the last thing she needs is for you to not be open and honest with her. That's one thing you've always been good about; you're a very honest person and like you said, she'll notice and will wonder if she can trust you. She needs to be able to trust you for you to be able to help her get through this.

"So be honest with her that you do care about her, just not in a boyfriend-girlfriend way; you just want to be friends, but be sure to mention that you are definitely there for her. You can even say 'I know it's bad timing, but I need to be honest with you.' Then just tell her the truth."

Max sighed a deep breath of relief but was still nervous. Still, she was probably right, so he replied, "Yeah, I guess you're right. Thanks, Mom. I'm still very nervous, but you've never steered me wrong so I will take your advice. I'll tell her and hope for the best."

Max's mom replied, "She'll understand, and she needs you right now Max, because really, a boyfriend would just be a distraction anyway. Don't tell her that, of course, but she needs a good friend to be there for her right now and that'll be best for her.""Okay, thanks. I love you, Mom, I'll try to call you sooner next time.""I love you too, Max", both hanging up as

Max headed for the girls' dorm and knocked on Shakira's door. He did as his Mom told him; after having finished saying it, he felt a couple tears go down his own cheeks.

"I... Thought it'd be easier to say than this. I mean, you're such an awesome person Shakira. I love you, I really do... and it breaks my heart to say all that. It really does, because you are an amazing person, a beautiful person... and well... I really wish we could have been something more. But maybe I should've noticed sooner, you know?"

He sniffed through his continued crying, saying, "I should've realized that we just weren't meant to be in a relationship of that kind, you know? You're still an amazing friend and I never want to lose that. I just hope you stick with me... Despite all this.""I understand... Thanks for being honest with me, Max", her comprehension transcending through their sharing of hugs. There was a brief silence as her cries came to a wipe, her jubilance significant as she said, "I'll definitely accept your offer, Max. Friends forever!" Through the sniffling, of course.

"That hurt... A lot. I'm glad she's taking it better than I feared, though. Not sure what it'll mean for Rally, but at least this relieves some of the tension. I really do care about Shakira a lot and I want to be there for her always."

****

Ikuto was nothing short of exhausted: he'd been teaching people fire powers, but nobody seemed to be catching on as fast as he was in his own training, except perhaps for Shaun. Shaun's fire was too fast and unfocused, though; poor Simon seemed to get it the least, as his own flames just kept dissipating. As he practiced he sighed, "I'm never going to get this!""Put that anger elsewhere, like in your fire powers. Think about what it felt like when you first used them, then just let them flow out."

Somewhat shyly, Simon said to his brother, "I know, I know. Why couldn't I learn as fast as you?"

Ikuto shrugged as he laughed a little, "How should I know... I'm new to this too. I just learned fast, I guess. Got good at my fire powers quickly; at least you're not like

Shaun. He's had to tone his down just to even try to control them and he's still having trouble. He nearly burned Rally, earlier!"

Rally heard in the distance and looked at them, nodding as she called out to them, "Trust me, it wasn't fun and if it wasn't for my ice powers that would've really, really, sucked!"

Ikuto sighed. *"Great. Now I'm going to have to check on Shaun next. He's always a pain in the ass."*

He said, "Speaking of which, I gotta check on him. Will you be fine for now?""Not like I'm going to burn someone on accident... Sure, I'll be fine."

Ikuto headed over for Shaun, who tried to hug Ikuto but Ikuto pushed him back laughing. "Nope. None for you!"

Shaun laughed, "Hey I got plenty more where that came from. You know what they call a gay drive by?"

At the somewhat surprising nature of this question Ikuto asked, "What?"

Shaun's wide grin came with the snack of his cheeks, as he said, "A fruit roll up."

The sheer immaturity of this question made Ikuto chuckle a little, but knew he couldn't hold off asking forever. Deliberating expressly, he asked politely, "So, how's your fire training going?"

Shaun pointed at the sky and sent small concentrated flames out, then a big burst thereafter. "I think I'm finally getting the hang of this!"

Ikuto whistled his say, remarking, "Awesome! That's actually quite a relief!"

A bigger burst of flame suddenly hit the sky with a danger, Shaun sighing, "Oops. Well, nobody is perfect!"

Ikuto nodded as he looked at the sky and then back at Shaun, an annoyance not withheld from himself or his pupil. He knew he'd have to keep helping him out, so he replied, "Well, I'll help you best I can."

As he began pointing out the targets and Shaun tried hitting them they decided to engage in casual conversation. "You know that whole story Allanon told all of us about those Phoenixes? You ever wonder if we kind of had it coming."

Ikuto looked at his student with a somewhat concerned expression, but Shaun replied, "Don't get me wrong, I don't want anybody to get hurt, But think about it... We hunted them down. We treated them like animals. It just doesn't seem right, ya know?"

Ikuto nodded, "Yeah, I guess so, but we can't do anything about that now. That was our ancestors. We didn't do that ourselves. Heck, most of us didn't even know phoenixes were real, until recently."

Shaun nodded, "Yeah, I just don't think that makes us innocent. I just feel bad for what humanity has done. Think about it, what about if the shoe was on the other foot and we had taught them how to fight dragons? Would they have hunted us?"

Ikuto replied, "I don't remember Allanon ever mentioning anything about dragons..."

Shaun sighed, "Great. Just great. I swear, sometimes me and my big mouth." Shaun suddenly owned a massive grin, one perhaps full of evil as flames began to surround him.

The students all turned and looked, with

Shaun laughing, "I won't go down as easily as #4 and #5 did. I may be #6, but I never showed them how strong I really was... They didn't know about me, Palnral the Magnificent. But you soon will..."

He jumped into the air and changed into his phoenix form. There lay a single scar going along his left eye, his wings massive and beautiful full of scars.

Ikuto used the flames under his own body to fly into the air next to him, yelling, "Looks like we're going to have to fight, huh?"

Shaun, obviously named Palnral, nodded. He flew forward launching massive flames at Ikuto, a wall of ice suddenly blocking it.

Rally created an ice pillar and went behind Palnral as she said, "Is this a private fight, or can anyone join in the fun?"

Palnral laughed, "You underestimate me. Big mistake."

He then uttered, "Magic... Missle", And bolts of lightning went in all directions, electrocuting both Ikuto and Rally.

Rally fell for the ground but Nero managed to catch her. Ikuto didn't waste any time as he sent flames at Palnral, but Palnral laughed haughtily.

"Fire? At me? I'm a phoenix. My natural flames are far hotter than any others, so I'm naturally immune to your pitiful excuse for flames! Besides, how long can you use flames to suspend yourself in the air, before you run out of energy and plummet to the ground?"

Suddenly he felt someone poking his shoulder and was sent flying backward with a single punch. It was

James laughing, "Perhaps you should try me on for size!", he said turning into his phoenix form.

Palnral was taken aback by this,"H-heliopolis?! From the Polis family?! Y-your strength among phoenixes is a legend! They say only the greatest phoenixes of all time surpass you, in strength!"In all of his phoenix-form glory Heliopolis laughed, challenging loudly, "Who's to say I'm not greater than some of them?", Heliopolis said flapping his wings rapidly. It was there massive flames began to engulf Palnral as he screamed in pain and became dust in the wind,

Heliopolis whispering, "No more humans get hurt, today."

He flew to the ground and turned back into human form a few feet above it, walking over to Rally and asking Nero as James, "What happened to her?"

Nero said, "T-the Phoenix said it was 'magic missile'. I-I h-hope she's ok."

James thus breathed a sigh of relief. "She'll be in a lot of pain either way, but I can heal her enough easily that she'll be fine. This is nowhere near as bad as what happened to Knoll."

James began tearing up, the drops hitting Rally's face and a green energy lightly going into her face as she slowly began to open her eyes in Nero's arms.

Rally jumped a back and demanded, "Ack! Let go of me bookworm!"

She then realized she was now standing up perfectly fine. "I- I'm not that bad!", until she started crying, "Ow. Ow. Ow. Ow!"

James chuckled, "You'll be alright. Your body will just be sore for a little while. It varies based on the person."

Rally thought for a moment and blushed, as she looked at James and said, "Wait... How'd you do that?"

James chuckled again with a very confident yet friendly countenance, saying, "Oh, don't mind me, I'm a phoenix. Healing tears are our thing. We're just lucky you weren't as bad as Knoll was."

Rally sighed, "It figures: get saved by a cute guy and he's not even human."

Everyone laughed and the day ended on a happy note, which they certainly needed to break the tension from all that happened earlier; it was here that their closest configuration as friends could be made lucid through the darkest of trying times.

Chapter 12 – Numbers

Shakira loved her Math teacher, Mr. McCoullach. His first name was John and she knew that's what his peers referred to him by. His math class was labeled to be for advanced learners, but she always found the class quite easy.One of her early problems was find the derivative of $\cos^2(\sqrt{x})$. Obviously she knew using the chain rule, "$d/dx(\cos^2(\sqrt{x})) = -(\sin(\sqrt{x})\cos(\sqrt{x}))/(\sqrt{x})$." It was simple math for her. Another one of the easier ones she saw was as follows: "Given that position of a car varies with a rate of r^4/e, find its velocity." Without fail she perfectly solved it. This one was an applied problem: "Velocity is the derivative of position as a function of time, so just differentiate (find the derivative of) the function: $d/dx(r^4/e) = 4r^3/e$."

She didn't see why others were still stuck on algebra. It felt like kindergarten stuff to her, but she sympathized with Max; he'd always struggled in Math and was not as proficient. He currently had to re-take an Algebra course because he'd forgotten what he'd learn in high school. It was a common problem for him, so she helped him from time to time.

But the real interesting situation was Mr. McCoullach and his math puns! Such famous ones as "Relatively find the relativity of that problem.", or "Pi r squared? That's crazy, I've been eating pie are round!" Other famous ones of his were "Don't imitate, integrate!", and "Don't drink and derive!"

He turned to Shakira realizing she was spacing out, saying, "That's unusual for you, Miss Nomura. Perhaps you can answer this problem on the board for me then?"

He began jotting down a bunch of things until he turned to her and pointed at the board. He was obviously trying to punish her daydreaming, which was so silly of him to do because she knew she could solve it!

Shakira smiled happily as she stood up looking at the problem. This was the Poincaré conjecture, something she'd studied because "Unsolved Math Problems" always fascinated her and this was solved recently. Still, they hadn't publicly shown the answer to it just yet, which made that she could figure it out more exciting.

She thought for a few moments, walking up to the board and writing things down. As time ticked away class had ended but she was still writing, by her end of class completing the problem.

Mr. McCoullach sat impressedly as he pulled out a sheet of paper and looked it over. He replied, "This piece has been solved before, though we'd hid from the students the answer, even editing our computers to not have any mention of its' solution. Even if you looked it up on a public computer, it takes a very intelligent mind to comprehend. I happen to have a piece that shows the answer and... y-you're correct! But that just can't be possible... can it?"

He paused astonishedly and responded, "I'll make sure the other classes excuse your absence for today."

Shakira smiled happily as she skipped out of class, satisfied with her usually successful mathematic self.

****

Max was doing sit-ups again; he learned that if you were late for class, the Theater teacher had mercy. He'd still let you inside if you weren't too late, but you would do pushups in exchange. It didn't help for Max that he wasn't in good shape, so he couldn't do a single pushup; fencing was somehow much easier regardless, so the teacher had him do sit-ups instead. Upon completing them he panted and headed back for the group.They were splitting up into groups again, this time for a play that they would be preparing for the remainder of this year. It was a Knights of the Round Table-centered play, a fiction complete with dragons.

He'd overheard the lesson plan, so he was assuredly prepared; it was incredibly ironic to Max since he knew Dragons were real and was taking fencing as well. He figured he had this down pat, but he'd also been working on his acting to its certain improvement. He was actually pretty decent at it now, easily as skillful as the best actors in the class.

As they separated into groups he was with TJ again, something he was now used to.. Instead of being with Syanne he was with the twins Fred and Mel, 'Mel' short for Melvin; for the latter it was a full name he hated, him and his brother playing two knights. Max was Arthur, no small feat for him to step to. TJ got Lancelot, Mel was Galahad and Fred was Tristin. The other knights wouldn't be featured for this little play for the sake of streamlining the fictional version, an interpretation that nonetheless couldn't spoil the fun.

TJ still delivered hammily with his lines, but by now he could more capably convince of their real. Given the proportion of more eccentric or usually comedic actors there were in entertainment it seemed that their characters suited them perfectly; TJ was certainly no exception. Despite this, TJ had by now learned he had to be somewhat good at acting as well. He couldn't just overact the whole time, thus choosing not to.

"'Arthur, it would appear the Saxons are breaching the north wall!'"

TJ delivered the line much better than he would have mere months ago, though he was also looking at the script while doing so since the scripts were doled out two days in advance.

Max nodded as he responded, "'We will meet them in battle then, Lancelot. Prepare the horses, today we go to battle!'... So how was I?"

TJ nodded, "Not bad, not bad. This Persian approves. All the same, I'm kind of glad I got Lancelot. Means I get the ladies."

He smirked a little on that last bit, obviously having somewhat dirtier thoughts but not outright saying them.

As the hour went by and they were dismissed, it was time for his next class; the accursed math.

Math was a mixed bag for him. On one hand it wasn't doing the lessons that was much of a problem; once he got a hold of things he did just fine, he just forgot how to do the problems often and had to relearn all over again. It was things like that which explained why he was in college retaking Algebra. There was one grace he always could look forward to in the midst of it, Ms. Ameena Kenny the math teacher.

Sure, it was usually considered childish to be attracted to a teacher, but her beauty piqued interest the way it would another besides him. He wasn't typically into African-American women, his perspective being that they were loud and obnoxious based on the ones they met. They weren't usually his type, but Ameena certainly had it to reach him with.She wasn't gossamer-thin as a supermodel and had ample measure of her buxom bane. She was also of lighter complexion with brown eyes, often wearing glasses and black dresses.

As he walked into class there was Miss Kenny, looking beautiful as ever. He wasn't one for types much older and she perhaps had a boyfriend, but the fancy to her was perfectly normal. "*I've always struggled in*

Math enough as it is. I need to keep my head in the game, so to speak", he thought

as she went over the lesson plans, him with complete self-distraction from her charisma.

The Math problems weren't too difficult in this case. $23=3a/567$ and problems like, fractions, always funny little mental nuggets. It was also interesting to him because sometimes these things would be answered using "Unsolvable" or "Not enough information." Sometimes there were trick questions, but not always. Just seeing the numbers gave him a bad headache; he just got stressed easily when it came to math, because it made him freak out and reach a kind of catatonia if he thought too much about it. He hated math so much! He knew it had its place in life, the reason for its difficulty lost on him.

People like Shakira were in Calculus and advanced math classes while he was sitting there retaking Algebra. It made him feel like an idiot; after the while he'd been stressing so much he realized class was over and he'd not done any of his math problems.

He walked up to the front after class and told her about his anxiety. "So, the same as it has been, but it's getting worse, huh?"

Max slowly nodded as he looked at the floor, so she put his hand on his shoulder as he failed slight increments of not blushing.

She said, "I'll tell you what: It sounds to me like you need a Math tutor. I'll call one up and in a few days I'll have one to help you after school. It sounds like to me you need extra help with your math and I'm happy to help arrange that for you. Okay?"

Max smiled a little and nodded, "Thanks. I really appreciate it.""No problem. Just remember, you aren't stupid. Some people just learn things at a different pace. Everyone has their talents and weaknesses. Never forget that."

Max nodded as he headed out of the classroom, *"I know, I know. I just still feel like an idiot, though."*

****

Brokk and Cael had their weapons at the ready as they hid behind the rocks while being fired at.

Cael laughed haughtily, "I guess my gang didn't appreciate me leaving. Now they want us dead too!"

Brokk grumbled, "Aren't you just Mr. Popular!"

As they continued getting fired at Brokk saw a bunch of other men on horses come up and attack what seemed to be mutual enemies.

Brokk smiled, "The enemy of my enemy is my friend." Brokk started to get up, Cael pulling his head down and shaking his head.

Brokk frowned with his face enraged, "Them too, Cael? Really?"

Cael frowned, this time his face more serious than before. "This is bad news. My former gang must have really, really upset someone big to see them turning up."

Brokk was curious about what Cael had said, most of all concerned; even Cael seemed serious about this, his partner asking, "Who are they?""Bad news. They're a huge gang. Very huge. They look small now, but that isn't even a fifth of the size that they get. Their boss runs a whole town too, but before that they were nothing but a bunch of crooks. They rob any trains that are unfortunate enough to have to pass by his town's station. I don't know what my old boys did, but to get their attention it could not have been small.""Doesn't sound good... Not at all. I wonder if the woman I love is caught up in all this? For all I know, she's in there, scared. We have to check it out... At least see if she's there."

Cael sighed, "Alright. I'm in... But if we get killed, it'll be your fault this time."

Brokk allowed a small grin to form on his face, though it was hard for him to be happy in times like these. "What can I say? Maybe you're just a bad influence on me, Cael."Cael returned the expression, then lost it when they both saw the men shot. Those were Cael's old friends, killed right in front of him. They'd parted ways, but Brokk was pretty sure that didn't make it hurt him any less. He decided that Cael would lead the way, since he seemed to know where it was located. Cael might not show it, but he was upset to see his boys shot up in front of him.

They didn't have much of a plan. The whole town was ran by this band of crooks, so the only option was simply to go in and get out if they didn't see her. Brokk had a feeling it'd be much more than that, since they'd shot Cael's former comrades. There'd be hell to pay, and Brokk would probably help him.

As they continued on their long walk to town, Brokk couldn't help but hate the insane heat. It was desert for miles, sunlight nowhere. He heard their destination was a few miles from the ocean, which would be nice since Brokk had never been there. It was a small comfort, considering this villa's jagged edge.

From what he'd been told the people there were always either fiercely loyal to the crooks who owned the place, or had their family threatened to their own resultant obedience. There was no time for sympathy, either; they'd both try to kill them upon sight, and it was very likely they'd be seen.A hard gust of wind starting heading their way, almost like a mini-sandstorm. Brokk pulled his cowboy hat over his face, glad he always wore his trench coat. It was going to protect his skin from the sand as it often had, Cael fit with a bandana for the same reason. Brokk sort of wished he had a bandana or a scarf himself, relying instead on his hat; Cael didn't have one, making less certain his hopes for shielding. The wind passed through almost as quickly as it had arrived and they kept walking as it stopped; they could barely stand then, so it was always wiser to wait for it to pass.

As sweat slid their brows they noticed the town was in view, hiding behind rocks as they heard horses passing by.

As they hid Brokk suggested, "We'll take their horses."

Cael smirked, "I like the way you think."

They ran behind the men and shot them the backs, the horses starting to rear up until Brokk walked over slowly, patting the side of the black horse to a gradual calm. He pointed towards the brown horse and motioned at Cael, him performing the same ritual."Let's go... 'Midnight.'"Getting in on this, Cael laughed, "Calling him by a name, are we? Fine... Mine is 'Sugarcube,' because it's a girl horse."

They both giddied up, signaling their horses to town. If being discovered was inevitable, it might as well have been in style. They both fell off their horses immediately after rising, both escaping from under and running toward the destination. "Oh yeah, we were handcuffed together, weren't we... I'd forgotten about that part."

Cael spat sand out of his mouth as he titled his head up from collapse. "... Sadly, so did I." He looked down at the handcuffs' links and remarked, "Though it would seem the length between our handcuffs has widened, or we wouldn't have been able to get on the horses."

Brokk looked down at the handcuffs, both further apart. He tried to think about what had changed, then said, "I... I don't know how to say this... But I think they get looser, depending on how well we get along. It can sort of... detect if we work well as a team and loosens up accordingly", standing up seconds later.

"I've read about old rune technology of this nature in one of my books I studied back home. It wasn't created intentionally... In fact, it was created accidentally with certain rare runes that looked almost identical to the ones used for Jade Lights, but were made of something called 'Onyxephon.'""Looks like the world has a sense of humor.""Either way, we're still handcuffed together, but at least we can move slightly more freely this way... I hate losing my horse, though."

Cael laughed, "Hey at least you didn't end up with a mouth full of sand!"

****

Max sighed. It was the next day and time for fencing; June was rapidly approaching and he couldn't wait for his birthday to come up. Still, he hoped their Phoenix detector would help the current situation because he wasn't sure how much more he could take of the predicament.

As fencing was about to begin, the instructor Mr. Klaus Einslaughter was talking. The first day he'd done fencing Mr. Einslaughter had pitted Jericho and Max against each other, something that seemed odd at the time because Jericho was the team captain and Max was a newbie. The teacher likely anticipated they'd be a good match up, a tough call to make from anyone else. Max figured he was just overthinking things again, a habit he needed to improve.

Knoll wasn't in for fencing either, which was understandable as he was still recovering. He said he felt fine, but surely the recovery process took place well after the preceding events.

Instead of Jericho his opponent was a guy named Christian, someone with long brown hair and a goatee who seemed to stay in decent shape. He wasn't amazingly muscular, but one could tell he stayed healthy and exercised regularly. He was someone Max had fought a couple times before who wasn't on the team but was pretty decent, possibly better than Max.

"Play... Ale!" They fenced, but Christian quickly got the first point; this frustrated Max, but he tried to keep his cool. They went again and Max finally managed a hit, thinking to himself,

"*Good. Not bad.*"

Then Christian got another hit. "*Damn. Time to try again.*"

Christian got another in and the match ended, Max sighing, "Oh well, can't win them all."

He shook Christian's hand and thanked him for a good match,

Christian smilingly returning, "Same for yourself. You aren't bad for a newbie at all. I've been doing this for a long time, so don't sweat it."

As Max headed out of the classroom he heard Lance, James and Draco; they were fighting, again.

"Look. I'm friends with both of you. Let the past be the past!", Lance yelled.

Draco huffed in reply, "You may be my friend, but I would never befriend a stinking Phoenix skum! And how dare you side with him! Do you know how much the other Dragons mock me for befriending you?"

Lance remarked, "I am doing no such thing! I said it before, I'll say it again. I think of you as equals! Besides, what if someone overhears us?!" "What's the matter 'Draco', scared after our last fight?", James taunted. "Scared? Me? Of you? I'll rip you in two!"

Then Allanon appeared before them, teleporting there from seemingly nowhere as time seemed to stop and he shouted, "Silence! All three of you: to my study, immediately. I will re-join you there, understood!"

James squinted his eyes as he angrily remarked, "Fine!"

Lance simply nodded obediently,

Draco growling a great deal as he heeded, "... As you wish."

Allanon gave them a threatening look as they walked off, much like a litter with tails between their legs.

Max walked up to Allanon as the other three were already headed for his study, very curious about what was going on. "Excuse me, Allanon. But uh... what's their story?"

"Nobody can hear us, so I'll tell you... But I must keep it brief, as they will be waiting for me. There was a small war that occurred between the Phoenixes and Dragons. As I said before, they'd been fighting for thousands of years.

"Humanity had simply made them go underground, so to speak. While Alexander was fighting the Wizard's guild, some Phoenixes who had not been in the Mage's Guild decided to take it upon themselves to ambush the dragons and attempt a strike to kill them once and for all, while we were distracted.

"It failed in the end, but among its two new heroes were Heliopolis and Goron. They had been around for a long time, but in this battle Goron gained his title 'The Destroyer.' Because he'd slaughtered hundreds of Phoenixes in this battle. In turn, Heliopolis had done the same to the Dragons. In the end, Heliopolis and Goron fought each other to a stalemate during this battle. "

Max whistled, "That's... That's a lot to take in. I had no idea they were both so highly regarded. I feel honored to have Heliopolis more so now than before."

Allanon nodded, "As you should. In any case Heliopolis retreated, realizing they were too equal in power. He knew if he kept fighting Goron they'd take each other out; furthermore, the remaining Phoenixes were losing more numbers than the Dragons were, so the Phoenix in charge, 'Nyle' was his name... ordered a tactical retreat. Ever since then Heliopolis has gained the status of being considered one of the strongest phoenixes alive, and Goron one of the strongest dragons alive. But you can see why they'd still hate each other even today, after all, these years."

Max was truly taken aback by this story as Allanon took his cue to have a serious talk with the three of them. As such, the story stayed in the back of Max's mind the entire remainder of the day.

Chapter 13 – Great Untold Battles

All was quiet as the others tried their best to listen, a hush presiding over the crowds. Allanon sighed and spoke, "It is to my embarrassment that I make this announcement. There is something wrong with the books I provided you all."

There was murmuring and then another hush. Were the books unreliable? What was wrong with the books? These questions

Allanon chuckled nervously at as he said, "No. The books are fine. For all our healers here I provided you with books for Clerics. It should help you greatly. And for everyone else here I provided books that are double the size of a cleric books, because they provide lessons for both Sorcerers and Druids.

"Which I figured would cover all of you, but therein lies the problem. Perhaps I was having a senior moment in my old age? But here's the thing. As many of you recall, some of you joined this school for your imagination, or your artistic talents and the like... but before that many of you joined because of your intelligence. This was because back in my day every magical human was a wizard.

"Sure they had Sorcerer abilities as well, but they started off as wizards and that was their foundation. Unfortunately, therein lied the problem, which is why I expanded to allow students with imagination and artistic talent to join... Because I'd discovered

Sorcerers and Druids. I'd discovered not all magic users started as Wizards. Then it got more complicated, because you all discovered your magic the way I expected most to: by complete accident. This lead me to believe none of you were wizards, but I was wrong. Some of you may indeed be Wizards, or at least part-Wizard. I'm not entirely sure precisely if my findings are accurate. As I said, humanity is new to the concept of separating Wizards, Sorcerers and Druids from each other.

"However, it is my belief that the following are at least part Wizard: Nero, Shakira, Maverick and, whenever he is fully recovered, Knoll. So, as you see, this would explain some of the frustration they may face. Especially for Maverick, who I should have been giving a Wizard book all along, but also for others who had their own complication; Shakira being a summoner, Nero and Knoll not being completely Wizard.

"In any case, this will be resolved now and I shall provide Wizard books to any students who wish to read them. They belong to me and they aren't great in supply, so please be kind enough to share as well as make sure the people I listed have one when they need it. Thank you."

As the students looked at the books they found interesting material, but were baffled at the books. Their overall meaning was difficult to decipher, but Allanon did the best he could.

He pointed out strange symbols to Nero and said, "I know these are difficult for you, but as you can see, if you use these they will greatly improve your chances for spells. You see, unlike Sorcerers or Druids it takes a great deal longer for you to do your spells. Aside from, for example, your Earth element which is part of why I was confused."

Nero was clearly still confused as he replied, "Uh…okay…."

Allanon continued, "Wizards depend on a lot of studying to create their magic. They must really examine their study books, begin to truly understand magical theory and practice minor magics whenever they can.

"For a wizard it does not come as natural to you as it does for Sorcerers, or Druids. It's a difficult but rewarding art, much like it was for me and my peers back in the day. Until then, though, you can still use your non-Wizard abilities in Earth as well."

Nero clearly still did not understand; all in all it was an awkward day and Allanon held his head in frustration. This was going to be a really, really long day as he'd try yet again to explain it all to them.

****

Back in Dark World as they headed for town, Brokk and Cael hid among some barrels as they surveyed the area. "I don't see her anywhere, but there is no way to be sure she isn't here.""Only one way to find out…", he said fired into the air with a grin famous to

Brokk."*Of course, he'd do that. Oh well, no use hiding, now.*"

Brokk and Cael waited until fired at. Cael shot back at them, Brokk carefully timing his own shots the same. He fired at a man on the roof, a man behind them, then a man to their right. He did it all in one swift motion and didn't miss any of them,

Cael asking, "Since when could you shoot like that?""Not sure. Been doing this for a while, so it just comes natural. No time for talk, though, we got more coming at us."

This time they had to move out of the way as their barrels were shot to pieces, forcing them to take leave of their narrow alley. Out in the open wasn't much better but at least they weren't wedged in.

Brokk and Cael continued firing at any men firing back at them, some dumb and charging falling quickly. Some were smarter in concealment, which meant Brokk and Cael had to keep moving; they'd gotten good at keeping up with each other, but the longer length for the handcuffs quite helped.

As more and more kept heading their way they did quite well betwixt the two. "You made it sound like they were something to worry about!"

"They never send their best at us first. It's how they operate. The weaklings go first."

Brokk and Cael ran into a room stumbling upon a series of munitions, such as was ripe for this personal mission. They reloaded but Cael spotted a man hiding with a rifle across the street, about to aim at them as Brokk was reloading. There and then Cael shot him, leaving his corpse rancid with blood.

"I owe you Cael."

"I know you do."

They headed back out and picked targets from off the rooftops, but as soon as the shooting seemed to stop a man came out of the maelstrom. He had a rugged face, a black jacket, and black jeans, a clean white dress shirt underneath and a large bowtie.

Brokk could tell by Cael's expression this man was really good.

Brokk held his hand by his pistol, which was sheathed on the side of his body. His fingers itching to grab the revolver and pull the trigger, it was a stand-off as the man clearly did the same. They both looked each other in the eyes, wondering who was going to pull the trigger first; the tension mounting, the seconds seemed to dragon in sheer length.

Brokk was already sweating, as was the other man; they knew they'd have to kill each other here and now, when Brokk pulled out his gun first and shot the pistol-ready man multiple times. If Brokk were even a fraction of a second off he would be dead, his opponent standing in for him in death while laying upon the desolate ground.

Cael whistled,

Brokk holstering his gun and looked around. He saw a woman in the house and he walked up to her, describing Morrigan and asking if she'd seen her.

She shook her head, spelling sadly, "Nobody has been here for years aside from us. Too smart to try to attack this town, no offense."

Cael smirked, "None taken."

The woman called, "Please don't leave us, though! We've been forced to follow these awful men for years... If you save us, I assure you we will repay you however we can! My husband has been working for them for a long, long time and I know that if he had any other choice he wouldn't be. He was an honest working man until those good-for-nothings showed up!"

Another woman nearby gasped, pulling up and smacking her. "Do you know what they'll do to us if they know these words you are saying? I have a mind to report you for some gold pieces!"

Brokk looked at the woman solemnly as he stammered grim, "If you strike her again for such things, I swear I will shoot you myself, got it?"

The other woman gulped and nodded as Brokk helped the fallen dame; he then turned to Cael, asking, "What do you think, Cael? They killed your old buddies anyways, what do you say we kill these bastards?""I agree."

"Then it's
decided."*****************************
***

Alexander stood on the top of a massive mountain as he looked down at what was headed his way, his flowing long red hair blowing with the wind as his cold-looking green eyes hid an inner fire of great ubiquity. Before him was an army of Phoenixes in the thousands, each one greater than the next. Not a day didn't go by that Alexander questioned what was going on.He didn't have much of a choice, for he would not allow the phoenixes to kill everyone he knew and loved. It shouldn't occur and at present it was down to himself and these headstrong rookies. There were a few teachers, but they were merely supposed to be non-combatant professors of novices. It was precisely why he'd volunteered to hit this battlefield, since the Phoenixes thought they could gain an easy win by ambushing an outpost full of rookies. He decided to head them off, but it turned out a spy among them was from the Mage's guild in disguise as a human warning the troops.

The Mage's guild decided to stick to the plan, but reinforced their troops with even stronger. None of the more powerful wizards could be spared as they were being hit from multiple fronts, so he, the rookies, and his master Allanon were the only ones available. As the legions and legions of Phoenixes marched forward a lone soldier gulped in his fear.

Alexander placed his hand on the grunt's shoulder and said, "Do not worry. You will not die on this day", then turned and shouted to the rookie Wizards all around him, "The rumors are true, I can cast spells without the use of a wand nor a staff. And yes, I will be fighting with each and every one of you.

"Know that I am where I am today through hard work alone; you could all someday be as great as I. No one person is more important than another. You are all important to me, and today you will fight so that someday you can rise to be the greatest wizards that ever lived!

"I will see to it that when this battle is all said and done, this battle will not have been in vain! I solemnly swear that on this day, not a single Phoenix shall leave this battlefield! Not one of them will survive! We will be victorious and on this day...", pausing as he shouted even louder for the phoenixes' hear, "We shall be victorious!"

The hundreds of young wizards and their teachers all cheered, Allanon placing his hand on Alexander's shoulder and saying, "That was a great speech, Alex. I know with you by our side, we can win."

Alexander smiled, quietly saying, "Thank you, master. But I'm glad you came with me. I could not do this alone in a million years." He turned to the other Wizards and shouted, "Begin the barrage!"

At that moment arrows of lightning fired at the Phoenixes, 'Magic Missiles' their moniker. They were very powerful attacks indeed, ones that normally could easily cause an army of humans to fall; it was easy as a basic spell to learn but difficult to master, for some. These weren't mere humans, so it merely slowed the Phoenixes down in this case. Meanwhile,

Alexander shouted as a small tornado formed under him and he ascended into the air, looking on as the Phoenixes began to fly upwards towards him.

He sent gigantic lightning bolts at them and fired them in rapid succession, then turned and formed a gigantic wave of water, the size of which could hit a mountain.

The water and lightning's mix electrocuted them viciously. As the phoenixes caused the massive amount of water to melt he'd prepared hundreds of stone arrows around him that were incrusted with runes and enchantments standing up in mid-air.

He fired them in rapid succession, each one having lightning surrounding them and the phoenixes starting to fall one by one. The lightning element was of the highest caliber, on such a level that it could fell a creature of no less than one hundred and fifty tons a creature for electric shock alone.

Still, it only could do so much as he caused more and more to appear around him while launching at phoenixes.

As he used his own magic to maintain the continuance of the spell he pulled his gigantic skull-blade out, a great sword that was no shorter than ten feet long. He began slashing down upon the phoenixes with his blade encased with arcane magic, phoenix after phoenix falling while his magic was still on artillery autopilot.

There were screams as he heard humans fall, enraged as flames formed around his shouting body to a sudden covering of flames. Allanon was already nearby firing many divine spells at hundreds of phoenixes with his staff, which had used a spell to make it as sharp as the greatest of blades.

Then there was General Irgoph, Alexander shouting toward the evil phoenix."You were foolish to come here human Alexander! You cannot defeat us! You may have begun this war when you first attacked, but we phoenixes will end it!""You stupid scum! It is you who intended to strike us down, do not think us foolish enough to simply wait for you to be ready to kill us when it is we who strike you down! This is for my comrades, my friends who you Mage guild scum have killed!"

Alexander pointed at a nearby volcano, causing it to erupt with his magic-wielded lava. "I know my flames are less effective against you Phoenixes, but how will you handle lava?""Foolish human! Lava has no effects on us, either!"

As the phoenix redirected the lava at humans, Alexander quickly made the lava fail from hitting his allies. It was nonetheless room enough for the phoenix to dig his talons into Alexander in a tearing of flesh.

Alexander slashed the Phoenix in retaliation, causing it to back away until they collided again, talon and sword meeting as one.

The Phoenix growled, "We can do better than you!"

It growled as a gigantic amount of lava and flames formed a no less than six-hundred-foot-tall sentient lava/flames that were meant to resemble a phoenix.

Alexander smiled in a cocky, almost evil gesture, virtually screaming, "Call forth Nogaroth!"

Allanon shouted, "No Alexander, don't do it! You don't know if you can control it!"

A gigantic light suddenly went out of Alexander's hands as he looked up at the sky with his hands in the air.

Allanon shouted, "No!"

It was then a humanoid creature of six hundred feet appeared, having sixteen eyes and six arms. It had sharp teeth and looked like a human without skin and a likely revelation of his musculature. It growled as a brutish creature, Alexander knowing it could speak but never chose to.

Nogaroth was a creature of legend, stronger than any phoenix or dragon. It was said it didn't know friend from foe because it had no acquaintance with mortality. It only wanted destruction and would annihilate anything in its wake.

Of the thousands of spells Alexander knew, it too knew every single one of them and it was said nothing on this earth was as strong as this. Alexander had vowed that someday it would belong to him as his summon and it seemed the time had arrived, upon this enchanted battlefield.

It swung its arm at him but he held the arm in place with his bare hand, the sheer strength he had being superhuman due to his magic. The hand could not have been stopped by Alexander alone, otherwise; he used some of his arrows to harm the beast, forcing its' pained screams and shouting, "I am your master and you will obey me! Now... Destroy the creature these phoenixes have summoned!"

The creature growled at him, forcing him to send more arrows to its' torture. The creature had the same ability, but Alexander wielded much greater. It obeyed by swinging at the sentient mix of magmas and fires, destroying it in one thrush.Alexander sent another bunch of arrows at it, but the creature blocked these almost innocently in the blindness of his malice. Alexander had lost control of the beast, for it was destroying everything on the battlefield in hot rage.

As it began its whirling dervish of magic missiles thousands did indeed die that day, as the earth quaked with every footstep it took and the world trembled before its might.

At the folly of his callous instincts

Alexander stood in shock, unnerved to his depths by what was meant for good in his eyes; no one of will would kill their fellows, himself yelling at the end, "What have I done?"Humans and phoenixes alike were slaughtered while Alexander formed a tornado under him, shouting greatly to Allanon,

"Master! Could you please use your Divine magic to try to hold it at bay! I will attempt to reopen the portal and send it from whence it came! If we do not stop it now, the thousands of spells he and I both know... You know what he is capable of!""Of course! It will be done!"

Allanon began to use his divine magic as a ray of light holding the creature in place, the same spell that years later he'd use to hold Goron in place at the school.

The creature growled and shrugged it right off like it was nothing, Allanon sending magic missiles at the creature alongside various other spells. It delayed the creature, but Allanon in all his great strength couldn't hold with it forever.

Green light surrounded Alexander, continuing to chant as he levitated mid-air with his arms folded. The general now furious, he ran for the creature and was killed with its own element; flames flew toward the phoenix as it was reduced to dust with the behemoth's simple spell.

As the green power formed Alexander opened up the portal and sent all the energy he had to send the beast back through.

As he fell nearly unconscious the portal was closing. He then saw that roughly only fifty rookies remained of the hundreds he'd seen earlier, feeling like a complete and utter failure as he wept deeply in regret.

He'd been right about one thing, though; not a single phoenix survived the battlefield, that day.

Chapter 14- Allanon's Plight

He'd gone by many names; Mages Guild Spy #6; Shaun Balthier; Weabdged, to name a few. Right now, however, he was Greggory Sprouse. He'd killed the real one, but it would take them quite a while before they found his body, making his disguise human. He will have done much more damage by the time they'd find the real one.

The thing about humans was that they believed death only when they saw it, never remembering the phoenix clan. Things were nonetheless far from perfect: #5 and #4 slew one another permanently. They had turned to ashes, but somebody destroyed them and nobody knew who, but it went right along with their other suspicions.

They'd succeeded in spreading fear even if he'd failed in staying alive that time around. His next task was something that made sense, #7 having not reported in. It was likely he was either apprehended, or killed for good. If it was the latter there was a massive unknown threat in the school, meaning this individual needed to be neutralized immediately.

That would be consistent for why "Sarah Mang" and "Charles Rojas" did not resurrect, as it didn't seem to be Allanon who did the task. He wasn't close enough at the time, as #1 could confirm since #6 had proven himself to be greater than #5, whom herself was considered an equal to #4. This was notwithstanding that they were now both deceased.

He was hoping for a promotion in his rank, though he understood when he was told that would come later. Their positions were also their call signs and avoiding confusion was best while in the field. It amounted to the same anyway, but he liked the formality of it all. He'd accept it for now because his task required precision, and would not fall as quickly this time as he had to Heliopolis.

  #1 had given him insurance to assure that, so #6 looked down at the stone in his hand and grinned...

  He'd gained a lead, however.

  It'd been days since he'd come back from the dead and in his hand was a piece of hair. He'd checked the scent. This clump was so small as to be unnoticeable to humans, but he'd detected it. The scene was that of Anna Smith the school nurse, whom he didn't need to kill because she was clearly a threat. The fact she even knew magic was also suspicious; Allanon didn't seem to show any indication of being aware of it.

  However, as he entered the nurse's office, there was a letter reading

"I know who you are. I've given Anna a distractive errand helping an injured Nero. Come outside to the forest behind the school. Come alone, or I will reveal your secret."

  He crumbled up the paper; could be another threat anyways.

  As he headed out the door he saw the forest. Likely a trap, but he didn't feel it mattered. Nothing could beat him this time. As he pressed on, Draco stepped before him and

  said, "I'll make a deal with you. All you have to do is beat me and I'll pretend I never even heard of your little secret... But if I win, I'm going to kill you, so fight like you mean it. Deal?"

  Shaun smirked, "What's to stop me from killing you if I win?"

  Draco laughed, "You won't win."

Shaun pulled out his stone, threatening, "I beg to differ."

Suddenly Draco held his chest in pain, yelling, "D-dragon's rose! Where did you find that?!"

Shaun laughed, "Funny story, really. It works on dragons or phoenixes, but the wielder is unaffected. It works better on dragons though, making this easier than I thought it'd be. It forces you to remain in your human form and brings your level down to mine, but with the added benefit of temporary heart murmurs! It's a tool for combat, as anything is fair in love and war and I do not love you dragon filth!"

Draco shudderingly spoke, "F-feeling's…. Mutual…. b-birdbrain. Centuries of f-fighting…. between … our races … doesn't just … disappear!"

Shaun slashed his hands at Draco, the latter's dodging and kicking at the phoenix pushing him back. Their human personage did not prevent their aged conflict's resonance, so Draco would prove it wasn't just his raw power equaling Heliopolis that made him great; he possessed true combat grit and abilities. He ran forward as he unsheathed his blade to slash down upon Shaun. Shaun blocked with his arm that had become easily as sharp due to phoenix magic.

Draco growled, "Y-you w-won't win foolish phoenix scum! Its because of… of… -y-your kind that my father, and my father's father, and his father died! I will… Never… Forgive you!"

Draco forcefully slashed downwards with dragonic flames forming around his blade. "The only flames capable of hurting a phoenix is that of a dragon!"

"However, phoenix flames can also hurt that of a dragon!"

Shaun surrounded his own body with split embers and charged for Draco, who swung his blade at Shaun. This thereby forced Shaun to dodge it and volley magic missiles at Draco, who jumped out of the way with a speed no typical human could. For a dragon it was second nature, Draco resuming his assault.

Shaun formed a massive grouping of acid meant to hit Draco's blade, but the dragon growled "Ro Maguth!" and the acid flung to the nearby wall. Draco then shouted "Rah Ro!" and suddenly Shaun was knocked against a wall. Shaun growled as the flames around him turned blue, turning to laughter at its' slight incredibility.

As the laughter grew he said, "T-this is amazing! I've been blessed with the rarest of honors... Not even our leaders, nor Heliopolis have been granted this blessing, one not seen in years! That of the blue flames! Hahahahaha!"

Draco grinned, "But let me ask you a question... With blue flames, what level does that make you? In what tier?"

Shaun looked down at the stone he had as it crumbled in his hands, yelling "N-no!"

Draco smiled, "Yes!", gigantic flames engulfing Shaun as he was burned to death. He'd fallen just as quickly as he had before to a similar attack from Heliopolis. Better than the rest still wasn't good enough and being granted great power you didn't yet understand wasn't always a blessing. Draco knew that, having stalled a feeling that something like this could one day occur.

****

The Fencing instructor asked Allanon to give him a hand with something in the fencing room, which was at present vacant since all fencing classes took place simultaneously. At this moment the fencing team was not there, as it was not yet time for practice.

Allanon walked in, the sound dampening spell activates; Allanon's eyebrow lifting couldn't predict the math teacher's fire blast at his back; he was the only one among them who could break through Allanon's divine spell, engaging an immediate blitzkrieg. The headmaster nonetheless easily defended himself while t
he science teacher blocked the exit and locked the door behind her.

Shakira's math teacher was on full assault through the use of claws, and elbow feather blades, saying

, "I'll be keeping him busy", while the other two began throwing knives at him.

While the math teacher continued Allanon tried to counterattack the pair other two put him back on defense with fireballs by throwing feathers. Allanon's defensive shield could block them from attacking, but not the math teacher as he pressed forward.

Allanon pushed the math teacher back and the science teacher used an arcane spear, slammed through the shield and overloaded it. As it fell Klaus revealed a hidden spear and enchanted it to get break through the barrier,
Allanon chanting quickly "Divine Ensnare!"

He hoped to get all three of them but only caught the math teacher, as the other two jumped out of the way of the onslaught.

Klaus tried to assault with the sword, the science teacher using fire feathers above. Allanon performed a full spin to deflect the strike all at once, as well as knock back the fencing instructor; this personal tornado fantastically formed a temporary arcane shield, a lightning spell sent all the while.

She used rocky spikes at his feet to trip him, but it conversely clipped her wings from human form, thus causing her to collapse in disorientation. Klaus lunged in with slashes that Allanon deflected with his staff, the rod itself breaking the sword to the fencing instructor's own winged evasion.

The math teacher broke free and roared into the air, causing Allanon to be temporarily deaf; meanwhile

, one of the phoenixes then spoke," Shadow Entanglement!"

The ground under Allanon went dark and ominous shadow vines wrapped around him with an attempt to penetrate. He here broke free, but not without a minor struggle and minor limb and leg cuts up and down.

Allanon still found himself completely deaf for the moment, deciding that if his foes would remain silent he would do the same; he then slammed his staff down and a lightning storm fired from its top at his assailants.

They attempted a block with the magical shield, herself standing up and attempting to cast; the weakness of her defense could not hold against what would vaporize her completely. As her ashes

rose into the air Allanon fired a green energy which destroyed them completely, which caused her to be unable to rise from them the more.
The other two were infuriated, a shadow spell filling the room to blind Allanon alongside his all-ready deafness.

Before being blinded he saw Klaus summon demonic weapons, allowing Allanon to utilize his knowledge of wind magic to substitute his own hearing with room vibration. Every time Allanon's staff collided with the blades green flames came out.

The math teacher was maintaining the shadow spell, slicing off one of the fencing instructor's arms; in his rage the teacher ran forward and attempted self-detonation on Allanon, who was able to defend against its admittedly exhausting force.

Suddenly a man walked in having long black hair and the crest of the phoenix guild, saying, "This place... It's been marked. I've been gifted with prophecy, and I have foreseen a great disaster that will befall this school. I've told the others... and I will telepathically send my vision to you."

After this the foes around Allanon began chanting as they burst into flames, their ashes swept away with the wind.

Allanon won, though puzzled as to why and how it happened. As far as he could tell all the Phoenixes that attacked him were long gone from the school grounds; as

the days continued onward, none of the other phoenixes showed themselves, some students in the school having left; it was perhaps that phoenixes were also sent eerie message from their own fears within, the cause of it remaining to be seen in the coming days.

Chapter 15 - Secrets and the Dragonsouled

The heat of the desert was so excruciating that even Cael seemed exhausted for a change. Brokk wasn't about to let it get to him, though; they were in the middle of nowhere and even if there was no sun, the heat was murder. It was the hottest time to be out and probably would've been during the day if there was a sun to see.

It was so fetidly hot that creatures tended to prefer not being outside either, usually burrowing or hiding in what little caves were occasionally around. Sweat trickled down Brokk's face as he was by now wishing they weren't handcuffed, so he could take his shirt off. As they took another step each one felt like it could be their last before they collapsed to the intense heat.

Step. Step. Stumble, fall. They both laid there unconscious for a few minutes until they felt someone pour water over their faces. They opened their eyes to see the woman who had arrested them earlier looking down at them, saying, "Guess this isn't your lucky day, boys. You're both coming with me."

Brokk and Cael reached for their guns only to realize she had them already strapped in her belt. She pointed hers at them and said, "On your feet."

They did as instructed as she stood near horse, keeping her gun trained on them. "We're headed back to the City. I'm sure they'll be happy to see your sorry asses again."

Suddenly, something headed for them. As Brokk saw the individual pursuant of them he heard Cael slowly say the words, "Man, he moves fast."Then he realized it wasn't just Cael's mouth that was moving slow. Everything but the man running forward seemed to be moving slower than him. It was a small wonder Brokk could see him at a decent but believable speed. Clearly this man had a spell allowing him to slow down time; everyone else was meant to perceive it as if he were cheetah-moving, but Brokk could somehow tell the difference.

The man had on ragged clothes and seeming to be of Paraian descent with the darker sort of olive skin tone of that region. He headed quickly toward them with his twin scimitars, knocking her to the ground. Then he cut the gun she was holding in half, clearly before she could even react in time.

As time returned to its normal self the man smiled. "Zeke Darkholme at your service, men. This lady will make a nice hostage." He knocked her unconscious with the hilt of one of his blades, then turning to them to say,
"I will only say this once. I can get you out of those cuffs, but if I do you owe me a debt; I expect that debt to be repaid immediately. Join my boys for a little heist, and you're free to go on your way. Deny this offer and I'll simply kill you both. This is what I'll do if you agree and betray me as well."

Cael smirked, "I'd like to see you-"

Brokk interrupted, "The idiot isn't with me. I accept",

Cael happily adding, "Well now", pausing to continue, "... Alright, I'm in. If it means I can have some fun, then who am I to object anyways?"

Zeke nodded and with one slice of his blade, the handcuffs were off. "Before you ask, No, these swords aren't normal, and No, I will not explain them.""I have a better question, isn't Zeke Darkholme the name of the prince of-"

Zeke stuck a blade to Cael's throat quickly, interrupting, "My people are long dead. If you don't want the same, you will speak no more of this."

Cael decided not to reply, Zeke confirming, "Wise choice", removing the blade from Cael's throat.

As they headed for camp, Zeke was holding the unconscious officer on his shoulder.

They finally reached camp later and there were about ten people working for Zeke, all to be the cut-throat type. One immediately caught Brokk's attention, however: she had long brown hair, tanned skin and blue eyes, features he'd recognize her with immediately. "Morrigan!"

They all looked at her and she seemed visibly upset, saying, "I'll be back, men. If you start lunch without me, I'll cut all your nuts off."

The men remained silent as she took him aside and they went outside of camp, Brokk nearly at tears. "I-I've finally found you. After all this time."

"You should go home Brokk. It isn't safe here for you."

"Come back home with me, Morrigan! All those years we spent together can't mean nothing to you!"

She smacked him yelling, "How dare you! Do you remember nothing of what happened?"

Brokk looked back at her with a sad expression, "What do you mean?"

Morrigan sighed, "I'm not the woman you used to know, Brokk, and I never wanted to do this, but it's time you knew the truth of what happened back home."

Brokk was confused, "T-truth?"

"Shush. You're not making this any easier for me. Brokk, look. I wasn't there with you for years. We were only together for one year."

Brokk shook his head, stammering and stuttering, "No, I remember, you were there for me for so many-"

"That wasn't me! You were talking to yourself!"

Brokk went pale, asking, "W-what do you mean?"

"You created me... In your head, at least. You were so lonely as a kid, being the only survivor of our home, so to fight off loneliness your mind created 'Morrigan.' A second personality, a female one. She was all the things you wanted. A sweet, innocent shy girl, so different from anyone else of this world... Untainted by its corruption.

"Had anyone seen you they'd call you crazy, but ironically it's probably what kept you sane. Eventually you dabbled into the magic arts and found out how to create life itself, thus creating a living, breathing human being from nothing but a mix of dirt, animal ingredients, and black magic. You created me, the person you are speaking to. You had assumed that you'd transferred your other personality to my body. But, all you'd really done, was gave me one just like hers."

Brokk shook his head, "No! No! This can't be real!"

She smacked him again, screaming, "Shut up and listen to me! Morrigan wasn't real! She was something your mind thought of! The only real Morrigan was me, but I'm not a real human either! I'm some creation you selfishly made just to make yourself feel better!"

She then sighed, after a few moments of silence continuing, "At first, just like your creation Morrigan I loved you. You made me that way, so what else could I know? But then one day, she spoke to me. Morrigan spoke to me, except she was contained for so long she resented me.

"She cried and said she hated me for taking you from her. She told me everything, all the details of how she'd come into being and warned me not to tell you. She's purposely made you forget, because she thought it would be easier for you if you thought she was real. I realized right then I could never compete with someone inside of your head.

"I was terrified, so I ran and I ran and ended up in this world. A sweet, cute innocent girl like me went through all kinds of hell in this cut-throat world. But I eventually found my place, in this gang. I renounced my old name; my name is Alice now. I've adapted, I've survived. You should go home, with your Morrigan. Obviously, she made you happy, kept you stable."

Brokk stood silently bewildered, the look in his eyes turning cold, distant, and even creepy.

Alice shouted at him, "There's nothing for you here, Brokk, just go! Leave me alone! Go away! I don't need you, anymore!"

Tears went down his eyes as he turned around and ran from the camp, Cael and Zeke on his trail. It didn't take long, as this time Zeke's abilities allowed him to catch Brokk and tackle him to the ground.

"You aren't going back on our deal, are you? I told you what'll happen if you do that!", Zeke yelled as

Brokk sat emotionlessly muttering, "E-everything. It was a lie. All… a lie."

Cael looked at Zeke as he helped hold Brokk down as he struggled to get up, asking, "What is he talking about? Why was that woman shouting at him?"

Zeke sighed, "So that's what happened. Who knew of all the people I'd meet, you were that Brokk."

Before they could continue or ponder on this multiple Red Dragons flew overhead breathing fire down upon the camp, flames engulfing and people running in fear of what was occurring. None of them were strong enough to take down Dragons
, one appearing with glowing gold eyes, a golden hide, and enormous scales. Its size was easily around six hundred feet tall, roaring at the other two as they fled the scene.

All hope seemed lost as Cael and Brokk stood there in shock at its standing overhead.

Zeke shouted to them, "Run you, idiots, run!" Alice tried to help them but Zeke grabbed her and they both ended up fleeing. The Dragon swooped down at Brokk and Cael, the only who were not running away from him.

Cael tried attacking it by pulling out a gun and firing. The shots did nothing, as the Dragon stood there staring blankly at them. Brokk formed magical flames around himself, firing a massive burst at the Dragon but it remained still in stare.

The Dragon spoke, "You two…are worthy."

With nothing more than a casual nudge it smacked the two hard onto the ground, sticking his smallest toe into their chests and plucking out their hearts. He then breathed upon them lightly, forming magical enchantments onto them before returning the hearts to their original possessors.

"I am the Golden Dragon Abraxas. There is rarely ever more than a single Golden Dragon for thousands of years; I've placed in you the Dragonic magic and a piece of my soul into both of your hearts. You two shall be henceforth known as the Dragon-souled. When the day comes, you both will know what to do with your new gifts", Abraxas said, making that last thing Cael and Brokk saw that day. They rose again, alive from their unconsciousness and unknowing of what great lay hidden.

End of Arc II

Arc III

Chapter 16 – Back in our world

It was June and everybody had been acting weird since April, so perhaps it was just Syanne's imagination. She nonetheless had to prepare, removing her beautiful white dress in preparation for fencing. Her nude body changed from wearing a black thong to some more modest string-tied based regular panties.

She placed her fencing uniform on, her hair brushed many times. Syanne was curvy but slender, hips making rotund her buttocks and large her breasts; her long brown hair curled with her pale skin against blue eyes.She was now applying makeup, something of a duration. It wasn't easy for a woman to make herself beautiful, but Syanne knew how. Not that it mattered anyways, since she tended to get sweaty and messy after fencing classes and would have to go back and do this again before Theater. She still preferred looking her best, anyways; to be beautiful and presentable. It hid well the darker days of her past.Her life was hardly inglorious; she wasn't poor, without food or without her amount of personal possessions in life. She was borderline spoilt with all the gifts her family and 'friends' gave her. People were only nice to her because they wanted something out of her, so that she looked at others with such cold disdain was unremarkable. It didn't help that her parents were killed in a car accident, something providing resentment toward the other vehicle's drunkard. She tried to maintain a normal life afterward, but it was difficult.

If she tries to be nice to someone, the bottom-feeders obviously want something from her. Sometimes it was sex. In fact, some people thought she was a whore simply because in the past she was easy to lay. Not anymore. It was now not for anyone, no matter the who. It was late for love, the names people called her hurting too much to excite or offend the more. She once said "If people are too rude to treat me like a princess and with respect, then I shall simply look down upon them with disdain and prove myself superior to them in every possible way."

She headed for fencing class, where everyone often seemed more close-knit than her. She often sided with Jericho in arguments but didn't seem in kind to particularly like her. Here he nodded, "Well Max, you'd do better if you parried that last stab."

Jericho's appearance almost connoted kindness, at least from his perspective. It truly disgusted Syanne while

Max smiled back at him, "I'll remember that. Seems just when I catch up to you, you surpass me yet again."

Syanne felt the two were almost friends, something to her weird, stupid and droll! She walked up to Max with usual cold in her eyes, planning that she'd presently set him straight.

Syanne spoke charmingly, "Hello there, riffraff. I've come to challenge you to a duel. Do you accept?"

Max smiled nervously, but nodded, "Sure. Whatever, I guess."

Syanne nodded, "I believe this just won't do at all. Regular fencing grows tiresome for me. That's why last week I proposed something that I've heard this morning to be approved… we shall have a kendo match."

Max shrugged, "Alright. I took Kendo for a few months before, can't be too hard."

Syanne grinned, "I'd hope so for your sake. Now, let's just get this started."

She walked over and grabbed a wooden katana-like sword made of what looked like bamboo, which was known as a Shenai, handing Max one as well. They both bowed and she headed forward with a swipe at him, who blocked it instinctively. She swung at him again, only to the same result.

Syanne was being very aggressive, performing multiple swipes but never managing to a counter from him due to her speed. Eventually she swiped and hit him in multiple spots for points, winning the match swiftly and quickly. Yet she didn't feel any better at all.

Max seemed prepared to ask for a rematch, but before he could she held up her hand and said, "I have no desire to face you further today" and went back to training by herself in the usual fencing again.

She was always bitter. She couldn't help it. Life wasn't right for her. She was just sick of it; sick of people not giving her proper respect; sick of feeling alone, with the closest thing to comfort being when a man was hitting on her for the one thousandth time; she'd at one point found solace in her opera career, but it seemed like opera wasn't as popular as widespread professional categories like pop, rock, country or tther genres.

She'd made a popular song in that lane but essentially became a one-hit wonder, so she was surprised she made it into Allan's. Sure, she'd done more than a single song, but only one of them received great notice.

The next half hour or so was spent putting her makeup together. It was fortuitous that fencing was spread out before other classes enough to make up for the sweat she tended to have, except on slower days when classes lasted longer.It was now time for theater class and she was ready to head on for it. They'd all been preparing for a big play, but today was a bit of a free day since they'd been exhausted from all the recent classwork. The Play was *Swan Lake*, but done in a new, more dialogue-heavy twist and focused less on the dancing. Syanne was the swan, but that didn't matter on this occasion.

Suddenly she felt a rash itching on her left arm, scratching and making it worse. She scratched some more until she realized she'd scratched it so much it was bleeding, so she left to see the nurse.

This college was a little bit odd with the nurse being the school psychologist, but figuring out the source of her rash was more imperatively necessary to find out. The nurse had short brown hair and green eyes, slender but with a little muscle tone to her. She wore a white lab-coat, yellow v-neck t-shirt with green trim and wore a short brown skirt, looking at Syanne's arm intently as she said, "This will do the trick..."

She placed an ointment on her arm and it subsided, Syanne not even bothering to thank her except by nodding. Whatever it was, she was glad it was over.

As Syanne headed outside she heard a voice speak to her:

'You can't ignore me forever.'

"W-who's there?"

'I'm your summon m'lady. Or did you forget your promise?'

"P-promise?"

Suddenly a ring of magical energy formed around her as a cat came from the ground underneath her saying, "You're not ready, nor are you worthy. Figures you'd resort to something as stupid as reincarnation. Forget it. When you're strong enough, come before me again."

With that the cat vanished, the nurse hiding against a wall peeking over the corner. Anna quitley said, "Ah knew that's what it had to be... So much for suppressing it. Looks like their plans are acceleratin'... This ain't lookin good. How much longer will ah be able to hide from Allanon? And do I really still wanna kill him? Ah'm havin second thoughts about it. Ah guess Ah'll see."

****

It was roll call time by now, so this was bound to take a while; the three people in charge were still Allanon, Ikuto, and Connor, though on occasion Jared and Nero helped. Even though others were making some headway, in the nearly two months that had passed progress in learning magic was still slow for most of them. It used to be a private little area to train in magic that was secret, now host to many students secretly training.They first went through the healers, of which there were about ten; among them were Colleen, Sarah McKnight and Sho Carter. The next were the elementals, which started with Simon and Ikuto the "Crimson Twins." These had certainly developed, but

The next three were known as the "Sparks" for being lightning users, all three of which trained under Connor. They weren't nearly as good at it as he was, but they managed well enough. One of them was actually Shakira's friend Joey.

After that was Knoll, the only wind user of the group. His elemental gifts weren't capable of being used for offensive purposes yet and were meant as mechanisms to help himself speed up the process of his learning.

Next were Nero and Jared, both by now having formed a bit of a rivalry.

Nero with earth and Jared with lava were the only users of their particular element; both were nearly as skilled as Ikuto and Connor at their gifts, though somewhat weaker.

Next were the "abnormals", which included Maverick Williams the magic mover and Zack Gordon, who could create a false mirror image of a specific object.

Next were the "spooks". They went second-to-last because everyone found their abilities unpleasant; this included Sam, who could grow multiple arms and create more that could be controlled out of floors and walls. There was Vincent Kleiner the illusionist, Tim Mason the ghost communicator, Roger Haven being able to detonate people into pools of blood through mere speech and Miles Celtic, something of the ultimate ventriloquist.Last but not least were the summoners Max, Jericho, Leon, and Shakira.

After roll-call Allanon had an annoucement to make, one that seemed important by the look on his face. He cleared his throat as he stuck his staff onto the ground to project his voice via magic."Everyone, I have an annoucement to make. As you know, among you are Wizards, Sorecerers and the exceptionally rare Druids. Now that you have all been studying for a time, you may have realized something.

"You all have been performing magical spells with merely your bare hands for the most part, while I myself use a magical staff. That is because the majority of you are sorcerers. In my age, 'Sorcerer' was a synonym for 'Wizard.' However, in more recent generations there is a distinction: wizards perform magic based on intelligence; sorcerers use their imagination and creativity to perform magic.

"Do not get me wrong, both are capable of them as incumbent upon the individual. However, in the old days it was considered normal for a magical user to train using only their hands for most spells, being given given wands or staffs upon learning better control.

"A magical tool that all magic users used to use, as a way to make their magic even more powerful by using it as a conduit. Even elemental spells, while they look the same, can be much stronger. A flame the size you make without a wand is even stronger with a wand, even while it appears to be the exact same at first glance.

"My first student Alexander was the first magic user to have no use for a wand, nor a staff. He could perform magic at a powerful level regardless if he had one or not. Thus, the sorcerer term now refers to those like him; I don't have enough resources to make wands for everyone who might be potentially a Wizard, so instead I had to choose carefully. All the wands are made of American Elm Tree wood, but have different cores to suit the personality of the person I created them for. Among the summoners only Shakira is a Wizard, so first, Shakira step forth."

She did as told and he handed her a wand, Allanon continuing to say, "Your wand's core is a piece of your summon's hair. His name is Uriel, by the way. I did so to hopefully strengthen your bond with him."

He then handed her a wand carved with words in Latin all along its edges. As she walked back into the crowd, Allanon continued, "Next is Sho, Nero, Colleen, and Maverick", these proceeding to their three identical blue wands.

"Your wands were made the same way, a fairly standard method so that they would be easier to make: unicorn hair is the core. Don't take the lack of orignality in nature of them lightly, for I couldn't make wands for everyone. Still, I chose the four of you to have these."

As they took their wands and walked back down, Allanon stated the next name to receive: "Simon."

As Simon came forward Allanon announced, "Simon's has a Phoenix feather core. This is fairly rare in material, but it suits your personalities the very best and I felt it appropriate. Take good care of it."

As he walked off Ikuto spoke up and asked, "Why did Simon get a wand and I didn't?" "The two of you are very different in nature; his greatest asset is his intelligence while yours is your creativity, though you may not fully realize it yet. Simply put, Simon is a Wizard and you are a sorcerer. You may be the Crimson Twins, but you don't have to be exactly the same."

Max felt this was awkward for Ikuto, but wanted to congratulate everyone who got a Wand. He wasn't sure what to do, so he awkwardly clapped and everyone applauded after.

Sometime after that, everyone went about their usual training as the four summoners were called to Allanon's private study via his teleportation technique.

Meanwhile, out of the many people out there training three of them couldn't concentrate;

Colleen turned to Knoll and said, "Something doesn't feel right. I don't know what it is... but, I have a bad feeling."

Knoll nodded, "I can sense it too. The wind feels... bitter. At first, I thought maybe it was just me getting used to my wind abilities, but each day the wind has felt harsher and harsher, like something isn't right."

Zack nodded to both of them, saying, "I feel it, too... Almost like today wasn't a good day to wake up to. I feel like we're all going to have to prepare for something huge and it's coming today. Best to keep it to ourselves for now, though.""Yeah, if we are right, it'd only cause panic."

Meanwhile, in the study Allanon was speaking to the four of them.

"I brought you here because if I told everyone at once, it would only cause panic. You've learned to summon your creatures at will, but you still are not on good terms with your summons. Thankfully we still have time, but I need to inform you of this, because I sense within the next few days I might not get another chance to."

Max, Jericho, Leon and Shakira gained serious looks on their faces as they listened intently.

"Many years ago, I was simply just awaiting the day the four of you and your fifth destined incarnate would be born. I took it upon myself to have an apprentice, as well... His name was John. He was a very valued student, like another son to me.

"Then the heavens seemed to shudder as a small army of magic wielders fell from the sky and descended upon our private study, the same area of land that I would later build this school on. They used magic, but not like the kind known to you or I. It was one so foreign it was even unlike the magic among any of the others still out there training as we speak. It was a very evil, dark magic.

"Their leader's name was Zack Gordon... No, not the Zack you know. Zachariah was older, considering the one you know today was not even born... Though I suppose the fact he looked the same and had the same name is something that even today reminds me of where these attackers were from. He claimed to be from another Earth like our own, but one encased in darkness.

"A parallel world to our own, in another dimension. According to him, he was the leader of this group that'd been sent to our earth and they'd been sent by their lord to find a new world to live on, as theirs was in turmoil. They were merely scouts, and they'd now send for their lord to announce they could invade our world and take it over by force."

"We could not allow this to happen, so John and I retaliated. As the many fights were waged, me and John gradually grew apart, with John and I disagreeing with the way to handle the threat. We just barely managed to win and after defeating Zack, he claimed his lord and their men would be back someday and get revenge for their deaths, for Zack was the son of the lord of their world... thus, the prince. After that, John finished him off."

"I grew angry at John for attacking a defenseless foe. John then attacked me and our bond had been broken. In the end, I easily won the fight and exiled John from my presence, for I could never kill him. John left and I never saw him again, but I knew something now... I needed to take on many more apprentices; I had no choice, fFor if I did not, this world would be unprepared for when the Dark Worlders would return to invade us again, ...as that left John and I the only magic users left on this earth.

"Im sorry for lyig to you about being the only survivor, but I did not want to scare away earth's only chance survival. That is why I've been training you all... T...to protect the earth from the coming invaders, t. Though it is indeed a pleasant bonus to have finally found the re-incarnations of Alexander as well."

Suddenly the ground began to shake, Allanon going a ghostly pale. "Not now! It's too early! We're not ready!"

The sky turned black as thunderclouds formed above them and the thunder rolled, and the lightning striked the sky. A massive force-field formed around the school ground, encompassing the area and its buildings into what appeared to be a magical dome as a man roughly seven-feet tall appeared.

He had long black hair that went down to his behind and had an all black button-up dress shirt, ablack cowboy style vest over it with black jeans and black cowboy boots on; . s shirt was slightly unbuttoned and he had a slight "petty boy boofile, himself hiean shaven.

A man with short red hair and a scar across his eye kneeled to the black-haired man and with a strong voice said," Orders, Mortas, sir?"He coldly and quietly said in reply, "Yes, Aldos. Tell the men to leave Allanon to me. As for the remainder… Wipe them out… All of them."

Aldo smiled evilly and replied, "Yes sir!" Out of the portal came five long lines of men holding rifles with runes attached to them for magical necessities. The lines doubtlessly led to an amount of men that numbered in the hundreds as they marched out.

People from inside the school buildings slowly went to the windows, clearly confused and some scared. One soldier threw a grenade into a room and it exploded as people inside all died at once. Screaming and panic ensued as the men fired at students through their school-bound march.

Mortas licked his lips and snapped his fingers, all wands in the area vanishing at an instant. It would appear their previous carriers would have to make due, though for some reason Allanon's Staff had not vanished. "Allanon's staff is immune to my teleportation spell... It would seem I can't take his tool so easily. How fun!"

Roger and Sam were already outside and on the scene, Roger opening his mouth as enemy soldiers started to explode into pools of blood. He thought back onto how this all started and how he used to be a student who spoke a lot about his life. He loved chatting it up with everyone and was the type of person who rarely ever took anything seriously. That was Roger Haven, a socialite who talked so much, t even got on some people's nerves.

He felt overjoyed to be in the band with Max and Leon as their bassist, though he never really felt he fit-in with them. They were nice to him, but he somehow couldn't help but feel like the odd man out. He nonetheless was entirely social, one day speaking to someone and causing their head to explode into many pieces with a great blood splattering.

He was greatly terrified, but Allanon took him in and taught him to control it. He was scarred by that for life and was often quiet through his ability, the control remaining difficult even now. It was ironic that the same ability was being used to protect the campus, making him almost half-smile with every falling soldier.

Sam was aiding him, keeping a safe enough distance to not be caught by the attack but using his power to sprout arms from the ground and snap enemy soldiers' spines.Mortas ran forward at blinding speeds and swiped his rune-encased sword with a slash right through Roger's neck, blood splattering out as his head fell off.

Mortas licked his blade and smiled, "You know they say that people don't die until ten seconds after their head is removed."

Sam stood right beside him, yelling, "Y-you bastard! He was my brother!" The shout prepared Sam to lift arms out of the ground in multiple rows of limbs; without hesitation Mortas ran forward and swiped his blade at Sam, decapitating him as well. Maintaining his cold demeanor, he stated, "You can die the same way he did then. Know these as the last words you hear." He paused as he allowed himself to smile and briefly lose control. "I enjoyed every minute of killing you both. Hee-heehahahahahaha!"

Allanon appeared right in front of him with a large staff that he swung at Mortas, who easily blocked it and yelled,

"At last, you appear before me, Allanon! Was wondering how long it'd take before you got the message!"

Allanon shouted with fierce anger, "You will pay for harming my students!"

Mortas smiled at the same time as his eyes went wide, placing his sword on the ground with its tip dug in. Hunching over and allowing his arms to sway side to side, he defiantly yelled, "Go ahead and try! I'll let you take the first shot! Come on, now! Don't be shy! I can't wait to kill you!"

Allanon made careful preparations and in a hidden area of the basement the ten healers were working as hard as they could on healing fellow students' wounds. It was much more than they were prepared to handle, however, especially after the school nurse disappeared. It didn't help that this college didn't have any medical students, nor a medical teaching area.

Sarah was in charge, even though Colleen was the best healer; this was due to her shy nature and Sarah was the second-best healer to begin with. Sarah was a natural leader, something she might have gotten from Leon's side of the family. Either way, she took charge regardless.

"I need you three to focus on that man over here, he might still make it", the healers nodding.

Then she saw Jericho's friend Sho was over a man's body, Sho with his glasses on. Sho's green eyes, but these were focused on healing the person in front of him if possible. Sarah touched Sho's shoulder saying, "He's dead, Sho. You need to move on to someone else."

Sho pushed her hand away. "I-I can't. This guy is my friend. He and I used to be bullied all the time, then Jericho stood up for us and the three of us become like brothers. You have to understand, I can't lose my brother!"

Sarah turned Sho and looked him in the eyes with sympathetic eyes and said,"I'm sorry, Sho… He's already gone. He's dead."

Sho allowed for a couple of tears to form in his eyes, before he wiped them away and slowly nodded in agreement."Can I trust you to make sure nobody else's brothers or sisters die?"

Sho slowly nodded again, Sarah hugging him and getting up to continue issuing orders to the other healers as people were brought in. The worst part about it was that some came in some badly damaged. The healers had only been learning healing for two months, the critically wounded having almost no hope of survival. With the magical force-field the enemy had up nobody could leave the school grounds, either.

Meanwhile, Joey was fighting as well. "I hope Shakira is alright… I haven't seen her yet."

He still grinned as lightning bolts fired out of his hands. He was taking on his opponents without as much difficulty as he expected, on a kind of autopilot. If he didn't react automatically, he'd probably stop in place and go into shock. After some skirmishes he continued looking to see if Shakira was safe.Jared and Nero were outside elsewhere,

Jared saying brashly, "I'll bet I can take out more guys than you can."

Nero sneered, "Y-youre on!"

One of the Sparks, a man named Jermaine was there as well. "Hope I can join in the fun!""The more the merrier."

Jared sent lava at several of them as he saw the men scream in pain melting. Nero caused the earth under a bunch to quake. Jermaine sent a burst of lightning at these assailants, which was when they saw a man with green hair of short stature no taller than five feet.He had a feminine appearance but was distinctly male, perhaps somewhere between eighteen and twenty years of age. The man smiled creepily as he kept his eyes closed through his calm and polite speech.

"Hello there, my name is Vorkalth. I'm here to kill you. I think it will be most pleasant to see your insides smeared all over the walls, so please don't resist."

Jared shouted, "Like hell, I won't!", then shot lava at him. Jermaine smirked, "Yeah! Guy's got it coming!" He sent lightning bolts simultaneously to Jared.

"I'm the one who created the force-field. Please permit me to show you a taste of my power."Redirecting the attacks he then pointed at Jermaine, who sas suddenly floating in mid-air as an extremely clean cut severed his torso from his legs to a bloodless separation. Vorkalth smiled and thmoved tos arms, following with ilike severance of headseIts levitation ceased the sudden, daming these various appendages and sections to fall to a shock of bloody pool aAt this

Nero went ghostly pale, turning and running as he yelled, "Well screw this!"

"Well... If he's a coward, then I don't want to bother killing him."

Jared said, "I'm not done yet! You'll pay for this!"

Joey and Shakira walked out, Joey seeing Jermaine on the ground and tears quickly went down his eyes. "J-Jermaine. H-he was my friend. We trained together under Connor... You'll pay for this!"

Suddenly lightning formed all around his body as he rapidly shot bolts of lightning at him. These projectiles showed sport, but Vorkalth simply gleamed.

Without even moving, he pointed at Joey

and caused him to freeze in place, his eyes widening as Volkarth smiled.

"Where should I begin, first?"

Joey looked at Shakira with terrible expression as he said, "S-Shakira... Thank you for always being there for me... Y-you were the best friend I could ever have. T-Thank you for all the good times we've had."

Vorkalth snapped one of his fingers, Joey instantly shouting in pain.

"STOP IT!"

"Alright, I'll make this quick", Volkarth immediately and simultaneously removing Joey's arms, legs, head, and torso to a collapse on the floor.

Shakira looked down in horror at the pieces of him as her breathing became erratic. "N-no... This... This can't be happening..."

She looked at what was left of him, but it was futile;

Joey was dead.

In the interim of all this, Nero was running into an area where there was nobody around and started digging into the ground."Its just a dome force-field. If I dig under the ground with my earth abilities, I can run away! I must get out of here! This place is crazy!"He then saw that the force-field wasn't a dome at all, but a sphere. There really was no escape, not even from underground. He sat there several feet underground, crying hopelessly in discovery.In the cafeteria, Aldos was grinning as he punched a whole in a wall yelling, "Come out and play, everybody! It's boring, if you all hide from me and my wonderful men!"

Vincent stood before Aldos, dignified and triumphant as he asked, "Who's hiding?"

Aldos grinned, "Ho ho, a tough guy, huh? Great! I could use a good warm-up!"

"Good, I'll give you a whole main course."

Vincent projected clones of himself, Aldos saying, "Oh a multiple-man spell huh? Pssh, like that'll even work on me."

Aldos pulled out his runed-gun and fired at all of the different Vincents, causing these illusions fizzle away as he yelled, "Illusions... Shouldn't have skipped that school."

Vincent's voice echoed throughout the cafeteria, "No. You shouldn't have."

Suddenly Aldos felt a tap on his shoulder as he was punched backward. "That hurt, you punk!", he said firing at Vincent. Another illusion.Vincent appeared before him and an arrow appeared in front of his hand,

Aldos laughing, "Heheh, it's not a real arrow. Illusions can't harm me!""Oh, can't they?"

He sent the arrow flying at him, causing him to cough up blood as he flew backward into a pile of fruit boxes in the kitchen nearby. He got up and threw them aside. "I'll get you for that!", Aldos said firing at him and missing the more. He heard footsteps behind him and pretended not to notice, looking around the room to feign combative uncertainty. He even shouted "Where are you?" to keep up the ruse, a pentagram instantly forming underneath Vincent.

As Vincent's feet magically froze in place, Aldos turned around and laughed, "You think I didn't hear you, there! It was only a matter of time before you came out of the woodwork! Now... Enjoy spending the rest of your life in eternal pain and tournament! Away with you, into the void... Forever!"

Vincent spat on Aldos and said, "Get it over with." Aldos stomped his foot as Vincent descended into the ground, Max and Leon had walked into the room just then. "It's rude to spit, kid."

Max and Leon appeared shocked for a moment, then shouted as the room shook. Vincent was their drummer, but was also more than that to them, a friend who they saw sent to hell.

Two portals opened above their heads as the incarnates of Alexander brought forth their summons.

Max shouted, "Heliopolis, please help us! The school is under attack!"

Leon nodded, "Yes, this son of a bitch killed our friend Lucian, we cannot allow this madness to continue!"Heliopolis and Lucian stood there and looked around, then turned to Max and Leon in perfect unison. "Why should we take orders from you?"

Chapter 17 – Despair

Leon looked surprised in his saying, "You said I'd earned your respect when we first met. Why is it that last time I summoned you and this time you won't help me?"

Lucian smirked, "Just because I respect you doesn't mean I have to take orders from you, kid", he said combing his mane.

Max looked at the Phoenix and said, "I take it the same is the case with us?", Heliopolis only silently nodding.

The last remaining spark alive walked in with a sad look upon his face. He mused aloud, saying, "The amount of bloodshed I've seen today is enough. I don't care if I live or die… Before this day is through, you will die!"

He pointed at the red-haired man, Aldos. "Oh, and these are for you guys." He threw bokkens to Leon and Max yelling, "They aren't much but you gotta have a way to defend yourselves!"

Aldos laughed, running forward and firing at the spark as it used the lightning to block the shots, the adrenaline rush making him more competent with the volts. Suddenly pots and pans were flying at the red-haired man, knocking him upside the head to a shout, "Who's there?"

Maverick's voice said from the shadows, "The last person you will ever hear speak", the kitchen stove going off its hinges and thrown at the red-haired man. Maverick knocked him through the wall and out the other side, appearing from the shadows and grinningly. Both he and the spark were floating in mid-air and heading straight for Aldos' general directly. The red-haired man meanwhile stood from his crater.

He smirked, "That old spell, huh? I know that one. I can do it quite well myself, as you can see." Maverick shouted, "Max! Leon! Cover your ears!"

As he headed forward, Maverick managed to clap his hands and the soundwave hit Aldos as suddenly a ringing sound filled the room. Blood from his painful ears caused him to growl as the spark laughed and sent him more lighting. Aldos stopped the spear in its tracks and sent it back at the spark, with the lightning of his own within the bolt. This lightning was instead colored red, instead of the usual bluish-yellow.

He smirked, "Oh yeah I forgot to mention it. Yes... I can launch projectiles of my opponents back at them... with a little bit of my energy added to it for good measure! Bet you didn't see that one coming!"

The Spark was electrocuted and fell over dead,

Leon and Max were alreading heading for Aldos swinging their bokkens. He laughed at them, this providing the required distraction as Maverick pointed at the man to the effect of his pupils turning white.

Aldos was hit with Leon and Max's bokkens as he shouted, "W-what the hell? I can't see!"

Maverick fell over as Max caught him, the latter softly speaking to him, "You idiot! You didn't have enough energy left after your other spells to cast that! Especially since you were just beginning to learn your sense-blinding spells!"

Maverick coughed as he said, "Guess that's what I get for being the first among us to learn a second spell field. I-it's ironic since I took longer to learn my first field than Ikuto or Connor did."

Max cried as he said, "W-well... I know you don't necessarily believe in heaven... and I couldn't convince you otherwise if I tried... but I hope whatever happens to you, you were happy with your current life.""Y-yeah, it wasn't so bad...", Maverick dying by his words, Max closing his eyes.

"I hope you're fucking happy! Now two more of my friends have died because you refused to help us! Well, if you won't fucking help us, then I will fight this red-haired man myself with just as much energy as Leon is fighting, right now! And I don't care if I get defeated, I'll get back up and I'll do it again and again and even if I die, my ghost will haunt this man for all eternity if that's what it takes to take him down!"

Heliopolis's eyes went wide for a moment, the great bird pausing as he said, "I'll agree to a temporary alliance. Nothing more. Sound good?"

Max nodded, "Better than nothing! I'll be kicking his ass with or without your help anyways!"

As a result, Lucian looked at Heliopolis and Max, then at Leon fiercely fighting Aldos and said, "I will do the same."

The Phoenix then cawed its cry of anger as the Wolf growled getting ready for the battle; regardless of the circumstances of their unison they were finding common foe.

****

Meanwhile, Vorkalth smiled coyly at Shakira as she screamed with fierce anger.

Suddenly a monkey roughly the size of herself appeared beside her, scratching his butt saying "What? I was having a good nap before you called me here! What do you want woman?"

Vorklath smiled, "A summon, is it? My my, that is quite impressive... but he appears far too weak to be useful against me."

The Monkey took one look at him and chirped, "Eep! Screw this woman! You're on your own!"

The Monkey went back into the portal he came from as it closed behind him.

Shakira felt as the hope slowly left her face, wanting to fight to avenge Joey but lacking ability to fight a foe of this magnitude. She couldn't help but feel utterly useless, crying as the Vorkalth smiled at her and said, "I have no need to kill cowards, so it's okay if you'd rather run away."

Shakira sat up slowly and yelled, "No! I may be too weak to fight you, but that won't stop me from trying to with every bit of energy I have, which I'll have you know is an awful lot!""Alright, then, but as the monkey said... You'll be on your own."

Suddenly a voice said, "No, you're not", a voice appearing from nearby as two flame balls fell down from the area above them. They were Simon's, meant to strike Vorkalth; he merely levitated backward as they missed,

the two big balls of flame subsiding to reveal Ikuto and Simon the Crimson Twins.

He pointed at them to freeze them in place, but they both easily dodged.

Vorkalth smiled, "Well, this is most definitely interesting: someone who can dodge my force field abilities."

Ikuto and Simon didn't say anything as they engulfed the floor in flames while circling around him. Vorkalth smiled as he used the force-fields to push the flames away, suddenly coughing. He looked at them, his calm demeanor now gone as he yelled, "Y-you did this on purpose! You're cutting off my oxygen! You little fucking half-wits! I'm going to wrap your fucking tonsils from your motherfucking throats, you pitiful excuses for meatbags!"His force-field abilities weren't as invisible as he launched and missed firing transparent bursts of them at Ikuto and Simon. They were both on opposite sides of him, in perfect unison as they dodged his attacks.

They then both launched flames at Vorkalth, who easily deflected them. Suddenl, Simon tripped over some of the rubble and Vorkalth stopped him in place.

Vorkalth smiled, "A most perfect opening. Fufufufu."

****

Syanne was panicked within this mess, the voice saying to her,

'You aren't worth helping. Save yourself.'

Syanne hadn't asked for its help, but it was clear the cat from before wouldn't be providing it even if she wanted it to. Suddenly a few zombies ran at her. She continued to scream, when suddenly an object moving at quick speeds sliced the zombies in half. It stopped and looked at her, having black hair and creepy eyes with an extremely eerie-toothed grin. It was a puppet. "I am your best friend! Don't worry, you are safe now!"

Miles appeared from the shadows. "My Puppet can handle these things, you better run if you don't want them to get you."Syanne decided to do what was told, eventually slamming against a locker as she ran through the halls.

It was the school nurse of all people, asking,

"What game are ya playin Syanne?"

Syanne maintained her composure as best she could, saying incredulously, "I do not at all understand what you could possibly mean!"

The nurse growled, "You don't remember me? It's Anna! Or maybe you remember me better as

Alexander! I don't care... all ah know is if you brought these people here, I swear I will kill you right now where you stand!"

Syanne was offended, "How could it have possibly been me? I lack the ability to conjure any of these bizarre occurrences!"

Anna sighed, "Ah don't detect that you are lying. You must've cleared your memory after ya reincarnated... Ironic, since you still have the same name. That means it couldn't'a been you that started all this."

Anna seemed deep in thought, when suddenly more soldiers came in firing their runed guns at them: Anna formed a giant shield made of green magical energy in front of them while shouting to Syanne, "Hide somewhere, quick! I'll hold them off!"

Syanne began to protest, when Anna gave her a look that showed desperation and determination. Syanne decided not to say anything as she headed for the quickest hiding spot she could find.

****

Meanwhile, a woman who appeared to be in her twenties with really long purple hair and a flat chest walked the halls. She hummed to herself as dead bodies of students surrounded her on the floor, electrocuted to death.

Two ice users appeared before her and fired their element at her, the purple haired girl smiling and sending lightning from her hands at both of them to an electrifying end.

Rally was running to catch up, huffing as she reached the right part of the hallway and said, "I'm here to kick your butt! We won't be pushed around by you!"

The purple haired girl smiled gleefully and clapped her hands, laughing, "Yay! A new opponent! Please don't die too quickly, okay?"A burst of lightning shot toward Rally, who narrowly dodged it. Suddenly a block of ice hit the purple haired girl's arm, freezing the woman's left limb.

Winter said, "I got this! Nobody hurts my friends!"

Rally gave the thumbs up, yelling, "Alright! Let's kick some ass, Winter!"

"Pssh, as if we wouldn't kick some serious ass!"

Winter and Rally had become good friends, the fact they utilized ice a very helpful feature. That the former's name fit her element was also an inside joke between them, the purple haired girl yelling, "Ooh! Not bad! Your ice powers are really cool, but I can do better!"She shot icicles at Winter with her right arm as flames surrounded her left arm freeing it, immediately firing flames at Rally.

Connor ran from the other hallway and jumped in front of the blast just in time to cut it in half with a bolt of lightning.

"I'll be joining this fight!""Yay! Another cool person is going to play with me! And he uses my favorite one I have: lightning! Woo-hoo!", the purple haired girl then frowning, "But people always die so fast with that one... No fun. Guess I'll use fire for now!"

She sent bursts of flames at Connor, who kept cutting through them as he failed to approach.

The purple haired girl was spinning in circles as she sent fire every direction, causing the building to catch on fire and causing Winter to put them ou. Rally had already run to Winter and protected them both with her own, while two more ice users joined the rescue fray.

The purple haired girl gleefully jumped up and down with glee as more around her caught fire, yelling, "Yay! Even more, people to play with! Time to have some fun!"

She ran at the ice users and sent flames at them, who tried to block with the ice but were simply outmatched as she killed them in a volley of burning melees. From one with fist to another with an immolating kick, this woman meant business.

She then ran for Rally, but Connor ran to her and kicked her in the face to a locker-bound fly.

She spat blood as she got up, murderous in countenance. "Y-you hurt me. Nobody hurts me!"

Her expression changed entirely to sheer rage as she ran for Connor and sent bolts of lightning at him, but he easily blocked with his own. "I'm a fast learner with lightning, you'll have to do better than that!"

She tried to create a whip of lightning and hit him with it, but he used his own to deflect it. Rally thought the distraction gave a good time to fire ice at her back, but the purple-haired girl blocked it with her own ice while sending another bolt of lightning at Connor.She turned around and ran for Winter with the lightning underneath her feet propelling her forward, creating a sword of pure lightning. With her other hand she created a dagger of flames, giving a rapid thrust with the sword through Winter's throat and the knife through her chest.

"No!" Tears quickly went down Rally's cheeks as she sent a massive blast of ice at the purple haired girl, but she easily blocked it in a fit of rage. "You're next, other ice girly!"

She ran forward and sent a bolt of lightning at Rally, but Connor jumped into the way and protected her with his own. Connor spoke to Rally as he was doing so, "Maybe we can take her out if we work together!""I'm willing to try it!"

She suddenly coughed blood as she hit the ground; behind her were the soldiers with runed guns, having entered the room silently, who were now firing in that direction.

Connor jumped out of the way of the shots he landed into a big room, one probably meant for storage as he was followed. She turned and looked at them, "Do not interfere with my plaything!", frying them later with lightning.

Connor was beginning to breathe irregularly as he said, "I-I'm really outmatched, here... What am I gonna do..."He then heard a voice behind him say, "Don't ya worry your sorry little ass, man, I got this one!"

****

TJ and Kathy were hiding in the theater room with their teacher Mr. Goodman,

Kathy huddled up against TJ and worriedly muttering, "I-I'm scared."Holding her close, TJ reassured, "It's alright, I got you. They haven't gotten here yet."

A voice deep and intimidating said, "I wouldn't say that. I was just waiting for the right moment."

Kathy went wide-eyed and ghostly pale, TJ turning and failing to see anything.

Suddenly there was banging on the outside door; there weren't windows, so they couldn't see what it was. They saw on the side door what it was as if another banged on the door with a window. The man was disfigured and appeared lifeless, himself host to areas of rotten flesh and eyes milky white. It was apparent that a spell of confederates he had

308

around him were in fact zombies."I'm a necromancer. I'll be killing you all now," his deep voice calming no one.

Zombies destroyed the doors and began feasting on the students in the room, TJ grabbing a prop sword and swinging it at the zombies to protect Kathy. In spite of his efforts he was quickly devoured as they ripped his insides apart.

Kath screamed as she backed up against a wall being eaten her as well, the hordes ripping her shirt off and biting down on her chest first, followed by her neck, arms and legs. Suddenly a wind gust came in and knocked them over.

"This is disgusting!", Knoll's voice called as he flew into the room swinging a long sword yelling, "You'll pay for killing all these people!" He'd purchased the sword because he occasionally liked going to the Renaissance fair and was planning to bring it to the next one. At the sight of this Zack remarked, "Going for the flashy approach I see. All the same, he's right. We won't allow you to do this any longer!"

The necromancer laughed,"Well well well, if isn't a couple of people with actual guts... And look at you, magic users, too! Is that supposed to impress me?"

Knoll shouted back at the voice as he was swinging his longsword to a zombie's slice each time. "Says the coward who won't show his face."

The necromancer laughed as he appeared from the ground in the center of the room. "Oh, I'll show you my face, not that you'll get anywhere near me", pulling out twin guns modified with runes.

Knoll laughed, "Six-shooters, really?"

Zack looked to Knoll, "Careful my friend, guns are no laughing matter.""This gun doesn't just fire bullets. Besides, the chambers have been modified to fire much more rounds than that... If I was relying on bullets. Luckily, I'm not. Those are optional", the vile user quick-firing shots of green energy at them. Knoll was fast enough to grab a hold of Zack as he used his wind abilities to narrowly dodge each shot, the blue haired man laughing, "Hahahahahah! See? It doesn't matter if you see my face, if you can't get anywhere near it!"

Zack began to confuse the zombies by casting illusions that made the zombies start to attack one another, their visual images now that of the living.

"That'll thin their numbers down very quickly.""Impressive. Between the swordsman and you, you're taking down my zombies rather quickly... but I have an arrangement for that."

The blue haired man stomped on the ground as a giant pentagram filled the room. He ordered his zombies to go forth throughout the rest of the school as the room started filling with a bright light. Suddenly a creature came out of the ground that was ten feet tall, one with for anhe eye on his head.

"Who says all my zombie minions are human? Say hello to my cyclops!"The cyclops growled as it swung its arms at Zack and Knoll, knocking Zack over for a second. Knoll shouted as he swung his sword at its legs, causing the cyclops to shout in pain. However, it seemed more annoyed than anything else, Knoll using his wind abilities to fly around attempting rapid swings of his sword. It was leaving scratches all over the beast, but nothing too deep.

Zack slowly got up, disoriented but alright. The necromancer attempted to shoot at Zack but it hit an illusion, himself growling, "Great. Now I've got mirages to deal with."

Zack's voice echoed in the room as he said, "You'll deal with far worse than that."

Suddenly the cyclops turned and knocked the blue haired man backward.

"W-why are you attacking me?"

Cyclops growled as it proceeded to pick him up and squeeze him;

Zack appeared behind it and stated, "It's simple, really. It thinks I am you, and that you are me. A simple switch really with my abilities."

The blue haired man screamed as his body exploded upon a firework of entrails and blood; once the Cyclops was freed from his summoner's magic due to the Necromancer's death, now the beast would do whatever it willed without someone to control it.

Zack dizzily stirred, "I-I've used as much of my powers as I could right now. Fooling the cyclops took a lot of energy... I won't be able to fool it for much longer, Knoll.""I'm on it!", Knoll said, deciding it was all or nothing. He had to take down the cyclops before it could do any more harm, therefore

he focused all the magic he could into his blade as the wind started to power through it. He flew forward as fast as he could and sliced the head clean off the cyclops, its terrible being falling to the ground as dead.

"Zack, we gotta see if anyone else needs our help. I know you and I are both low on magic, but we gotta try! You going to be alright?"

Zack nodded, "I'll manage. Let's do this!"

311

Chapter 18 – Hope

Tim walked forward casually as he said, "Gabriel, I need something to give this girl a little spank."

A ghost appeared before him. He a was tall old Englishman with a gray beard who was obviously a blacksmith, though nobody but Tim could see him.

The ghost Gabriel spoke, "Well first, you're going to have to get close and I have just the thing." The ghost turned into a tower shield that appeared on his arm. "She's likely to be playing at range."

Tim nodded, "This'll do." Placing the shield in front of him he charged forward, her launching attacks at him and him sending lightning back at her. She used her other arm to launch lightning back at Connor to cancel out his,

Tim plowing through all the boxes on the ground. As he approached the purple-haired girl she was firing lightning at both Tim and with her other hand Connor. As Tim got closer she jumped back into the hallway and focused her lightning on Tim.

Maniacally she laughed, "You guys can't try to distract me if I'm in this hallway!"

In return, Tim laughed, "It's a two-way street, doll!"

He jumped forward as the shield turned into a crossbow, landing in a roll and firing the arrows into the doorway.

She blocked with her lightning, Connor looking to Tim and said, "Anyway I can help?"

Tim shouted, "Get around her", subtly pointing his face to the wall.

She laughed, "You think this'll stop me?" She fired icicles at him with lightning manifest from their centers.

Tim dropped to his knees as his crossbow turned into a shield again to shatter ice, the lightning shocking him.

"This little girl packs a punch! That almost hurt!"

Tim wouldn't admit the shock had destabilized him, meaning he wouldn't be able to walk perfectly straight. He quietly said to his ghost, "Woo! Getting dizzy, Gabriel, any ideas?"

Connor was electrocuting the wall as much as possible, though it'd take a minute or two to break through. In the meantime

Gabriel said, "I got an idea but you'll have to toss me."

Tim nodded, "Alright! Dead man coming up!"

Gabriel turned into a dagger and Tim tossed it at her. As it took flight it turned into a mace with her dodging into the big room before its' transformation. She made a huge leap that put her far from the weapon, firing an enormous burst of lightning at Tim. He

 ducked to roll away from the exploding boxes, her shouting, "I'll kill you!"

Connor ran forward at her and was trying to hit her with blasts of lightning, which she easily blocked; she then kicked him backward with lightning in her feet, which caused his electrocution to render him sleeping.

She slowly walked to the flaming boxes, yelling, "Come out, come out, wherever you are! Can't have you die that easily! You're more fun than any of my other fights so far! It'd be no fun if you died!"

"Game's over, bitch!"
He came out of the boxes with a shovel that had spiritual flames encasing the end, thereby hitting her in the chest.
She laughed in her bewilderment, "Flames? Really? This can't-", her face suddenly showing a great deal of pain.

Tim smirked, "Flames and spirit fire are two different things. What this does, it'll slowly burn away at you from the inside out, burning your soul. It's not real flames, so in short, you can't put it out. Hurts, doesn't it?"

She screamed to an echo throughout the building as she slowly clawed at the invisible flames only apparent to Tim. As it slowly deteriorated her, it engulfed her in the blue embers.
Tim then walked over to Connor and taunted ,"Hey! Hey, are you dead? I don't see your spirit, so I think yer still alive!"

Connor slowly opened his eyes and said, "Whoa… What happened?"

"Fried me a pre-schooler. Do you know if its Taco Day? I'm thinking burrito."

Connor heaved, rising to walk to Rally and Tim continually goading, "No use livin' in the past man."

Connor checked her pulse and looked up, yelling, "She's not dead yet! I don't care what you do, but I'm taking Rally to the medics! She just might survive!"

He then picked her up, heading down the burnt hallway. As he looked around he saw students' bodies littered throughout, ones that were victims of the purple haired woman that Tim had just beaten. This included Rally's friend Winter as well as the other ice users, making her the last ice user.

As he continued he heard Allanon's voice in his head speaking to him telepathically. "Be strong, Connor. You are a leader. I have my hands tied fighting Mortas and Ikuto is busy as well, which leaves you the best bet at helping the students and teachers who can't defend themselves. After you get Rally to saftey, they'll need you, Connor."

Connor nodded and allowed his thoughts to direct themselves to Allanon, asking, "What of my personal students... The Sparks?"

Nothing for a few moments and then Allanon's voice was in his head again, "... They're all dead, Connor. I'm sorry. Just like Rally, that leaves you the last of your element among us."

Connor thought back, "To hell with that reasoning, it also means these sons of bitches killed my friends! Yes... After I've brought Rally to safety, I'm giving them hell!"

Suddenly some more soldiers with runed guns arrived.
"Hahaha, these students are too easy!"

Connor sighed, "It would be too difficult to fight with Rally in his arms. He'd have to try to dodge the shots, but it'd be unlikely he'd last long."

A gust of wind then blew in and knocked them over quickly.

Knoll came in, sweating a lot.

Zack said, "W-We'll take care of this."

Connor looked at them both and said,"You guys are exhausted! I can tell you're both low on magic! If you use much more of your magic, you might die!"

"You have to help people, and we have to help you. Now go! Or you trying to rescue her will be for nothing!"

"Alright! But you guys better not die!"

Zack gave a thumbs up while

Connor continued towards the medics; with the likelihood Rally might not die, hope was somehow applicable.

****

Vorkalth laughed, "Gave me a fright for a minute there, but how best should I take care of your brother Simon, eh?""You won't!"

He jumped off the walls as flames filled the room, then he shot fire at Vorklath's feet as he snatched Simon.

Vorkalth narrowly dodged as he was set off balance and fell over,

Jared taking this as an opening and firing lava.

Jared smirked, "I waited patiently, figuring you might forget about me with all the distractions. I knew if I kept attacking you'd only block me, but I'll bet you didn't see me coming now!"

The lava was just barely deflected,

Vorkalth gnarling, "You stupid little-"

He stopped for a moment and nodded. "It would appear I'm getting low enough on magic that if I keep this fighting, I won't be able to hold up the shield. Guess I gotta go for now. Alright, go ahead and teleport me!", Volkarth suddenly vanishing.

Ikuto sighed, "At least Simon and Jared are spared. Shakira, how are you holding up?, only to look over and see as Shakira sat the ground in absolute shock, her eyes wide and her face wordless.

***************************In his dorm room Jericho opened up a large closet he'd had to work a part-time job to pay for. Inside the large closet was his sword collection. He was a sword buff, one who had a decent number of swords he liked.

He grabbed his favorite one, the claymore. The blade alone was almost as tall as he was, with a long handle with a skull insignia at the base of the blade. He'd sharpened this sword regularly, simply because he thought it was cool to do so. People who knew thought it was a bit nerdy, but Jericho would have his day to confound those in memory.

He grabbed the sword and went down to the dorm basement, then summoned Goron.

"Why have you summoned Goron the destroyer?"

Jericho pointed his sword at the dragon stating, "Last time I summoned you I learned how to summon you at will, but you said you refused to serve me because you did not respect me. Today you will."

"Oh? How will you do that?"

"By defeating you in combat."Jericho's confidence astonishing, the dragon huffed, "Go ahead and try."

He breathed fire at Jericho, but he jumped out of the way and attempted a slash at Goron, who jumped into the air to fly but hit the ceiling.

Jericho laughed, "The basement doesn't have that high of a ceiling", jumping easily into the air to swing again. Goron flew out of the way and breathed more fire at Jericho, but Jericho was able to avoid it due to simply shifting his weight to allow gravity's pull. He came back down quicker and rolled on the floor, placing a huge scratch across the dragon's chest area hide.

The Dragon growled, "That will leave a scar! A scar on my flawless body you little-", then paused for a moment. "You still haven't beaten me."

The Dragon swung its claws at Jericho, but he rolled out of the way and took another swing at him. The Dragon also dodged and breathed more fire, Jericho ducking the flames as they hit the basement. It was a courtesy of the heavens the dorms were empty in the case of the basement ablaze.

The Dragon swiped its tail at Jericho, but he jumped over it and slashed it, hitting the spikes and forcing the tail down for a moment as he picked the sword back up. He proceeded to run along the tail in a surprisingly quick dash for someone holding a claymore, jumping on Goron's back with the blade to the dragon's throat. "Respect me and acknowledge me as your summoner…,or die. Choose."

The Dragon growled with fierce anger and then said through clenched teeth,"I... I respect you as my summoner."

****

Heliopolis and Lucian had been trying to attack Aldos, but he'd been either dodging or launching Heliopolis's fire attacks back at him.

Max and Leon were getting lucky, their wooden swords not doing much more than annoying him. Between them and their summons he hadn't caught anybody yet either,

Aldos laughing, "I may be unable to see, but I can still hear you and I can still feel your magical energies around me."

He fired his gun at them as they all dodged as best they could,

Max suddenly thinking, "Heliopolis... Let me ride on your back."

Heliopolis huffed, "Why would I dare ever stoop myself as low as to-" "-I know you don't respect me as your summoner enough to let me order you around, and I know this alliance is only temporary, but either you let me do this or your help will have been for nothing! Can your pride take a loss in battle or will it take me riding your back for five minutes instead? Choose!"

Heliopolis bowed as Max climbed onto its back. As expected through summon, the Phoenix's flaming areas did not harm him. He then shouted to Lucian and Leon, "Keep attacking him!"

Leon and Lucian nodded as Leon swung his wooden bokken at Aldos; the Wolf kept using its claws at him while he kept blocking them with his attempts at firepower. Heliopolis charged for Aldos and he shot at it, Max yelling, "Take the hit. Your healing tears can handle the pain."Heliopolis did as told, Max jumping off his back and winding with all his energy at his opponent. All of a sudden wind formed around the wooden sword as he swung down and hit Aldos, the added torrent quickening the swing necessary to knock Aldos unconscious.

Leon looked at Max and whistled,"Looks like we know what your second area of magic is... Wind! Congrats!"

Max panted with a thumbs up; they'd knocked him out, which then meant they had to figure out what to do with him.

****

**"You may be several times younger than me, but I still have it."

"How cute, you can block my sword with your staff! We've been fighting for a while now, so shouldn't you be tired? Ah, well."

The candor of his opponent was making this wisened sorcerer exhausted with the notion he had to keep going. "I'm not done yet", Allanon said as he sent a blast at Mortas launching him backward. Mortas regained his footing and sent his blasts, propelling himself forward and attempting rapid slashes.

Allanon dodged them each and tried to hit Mortas with his staff, but it did him no good; the dark haired man launched fire that would singe his shoulder, laughing, "Be careful not to burn yourself!"

He launched more flames at Allanon who easily deflected them, but Mortas appeared behind him to attempt a swing with wind enhancing its speed. Allanon blocked and sent a magic blast of energy at Mortas, who easily deflected it while Allanon jumped several feet backward from Mortas.

Mortas laughed, "I can read your mind, remember? Anything you do, I'll see it before you even do it! I already have troops going after Connor! Once they find out where he's headed, your medics will be next on the chopping block!"

Allanon sent a gigantic burst of light energy at Mortas, the latter retaliating with a gigantic burst of dark energy forcing a clash of their powers.

Mortas laughed, "Didn't expect you to be equal in strength to me! Hahahahah! How amusing, but no matter!"

He shouted with fierce anger as he put more dark energy into his, but Allanon did the same with the light. Whichever blast hit would kill the other, the streams continuing to flow endlessly.

Allanon knew he wouldn't be able to hold up for much longer.

"I- won't be able to win this fight. Just know...that I love each and every one of you as if you were my own. You have been my students..whether it be in magic, or in more traditional studies..and that all these years I've lived on my life, I'm a happy man. I will die in piece. Keep up your studies, and never stop fighting, whatever you do! Go for your dreams and aspirations, but again most of all..do not stop fighting for them, and do not stop fighting whatever obstacles you face in life! Goodbye."

These telepathic words reached the entire school as the dark energy overtook his force, Allanon encased in the darkness as he fell over with dying screams of pain. Here

Mortas laughed a'jackal, yelling, "Oh come on, man, surely you were better than that!"

Jericho appeared and swung his claymore at Mortas's back, the latter turning around and jumping to the right.

"That would've been a swordsman's shame, if you'd hit me."Goron landed beside Jericho, now his size as

Mortas laughed, "How amusing, but it looks like you lack even the strength to summon a Red Dragon at its true size. Allow me to show you how it is done."

He snapped his fingers as a dark portal opened, an enormous Black looking-dragon appearing and breathing purple fire into the air.

Mortas laughed, "Say hello to Fafnir! He's one of the legendary eight dragons in all of my world that gained power comparable to that of a Golden Dragon! His power is truly immense! Guess how long it took me to defeat him and force him to my will?"

Jericho was scared, but he didn't give off its appearance as he asked, "How long?""Thanks for asking. Two minutes. It took a total of two minutes to defeat him and bend him to my will."

Jericho knew right away that he couldn't win against the man who took down his mentor, but he didn't care. He wouldn't allow him to go any further, suddenly feeling a hand touch his shoulder.

"You don't have to face him. I will."

It was Anna the nurse; piqued of incredulity,

Mortas laughed, "You? What can you do?""I should've known what you were from the beginning. My father told me of your kind and how he defeated you all when he fought alongside his master Allanon... before Allanon betrayed him," she said breathing deeply.

Jericho looked at her, "Y-you're the daughter of John?""... Yes... Yes I am. But most of all."

A giant blue burst of energy surrounded the area as a white horse came out of the ground. The horse itself wasn't normal, having a single horn protruding from its forehead like a unicorn and Pegasus-like wingspan. "This is my Alicorn, Perseus... And I am the first to have re-incarnated from Alexander. I represent hope; the hope people need to keep fighting even when all seems lost and I'm here to destroy you! Allanon may have betrayed my now deceased father, but I still view him as if he was my own grandfather... and the students of this school as my siblings. No one shall shed the blood of another member of my family again!"

A blue light filled the entire area as anyone not of dark world who was not dead felt their wounds rapidly healing and their fatigue leaving their bodies; in the case of magic users their power levels also returned to full strength, the great healing powers of Anna seeming quite resonant in their strength.

"Now you will face us all that live yet again, at full strength. How much longer can you last?""T-this is too rich! This is hilarious! But! This has gone on far enough", running and punching Anna in the gut before she could even see him coming. She then coughed blood and fell to the ground.

"I should kill you now where you stand... but I have a better idea."

Vorkalth had been watching and appeared next to him, "What did you have in mind?"

Mortas laughed, "I won't be just teleporting you."

He snapped his fingers and all the living commanders of his forces appeared before him;

Mortas first walked up to a now-conscious Aldos and punched his fist through his chest, ripping out his heart.

"You were useless to me; I read your thoughts the whole time. You are not worthy of second-in-command", looking at Vorkalth and saying, "You are my second-in-command now!"

As Vorkalth nodded confidently, Mortas said,

"As for my plans… It's simple. A combination of your powers and mine. Your forcefields, and my teleportation and portal abilities. I shall name them off and send their appearances into your mind, so do this carefully as we do so, for we are sending them to our home."

Camp One: *Max, Jericho, Leon, Shakira, Zack and Knoll. They were sent to the ruined city of Jariahville, which was currently under attack by Dragons.*Camp Two: *Anna, Simon, Ikuto, Connor, Rally, Jared, and Tim. They were sent into a massive desert filled with Jackaloves and Bregals and no cities for many miles any direction.*Camp Three: *The force-field would remain over the school grounds and school buildings, which would be uprooted and intact as anyone remaining in the entire school that wasn't in Camp One or Two was sent along with the grounds and buildings themselves to a place on the other side of the planet from the other two camps; an area also surrounded by Jackaloves and Bregals. Vorkalth would leave the force-field over them, but not have to concentrate to maintain it due to new rune tech that would maintain what he created for him without draining his magic. The force-field would have new rules: they could at any time they wish as well as return back into the dome anytime they wish, but* *the area was surrounded by Jackaloves and Bregals. Meanwhile, the dome kept the Jackaloves and Bregals out, making it very much a prison.*

Mortas laughed, "That... should keep our lord distracted for a long, long while. Meanwhile, we will take over this world while he is busy handling these people in our world. Why should our lord be the ruler of this world after he messed up ours? Of course, if they die...they weren't worth us dirtying our hands by killing them anyways, but if they survive, will make huge problem for our boss huh?", laughter leaving his contemptuous lips the while.

With that, the deed was done. Everyone's fates were now unclear, as the students of the College for the Gifted were now in Dark World and they would never forget Mortas, Vorkalth, and their army of invaders.

End of Part I

List of deceased due to Dark World invasion: Sam, Roger, Jermaine, Joey, Vincent, Maverick, Winter, four ice users, two lightning users, Allanon and roughly half of all campus populace.

Part II- Dark World

Arc IV

Chapter 19 – Dragon Slayers

They landed in Dark World, hearing a voice in their heads laughing that these would live in their world during an invasion of Earth.

Suddenly Knoll punched Max across the face. "How many people died because of you! I'll bet anything it's because you were one of those destined children! It's all that Alexander crap, isn't it? If you had died when your name was Alexander then all our friends wouldn't have had to die, would they?"

Tears were rolling down Knoll's face as he started randomly swinging at Max. Max was still surprised by it all and was taking the hits rather poorly, but he wasn't complaining. If he did, it'd only add accent to a bad situation.

Max stumbled to get up, which was difficult after the volley of swings. Max shouted back at Knoll, "It wasn't my fault! This had nothing to do with Alexander! Allanon told us-"

Knoll interrupted furiously, "How dare you blame this on Allanon! He died for us!" He punched Max again, knocking him to the ground.

Max was more determined than ever as he yelled, "Look! Listen to me! Even if it had been Alexander's fault, I'm my own person just as much as Jericho, Shakira, and Leon are! We're our own people. The faults of Alexander are not our own!"Knoll fell to his knees; he knew that Max was right to say that, but it was hard to handle everything that happened and it was easier to shift the blame on his friend than to continue to feel powerless. In that moment he felt so without strength that he broke into tears from the front. "Even after I took down a cyclops, a fucking cyclops... there were still so many people I wasn't able to save. And the worst part is... I'm not even sure who to blame for it all."

Max looked at the floor and then said, "The people who did this to us obviously worked for someone. I don't know if we'll ever find out who it is, but they wanted our world and were willing to do whatever it took to take it from us. The point is, though, I didn't expect this either."

As he turned around to look at the area he realized Shakira was with them as well. She was wide-eyed, sitting on the ground with her legs tucked in under her arms quietly breathing to herself "Joey's dead... Joey's dead... Joey's dead."

As Max watched Shakira's mental state begin to come apart at the seams, he stomped his foot on the ground angrily as he said, "This is crazy! None of this makes any sense! Just a few minutes ago we were at school, back in our world. Now, look at us!"

Knoll slowly nodded, "It's fucked up!""All fucked up."

Max remembered the first day after Leon had joined them as a summoner. He went out on a date with Shakira that day.

'We went on a few dates.. we got along really well at first. Boyfriend and girlfriend, that was us! We ended up realizing that while we had a lot in common, we ended up fighting often. We then realized we were better suited as friends, but to me she's more than just my ex... she's one of my best friends. Now she's sitting there in shock over the death of her best friend and I can't do a damn thing to help her! Hell, not even I know what to think!'

He continued aloud, "I'm stuck here trying to piece together. Did all of that really just happen? Did I just see that many people... That many dead bodies? All of this has to be some sort of bad dream, something we should wake up from any moment now."

He paused for several moments and then continued his monologue externally, spluttering, "… But I know it isn't, no matter how hard I wish it was…"

He saw his bokken on the ground beside him. It wasn't much, but it was better to go into an untelling situation armed. As he slid the bokken under his belt he realized he hadn't even looked at his surroundings, the rubble and ruin of a blue building all about them. Somehow the walls were intact, despite their shabby state and the darkness.

He took a few steps outside of the unstable building to see what was going on, immediately greeted by the sight of an enormous Red Dragon hovering right above them in the night sky. The hair on his neck stood up on end from his instinct to his skin, forcing him to grab Shakira and Knoll and jumping out of the way as the flames spewed from the dragon to their location.

As Max watched this eerie ballet of fire and fury, death and destruction, he didn't feel the same way that he would have expected. It felt as though in the next few seconds someone would cue the orchestra, but it remained eerily silent all around. He wasn't afraid, the dragons' soar overhead a beauteous endeavor.

Then he remembered something the evil man had said: he didn't specify where each camp was in the telepathic messages, knowing where they all were. He did say, however, who was there with him in what he called "Camp One." He'd said the others there were Jericho, Leon and Zack, which meant the three were somewhere in this city. He could only hope they were okay.

Luckily the dragons seemed to pay Max and his two friends no bother, at least for now. He remembered the dragon that had set fire to the building he was just in, turning around to see it and the Dragon flying behind with deceptive silence.

Its immediate growl caused Knoll too look way, two figures rapidly running past them. They were moving way too fast for Max to be able to tell who they were, but he could hear their voices.

The first voice cocky and reckless said, "I'll bet I can take this one down faster than you can!"

The second voice was equally arrogant, but seemed to exude experiential weight behind it as he yelled, "Please! I may use to have been a total killjoy, but I've always been better at this than you have!"

"Those were just lucky shots! You'll see, Brokk, my time is coming! Besides, there's no way you could've taken any of them down without my help!"

"Fair enough, Cael, fair enough."

Max began to wonder if having his wooden bokken really mattered at this point. It was nonetheless better than nothing.

Cael jumped into the air flying as he pulled out a long blade with a dragon wing design above its guard, a blue crystal in the center of it; an elegant blade. He slashed so quickly that hardly anyone could see him as he went around the Red Dragon in the sky.

Brokk was helping as well, slashing the dragon with his sword drawn. His was a claymore, the blade large and comparable in size to Jericho's favorite blade back home. In its center there was a green crystal and its handle was simplistic in design, likely more for function than anything else.

They were not stopping for a second, for the dragon was too strong to let up; that didn't stop them from holding a conversation while they did,

Brokk saying, "I still find it funny. We both relied on guns so much, it's ironic that now we're at a skill level where we're even greater with swords. Hell, you don't even use your gun anymore."

He narrowly dodged a breath of flames from the Red Dragon that they were still fighting. He looked down at his revolver; Cael didn't use a gun anymore, but Brokk on occasion kept his."No, what I find funny is how mad Harding and Nrath still are at us."

He slashed at the Dragon's tail swiftly right after saying this,

Brokk sighing as he dodged another bit of flames, "Yeah, you'd think they'd be grateful to us. If we hadn't come in when we did, their cities would've been as bad off as Jariahville and the other four cities the dragons reduced to rubble in the past few months. We at least sort of saved their cities… mostly. I don't see why they blame us for everything."

Cael laughed, "But wasn't it you who caused us to go into a place where we awoke the dragons in the first place?" This time Cael created a long slash along the back of the dragon. "They don't know that! They are just mad because we took out the dragons and they didn't! Way to miss the fucking point, guys! Am I right?"

Cael nodded, "That's true. But I kinda like the high bounties we both now have, means lots of fun fights!""Fair enough."

While the insanity was occurring, Max heard a voice in the distance and ran for it leaving Knoll and Shakira where they were; with this, they wouldn't so much as think he ran off. He then reached the sounds of the voice emanating from Jericho being held back by Leon and Zack.

Jericho growled, "If you both don't let me go, I will have to take you down by force!"

He looked like he could do it, too, having his claymore strapped to his back; Max had to admit it looked somewhat dippy when you considered they were all still in school uniform. Leon's bokken was on the ground beside them, himself replying, "We can't do that Jericho, you are talking crazy! These Dragons are way out of our league, we need to stay back here and hide! I understand you're mad about what happened back home, we all are, but this isn't the way to handle your anger!"

Zack nodded, "Letting out your anger on those dragons won't make anything better for us, it will just get yourself killed!"

Max sighed as he said, "Glad to see you guys are alright, and that Jericho hasn't changed!"

This startled the other two long enough for Jericho to break free as he ran forward and summoned his dragon Goron, but he had darker scales than before, and a look in his eyes frighteningly different. Jericho paid no bother of it and jumped on heading for the Dragons.

Max turned to Leon, yelling, "I'm going after him! I have the only flying summon!"

Before they could reply, he summoned his phoenix and jumped on, Heliopolis shaking him off and saying, "It was a temporary alliance, you stupid human!"

Max looked at his Phoenix, someone who didn't normally talk like this and there he sensed something wasn't right at all. He looked into its eyes and saw some irrational anger within them, stuttering, "W-what's wrong with you Heliopolis? I need to save Jericho before it is too late!"

He'd not even noticed what was occurring above them. The Red Dragon looked like Jericho's did, but Jericho's was much smaller than the others.

Suddenly Brokk appeared next to them holding Jericho's unconscious body, looking at Max and asking, "Who are you? You seem different than anyone else I've met. I can't figure out how, but you feel… untainted. Either way, you need to watch your friend here! He nearly got himself killed!"

Max looked back and said, "I… I know. We tried to stop him, but he's been through a lot, we all have."

Brokk nodded in understanding, not necessarily knowing the specifics but having a feeling he cogitated enough; there were those who had lost their loved ones to the dragons. "I'll be back, however many of you there are: gather here and I will return to you."

With that Brokk flew into the air as the wind around him guided him there. Jericho's Dragon was swatted away and crashed onto the ground beside Max, causing him to jump a bit. Brokk continued forward, pulled out his sword and shouted with fierce anger as magic surrounded his body he swung and punctured the chest of the dragon that had taken down Jericho.

The Dragon let out a great scream, hurt but not defeated. This was still enough for it and the other dragon remaining of the ones who attacked the city. Both flew out of the city in sheer terror of Brokk and Cael, which actually worked to their benefit as there was no guarantee they'd be able to take out them all at once.

They came back to them, and by now every one of Camp One was gathered, and the summons had vanished, no doubt going back to where they'd come from.

Cael and Brokk stood there a few feet in front of everyone else, obviously on their guard and unsure of what to think of these strange people. Brokk wore a black cowboy hat with black boots and a dark blue trench coat over all black clothing, the blue faded with sand all over it. Cael had on his usual gray denim jacket and a basic white shirt and wore black pants. They also both had on white scarfs used to cover their mouths from the sand.

Cael threw a longsword as it hit the ground, asking, "This belong to one of you?"

Knoll ran to it and took it out of the ground, saying, "… Thanks.""No problem. It's a nice sword, you should take better care of it."

Knoll nodded as he walked back to the others,

Cael asking, "So who're they? They all have matching outfits, but definitely not from around here"

Brokk shrugged, "We're about to find out. I'd rule out soldiers; they do look like uniforms, but they fight horribly."

Max imagined that if Jericho were awake he'd take offense to that, so Max decided to speak up instead without protest. They'd need to make friendly contact, especially since these two just saved their asses big time.

"I'm Max. The one you guys saved is Jericho. This is Leon, Zack, and Knoll...and... She's Shakira. We've been through a lot."

Leon sighed, "A lot doesn't even begin to cover it. We've been through hell, and now we're not even on our own earth!

Cael sighed, "Well this is interesting, what happened to you guys?"

Leon told them the tale of what had happened to them as best he could, trying to where they were from as best he could as well; when his tale concluded Brokk was the first to speak, turning to Cael and saying, "I-I think this is what the Gold Dragon meant. This is what we were supposed to use our gifts for."

Cael laughed, "You sure it isn't just killing dragons? Cuz that's pretty fun!"

Brokk sighed, "Oh come on, use your head. Why would the Golden Dragon have intended that for us? In any case, I think we should help them."

Cael shrugged, "Why not. Guess it means more company, so couldn't kill us. But what about the girl?"

There was brief silence and Max said, "I'll carry her... and what Golden Dragon."

Brokk sighed as he started to speak but was interrupted,

Leon looking at Max and saying,"You crazy? You're too skinny, there's no way you could carry her the whole time! Besides, should we try talking to her?"

Max replied, "She's in shock and isn't responding to any verbal communication, and we can't just leave her like this..."

Zack nodded, "That's true, but we should be reasonable about what one can carry."

Knoll nodded, "So who here is the physically strongest?"

Max nodded, "Well that'd be Jericho, but I don't trust him to carry her..."

Jericho just awoke to hearing that, sitting up as he said, "Why not?"

Max felt uneasy, "W-well, I mean... No offense dude, but you kind of have a reputation for-"

Jericho looked at Max and said, "Max, sometimes you just need to learn to trust your friends: I'll carry her. I promise I won't do anything crazy while carrying her. Just let me help you guys out alright?"

Zack nodded, "I'll agree to it."

Leon nodded slowly, saying, "He seems sincere enough, I guess. I'll agree to it"

Knoll spoke up, "I don't think it's a good idea, but if everyone else is for it, fine then."

Max sighed, "Alright, but if let her get hurt, I'll beat your ass."

Jericho smirked, "Come on man, you can trust me. Besides, you couldn't beat me if you tried. Oh, and one more thing..."

He pulled out his sword, saying, "Since your so worried about her, carry my claymore. It'll build up your muscle having to have it around on your back, and besides, if I have to carry her, there's always the risk the sword could cut her skin."

Max was a little surprised. "... Really?""I won't make this offer twice.""I-I'll do it."

"Careful... It's sharp."

Max sighed and decided to let it one go as Jericho walked up to Shakira. She was silent, her eyes showing an emptiness to them as her mind was clearly elsewhere; Jericho hoisted Shakira onto his back, asking in time, "So, where we going?"

Brokk nodded, "The nearest city is a long walk since all the other cities that were anywhere near here are now ruins due to the dragon attacks, but I guess it'll be less boring with more people to talk to. The next city is in the land of Mu. I warn you, though, the walk will be very, very long and perilous.

"The soonest we'll reach the land of Mu is probably a month from now, and even that's generous. Nothing but desert between here and there, as Jariahville is the last city you stop by before heading for Mu. I gotta admit, I've never been there, so not sure what to expect. You guys sure you're up for it?"

Knoll replied, "Not like we've got much of a choice."

Cael smirked, "Not really."

Max spoke up, saying, "There is something that concerns me, however. My summon and Jericho's... They were different.""A summoner. That's impressive."

Brokk looked around, his sense of their culture immediate. "I'm going to assume you guys think it's nighttime, right?"

"You mean it's not?"

Brokk shook his head saying, "No. The sky has been blocked out for as long as I can remember. It's always this dark outside. I've been to many cities all over this land and it's all the same; no sunlight... At all. Ever. They say it's because the magic of our world corrupted the sky as much as it corrupted our lands and its people.

"My bet is that your summons are being affected by the dark magic of this land. It'd make sense because normally people use the magic of the area around them to help power their summoning. You've been so used to doing so you didn't realize that the magic you draw from here is different than that of your world."

Everyone had a look seeming somewhat confused by this revelation. Max started to say something but Brokk interrupted, "We'll have to discuss this on the way there, because we can't stay here for long. More dragons will arrive, and in greater numbers. Cael and I might be good at what we do, but make no mistake... we are human. We're both too low on magic to fight the number that will be headed for here, so we best go now. I promise I'll explain everything as well as I can."

With that they started what would be a very, very long walk.

****

The school grounds were certainly a dark place. Merely minutes ago everything had gone to hell, Mortas having said that if they tried to leave the force-field various monsters would greet them to a diet of worms.

The male dorm had been burned down to a cigarette, but the female dorm remained intact. The cafeteria was somewhat cluttered, but otherwise the food was fine. There had been damage throughout the buildings, but that was to be expected. Any surviving people were healed and refreshed, thanks to Anna. Interestingly enough, the invaders overlooked Miles; he'd been fighting, but for some reason they missed him entirely and perhaps on the basis of combat's ever-changing goals. There was someone else they'd overlooked, too: Nero.

Nero came out from his hiding spot only to be greeted with people throwing things at him, cursing him and stating the direct truth of his cowardice. He thought to himself and even said aloud, "I couldn't help it! Everything was so crazy! I panicked!", but nobody listened and then he let it all sink in. Merely fifteen minutes had passed, but in that time Nero was now hiding in the earth, this time from his fellow students. As he wept and cursed his own existence.

After about a half-hour from when they'd arrived in Dark World an announcement went over the intercoms from Sarah McKnight. "We will be performing a headcount, so please everyone, perform the standard campus intrusion drill and arrive in an orderly fashion to the school auditorium."

People arrived and it was over-packed, people mostly drained and scared. Everyone was getting restless, but they managed a rough head count after a little while and found half of the school still alive. It was certainly better than they expected at least. They also knew who comprised 'Camp One and Camp Two', though not where these camps were. That it was a new world made this of slight irrelevance.

After a bit, everyone got restless and someone shouted, "We're all going to die here!"

People started crying and panicking as they screamed up a chaos,

Sarah damning the microphone, "Everyone, please calm down!" It didn't help through the fear's chorus, Sho then damning, "Quiet! Everyone calm down!" With that their surprise left a pin drop the loudest; Sho's general quietude made for a more astounding realm of his voice's gravity.

Since he had their attention, he decided he should say a few things that he felt would be helpful. "I think we'll need to ration the food in the cafeteria to make it last. That means we'll have to have someone guarding the food.

"Also, we'll need someone to guard the agriculture department. We have our own soil underneath us, so we know we can grow our own food on it still. Now... With everything going on, we'll need a way to keep ourselves occupied and help us keep calm; panic won't help anyone. Any ideas?"

Someone in the crowd replied, "The library is fully intact.""That's a good idea. Any additional ones?"

Another voice said, "Well, we have the fencing/kendo room.""Good: a place where we can train defending ourselves, that's a bonus... Alright, we can't have everyone in those places at once, so we'll have to set up a rotation for them. Also, for sleeping some will be permitted to sleep in here, some in the girls' dorm, and others can sleep in the storage room.

"We'll throw out the boxes and provide make-shift beds. That should help us some, but if you want to sleep elsewhere that's fine... Alright everyone, I know we can make it through this, so please everyone, remain calm!"

Sarah decided she should add something so she said, "Also, we noticed that it isn't all grassy plains outside the dome around us. There is in fact a forest behind the school outside the dome, as well. We'll let you know if and when we will go there, so for now don't do anything reckless and try to journey through the forest right now! We know there are all kinds of dangerous creatures outside the dome: the last thing we need is more lives lost."

Chapter 20 – Weakness

The ice was frigid, for they'd been sent near the South Pole of Dark World. They'd only said that to themselves silently after distinctly telling everyone else they were in the middle of a desert. The black-haired man had strangely lied to everyone but Camp 2 itself. Simon and Rally fell to their knees and began puking from the recent events.

'*Aw, shit its cold. Aw, shit its cold.*' Tim looked around the horizon and shouted into the sky, "Why are we in the South Pole!"

Tim checked around for status of the group; Anna was unconscious on the ground, Ikuto seemed distant in thought with curiosity of his surroundings. Rally was crying and Jared seemed to be partially in shock, but Tim on him being here. Connor was hard to read but at least seemed least affected by the situation, something that couldn't be said for Simon.

Tim turned to Connor and said, "You should grab Anna and we should get going somewhere safe."

Connor nodded slowly and said, "There's a cave just a couple yards ahead of us, we could head in there. I think Ikuto and Simon could also make us a campfire too."

Tim nodded, "Good, get it done." Let's take a look at the situation.

Gabriel appeared in front of Tim, the latter remarking, "Oh, so you're still here?"

Gabriel nodded, "I never left. I stepped out for some tea though, I guess."

Tim replied, "Ghost Tea?"

Gabriel smirked with a look on his face with punchline as he said, "Is there any other kind?"

Tim blinked a couple times, then looked around. Connor managed to get everybody moving along except a still cying Rally. Tim moved over and slapped her. At this she shouted, "What was that for?"

Tim remarked, "You can cry all you want once you get in the cave! It's not safe out here! I'll keep watch. You head over with the others!"

Rally sighed and nodded as she headed in the direction of the others. He looked in the distance to keep watch, then turned to Gabriel and said, "What the hell are we gonna do? Any ideas?"

The two stood in silence for a bit as the bitter air continued.

Some time passed and they were now huddled up in a nearby cave, keeping warm with Ikuto and Simon's fire powers. Tim was walking in as he said, "It looks like there's a storm a'brewin'! … So. We're gonna need a plan. I suggest we stay held up in here for the night, keep warm, and leave in the morning. The campfire was a good idea, but I suggest Rally seal up the cave so the harsh winds don't come in, but leave an airhole so we don't suffocate. "

Rally walked over and did as told while the ice filled the entrance 'til there was just enough space for air. She slumped over against the wall, depressed and waiting as they all took seat.

After a large amount of time had passed Connor walked up to Tim and told him, "It's been twlve hours.""And?""The sun still isn't out.""You sure it's been twelve hours?"

Connor pulled up his sleeve to reveal a watch and said "Dead sure. Also, Anna still hasn't woken up. I've tried waking her multiple times... I even checked for a pulse: there was one, but she's still not responding to anything."

Tim sighed, "Guess now we'll have to carry her around with us. Well fuck, looks like we're going at night."

Connor replied, "I'm beginning to think that there isn't a daytime around here."

Tim replied, "Don't jump to conclusions!"

Ikuto replied, "I think he might be right, though."

Tim nodded and said,"Well pack your bags, kids, we're goin on a trip."

Then suddenly they heard a loud growl from deeper in the cave.

Tim had a look on his face of sheer fear and replied,"And look kids, we're leavin a lot sooner than planned. Go go go!"

Connor grabbed Anna and placed her on his back. As they exited the cave, behind them they saw a Polar bear on all fours, that seemed to currently be at about seven feet tall with a beautiful white wingspan that was massive on it's back. If it stood up on two legs, it probably would double in height.

Jared looked surprised as he said, "Well you don't see that every day."

Rally replied, "Well no shit!"

Tim patted Jared on the back and said, "Well good luck with that buddy." And began running.

Everybody followed suit and were running in the direction Tim was running.

As they ran Tim thought to himself. I wonder if it's still behind us. He turns around and sees it flying right behind them, growling at them, following them.

Tim shouted back at Connor, "Hit it! hit it! Hit it!"

Connor prepared as much lightning as he could and sent it at the creature. It fell to the ground and growled, but managed to get back up again. Its wings seemed harmed, but it still ran after them.

Tim shouted back at them as they all continued to run. "Lava-boy you're up, make em crispy!"

Jared turned around and concentrated, as he did so a massive spurt of Lava hit the bear, charing the skin and setting it aflame. It scorched the bone as the bear collapsed.

Jared replied, "Uh...guys....I didn't mean to use that much lava. And the weirdest part is.. that only took as much magic out of me as the amount that I meant to send."

Tim clapped, "And that's how you do it!"

Ikuto asked Tim, "You're in front, you see anything?"

Tim looked around and saw a whole lot of nothing, but decided to comment on it anyways.

"Snow...Snow....more snow...Darkness...more snow....oh look a rock...no wait it's a speck!"

Connor replied, "I see it. Looks like it could be anything, a building, or maybe a huge rock. But you're right. There doesn't seem to be much of anything else anywhere. Maybe we should head that way?"

Tim replied, "Sounds like a trap to me!"

Rally replies, "Even if it is a trap, do we have much of a choice? I mean we could head back for the cave, but what if there are more bears there?"

Tim replies, "What makes you say that?"

Suddenly another large growl is heard from the general area of the cave.

Tim had a look of fear on his face as he nodded and said, "Well look at that kids, off to the speck we go!"

****

It was a walk that seemed to stretch on forever. But everyone was really quiet, even Max. It was just still a lot to sink in. They'd lost so many friends in the past few months. First due to the Mage's Guild of all things... and then due to the invaders.

It just felt like the past few months went by so fast, and all this bad stuff had hit them all at once. Max wasn't sure how to take it all in. He was beyond the crying stage, he did some crying earlier as they walked, though he kept his tears quiet and without sobbing.

And now what? They were in some world that was in eternal night. With no idea where they were going, even their guides didn't know what the land of Mu would be like.

Brokk spoke,"Alright, let's all rest and make camp. We did a lot of walking today, we earned a break."

They sat and made a campfire. There wasn't anything dangerous in the area, so they were lucky. Still.. all was just surreal. It was hard to take in at once. Everything that had happened. Some might have called the fact he was dwelling on it redundant, but it was just so much to cope with, and Max was known for overthinking things at times anyways.

Max reached a decision, "We should all say something. Like a sort of.. funeral. To honor those who died. Not just recently, but everyone and anyone who meant something to us, and died in the past few months. I feel like it's what we should do."

Leon slowly nodded, "I agree. May I start us off?"

Max nodded.

Leon sighed and spoke, "We lost a lot of good friends. Some of which were among my best friends. We all lost people we cared about... and today we honor their memory. I know we didn't know all of them, but they were all equally important. I think it best we all say a little bit about those who meant the very most to each of us personally. I start with Charles.

"That was merely months ago, yet it still hurts even today. He was a good friend, who protected Knoll to his last breath. He didn't like fighting people, but he knew when it was the time to do what was right. He also was pretty fun to play against in shooters. He was a good friend, and I'm sure we will never forget him."

Knoll cried a bit, and Max patted him on the back.

Leon continued,"Then there was Vincent. He always had a good sense of humor. He made us laugh, and he impressed us with his illusions. He even helped Zack with his Illusions from time to time. I remember one time he mentioned how he hacked into several government websites and went to prison twice for it.

"He had serious balls, and he used those skills to make 3D Models and was thinking about working on his own video game. He was one of my very good friends, as well as a good friend to Max as well. He will be missed."

Everyone was crying in some manner or another by now, except for Brokk and Cael of course. Guess the memories just flood all at once when you think about the ones you'll never see again.

Max spoke, "I'll go next. Roger wasn't always liked by people, but he was a good friend. He spotted me a good twenty bucks once when I needed it. I still wanted to pay him back eventually for that. He also always liked Wolves, something he and I shared in common. Beautiful creatures, and sometimes we'd joke that we were from the same pack. I didn't hang out with him nearly as much as I should've.

"Probably because he got on my nerves as much as he did everyone else. I regret that. All the same... he was a good guy. There's also the sparks. I didn't know them personally, but Jermaine was a hard-working guy, trying to get a degree so he could help make his grandma proud. She already was, since obviously, he made it into this school. But he really wanted to do something more. I only talked to him a couple times, but I know that much. He was a hardworking guy, and I can say that much. Among the Sparks was also Joey."

As he said this Shakira gazed at Max, though her eyes were still half-empty looking. He had her attention.

Max continued, "I only met him a few times...but he was a very nice guy. He and I both liked anime and manga, and he meant a lot to all of us. He was very friendly and kind, I'm sure we all will miss him. And as Leon said earlier, there was Vincent. I used to talk to him online all the time back in the day. I'd known him before we went to the college. He was always very easygoing, and easy to get along with. I remember anytime I had a request for something I want him to photo edit for me, he'd do it without even a second thought. I'll miss him. A lot. He was a very good man."

Shakira had a few tears go down her cheeks as she heard all this.

Zack nodded, "There was Shaun. He was my roommate from the day I joined the school. He always liked to crack a good joke. He picked some really nice places to eat, and I remember I taught him how to treat a lady once, when he had a girlfriend for a little while. He liked to joke about himself being gay, but he really liked women too. He was a really good friend….I miss him, but I figure he's in a better place now."

Knoll nodded, "As Leon mentioned earlier I'll always miss Charles. He risked his life for me. We went to high school together. I remember one time we were on the school bus listening to music and we got into this argument about which band was better. I don't even remember what the bands were, but by the end of it we were cracking up laughing because we ended up finding the most ridiculous song ever, and it was a collaboration between the two! The song was hilarious! I'll always miss him. I also want to honor Allanon. Our headmaster. He taught us all magic, in his own way... and he will be sorely missed."

Suddenly Brokk raised his head and looked into the air,"something's coming! Put out the fire and everybody hide behind those rocks NOW!" He pointed to some nearby rocks that would take a little bit to walk to, but were close enough by that they could make it. They'd decided not to be on the rocks because they were uncomfortable, but stayed close enough that they could hide on them if any trouble came.

They all scrambled to do as told and hid behind the rocks as they looked down from the ledge at what was passing through.

They were riding Jackaloves. They were no less than eight feet tall, possibly taller, and while they looked humanoid, they had an almost flat nose, sharp monster-like teeth and slimy skin. Some had deformed faces, some were more humanoid looking in their face than others. They had brownish green-skin, though again, their skin was slimier. They had yellow eyes.

Brokk whispered to the others,"I-I've heard legends about Goblins. They were from before my time, but legend has it god killed them, as his only act of killing a race, only allowing a few to survive. But they were only about three to five feet tall..these...these are different."

Knoll whispered,"Max and I recognize them. But not from reality. We used to play tabletop games over the internet with each other on occasion...."

Max nodded and whispered,"Orcs."

Leon shushed them as quietly as he could.

The tallest Orc had long messy black hair and looked to the one with the most deformed face,"You're sure there was a fire here?!"

Deformed face said,"I swears it! We're within reach of man flesh! Just smell it, they were definitely here!"

The tallest Orc sniffed the air,"I do smell it."

Cael jumped from the Rock and as he swung his blade the blade went straight through both the Deformed face's head AND his Jackalove's head in one stab.

Brokk smirked,"That's Cael for you. Looks like we're in for a fight guys! I know your blades aren't much, but give me one moment to fix that."

Brokk ran forward and stabbed a bunch of Orcs, killing two rather quickly and then threw their blades to Max and Leon. "That should do it for now!"

Max gave Jericho his blade and as him and Jericho headed for the Orcs, Shakira was left behind being watched over by Zack who stayed back from the fight. Max tried his best, but couldn't overpower the Orcs, who were clearly way physically stronger than he. Jericho stabbed one before it could kill Max.

Max cursed his own physical weakness. He just wasn't strong enough to fight off Orcs! Leon faired better, as did Jericho. They weren't perfect, but they could manage to take out a couple each, though their strength still did not match that of the Orcs.

Knoll couldn't overpower the Orcs either, but his wind magic seemed to work just like it did outside of Dark World, and he was able to dodge their attacks before they could strike, so he managed to stab them with fatal wounds, even if he couldn't overpower them in strength.

Jericho shouted to Brokk and Cael,"We need to retreat! We can't hold this up!"

Cael groaned,"But we'll miss out on all this fun!"

Brokk sighed,"As much as I agree Cael, we-" he swung down into another Orc and continued, "He's right, we need to retreat as soon as we can."

The Orc leader swung his blade at Brokk who blocked it. "I'm not like these others. I'm a dragon-souled." He shouted with fierce anger and the head Orc flew backward.

Brokk turned to the other people in Camp Oneand yelled, "We retreat! The Orcs might only grow in numbers if they're anything like the Goblins of old! I may be able to take out dragons, but these things we fight now are no laughing matter! Regroup! We must go!"

The Orcs continued fighting the others as Leon shouted, "Where would we go to? There's nothing but open desert for miles!"

Brokk growled as he grew taller than the Orcs and his muscles grew in size. A glimmer of a smile leaving Cael, dragon-like wings grew out of both their backs and their eyes became lizard-like slits. These had to be their dragon forms obtained from the Gold Dragon earlier, as they breathed fire at the Orcs. An Orc grabbed a horn of one of them and began blowing into it. Reinforcements were on their way.

Max was still trying not to get hurt, as it was impossible for him to overpower an Orc; as one of them swung down Max narrowly dodged and stabbed it, dodging more swipes as it growled. The puncture did hurt it, but Orcs were clearly quite tough as he pulled the blade out continued to face its might. Max knew he couldn't last much longer against this. He was managing to stay alive, but he lacked the strength to overpower them.

Leon and Jericho were managing, barely. As it swung its blade down upon Jericho, Leon managed to slice its head off.

Leon smiled, "You owe me, Jericho."

Jericho smirked as he stabbed another Orc from behind Leon, chuckling, "Not anymore, I don't", then decapitating it as it fell.

These Orcs were tiresome, but from Jericho's perspective, he was somewhat enjoying the fighting. It gave him a chance to unleash his pent-up and he certainly needed it, after all that had happened.As usual Knoll was using his speed to dodge and still managed to harm the Orcs, inquiring to Brokk with shout, "Why is it I'm using my Wind magic so easily? Shouldn't it be affected me?"

Brokk shouted across to him, "I've heard rumors that Wind-based spells are the only element that can't be tainted by darkness", striking down an Orc and continuing, "Perhaps the rumors were true."

Cael and Brokk began digging their blades into the Orcs as Brokk pulled out his revolver and shouted the words "Nah Ra Ro!", a spell launching suddenly from his gun that began tearing an Orc to shreds.

Brokk shouted to the others as his voice was deeper now, "Cael and I cannot maintain this form for long. We'll fight as we attempt a retreat: we may have nowhere else to go, but we cannot remain here!"

While the others were still fighting, an Orc had managed to climb on the rocks while the others were still fighting. It looked at the sitting Shakira who was still in shock and at Zack as he looked back.

Zack pointed at a nearby bush, the illusion cast being that it looked like them and they looked like the bush. It was quick thinking that bought them time, as the Orc began attacking the bush.

Zack turned to Shakira and he picked her up jumping behind the rocks so they were further from everyone else. He yelled to Shakira, "You need to wake up! I can't carry you the whole time, you need to wake up! Shakira! Shakira, wake up!"

Chapter 21 - Friend or Foe

Nero stood wide-eyed at the forest around him. Nobody liked him anyway... and why should they? He was just a coward. A worthless, useless coward who when things got thought, he hid. He hated himself so much for that.

He thought back to the days when the Phoenix paranoia was going on... he'd been a complete jerk back then as well. One thing that'd surprised him was that they still had electricity. It seemed to be that the dome protecting them, also kept their basic heating and lighting on. No internet access nor plumbing, though, obviously.

In any case, Nero had began to realize more and more as he laid there hiding from everyone earlier... he really did hate himself. Well, no more. He was prepared to prove he was worth something. Earth was his element anyways, how hard could this whole hunting and gathering thing be? He would get enough to provide a lot of food for everyone. Maybe then they'd accept him again. Or at the least, that'd be a start.

The funeral was incredibly depressing. Some of the people who'd died were nice to him. That wasn't a common thing, because everyone found his wild conspiracy theories and rambling to be crazy and irrational. They'd buried them beside the flower gardens, so people could visit them. They were given as nice of a burial as they could but, the graves had to be mass graves because there wasn't much room to bury them anywhere else without being a constant reminder to everybody.

Nero had thought about asking Miles to come with him, but the guy creeped him out too much. Especially since they'd landed in dark world. Nero tried to search him out, hoping for some sort of kindred spirit among them, since as far as he knew, they were the only non-healer magic users left in Camp 3.

He'd began making a lot more puppets, and kept a room to himself as his own private workstation. Everyone in charge didn't know, and anyone who DID know were too busy trying to pretend they didn't. Miles was a bad idea. Besides... this was something Nero should do alone.

It was dark outside, but it had been long enough everyone had figured out it was probably always dark outside in this world. Nero was good at seeing in the dark anyways, though, so it effected him little. Perhaps everyone's eyes could adjust to it anyways when not indoors.

He formed a bow and arrows out of hardened earth. He'd gotten to where he could make it as hard as a rock. It would do the trick as he aimed at something resembling a deer. As he did so he heard a loud shake, and out of the ground, the deer turned out to be an ornament, a sort of front horn to lure in food.. belonging to a gigantic creature with sharp teeth and fur the same color as a deer. It stood on two legs but could clearly also run on all four, with a mouth big enough to swallow a paddle boat whole with no problems.

Nero yelped as he ran, but then stopped. No. He would not run anymore. He turned and stomped on the ground as stone pillars came out of the ground and sent the creature flying backward. He fired a few arrows at the beast as it flew back, the arrows pierced its flesh and a loud roar of pain could be heard from the beast.

He then dug his hands into the ground and then used the earth to form a stone sword in his hands, a two-handed longsword. Not a great sword/claymore mind, those are bigger. In any case, he swung at the beast and managed to puncture its skin. It screeched but scratched his arm, leaving a long scar along his arm.

Then a werewolf jumped out from the clearing and began beating up the creature. As the werewolf turned and looked at him it said, "Don't worry, I won't hurt you. Hi. I'm Christian, I am a student at the school too."

Nero fainted.

Christian went into human form. He thought on how a werewolf had bitten him when he wandered outside the school recently. Christian wondered if it had been bad to reveal his secret to Nero like that. But Christian wanted a friend. He then rolled Nero's uncurious body in the the dirt. He then took Nero's hands and placed it in the monster's blood, and wiped it on Nero's shirt, as if he had just whipped blood off of his hands.

After he's done he threw one of Nero's arms over his shoulder and lifted him up by the waist. They headed back to camp. One of the students saw them coming from the forest and shouted, "Oh my god! Students coming back from the forest, they appear to be hurt!"

As students gathered to stare at the sight of the bloody-shirted Nero and Christian beside him with his shredded and torn clothes.., as well as covered in wounds.

The students said, "Are you guys nuts?! We were not supposed to go there yet! Not until they checked it out!"

Christian sighed, "I went out to search for food and Nero was with me. I was nearly ripped to shreds by a monster. Nero saved my life."

The Students say, "So what happened to him?" Pointing to the unconscious Nero

Christian, "Oh he was amazing. He fought off the beast with his earth abilities using them to create arrows and even a sword, he was so fearless it was amazing and if he had not been there I'd be dead right now. But unfortunately, he was exhausted and passed out. So I felt the least I could do was bring him back."

One of the people in the crowd said, "You should've left the spineless coward!"

Christian walks over to the boy and knocks him to the ground and says, "You wouldn't be talking so tough if it was you!"

He kicks the guy, now on the ground and says, "dumb bastard!"

As Sho had just walked outside, Christian looked toward him and said, "You took charge yesterday, perhaps you can help him."

Sho nods as they turn around to head back. Sho says to the other, "Return to what you were doing." He turns to Christian and says,"Gimme a hand with him."

As they head towards the medical area of the School, Sho asks: "Did he really do all those things you were talking about?"

Christian chuckles, "Well, he was fairly brave, for Nero anyways. He did make those Earth weapons I mentioned. But no, it was me who saved him in the end. I was just helping him out, you know what his reputation is."

Sho nodded, "Your secret is safe with me."

And with that, they headed to the medical area.

****

Back in the forest near Camp 3, where the dead creature lies, a few men were talking amongst themselves.

A man with short brown hair and wore a black fur vest, shirtless underneath and scars all across his chest, wearing black jeans and black boots said, "Looks like we're not the only one around here. Makes me wanna howl with excitement."

Next to him was a man with white and black fur. He looked like a hybrid as his head was like that of a white-tiger but his body that of a man covered in white and black striped fur, black claws along each of his fingers. He wore red jeans and a white belt, with a gold buckle. He wore a white shirt under a long black jacket. "Indeed. This could prove to be a problem. We isolated ourselves from all other continents for a reason. The force field could be a problem, though."

A slender girl with medium hair which on the left side was platinum blonde and black on the right side was behind them. She had a large bust and was wearing a brown leather jacket over her white shirt and wore leather armor under her white pants. She was holding a halberd spear and said,"Hmph. As long as it's a good fight, I'm up for anything." She then allowed herself to do a large shout as she turned into a hybrid, much like the tiger with her, but was part bunny instead.

In the distance at the school, the weird shout could be heard among the bewildered students.

****

Zack realized his prompting wasn't working. But if he didn't wake her, soon the Orc would be upon them. He heard the Orc had already figured it out, "Trying to pull a fast one ey? Where are you? I'm gonna skewer you both!"

Zack smacked Shakira firmly across the face, "Shakira, I know you've been through a lot and you miss Joey. But do you think he'd want you like this? If you don't snap out of it, his death will be in vain! You have friends here and now. I'm your friend, Max is your friend... we're your friend Shakira and if you don't snap out of it, we might die too! You need to wake up!"

Shakira blinked and looked at him. She stood up and suddenly the ground under them rumbled. Zack instinctively dodged as a massive eruption of lava came out of the ground and hit the Orc in front of them, briefly. She then stood there and said, "I'm...I'm sorry about that Zack. I'm ready!"

Suddenly they both heard Brokk shouting, "Dragon!"

Sure enough, a purple dragon was flying above them. It swooped down and began eating the Orcs. Max headed in Zack's direction.

He looked at Shakira and smiled, as he teared up a bit and hugged her. He was overjoyed to see she was ok, but the he noticed something as he let go and shouted to everybody, "There's a crevice over here guys! I think it's a cave! We can get away over here!"

The others ran for the cave and all of Camp 1 headed into it. As they headed through the cave, it was a narrow pathway that seemed to go on for a while.

As they continued their walk, they eventually reached an area where they noticed a light coming from the sealing. It was a jade light. And before them was a ruin, somehow within the cave.

It appeared that the ceiling wasn't always there.. it was like something had dug it out. And before them was a ruined castle. On the front of the castle, it said the words "Gallindor".

Brokk was wide-eyed, "I'd heard about it. Gallindor. A kingdom that fell many years ago. But they say that right before the kingdom fell, the castle mysterious disappeared and was never found… this..this must be that castle. At any rate, we can rest here. I'm sure we could all use it, since we still haven't gotten any sleep yet."

They walked into the massive Castle. It was big, and beautiful. But everyone was exhausted and tired. Especially, Max, he could barely keep his eyes open. They found a large room, near the center of the castle. It had a red carpet that was faded and old, but was mostly rock floors and walls. There appeared to be a throne as well, but everything else was messy, like a battle had happened.

They all laid in various places. Max laid down on the floor beside the throne. Brokk slept on the thrown. Cael and Zack slept near a small well that was for some reason in the throne room. Shakira and the others were in various places on the floor.

Zack lay there asleep. He was dreaming. In his dream, he had on red and black armor. He was taller too. In both of his hands were swords, but the swords were wide in shape and had chains at the end of them, so they could be thrown and then pulled back to himself.

In the dream, he was standing above a man and there was red magical energy coming from his own hands and hitting the man. The man was screaming in pain.

"Please! Just kill me and let it be over with."

Zack smiled and said, "No. I want to see you squirm. I'll grant you death when I am bored with your screams of pain. They entertain me too much to stop now!"

Suddenly a woman came into alleyway they were in. "Harold! W-what are you doing to my husband?! Y-You're him, aren't you?! Zack Gordon! I've heard about you! P-please, I beg of you, let my husband go!"

Zack grinned as he threw his blade straight through her chest and tore down her midsection, killing her brutally as he proceeded to use the blades to tear her shreds right in front of her still in-pain husband who was crying but could barely make a sound out of the sheer pain he was experiencing.

While Zack was having this dream, Brokk too was having a dream. He dreamed of his ancestor, Josh. This was many years ago, in an age before this world was known as "Dark World". Brokk had heard Josh was a great knight, but knew very little else about him. But the dream showed a much more detailed story. The dream had himself looking through his ancestor's eyes. It was if he was his own ancestor!

Tearing through the enemy one by one, he wasn't sure what he was doing anymore. What did he fight for? What purpose did he have in this world? Not much time to think about it, but now it's all he thought about. He'd slash down the enemy with his sword. The blood would smear down it. Yet now he thought again... why did he fight? He was but a foot soldier. Not even a knight. Not royalty, just a soldier fighting for his king. Yet he'd seen many battles. Well more like 3 or 4. Fought in all of the ones he saw, of course. He'd just killed his last enemy when he stopped and looked around.

Bodies everywhere. This battle had been far worse than any other. He was the only foot soldier alive. Only ones on his side in battle who was alive besides himself was the Knights themselves. He'd only survived by pure luck. Though some would say it was skill. One of the Knights stopped to get off his horse, "Are you Injured?" He laughed, "Just a lot of cuts and bruises. Nothing a little rest can't fix."

The Knight laughed, "Impressive. What is your name?" "Josh sir." The Knight grinned, "Josh... Kneel." Josh did as he was told, in shock at what was about to happen. The Knight put his blade on either side of the man's shoulders and said, "I, head Knight Bartholomew, hereby declare you, Josh, Knight of Gallandoir. Rise." Josh again did as commanded. 'Wow, he thought to himself. This.. this wasn't at all what he expected to happen today. He actually was expecting to die.. he even wondered why he even existed, yet now.. he was a knight.

Barth smiled, "Ride with us."

Josh nodded, "Yes Sir."

Barth laughed," No need to be formal with me. Now let's go."

He headed over and got on a horse they had.

The Six headed back for Gallandoir, to report that the enemies had been killed, but the cost was great. The Kingdom of Gallandoir would be ambushed by a second wave soon. That just now WAS Gallandoir's second wave. It would be down to the Knights themselves and the wall guards of the Kingdom to fight this army. But that wasn't the half of it...Josh's Birth Mark mysteriously started to glow. Josh scratched it...it only tended to glow when something bad was to happen soon...this was a bad sign. Josh covered it with his sleeve, which had been rolled up, as he rode with the knights.

In any case, he rid his horse over to the castle.

On the way, he had to ask, "I notice each of you have a small number on your arm, probably showing what order you joined. Makes me wonder.. how did each of you guys become Knights?"

The Head Knight laughed, "Well, let's just say I've been one for quite a while."

The fourth knight, who was short but stalky with big muscles and was bald, laughed, "Oh come on Barth, you and the king are old chums. It's no secret. As for how, who knows. Barth doesn't talk much about his personal life, and we don't mind that."

Josh looked at the fourth knight, "well then, how'd you become a knight?"

The fourth knight laughed, "Me? Simple. My father was a knight of this kingdom before me. I wanted to be one too, but Barth here said I had to earn it just like anyone else, so I did. They say I fought an army of Cyclops while my arms were bound. That's what they say. I'll let you decide for yourself if you believe it. Names Hogar by the way."

Josh looked at the fifth knight, "And you?"

The fifth Knight was covered in black clothing. He was lean in build but muscular. He had no sleeves. He ignored Josh completely.

Hogar remarked, "That's Alucard. I wouldn't go asking him too many questions were I you, kid. He's got a mad temper. But don't worry, he won't hurt ya. You don't want to know how he became a knight, though, trust me. If you value having sleep at night, you're better off not knowing."

Josh laughed nervously, "Okay. Guess that leaves those two."

He pointed at the second and third knights, who were further up ahead from everyone else.

Hogar laughed, "You got a lot of questions, don't you? Well, those two are old friends of Barth. They were former mercenaries when Barth found 'em. Brothers those two are. Same father, different mother. Took a lot of convincing but they became knights alongside Barth.

"The three of them were the only knights we had for a long time because of the death of our first king and his knights against the Paraians. We only got a reprieve because of a short truce we had with the Paraians. As you know, we just defeated the them two years ago. Vicious lot they were. You're the first new knight since those days, well sort of. We'll be meeting with the sixth Knight when we arrive. He's guarding the king."

Josh was curious, "Sixth? How come I've not heard of him before?"

Hogar grinned,"He's one of the strongest among us. Definitely the oldest. They say his skill level is comparable to the head knight himself. He hasn't been doing much sense we beat the Paraians, and he wasn't knighted until after he had helped us win the final battle of that war. Ever since, he's been guarding the king most of the time. Opted out of fighting with us, and we respect that. The rest of us are like brothers, though, and you our newest brother. You and I should have a drink sometime."

Josh laughed, "I don't drink."

Hogar laughed, "Never hurt to give it a try." Josh just nodded.

When they arrived at the kingdom, the front gate lowered and they entered into the kingdom. It was smaller than some, but that makes sense when you note that Gallandoir only started about 80 years ago, making it much younger than most other kingdoms. As they began entering the kingdom, the dream continued.. as Brokk wondered how it was that he not only was seeing the memories of his ancestor, but knew what he was thinking at those moments as well.

Max had a different dream, two in fact.

His first dream was he was back home. There was a woman crying to her daughter, her daughter being in her early 20s. The mother was blonde. She spoke to the daughter while laying in the sand and covering her arms in the sand, and Max could see from the daughter's eyes.

The Mother said,"What were they working on there? Please.. just tell me what they are doing."

Max could see the daughter's thoughts. As he saw her think about the Zombie Virus and how it had failed because the enemy had necromancers. He then thought on how the US had developed gigantic humanoid robots and had already long deployed them on the battlefield in the "previous war", whatever that meant. In any case, they felt the "mechs" weren't enough now that the enemy had struck again.

Then he heard her say it from what felt like his mouth,"They've developed a machine. Powered by potatoes of all things. The goal is to see the future, but with scientific machinery. They gained the idea when the Schneider house head, Maxwell, revealed he had the gift of divination. Please, now get up."

The mother said,"I can't. They tried to kill me once before. They'd shoot at me the second I got up off this ground."

Max continued to see through the Daughters eyes as she looked at mysterious black car pulled up beyond the gate and two government agents dressed in black came out of it and they closed the doors.

It was very vivid..was he seeing the future? He felt like he was, though he couldn't explain why. Then the dream faded away into black and he was in a new dream. This time he could sense it was his regular dream... somehow.

He was standing in a gigantic white room. It was clean and beautiful. He saw a door. The door was labeled "Dream Hallway." As he walked for the door, suddenly the white room expanded into a massive cornfield. And he heard growls all around him. Creatures of some sort, and they didn't sound friendly.

He found himself more capable as a fighter in his dream, however, as when the first beast came out it was a shadowy creature resembling a cat and a dog mixed, he somehow knew martial arts as he did a karate kick to push it back and then used kung fu punches and swings to take down another.

He ran for the door, which continued to get further and further away. Then he jumped into the air and found himself flying, superhero style. He flew at great speeds and reached the door and opened it. As he opened the door he saw the doors were labeled.

The doors read "Jericho, Shakira, Leon, and Anna." He looked above the door he'd come out of and saw it read "Max". These doors must have led to other people's dreams! He opened the door labeled "Anna", and stepped inside….

****

Now we look back at Camp 2. They'd reached the speck. Turns out the speck was an odd bit of rocks gathered together. But they were shaped in such a way they look like they could provide shelter, like they'd been dug out into makeshift caves sort of. It was amazing looking to Simon. It reminded him of the cave they were in before. He'd been in shock at first, but he was quickly realizing they did not have time to just stand around doing nothing.

Oh, how he wished they'd stayed in that cave. The walk had been long, cold and he couldn't feel his fingers. Nothing but snow, everywhere and all they had to wear was school uniforms. They were lucky they hadn't frozen to death.

He felt like he might pass out even. But he wasn't about to allow that to happen. Everybody else was being strong during that walk. Nobody complained and they'd marched forward. He felt like the weakest team member, but he was determined not to show it.

Besides, he was one of the Crimson Twins... or was it the Azure Twins? People kept debating whether to call them off their fire powers or their last names. Guess that didn't matter now, though. He was the quiet type anyways, so he tended to let others do the talking.

Suddenly many arrows started heading their way. Him and Ikuto Instinctively blocked them by creating a bunch of flames in front of themselves, strong enough the arrows turned to ash. That was new. Their fire was clearly stronger in this world, just like the lava.

Ikuto looked down as he said, "That...was better than expected." Then he felt his hand and made a sound of pain as he noticed he'd lightly burned his thumb and a couple of his fingers on his right hand. "This fuckin hurts!"

Jared was the next to speak as he nodded understandingly, "Just like my lava. This worlds doing something to our magic, making it stronger, but harder to control."

Simon looked at his fingers, it would seem his were unharmed, for now. He remarked, "I wasn't burned, for some reason."

Tim nodded, "That is awfully weird. But right now I'm more worried about where those arrows came from, and why they stopped...and where did Connor go?"

Connor came out from the rocks holding a man who was apparently by now unarmed as he threw the man onto the ground.

Connor nodded, "I found this guy. I scouted up ahead and saw him about to re-arm his bow. I stopped him with a good nice shock from my lightning and decided to bring him here."

Simon felt immediately reminded of how he felt like the weakest in the group. Rally had ice element, so this place was a natural fit for her, though she did seem to be constantly scared by the expressions on her face, which was in its own twisted way at least a small comfort to Simon. Other than just now, Ikuto had been handling things well enough, proving how opposite twins can be.

Jared was handling the situation with his usual mellow attitude, almost as if this place hadn't affected him, which unlike Simon, he probably wasn't faking. Tim had taken charge proving to be the brains of the group showing just how much a hick's smarts can be useful in survival, and Connor was continuously proving why Allanon had made him one of the two in charge back home. Sure Anna was apparently in a coma, but it was because she'd healed the entire school at once!

What could Simon say? He was just another fire guy, while they already had his brother. He felt worthless.

Tim asked the man they'd captured,"You wanna tell us why you were shooting at us?"

The man was silent for a moment and then said, "No reason. I just thought you looked funny."

Tim looked to his side and then back at the man and said, "My ghost buddy tells me you're lying. I don't particularly like lying. Makes me unhappy. Connor, which part did you electrocute again?"

Connor replied, "His left leg mostly."

Tim kicked the guy's shin and he shouted in pain. Simon didn't like what he was doing, but he said nothing. It could be key to their survival to figure this out.

"Now care to rephrase that?"

The man seemed too stubborn to speak.

"Connor, give him a lil zap please."

Rally stepped forward, "That isn't right! He's a human being! Enemy or not, that's just cruel!"

Tim looked at Rally and said,"I know it ain't pretty, but we gotta stay alive out here. Do you want to freeze to death or worse get killed by this guys buddies?"

Rally looked at the ground, "No….but-"

Tim interrupted her, "But nothing. Connor and I are doing what we have to do to get it done."

Connor replied, "If it makes you feel better, you don't have to watch. The area I came from should be clear for now. Just stay on guard. Look, I don't like doing it either. But I agree with Tim. We have to do this."

Rally sighed, "W-whatever…."

It took a little while, as the man was very stubborn about not talking. But they managed to get some information out of him.

"My people are hiding after the war with the North. We've been barely surviving off of the food and water here. If anyone from the North finds out we're alive, they'll slaughter every man, woman, and child! I beg of you, don't report us! We're barely surviving as it is!"

Tim nodded,"We won't. But in exchange, you gotta show us your people. We need shelter."

The man grumbled but seemed to agree as he said, "It's several miles underground, directly under these rocks."

Ikuto replied,"Sounds like we've got a place to go to!"

Tim nodded,"That it does. That it does."

And with that, they reached a manhole cover and opened it. There was a ladder. Tim went down first.

Then the man that was their guide, then Connor, then the others, with Rally bringing up the rear.

As they headed down the ladder, they'd told her to cover the whole back up with the cover they'd opened, so she did.

As they went down the ladder they reached a massive round staircase. It took them a really long time to get down it. Apparently, he wasn't fooling. It was six miles down before they reached a dead end.

The man said,"She ga-ra-tie-lenthia."

Jared asked,"What language is that?"

The man said, "Snake language. My people can talk to snakes. We're quite proud of it."

As they entered the door there was a makeshift elevator. It was very cheaply made as a big cage with a door and held by normal rope. The man used his hands to wheel them down. This last a very long time.

As they got down he opened the door. There was another door, this time massive, no less than sixty feet tall.

The man said,"Eye-lewith-ydga-seth!" and the door opened.

Upon opening, they saw a massive castle-like fort in the distance, and a bunch of poorly made make-shift buildings with people on the streets. But right in front of them were many men dressed just like the man they'd brought with them.

They had their bows pointed at Tim and the others.

One man seemed to be in charge, he had ginger hair and a ginger goatee and was pale white, looked to be in his fifties. The man used magic to create a pillar of ice as he sort of surfed on the ice and headed for them, confidently and proudly, before landing on the ground in front of them, in between them and the guards. He wore the same standard leather armor as they did, and had two short swords, one on each side of his waist and a bow with its quiver on his back. His bow was larger than that of the others.

"I am King Terragon of the Southern Kingdom. You are my prisoners and you are coming with me, faggots."

Simon replied, "We're not gay, actually..."

One of the guards said, "He calls people that all the time, even if there is no reason. You'll get used to it, if you survive that long."

And with little other choice, they followed the guards into the kingdom.

Chapter 22- A new beginning

Jericho was in a deep sleep. He was dreaming..he could tell. But what he saw, looked very real. It's like he was watching someone's life story unfold. First, he saw two men. One had long brown hair and was built slender, in fact, his general build looked almost the exactly the same as Max's, down to the height even. The other was short and stockier but built well.. the same general build as himself. They were near the area where they kept the horses held up.

The first man said,"So I take it you're leaving soon, huh?"

The Stockier man was polishing his sword and continued to do so as he said,"Well duh. I never wanted to be King of Bretonoyama. Freedom is what I want. To do whatever I want, when I want. That's why I'm leaving. What about you, Cyril?"

The first man, obviously named Cyril was fiddling with a knife as he said,"Well Aiden, you may be my twin.. but that's not what I want. Don't get me wrong, I don't want to stay here either.. but your idea of fun sounds like anarchy. I'm not into that. I'm not exactly sure what I want actually. but I know it's not here. I'm going to wait for awhile after you leave, though.. with both our older brothers gone, if I leave now then nobody will watch after Connor."

Aiden laughed,"Whatever floats your boat man. He may be our adoptive brother..but the kid's just too weird for my tastes. Good luck."

Suddenly all went black and when Jericho could see again.. he saw Cyril again, alongside Aiden and a third man with short blonde hair. Cyril was wearing blue armor that was plated and metal, Aiden was wearing a dirty white shirt with a brown vest over it and black pants and had on black boots. The third guy had on blue armor but it appeared to be less bulky than the armor Cyril wore. Cyril had twin katanas, Aiden was holding a cutlass and a flintlock pistol, and The third guy had a rather long sword.

They were outside in a massive plain that had a mountain not too far away in the distance. The place reminded Jericho of Dark World a lot..except it was during the daytime. Maybe this was from before the eternal night had happened? In front of Cyril, Aiden and the third man..was another man wearing armor almost the same as Cyril's, but was the only person there wearing a helmet, and one couldn't see the mans face at all. The man in front of them was laughing like he was crazy.

The man said,"Red Bane, Red Bane, Red Bane. I'm quite glad I took up the mantle. SOMEONE had to when you became such a coward!"

Cyril frowned,"I was a monster as the Red Bane. I slaughtered many and I'm GLAD I revoked my old nickname. Now I'm simply, Raven. After the hundreds of years, I've been alive..I know very firmly. That is the name I want to be known for!"

Aiden shrugged,"Who cares about the semantics, Raven! This son of a bitch killed crewmembers of mine and he's going to pay for it! I'm still surprised you brought Thomas along, since this battle is personal to the two of us but he's just here because you allowed it!"

The third man, obviously named Thomas laughed,"Sometimes I tend to forget that I'm working alongside the most wanted man in history, the former Red Bane, Raven.. and his twin brother, the second most wanted man in history; the King of the Pirates...Aiden both older than my great grandpa yet you both look my age and-.Aiden's already attacking him isn't he?"

Cyril, who clearly was called Raven now nodded,"Yep. Let's follow his lead."

Sure enough, Aiden was already charging for him..but before anything could be done, this "new" Red Bane had already disappeared behind his men. A massive army of undead soldiers in Red Armor. They'd merely appeared from thin air and were standing there, awaiting the battle that was no doubt about to commence.

These soldiers had rotting skin but seemed to be able to move like they were living, breathing humans. But one look at their pupiless eyes told a different story.. they'd been reanimated. Jericho guessed probably by this "new" Red Bane.

Jericho was in awe of what he was seeing. Hundreds and Hundreds of men were going to attack simply three men. Jericho had a feeling, however, that it wouldn't be the death of these three.

Suddenly before Jericho could get a bearing on what was happening, there was a bright flash and suddenly he saw that there was a massive army fighting the other one..but being slaughtered like ants! This army could not even hope to stand up to the undead army's might! However among all the fighting.

It was a completely different story for those three.

Thomas sliced the head off of one man. Raven split someone in half horizontally, as Aiden did so to another 10 men Vertically. They slashed through the men one by one.

Raven shouted,"damn you, whoever you are! I'm going to make you pay for all the murdering you've done!"

The New Red Bane guy laughed as he still allowed his men to do all of the fighting. Suddenly, Raven slashed at the ground, cleaving the very earth apart. As the fissure continued to grow, many men fell into the earth below.

Thomas and Raven swirled their blades into the air it sent a wind gust sending men flying, enemies and supposedly allies alike. They seemed to not be concerned for anyone else's well-being at all. The three seemed to be only working together with each other, and not the army. Jericho was very impressed with the amount of swiftness they took them out.

Within mere minutes there was only Thomas, Raven, Aiden and the man they'd been fighting their way to get to. Everyone and everything else was mere corpses all around them.

The Red Bane laughed,"You cannot have my blade! It's mine, you hear me?! ALL MINE! IT GAVE ME MORE POWER THAN I'VE EVER DREAMED OF! BEFORE I HAD THIS BLADE, I WAS A WEAKLING. THE COWARD WHO RAN AWAY FROM THE WARS OF OLD! But now?! Now I'm the mightiest man on this earth! I'm the great and powerful second coming of the Red Bane, greater than the first! And today….I'm going to prove it!"

Suddenly the Red Bane slashed his blade onto the blade of Raven.

Raven growled,"that blade doesn't belong in anyone's hands! It's cursed! I should have destroyed it many years ago!"

Their blades clashed together but then shortly after Thomas and Aiden joined in the battle. There was a flash. Jericho was upset he was going to miss the best parts..he didn't get to see the rest of this fight!

When the flash ended, the new Red Bane was dead and on the stairs of the outside of a pyramid-like structure. Thomas was holding the apparently cursed sword.

Raven shouted,"Destroy it! Don't let it take hold of you, destroy it!"

Thomas said,"No....it's MINE." And with that, he slashed Raven and knocked him down the stairs.

Aiden saw what happened and went to help Raven as Thomas left the opposite direction.

Then another flash happened and Jericho saw...Gallindor? But it was different. if it hadn't been for seeing the outside of the castle he would never have guessed it was the same place. There he saw Raven being placed in a coffin and laid to rest. Odd.

Jericho awoke to see Knoll and Zack looking at him.

Zack said,"What were you dreaming about? You were talking in your sleep."

Jericho shook his head,"I have somewhere to be. Follow me if you want."

Knoll was puzzled,"Somewhere to be? We've barely spent a night here. Yeah, we're following you."

As they followed Jericho, he looked to the hallways. They were very different, but he could roughly understand which way to go. He then found a broken bookcase with a door behind it and slashed open the door. A staircase. The three then went down the staircase for a long, long way.

Another door. He slashed it open and they went down a hallway with many doors. Jericho picked the one at the end of the hall and it had yet another staircase. This one was dauntingly long..it felt like hours going down this one alone. Then they reached another door and Jericho opened it up.

And there was the tomb of Raven. Jericho opened the coffin. Raven was in it, but looked much older. Elderly even... but seemed to be well preserved and like he was in good health when he died. Suddenly he opened his eyes.

Knoll and Zack jumped backward with a fright! Jericho nodded,"I had a feeling you were still alive, Raven."

Raven sat up and looked at them."...Who are you guys?"

Jericho knelt down on one knee and said,"Raven.. my name is Jericho. I had a dream, you were in it and you were fighting alongside your brother Aiden and your friend Thomas and fighting the new Red Bane. You beat him but then Thomas turned on you. Then I saw you being laid to rest here, and I awoke.

"I knew exactly where the location was because I remembered seeing it in the dream.. me and my allies come from another world completely different from yours. We were brought here against our will. I came here because we need your help. We are in this darkened world of yours and are too weak to properly take care of ourselves. We need you to train us until we are stronger. I beseech you, please help us!"

Jericho figured using those words would help. He loved watching knights of round table type movies as well as Viking Movies and the like.. so he knew a thing or two about how to do this.

Raven said, "... I'm not even sure how long I've been asleep. I can sense great hidden potential in each of you..and the last thing we need is for you to become misguided in this corrupted world. My lust for power and desire to become the strongest man in the world turned me into less than a man..the blade merely helped me get what I craved.

"After all these years there's something I've learned: constantly seeking power for the sake of fame, or to be the "best in the world" or any other selfish reasons brings emptiness, not happiness. Especially as you see those around you pass on.

Instead, one should seek power in order to protect those around you, and focus on friendship to bring happiness.. not the desire to be the best. I will train you."

'This guy talks as much as Max does,' Jericho thought to himself. "Thank you, Raven.", He said.

****

Meanwhile, Max was still asleep..and his dream had gotten rather strange.

Max was wearing a black trenchcoat and all black clothes and was in a city. As he walked along he felt like he'd been in this city for years. He'd merely forgotten it all. How, though? He couldn't remember. Suddenly, he was attacked by police. He defeated them rather easily, though, with punches and kicks that simply felt natural to him. After doing so he heard sirens and ran instinctively, then found another door, pulled out a key labeled "Anna" and entered it.

Then Max entered a hallway..until he found a door labeled Anna. He entered the door and found it was on the hill near a cliff, and there she was crying.

"I-I've failed you! I've failed you all...I.. I can't ever live up to what everyone needs of me!"

As she did this, it started to storm, as lightning clashed, it got cloudy and windy and the waves of the water below began to move violently.

Max saw her breaking down. It reminded him of Shakira. He thought on what she was currently dealing with emotionally. He failed to help her so far, he wouldn't do the same here! He ran to her and said,"You're having a nightmare! This isn't real! Wake up! Wake up!"

He smacked her repeatedly.

Max continued,"If you don't wake up, you really will fail us! We need you but if you keep staying here, you can't do that! Wake up!"

Suddenly Max blinked..and it was he who was awake. Odd. Cael, Leon, and Shakira were still asleep. Brokk was out, probably still on guard duty. Clearly, it was still the same night that Max had fallen asleep. Guess that's what the kid had meant...if any of it was real. He had been dreaming, after all. So it's possible none of it was real at all.

Then he saw Jericho, Knoll, and Zack coming back up with an older man. Maybe he'd been asleep for longer than he thought.

The Man said,"I'm Raven. Your friend Jericho here, says you need my help to become better at protecting yourselves. I'm here to help. It's been no doubt hundreds of years that I've been alive...but I'm sure that'll help, not hurt my ability to help you. This old man still knows a lot about fighting."

Max felt almost like he was looking at an older version of himself..how odd. Still, maybe this guy can help us out? It's not like they have any other good news..suddenly Max' s mind shifted b ack to the dead bodies of all the students back at the school. It...it's a lot to see.

It's one thing at a funeral.. he'd been to one of those before. But it's another to see someone who's just freshly been killed. It's like, they were living their daily lives..and then it was all over. That just shows how fragile human life is.. and that's frightening. That one day, it can all be over. Just like that. The thought terrified Max. And seeing the dead bodies of people he'd met..that would scar anyone. But that also worried him. What if this guy wasn't completely trustworthy?

Max said,"I'm not sure we can trust you. We've lost so much already." He turned to the others and said,"I know you guys still remember what happened with the Mages Guild. I hate to bring up old wounds, but do we really want to risk the same sort of scenario?"

Knoll nodded,"I agree. I mean, isn't it a little too convenient that the one guy who knows all there is to know about fighting just happens to appear? Or well. that's basically who he is."

Zack sighed,"While I don't trust him, what choice do we have? We've lost so much already..and this could be our chance to protect ourselves and each other. Don't forget, we didn't know Brokk and Cael until recently either."

Knoll remarked,"True, but they saved our lives! This guy just appeared in a coffin. That's another thing..why was he in a coffin in the first place?"

Raven replied,"I don't expect you to immediately trust me. But I'm your only real chance you have. Take it or leave it."

Zack said,"I think we should hear him out. He's the best chance we've got. We've lost so much already..don't you guys want a chance to fight back?"

Raven nodded,"Jericho told me on the way back here all about what happened to you at your school. There's nothing I can say to change what you've seen. We can wait to start whenever you're ready. I won't rush you. I promise."

"I'll help train them." The voice belonged to Brokk, who apparently had been listening to the whole time, somewhere nearby..unseen.

Raven shrugged,"I've heard about you from Jericho as well. Perhaps. We'll see how that goes on a trial basis. You definitely interest me. In my days, dragons were considered fairy tales..I'd rather not say about my past experience with them. We'd only rediscovered magic towards the later parts of my life..so I'll be watching you with great interest."

Cael yawned and said,"what did I miss?"

Brokk grinned a little,"A lot."

Once Brokk had finished explaining everything, Cael sighed. "Boooooring! What am I supposed to do during all of this?"

Brokk sighed,"How am I supposed to know?"

Max mind shifted as he then said,"Wait a minute..there's something I need to do."

He then entered the room where Shakira was sleeping, as he lightly woke her with a small shake. She jerked upwards, scared out of her wits. As she did, Max hugged her.

"I've been very worried about you Shakira. I-..I can't explain it, but as I was sleeping last night, my dreams reminded me of how much I missed you! I promise.I won't ever let anything happen to you! You have my word!"

Shakira wept as she hugged him back. All she could manage was a weak,"T-thank you."

Without Max nor Shakira realizing it, Raven had entered the room as well.

Shakira shrieked. Max said,"AAAH!" her shreak had scared him as well.

Once he realized it was just Raven, he sighed and tried to reassure her. "It's okay Shakira..this is Raven. He's here to help us! He's how I'm going to become stronger..so I can protect you and everyone else!"

Shakira nodded slowly. Raven sat on the floor and told her and Max everything that had happened between himself and Jericho, as well a general idea of the dream Jericho had dreamt.

After he was done, Shakira listened closely and said,"I…I want to train with you too. I..I can't let what happened to Joey happen to anyone else again. I..may have to take it slow at first but. I want to become stronger too!"

Max nodded,"I..I think I might be ready too."

Raven nodded," then let's begin right now!" He then entered the room they were all sleeping in before alongside Max and Shakira.

Cael sighed as he said,"I'm going to go try to get a pet dragon or something. Later guys." And left the castle abruptly.

Brokk placed the palm of his hand onto his face and said," You guys go ahead. I'll keep an eye on him for now. Who knows? Maybe we'll run into a party out there...I'll make sure we aren't followed back." And with that, Brokk left too.

Raven said,"the first problem is conquering your inner demons. From what Jericho has told me, you've all faced a lot since you've came here..and while you all have handled it differently.You Must All Face it. This world is dark and corrupting and the dark magic in the air around us will change you. But we need to make sure you can move on from the past..otherwise, the change will be very bad.

"For all of you. Now. I want each of you to try summoning your creatures again. They will be corrupted by this world more so than yourselves, but don't worry. I'll help you keep them in line..but they will need to be a part of this too. Zack, Knoll. I'm sorry but that means this step won't include either of you just yet."

And with that..their training began...

****

Knoll and Zack both said,"I understand." And laughed a little about saying it at the same time, but then immediately switched back to uncomfortable because they were still in the presence of a total stranger.

Raven chuckled a little too and said,"Good. Laughter could be of use in times like these. Anyways, it is now time to perform your summons. Max, Jericho. You two go first."

Max and Jericho did like Allanon had taught them, and sure enough. Goron and Heliopolis appeared before them.

Goron growled,"..I'd ask 'why did you summon me' but I have a feeling it's because you need MY help again. If you hadn't beaten me in battle, I'd be kicking your sorry ass right now, Jericho! In fact, I'm feeling extra strong right now. Perhaps I should do it again?"

Heliopolis laughed,"You? Extra strong. Don't forget I'm right here beside you and I could throw you from here to the other side of town! Remember how great I was against those Mage's guild scum?"

Goron growled,"those were other Phoenixes, you birdbrain! I'm a dragon. Try it again against me and I'll flash fry you!"

Heliopolis got mad right back,"Let's find out right now!"

Suddenly, before anyone could see what had happened, both Heliopolis and Goron were on the ground, with a blade each on their throats..defeated by Raven!

Goron replied,"w-what happened?!"

Heliopolis was equally surprised,"I-I didn't even see you! When did you draw those swords even?!"

Raven smirked,"By the looks of it, I might be as old as you are. It's not common a human being can say that to a Dragon and a Phoenix..is it? Do the math and then you tell ME how it is that I beat you."

Goron laughed,"to be older than me you'd have to be-"

Raven interrupted,"Over several hundreds of years old? I am."

Heliopolis answered with the obvious,"What do you want from us?"

Raven nodded as he said,"You are to become partners with Max and Jericho over there. Your strengths are theirs and theirs are yours. The same goes for your weaknesses..and I'd bet two prideful races such as yours wouldn't like that.. so I'm going to be training you. All of you. If you've got a problem with that, we can have this fight again. And again. And again. I promise you that I will win. Every. Single. Time."

Heliopolis,"You have earned my respect. I will do it. I am curious what a human with as much determination as this Max kid will accomplish anyways. I just felt he should've been the one to beat me first."

Goron replied,"I was already beaten by Jericho before anyways. The kid already has my respect."

Raven got off of them and said,"Good. Next is Leon." He turned to him. "You know what to do."

Leon summoned him and as he did so, a Werewolf appeared. His summon.

He growled,"How could you spend so long without even so much as a hello to me?! I thought we'd become friends Leon! How dare you betray my trust and keep me cooped up like that for so long?! I'm going to tear your throat out!"

Leon replied,"Lucian, I'm sorry. I really am. A lot has happened!"

Lucian said,"Sorry won't cut it! I'm going to KILL YOU!"

In an instant, Lucian was in human form and on the ground, bleeding. His nude body had a blade to his throat as Raven was over him.

Raven replied,"Heel, doggie. You calm now?"

Lucian replied,"...I am. I'm sorry..I- I don't know what came over me."

Raven responded,"It's the darkness of this world, affecting your already negative emotions. It's understandable. I need you to try to remain calm. You're going to begin training with Leon soon."

Lucian nodded,"O-Okay. Sure thing."

Raven nodded,"Good."

He got off of Lucian and then headed for Shakira who was blushing as he approached her. "Well? Shakira. You know what to do."

Shakira backed off,"I-I can't."

Raven replied,"why not? I have shown I can put any summon here thus far in their place."

Shakira said,"I-t's not that. H-he..every time I've ever summoned him. It went badly...and the last time I summoned him-" her memories went back to the moment where she'd summoned him to try to rescue Joey.. and how the Monkey had run away. She began shaking in place, fearful.

Raven put his hand on her shoulder,"I understand. We don't have to begin yet if you don't want to."

Shakira shook her head,"N-no! I-I want to...I want to now."

Raven,"Alright. Then do it."

Shakira did as told and summoned the Monkey.

He immediately began throwing feces at Shakira, but Raven had long blocked it with his blade and had the blade to the Monkey's throat.

"Now, now. That isn't very polite."

The Monkey yelped. "YIKES! This dude is scary!"

Raven said,"You're going to be fighting with Shakira from now on."

The Monkey said,"S-sure whatever you say, tall dark and scary!" His eyes were shifting side to side..showing dishonesty that was likely only being said out of fear.

Raven replied,"I'll be watching, so you best not lie to me."

****

Connor sighed. His girlfriend back home had to deal with him being far away in college..now he was in Dark World. Would he ever get back? Who knows. He tended to let the others do the talking, only speaking up when he needed to. Tim seemed to have appointed himself leader anyways, so why not?

Most of the next fee minutes were just usual sarcastic jokes from Tim. They didn't seem to work so well with this places leader, but didn't hurt so far either.

Terragon spoke up,"Alright alright that's enough. So what are a bunch of outsiders like you doing out here?"

Jared spoke up this time,"We don't know even. One second we were in our world, the next we're running from a polar bear with wings and then we ended up here while running."

Tim nodded,"Pretty much what he said."

Connor could tell Terragon was the thinking it over. Then he said,"So let me get this straight, you faggots are from another world. Explain that one further to me."

Connor decided to say for this one,"Basically an alternate. A parallel world Similiar but different to yours, existing in another dimension."

Terragon replied,"Uh-huh. Sure. Whatever. Why not? Alright.. while I believe you..our wonderful and powerful kingdom has stayed alive all these years due to our secrecy. If anyone were to find out about us, it puts us in danger. We work best from the shadows really. That makes all of you..liabilities. Thing is, it gets really boring around here. So I won't imprison you..but you can't leave either."

Tim got annoyed. Oh boy. Connor knew that look, as he'd gotten to know Tim well enough by now. Tim was going to have things to say.

Tim said,"Oh I'm sorry I must have gotten some snow in my ears because I could have sworn that was a threat? I must be mistaken."

Terragon sat more upright on his thrown as he said,"More like a promise. If people found out about us, it would expose us to enemy countries. But why should I even have to explain it to you nimrods?"

As he said this, the guards got in between Tim and the thrown.

"Because this nimrod asked nicely." Tim says his eyes glowing with Soul fire as Gabriel appears standing next to the gentlemen his ghostly form flickering lightly with soul fire as he stared down Terragon.

Connor knew this could get ugly really quick. They couldn't afford to have a fight right now. He said, " Come on Tim this isn't the time for this"

Terragon jumps back ad he sheaths his short swords and pulls out his longbow and fires an arrow at the ghost, it goes through the ghost and doesn't faze his form, as this is happening The two guards try to stab Tim with Their spears

Gabriel vanishes and creates a shield before pushing forward towards the oncoming spear thrusts deflecting them upwards and shoulder slamming into the two guards pushing them back. He noticed how fast Terragon could move so he sarcastic responded," Oh you're a quick one!"

Jared suddenly placed a pool of lava suddenly on the floor in between Tim and the Guards and said,"Let's all calm down guys, before we do something stupid. Or, well...more stupid."

Ikuto nodded in agreement," this is crazy! We just want somewhere to stay warm and stuff!"

Rally replied," Well yeah, but being trapped down here would suck!" She then looked at the guards nervously and added,"No offense."

Tim glares at the group with soul fire in his eyes still before throwing his hands in the air in defeat " Fine whatever have yer fucken peace talks with this asshole for all I care" his should disappeared as he walked to the back of the group looking annoyed that his fun was stopped.

Connor was relieved. It would seem their designated leader was better at survival than talking.

Jared made the lava harden to rock, as he apologized to the guards and turned to the others,"Well, I don't want to take Times place as leader..so who should lead us?"

Ikuto said," I don't really want to either."

Jared laughed,"No offense, but I wouldn't want you to lead us either."

Ikuto shrugged," Back in the day, though, there was someone else who taught people other than me, that'd be Connor."

Rally agreed,"Connor sounds like a good idea."

Simon said,"I agree."

Connor was surprised by their choice. He wasn't sure if he wanted to be leader or not. But he may have little choice. He walked forwards towards Terragon.

Terragon smirked as he sarcastically said,"Yeeees? I take it you are the new leader?"

As Connor was about to speak, Anna awoke.

Anna got up and looked around,"W-what did I miss?"

Ikuto shrugged,"Not much."

Simon smacked the back of Ikuto's head.

Connor replied,"We were sent to another world covered in Darkness and now we have a leader of a country threatening us not to leave and saying he won't imprison us because he's bored. Outside is the south pole and is really cold.

"We were referred to as Camp 2, which is everyone you see here. Camp 1 is god knows where, surrounded by Dragons and might be dead. Max, Jericho, Leon, Shakira, Zack, and Knoll were sent in Camp 1. Everyone else and the school itself is Camp

3 and we have no idea where they are, but we were told they are safe for the time being. That's the gist anyways. "

Anna nodded,"That..sounds like a lot."

She walked over to Terragon.

"We come in peace. We want shelter from the cold. But if you try to keep us here for longer than we wish and against our will, I will have to force you to reconsider."

Terragon laughed,"You and what army?"

Anna said,"I don't wish to fight. I ask you again, can't we please just resolve this peacefully? We promise not to speak of you to outsiders. We merely wish for somewhere warm to stay for a few nights."

Terragon said,"I don't think so. Let's fight!"

Anna sighed,"If y'all insist."

There was a bright light as a winged unicorn, also known as an Alicorn.. suddenly flew straight at Terragon and had its horn to his throat before he could react in time.

Anna replied,"Order yer guards to back down and give us as we wish, or mah friend here will pierce yer throat and spill yer blood until it flows like a river down this entire room. And DON'T y'all think about tryin anything funny when my friend temporarily leaves. I know how to turn mah healing spells into something far more...dangerous."

Terragon growled,"Fine! Whatever! Do as she says!"

With that, the Guards backed down.

Anna smiled,"Good. Now we can start getting somewhere!

As the throne room had an eerie silence over the entire place, Connor looked around him. The Guards were baffled, and no doubt upset that they had been so powerless. Jared had his hands up in a manner that looked read for a fight..no doubt on guard, probably thinking this could get uglier quickly. Rally was hiding behind Connor. Poor Rally had been through a lot lately, he couldn't blame her for it really. Ikuto and Simon seemed to be just watching, unsure how to make heads or tails of what happened.

Connor was glad this had been settled. It wasn't exactly the way he wanted it to go, but she probably did a better job than he could have. But then there was Tim. He seemed annoyed. What would he say next?

Tim walked over and threw up his hands, "Oh I see how it is. SHE get's to have fun, but ol' Tim doesn't!"

Connor knew how to pacify the situation. Tim was stubborn and sometimes quite tempermental, but he wasn't an idiot. So, Connor put his hand on Tim's shoulder and said, "Dude. You were going to kill him. We wanted to END the conflict. Not start a new one by ending him."

Tim put his finger on his chin and looked up for a moment. He then nodded and chuckled, "Good point. Alright, I guess you got me there."

Terragon was less than amused, "What do you want?"

Anna sighed,"My name is Anna. And this here is, Connor, Tim, Rally, Jared, Simon, and Ikuto." She pointed at each of them as she introduced them and she immediately continued without pausing," We simply want somewhere to stay as shelter. I know you were being threatened earlier.. so this is less than an ideal situation. But I'm ready to prove we can, in fact, be of use to you. We'll go out and bring you enough food to feed about fifty people. Surely that would prove our worth?"

Terragon shrugged, "Not like we have a choice."

Anna nodded, "Good. Oh and one more thing. it's in y'alls best interest you let us back inside when we return. You don't want to know how much more I could do if you don't. Furthermore, I'll be having Tim, Rally, Ikuto and Simon staying here to keep an eye on things. If you try any funny business, Tim has my permission to kill ya."

Tim had a smirk on his face as she said that. Connor couldn't help but laugh quietly to himself at Tim's response. Still, it was interesting that she was bringing himself and Jared along with her. He'd wait until they got outside to ask her about it, though.

Terragon merely growled and nodded as he looked at the ceiling and said, "Whatever."

and with that, they went back the way they came and headed outside. Nothing but snow in all directions all around them, just like earlier. Connor took this chance to ask her what he'd wanted to earlier.

"Why did you bring us?"

Anna smiled,"I feel the two of you have the most useful abilities to use for our hunting for food. We're going to be hunting the biggest animals we can find, that way we don't have to carry back as many of them. Ah would have possibly taken Ikuto, but it's best not to split him up from his brother. Rally wouldn't be of much use in a battle of any kind in her current emotional state and I don't think it's wise to leave Tim there alone. So that made it easy to choose whom would come with me."

Jared grinned and said,"So it's because I've got Lava then?"

Anna giggled,"You bet! Plus, Connor has his lightning. Ah must say, though, I'll have to work on helping you both keep control of your magic.. this area had very dark magic in it's atmosphere. Ah can feel it. That's probably contributing to the lack of sunlight. Anyways, follow me."

With that, they followed Anna out into the harsh winter night. Though Connor wasn't sure it would be nighttime if it wasn't for the eternal night thing that was going on.

As they continued, in the distance they saw something that gave them a great pause. It was a 30 foot tall Polar Bear with wings on it's back, and there was a bunch of seven feet tall polar bears with wings all around him. 'Well, shit!' was the first thought that popped into Connor's mind.

Anna smiled,"Easy prey for me. Just follow my lead boys."

She ran right for them!

Jared was wide-eyed as he looked at her running ahead of them and said, "Crazy bitch!"

More crude words than Connor would have used but essentially the same. Still, she had to know what she was doing...right? Connor sighed and said,"Let's give her the benefit of a doubt. I mean, she DOES seem to be pretty powerful right?"

Jared nodded and said,"Well.. yeah but fuck that!"

Connor said,"Let's just go!"

Jared,"Alright, I'll go but if its gets to be too much trouble, I'm pulling your ass back out of there with me!"

With that, they followed her as much as they could, though she was obviously a faster runner than them and also had a head start. Then they saw the 30-foot tall bear collapse. He saw a man with two swords had done it. Hard to make out what the man looked like though. But in a single slash, he'd taken down the biggest threat there!

Then there was suddenly two more men. The first one began slashing them down one by one, and as he did so they were becoming frozen and shattering into pieces! The other one was doing slashes that were splitting them in two.. but each cut was clean and left no blood!

There was also a fourth man there as well, he seemed to be the shortest among them..but he was mostly running from the polar bears and occasionally throwing knives at them. Then suddenly a polar bear got too close and the fourth man was sliced in two! However, the man reattached his top half back to his bottom half and stabbed the bear in the eyes with his throwing knives!

The biggest shock was after the bears had already all fallen to these men, when a fifth man..seemingly from out of nowhere.. appeared. But what was surprising about him was that this fifth man was as big as the polar bear was on all fours..30 feet tall!

Anna already seemed to be talking to them as Connor and Jared continued approaching, by now not running while doing so anymore.

Anna laughed and said,"Howdy guys! Glad y'all could join us! Ah'd like to introduce you to these five gentlemen."

She pointed to the man who had two swords from earlier who'd taken down the biggest bear. He had brown hair with a lot of grey hairs in it that was short, was missing his left eye and had on dark green cloth pants, black boots and wore a brown fur coat and was shirtless underneath it. He was muscular in build but still somewhat slender. She said,"This is Ryo."

She then pointed to the man who had cut bears in half without leaving any blood. He had short brown hair as well though it had less grey hairs in it and wore a black fur coat with no shirt on underneath it, wore black boots and had on brown cloth pants his general build was the same as Ryo, but he had both his eyes intact.

"This is his younger brother, Yuji. They used to be from a place called Bretonyama, but joined the South Pole's military many years ago to help fight the threat of the Northern Forces at the time. The remainder here are also former members of that army."

She pointed to the man who could separate his body parts at will and reattach them, which he did so himself as he waved. He had long blue hair in a ponytail and it had many grey hairs in it. He interrupted her before she could speak to say,"I'm the great and powerful Argos! Like all these men beside me, I was a great and respect Knight of the South Pole's joint armies! None could touch me because I'm immune to all forms of cutting and slicing! I-"

Anna interrupted him as she continued,"And this is Zimri. He was the one using his sword to freeze opponents." The man she pointed too was a living skeleton! He had on black cloth clothing and black boots that matched the ones Ryo, Yuji and Argos wore. Connor and Jared nearly freaked out but the man laughed and said,"don't be afraid of me, I'm just all bones! I died in the last great battle of the south pole, but Yuji brought me back from the grave to help these others survive. We're all old friends so I didn't mind one bit, in fact it touches my heart...if I had a heart I mean." He then laughed to himself further.

Connor wasn't sure whether to be amused or creeped out. But then there was the elephant in the room that was, even more, standing out: the giant.

Anna seemed to be reading his mind as she said,"And last but not least, this is Tim. Dear me, that will get complicated when he meets our Tim, won't it? All the same. Tim is this man's name."

The 30 foot tall man was wearing what appeared to be black underwear and that was it. He had long black hair and a long black beared. He had grey hairs everywhere, though. He smiled in a friendly manner as he said,"TIM!"

Ryo grinned as he said,"Don't mind him. He likes to say his own name a lot. The big guy is still our friend, though!"

Anna said,"I've already told them who you two are, and now that we are all together. I have good news!"

She turned to the five older men before them and said,"We actually were just at your former home kingdom, and they are still alive! We actually came out here to get some food for them, so we could bring these polar bears to them as a way to do so and we'll even show you where they are hiding out at!"

Things were happening too fast for Connor's taste and it could lead to things getting ugly fast. He needed to say something quickly before it go tout of hand.

Connor replied,"Woah woah woah. Wait. Anna, what if these guys are lying and they're the bad guys?"

Jared nodded,"He's got a point you know."

Anna sighed,"If they are. We'll cross that bridge when we get there. I'm probably the only one strong enough among us to fight them anyways, so it's best if we just cooperate for now."

With that, she was already leading them back the way they came. As they headed back, they arrived at the kingdom.

The Guards immediately recognized them and one of them said,"Y-you're alive! We thought all our best warriors died in that war! S-sirs..you've missed so much! Since you've been away we've all been under Prince Terragon's rule, and frankly.. he's been in denial about us not being what we once were, but he's all we've had to stay alive! Now with you five here, maybe we have a little bit more hope! Come with me, I'll personally take you all to see Terragon now!"

Yuji nodded seriously,"If little Terragon is leading you I can see the issue. I remember last time I saw him, he was a child."

Ryo smirked,"Guess we'll have to set the little shit in his place. My loyalty was to the king, not some snot nose brat who grew up too big for his britches."

Argos gulped,"On one hand Terragon is probably really strong." Then he continued as he talked to himself,"but I'm with my knight buddies so this could just be another opportunity to use my status to get through this..hmmm."

The skeleton simply laughed and said,"With the King gone all I've had is my friends anyways. Besides, if Yuji willed it I'd be dead again anyways. Time for more fun I guess!" He continued lightly laughing.

As they entered the throne room Terragon saw the knights enter.

Ryo said, "So, you're leading our people, huh?"

Terragon said, "It was their idea. All our leaders and greatest fighters were supposedly dead. I do kinda like my role, though. I didn't know you were all around."

Yuji said," I've heard you are being a royal pain."

Terragon said, "Save it. Look, I could have tortured and interrogated these folks but I didn't. And as for your respect? I don't need it. As far as I can tell you knights have been surviving on your own all this time. You can continue doing that, or you can rejoin your people and gain glory in battle."

Argos said, "What Glory? On our way here I saw what's left of our people. It isn't much."

Anna interrupted, "Actually, I have a plan. My allies from my world and I are potentially powerful magic users. And am I right in that the only other magic users here are probably you five?"

Ryo allowed magic flame to briefly appear on one of his blades as he held it out and said,"Yes."

Yuji asked, "What's your point?"

"My point is," Anna added,"that you five can teach my friends how to perfect their magic and then just maybe we'll have enough strength to find this glory you all seek."

Terragon shrugged, "It's not like any of us have anything better to do."

Ryo and Yuji muttered to each other and nodded. They then talked to Argos and Zimri, Who both seemed to look positive.

Yuji said,"the four of us agree with your idea and I'm sure Tim outside would agree as well."

Terragon laughed, "Tim lived too?"

Ryo nodded, "the big guy is a big part of why we didn't all die..well except for Argos. He was able to retreat on his own."

Anna smiled, "Then it is decided."

End of Arc IV

Chapter 23- War of Shogun

Note:

Camp 1 - Max, Jericho, Leon, Shakira, Zack and Knoll plus "The DWD (Dark World Duo)" Brokk and Cael

Camp 2 - Anna, Simon, Ikuto, Connor, Rally, Jared, and Tim.

Camp 3 - Anyone else who isn't dead.

A few months had passed and Max looked at the darkened sky. He hadn't seen the sun once in the past few months, yet somehow there was just enough light to be able to see. Or perhaps he was simply used to it by now. The cold, bitter air. The darkness that surrounded them all.

But their mentor, Raven had done well to help them all overcome that. Max had been overjoyed when Raven told them their training was now completed. But then, just like that..he left. Merely days ago, he'd left them all behind. Now it was the big moment. Brokk and Cael had immediately set out to finish taking them to the land of Mu. Raven had called it something else, though..he called the land, Shogun.

The names both suggested Japanese origins, or at least this world's equivalent. What would they find once they arrived at Shogun? Who could say..but Brokk and Cael had to part ways shortly before arrival. Something about "Unfinished business" with men named Harding and Nrath. Once they were done with that, they'd meet back up in Mu at some point, but Brokk and Cael said not to wait up for them. That was merely hours ago.

Max turned to the others. Jericho, Shakira, Leon, Knoll, Zack....they were about to cross the border into Mu..and they had no idea what to expect, but they'd have to face it..on their own.

Upon entering the land of Mu, also known as Shogun..they saw trees that were half-dead but seemed to still be hanging on. It looked like a land that might have been once beautiful, had it not been for the darkness covering the sky.

Many buildings of a white concrete/marble design were nearby. Max looked to the others and said,"So..I guess we should figure out the name of the place we are at, right? The land may be called Mu or Shogun or who knows what it is at this point?"

He walked over to a nearby person selling newspapers. He asked for one and gave a piece of gold that Brokk had given him. The newspaper made it clear.

Max nodded," newstand says here we are in the Country called Freyala....and that it's one of six countries in Mu. It doesn't list the place as Shogan..so I guess it's currently called Mu still."

The man newsstand looked up and had a look on his face,"Shogan..where did you hear that name?"

Max replied,"A friend said it. He's a fan of past history."

The man in the news stand was a much older man with grey hairs and seemed tired and exhausted..but more of due to past experience. Like

399

he was an all around tired man. He slowly looked Max over, but nodded,"I'll say. Our land hasn't been called Shogun in a long, long time. Last time we were called that was before the Great War. A lot changed due to the war...the skies became darker, the people became angrier... I miss how beautiful Freyala used to be, in the days before it all. But that's enough of the past..it's best not to bring such things up further."

Max nodded,"I respect that."

The Newspaper guy added," You seem like nice people, so a piece of advice. You should leave while you still can."

Jericho inquired,"Why is that?"

The Newspaper guy said,"War. We're in the middle of one. Outsiders shouldn't be here. You'd get caught up in it, and most people won't be as nice as I am."

Jericho grinned,"That's what I like to hear. We have yet to test our powers against a real challenge yet."

Max nodded,"The very same."

The Newspaper guy said,"Okay fine, don't listen to me. I'm just a newspaper man, what do I know, right?" with that, the newspaper man spun his arms in a circle and the air currents formed caused his stand to be closed and the papers to fly up into a pouch on the roof of his stand.

Max whistled,"A wind element user, huh?"

The newspaper man grinned,"Everyone in Freyala is. Just like everyone in Aine uses fire, and so on. You really ARE outsiders."

Shakira grinned,"Nifty! That sounds fun!"

The Newspaperman started to leave, but Max and Shakira followed him. He turned and said,"leave me alone! I'm busy!"

Max and Shakira shook their heads and both said,"Nope. We're following you." in perfect unison.

Jericho shrugged,"We'll keep looking around. You two have fun pestering the newspaper man."

Max nodded and waved goodbye as the two of them continued following him.

Jericho, Leon, Zack and Knoll continued sight seeing around the city.

Leon sighed,"I do find it awfully strange they decided to follow an old newspaper man like that. I was tempted to go with them but I didn't want to be rude to the poor old guy."

Knoll said,"Seemed pointless to follow him in my opinion."

Zack shrugged,"Not like we are doing any better just wandering around town like this. We should get some disguises or something. We stand out like sore thumbs. That newspaper guy knew we were foreigners right away."

Jericho smiled,"Disguises it is then, I guess. We'll have to enter a store to buy some, though."

They entered a smaller store and prepared to buy what they could.

Meanwhile back with Max and Shakira, the Old man arrived at his home and said,"Fine. I guess I can serve the two of you dinner. Since you're following me anyways."

As they sat down he was in the kitchen preparing food.

Max said,"Oh, I guess we should introduce ourselves. I'm Max and this is Shakira."

The old man paused for a moment and then said,"..Akanu. If anyone asks ya though, forget you heard it. I prefer to keep to myself."

Max smiled,"So you just sell Newspapers huh? Someone with your talents should be fighting in that war you mentioned is going on."

The old man paused and said,"Who says I'm even that great? Freyalans all have Wind Element, remember?"

Shakira giggled,"Don't be silly! We could see it in your eyes and the way you moved..that's a practiced hand. You have the look of a former warrior to us."

Akanu sighed,"Guilty as charged. But I'm an old man, my days of fighting are behind me. Skilled or not, it's best for people my age to leave the fighting to the youngins."

Max said,"Can you tell us much about this war?"

Akanu shrugged, "What's to say? Ever since the Great War ended, everyone's been angrier. Things that would normally upset people just upset them even more. That and, plants don't grow as plentiful so food isn't as plentiful. Hungry people get desperate. It can get people angrier too in and of itself. Former allies become enemies and the like. It's split Aine even...as many people of Aine are half-Freyalan, while others consider themselves "Pure-bloods." So the poor Country is in a Civil War..with Freyala backing the half-bloods, of course.

"Meanwhile, Jigoku has turned against us Freyalans. Everybody loves the Jigoku people, so nobody is willing to fight them, and meanwhile we HAVE TO. Don't get me started on Raiterra, which wants to wipe out all of Aine in general. Fin'eowyn, meanwhile feels the same way Raiterra does and wants to wipe out all of Aine..but is hesitant because it doesn't want a war with us Freyalans. It also can't stand the Raiterrans.

"Only country neutral in all of this is Auron, who has sealed its borders off. Sorry, guess I should clarify some things. Like I said before, Freyalan's all use Wind Element and most people of Aine use Fire Element. Raiterrans ues Lightning, Fin'eowyn's people use Water, Jigoku people use Lava and Auron use Earth. It's all a bloody mess if you ask me."

Max said,"Then I guess I'll fight for Freyala. Why the heck not, right?"

Shakira said,"Yep! Sounds good to me too!"

Akanu looked at both of them,"You two are very strange people..."

A voice came from the background,"Might as well just accept them, Akemi."

The old man sighed,"I told you not to use my real name in front of people, Han."

Another older man entered. This one was a bit rounder in build but had a lot of muscle.

"They have their hearts in the right place. I know you want to stay hidden and all of that...but isn't this war the perfect time to redeem the Okami name?"

The old man, apparently named Akemi and not Akanu sighed. "This is my friend, Han. He defected from Jigoku because he disagree's with his own people's idea to go against Freyala."

Han laughed,"We should go with them. If they're going to go out and fight like this...why don't we? Sounds like fun!" Han briefly formed lava in his hand before it disappeared into ash.

Akanu sighed,"When you get like this, there's no arguing with you....alright fine. Not like any of this matters so long as we continue to be under the rule of the Northern Capital." he turned to Max and said,"My True desire is for Mu to regain its old name of Shogun..and to become independent from the North again.

"But those days will likely never come. One thing at a time though...Freyala coming out of this war on top is a good start!...fine! So be it, I shall lead the two of you and your friends into the battlefield!"

With that, they all set out to find Jericho and the others...which didn't take long once they heard a ruckus was happening at a local shop.

Cop, "You're under arrest for disturbing the peace, foreigner! Turn yourself in!"

Jericho smirked,"Hey, this asshole started it." He threw the civilian into the cops and they used wind to stop the person from hitting them.

Zack sighed,"That's Jericho..can't go anywhere without a fight being started. Guess there's no choice for us now..."

Leon shrugged,"I guess not."

Jericho shrugged,"I haven't used any of my magic yet. I'd say I'm doing just fine!"

Akemi and Han entered with the others.

Akemi sighed,"Stop. Stop Stop."

Jericho looked,"Why should I?"

Max replied,"We didn't come here to cause trouble, Jericho. Just humor him for a little while."

Jericho sighed,"Fine. What now?"

Akemi sighed and turned to the cops. "By Royal Decree, 2-11-359, I demand we see the king at once."

The Cops saluted,"Yes sir! We didn't realize they were with you!"

With that, they were whisked away to the King's royal palace. No telling how this would go, but at least they were off the hook for now.

405

The King saw them approaching his throne and asked,"what is it you want?"

Akemi replied,"Instead of throwing them into a jail cell for a minor squabble..I'd like to propose something grander. As you know, the Okami name hasn't gone as far. I'm the last of my family after the rest of my clan were slaughtered in the war that lead to us being conquered by the North Kingdom.

"You also know that my ancestor's cousin formed an Okami family branch in Raiterra, and they may soon be used against us. I propose you allow me to restore my family name. Han here, of Jigoku, is prepared to help us...as are these strangers. Old friend...I beseech you to allow me my chance...to allow all of us our chance..to fight for you. And help Freyala in this war."

The King thought to himself for several minutes..and shifted his weight a little and replied,"Normally, I'd have said no...especially since these are foreigners. But...you are my old friend, and I trust your judgment. So be it. But if you embarrass me in such a way I regret this decision in anyway..such as these foreigners proving to be a nuisance.. I will have you executed. Understood?"

Akemi bowed and nodded. Max was surprised. Everything was moving so quickly..but it was time. They'd spent the past several months training, and though they personally had no stake in all of this..they needed to test their strength. Not only that..but perhaps they could build potential allies from this. And while in this world..that's something they desperately needed.

****

406

Connor calmly took a deep breath. Apparently, there was a huge number of Orc Territories growing near the Southern Kingdom, and Terragon and the others would be in great danger if they weren't taken out.

Sure, Ryo, Yuji, Argos, Zimri and Tim could take them out.. but that wouldn't really help anything, because this was also meant to be a test for Connor, Jared, Ikuto and Simon. To see how much they'd grown in the past few months while training under Ryo and the others. Tim, Rally and Anna would stay behind with Terragon, as insurance if anything went wrong to help Terragon protect the Southern Kingdom if Connor and the others were killed.

In the months they'd been under the tutelage of Ryo and the others, they'd learned an interesting detail. Bretonoyama was a country of the North. Ryo and Yuji had left it behind. Not only that, but apparently it was a ghost town and many of it's former inhabitants had moved to...the Northern Capital.

In fact, nobody from the Northern Capital was originally living there.. they were all former inhabitants of either Bretonyama or any number of other Northern Kingdoms, they'd simply formed the Capital as a new Kingdom lead by the former leader of Breyonyama. Ryo Yuji had left and joined the Southern Kingdom's armies..believing their former home to be in the wrong. They'd earned the right to be as respected as Argos, Zimri and Tim.

In any case, there were the Orcs. Turns out that the Orcs of this world are located in the ruins of the fallen cities in the south, and have grown exponentially in their time of hiding, and are ready to hide no longer.

Connor didn't like Orcs. Sure, back home hearing of them in fantasy books was kind of cool. But he didn't like the idea of having to fight them now. Still.each of them had learned and gained something since their time training..and it was time to use it. Connor and the others silently made their approach closer and closer to the Orc settlement, until they'd finally arrived pretty damn close to it.

Connor shouted,"Hey ugly Orcs! Come out and fight us!" that would definitely get their attention. No need to be stealthy, since the whole point of them heading out here to the Orcs homes was to start a fight.

Out came about 50 of them, running at them in plate armor and growling as they held their swords and knives and axes and the like.

Connor formed his hands together and created a sword made of Lightning in one hand, and a sword made of fire in the other hand. He shouted,"Let's get them!"

Jared nodded,"Got it." and he suddenly grew to be 30 feet tall! 30 foot tall Jared began stomping on and crushing enemy Orcs as he said,"I don't have to use Lava to beat you guys!"

After a few moments of Silence as he stepped on Orcs he added,"...but I still got Lava." and sent some Lava down on a few of the arcs, for old time's sake, even if he seemed to not need to.

The Orcs tried to slice down Simon, but as it sliced straight through Simon, but Simon allowed his left half and his right half to reattach as he said,"I learned THAT from Argos!" Next Simon allowed his hand to detach from his body as it began shooting Orcs with flames from above as he then detatched his body from his feet and allowed Ikuto to guard his feet while the rest of Simon himself was flying into the air, using his own various detached body parts for combat!

Ikuto smirked,"You could say I'm the opposite of my brother Simon over there." He then formed a sword made of flames and sliced an enemy in two, but the cut was clean and left no blood, and the Orc was still technically alive while in pieces on the ground! Ikuto smirked,"I learned that from Yuji." He then pointed to one Orc and then pointed at another and suddenly the first arc had nothing but arms and the other Orc now had nothing but legs! Ikuto smiled,"You two look better like that...not by much, though."

Connor continued slicing through his opponents with his lightning sword and his fire sword as more and more Orcs kept coming in! Connor grinned,"looks like our test is going well..but one last thing."

He turned to Simon, Ikuto, and Jared. They each gave a thumbs up.

Connor sends gigantic lightning bolts outwards towards the home of the Orcs that they'd come out of. Jared did the same with his lava as a gigantic torrent of Lava was sent that direction. Ikuto and Simon did the same with their flames. The Orc's home exploded into many pieces as it was swiftly destroyed! Considering the eternal night they were under..this made the explosion shine all the more brighter!

Of course..this was merely one of the Orc settlements near to the Southern Kingdom. There were many more to go..but all in all...this was a success.

****

The rain poured down. The dark blackened sky was the only thing to greet them. It was hard to see, but Jericho's eyes had grown accustomed to the darkness. Right now, the reasons for the war didn't matter. Jericho didn't care, to begin with anyways. It was time to test what he could do.

Downhill ahead of them, Aine troops were confused and throwing flames at one another. It was very difficult to know friend from foe. But the Freyalan troops seem to know, at least. Which was more than Jericho could do.

Then suddenly, Raiterran troops came riding downhill riding lightning bolts like as if they were surfboards in the air. Jericho smiled. They were all his enemy in that country....he's know whom to strike down now. That was all a part of the plan of course.

Freyala would focus on helping Aine with its civil war..and the foreigners would focus on preventing the Raiterran troops from interfering for as long as they could...if they were to die, then Freyala would worry about whatever enemy troops were left. Freyala expected them to die. Jericho couldn't wait to prove that the 6 of them would not only survive..but take care of the Raiterran troops on this battlefield by themselves.

The rain around them seemed to not be affecting the troops...must be rubber boots and the fact the lightning was their own. None-the-less, the rainfall meant Jericho would have the advantage. He couldn't use his usual fire attacks as well as usual..but he didn't need to.

He opened up his hand at the falling rain and formed a massive torrent of water and sent it flying at the enemy troops, causing them to electrocute themselves, taking out a huge bunch of them. Meanwhile, Jericho ran forward sending a fireball down at some of the ones who had avoided the attack with his free hand. He pulled out his sword and began swinging, cutting down enemy troops.

Nearby, Max had his sword at the ready and was using Wind Element to move even quicker, sending torrents of wind to knock enemies off balance and then he'd slice them down with his sword.

Max then had a Raiterran troop send a bolt of lightning towards himself but he stopped it in mid-air and sent it right back at the troops. Max had lightning element. But then, so did Shakira as she began sending lightning bolts like mad at troops left and right. She was running forward even more aggressively than even Max, and was well into being among the enemy Raiterrans before even Max or Jericho!

Leon rubbed his hands together and then formed a massive, several story tall vally of raw arcane magic at the enemy! It disintegrated a huge portion of the enemy troops.

Jericho grinned,"Save some of them for me, asshole!"

Leon nodded,"Just try to keep up."

Jericho smirked.

Max formed wind around his blade itself as he began slicing through people, using the wind to make the cutting and slicing even more powerful. As they continued fighting, it became clear that most people of Shogun were swordsmen..made a lot of sense, but meant they wouldn't have to worry about any gunfire at least.

Jericho formed lava into his hands and covered some Raiterran troops in the lava!

Meanwhile, Akemi and Han were fighting the enemies among the Aine troops. As were most of the troops from Freyala. That was fine.Max swung his wind covered sword slicing through troops. Shakira placed lightning element around the outside of her fists and was knocking troops out with it, which was super effective given the rain made it even more potent. Leon was mostly avoiding using weapons and simply using his raw arcane magic as the way to fight. Jericho did what he did best..he had his sword at the ready and mixed up with whatever the situation called for.

Knoll sent large amounts of flames outward from himself, catching enemy troops on fire. He then threw a potion to Zack. "Drink it." Zack did as told, as Knoll got another one for himself and drank it.

Suddenly Zack and Knoll were twice as fast and twice as physically strong. Zack was knocking over enemy soldiers with his sword much more easily, as if they were weaklings!

Knoll nodded,"I made the potion myself. We won't feel any adverse effects for another 24 hours."

Jericho swung and knocked down several soldiers in one swing...the water around his sword was making the swings more lethal and he could defeat enemy troops en masse.

However while the fighting was going on, some of the Raiterran soldiers were trying to sneak around and get to the next battlefield.

Leon caught notice of this. He sent a wave of arcane magic at them, but it only hit some of them as some of the Raiterran troops used lightning element to block the attack! Slowly but surely, they were getting around the huge battle Jericho, Max and the others were doing!

Jericho meanwhile was swinging his sword and striking down soldier after soldier, occasionally sending bits of lava at some of the soldiers, then sending a bunch of water to drown some of the others.

Suddenly a soldier stepped forward. "Foreigners should not meddle in our affairs!" he swung his sword and it collided with Jericho's.

Jericho grinned,"At last, a worthy challenger."

The soldier growled,"You've killed enough of our troops! You face ME now!"

Jericho and the other man collided swords. Lightning went out and hit Jericho who nearly fell over but immediately got back up as green surrounded his body.

Jericho smiled,"I know healing magic. You'll have to do better than that."

The Raitteran frowned,"I will." He swung as Jericho and his blade both collided. Jericho tried to use the lock of blades to send Lava at the man's face but he backed off and dodged it and knocked it aside with lightning. Jericho didn't stop there and sent water at him but the Soldier threw a small device that gathered the water into itself and closed.

The Raitteran growled,"Hardly fair that you foreigners know more than one element."

Shakira shouted as she collided with another few soldiers and knocked them down one by one. She then turned into lightning itself for a moment and quickly took down several rows of troops before returning to her physical form. She'd gotten that skilled with her magic.

Training with Raven would do that. She turned and looked to Max. They then moved in perfect synch, both using the same technique Shakira just had as they both turned into lightning itself and took down rows and rows of troops, trading off which side they attacked in rapid succession. They both stopped and panted.

Max responded,"We should avoid using that technique too much more Shakira...we'll run out of magic that way."

Shakira sighed and nodded,"Yes, you're right."

Things then escalated from bad to worse as a humongous roar was heard.

Jericho looked into the sky and saw it. The dragon was bigger than the Black Dragon he'd seen Black Hair summon a long time ago. A lot bigger. More than 3 times its size. Jericho could only hope he MIGHT be ALMOST the size of its eyeball. The large dragon had gold and red scales.

The Raiterran he was fighting stopped and said with an alarmed voice,"ABRAXAS!"

Suddenly, another thing filled into the sky. A gigantic blue bird, with lightning forming around its wings at all times. The bird was the same size as this golden dragon apparently named Abraxas. This bird made Jericho WISH he could fee like an ant..because he'd feel bigger than he did now.

The Raiterran went wide eyed,"IT'S A ZIZIX!"

The Zizix spoke with a distinctly feminine voice as it said,"Abraxas, I see you've become a Golden Dragon."

Abraxas growled,"I've awaited the day I could kill you, Mangrielle!"

The Zizix, obviously named Mangrielle and Abraxas fought in the sky and then he saw it...dragons and phoenixes everywhere, fighting in mid-air. Many of the human soldiers stopped their fighting..and panicked as everyone went seperate directions and various cries of "RETREAT!" were declared. But it was too late as flames and lightning, and ice and all various kinds of elements flung everywhere from the battle above, hitting the people below. Clearly, the Phoenixes and Dragons were at war..and now it'd spilled out to the people of Mu.

Max shouted,"RETREAT!" and everyone followed. Jericho growled. He could hold his ground..or he could retreat as well. He looked at the battlefield..then back to his friends. He couldn't fight this alone..not a chance in hell. He would be killed. He turned to the Raitterran he'd been fighting and asked,"What's your name?"

The Raitteran responded," Gratho. Gratho
Okami, of the Raiterran Okami family."

Jericho shouted,"My name is Jericho.
Remember it. Perhaps someday we will fight again."

The Raitteran nodded. Jericho had said his
piece..and there was no way even he could survive
all of this. So, reluctantly..he ran with his friends to
retreat from the battle.

Chapter 24- Jigoku

Freyala decided now was not the time for war. With the insanity that was the Dragons and Phoenixes attacking, they decided it's time to negotiate a temporary peace. To fight a common foe: the dragons and phoenixes. But whom to start with? Han suggested his own people, of Jigoku. Akemi agrees and decides to accompany him. The Freyalan king agreed under one condition: the foreigners go with them. So now here they are.

It was all very funny for Shakira, as the politics of it all was confusing but she mostly followed it. They'd been taking more than a couple days to reach their destination, the capital of Jigoku: Dai Kaiju. Apparently named after a legendary dragon that had attacked them once, himself named Kaiju.

They were now walking in the lands of Jigoku..and Shakira realized why the people were lava element users. The lands they walked on were covered in lava, with certain paths designated for people to walk on and to live in. The building structures were sturdy and powerful looking. Shakira found it funny that according to their map, they'd at one point passed a city called "hahahahahaha".

Han had said,"there was a time when Jigoku was known for its sense of humor. Sadly that was a long time ago. But perhaps it's time they learned about those days again. The Jigoku people used to be allies to everyone, so it's awfully strange that in recent years they've been fighting Freyala, very peculiar even considering their long history of allyship."

After much more walking, they reached the capital. They entered and Shakira noticed the architecture was interesting. It was strong, sturdy but anytime they entered inside of buildings, it was extremely beautiful and welcoming. Mixes of reds, oranges, shades of black and white, but in a blend that was calming and peaceful.

Max turned to Shakira and said,"It's beautiful...isn't it?"

Shakira nodded,"Very beautiful! Yep,yep,yep!"

Jericho looked around. He saw paintings of the warriors over the years of Jigoku and said,"Definitely some powerful fighters by the looks of their paintings."

Leon nodded,"I like their taste in music they are playing. Strong, but almost..happy."

Shakira nodded and said,"But something...doesn't feel right."

Max asked,"what do you mean? I don't sense anything."

Leon said,"Me neither."

Shakira,"it's not exactly this building specifically..it's something..elsewhere. Elusive."

Jericho smirked,"Don't worry about it then. There's no reason to worry over something if you don't even know what it is."

Max shook his head,"I disagree. The fact only you sense it means it might be something that you specifically need to worry about...at the least." When they entered the palace, the King of Jigoku recognized them and said,"Come forward, traitor."

Han shrugged,"I am no traitor to my people. My people betray themselves, my king. Why is it that you fight the Freyalan people in this war? You used to be a happy people. Allied to everyone. What happened?"

King of Jigoku responded,"War happened. Many of our people since then have died to Freyalan soldiers."

Han nodded,"And what started the war?"

The King of Jigoku growled,"What does that matter? The point is, we've been at war with Freyala for many years now, and some simple words won't change that!"

Han sighed,"I know that. But did you not hear of what happened in Aine? The Dragons of old are back..and they've brought a war with the Phoenixes into our lands. This isn't a time for us all to be fighting each other...and let me ask..do you even remember what started the war?"

The King sighed,"I'd heard the rumors...but I wasn't sure if they were true.

Akemi replied,"We were there to see it for ourselves..the rumors are true. The Dragons and Phoenixes fight in Aine even now, as we speak."

The King continued,"In truth.I don't know what started the war between Freyala and Jigoku. Not many of my people do."

Han replied,"That gives even more reason why this fighting should cease...if you don't remember why we are even fighting, isn't it kind of pointless to keep doing so?"

Suddenly a large growl happened, the source of which was unclear.

The King replied,"...that...it's in the inner depths of the ground." Suddenly the king's eyes glowed and a voice spoke through his mouth..one that wasn't his own.

"The one called Shakira shall face me in the depths below. If anyone else comes, you fail this trial. Shakira, come alone. Face me and if you lose, I cannot guarantee the safety of the Jigoku people."

Shakira was surprised by this challenge. But her feelings told her..this was what the bad feeling before was about. If this would help the peace between Freyala and Jigoku..she had to try. "I'll go."

Max responded,"It's an obvious trap! Take one of us with you!"

Shakira shook her head,"No. I will go alone. If I die or something and don't return by tomorrow, you may come all at once and do what you want. But let me try to face this enemy on his terms. Trust me Max..I can do this. This is the kinds of reasons we trained for so long, right? Believe in me!"

Max nodded,"alright Shakira. Just please don't die."

The King pointed to behind his thrown as a doorway opened. Shakira entered the doorway and went down a long staircase..soon people behind here were distant as she descended further and further into the depths below.

As she finished walking, she stopped before a gigantic monkey. The monkey was probably about

15 feet tall while on all fours. Lava dripped from his mouth. It spoke.

"I am the origin of all of the lava elemental magic used by the Jigoku people. They originally learned it from me, and I learned it from the great elemental wolf of Shogun. It is I that decided that we should begin our war with Freyala. So I subconsciously sent that desire to our people. Too long did the Jigoku people pacify their enemies through humor. It's insulting. Such great warriors, never using their strength for war. It made me angry..but I didn't realize how angry it truly made me..until the day Jigoku and all the other countries of shotgun were defeated in the great war. I knew..it was time for war."

Shakira replied,"You have the same voice as before..it was you speaking through the king. But you are wrong..making people laugh and smile isn't a weakness..it's Jigoku's greatest strength!"

The monkey growled,"Enough! Summon Uriel! I sensed via my telepathy that he is your summon. The two of you will face me. If you win, I will listen to you. If I win...I will kill you..and the dead don't need to know what happens after that."

The monkey growled and made noises as he charged Shakira. She dodged as she put the magic into her hands and said,"I call for to thee, URIEL!" And her Monkey was summoned, but this time he was the size of the monkey she was fighting!

Shakira,"You've gotten big, haven't you Uriel?"

Uriel responded,"ha-ha. Almost sounds like a fat joke, girl."

Shakira gave him a look and he shook,"S-sorry! Please don't hurt me again Shakira! I'll be a good boy!"

Shakira smiled,"that's what I thought. Uriel, we have a bad monkey to defeat! Ready?"

Uriel nodded,"Sure thing! Let's do this!"

The enemy monkey sent lava at Shakira. Shakira blocked it with her wind element which caused it to turn into ash and peacefully fall downwards, due to the strength of what was used. She then sent a lightning bolt at the enemy monkey, shocking it! She pointed to Uriel and he summoned a spear made of pure light and he began throwing it at the enemy monkey, but the enemy monkey blocked it with his lava.

Shakira formed lighting around her fists, like she had during the dragons fight and began punching the enemy monkey, but he seemed to be tanking the attacks and swung his fists back at her but Uriel was punching the enemy monkey's fists away from Shakira to protect her while she continued sending lightning punches at him!

The Monkey growled and sent a gigantic torrent of lava all over the ground around them, obviously trying to drown both his enemies in pure lava! Uriel flew into the air and kept Shakira on his back as the Lava continued flooding the entire area!

The Enemy monkey growled and swung his fists at Shakira and Uriel but they blocked it!

The enemy monkey formed a gigantic sword made of lava and begun swinging it down, but Uriel blocked it with his light speer!

Shakira used wind element to fly in mid-air as she jumped off of Uriel's back. She then flew quickly from side to side so quickly it sent a gust of wind towards the enemy monkey's right side, a blaze of fire at the monkey's center, and a bunch of lightning at the monkey's left side..all at the same time! The monkey couldn't block all of them at once and was hit by it!

It damaged him greatly but the monkey wasn't defeated yet! It growled as it howled loudly. It caused it to hurt Shakira's ears as she was thrown off balance and was falling! Uriel caught her and put her on his back.

"You'll pay for hurting my master!", Uriel said. He lifted his finger and a series of various light spears appeared all around the enemy Lava monkey. They swiftly all hit him from all sides and rapidly did tons upon tons of damage to the enemy lava monkey! Uriel did it again, and it hit the monkey! Uriel then did it a third time, as they kept hitting the lava monkey again and again and again!

The enemy lava monkey fell to the ground as the lava he'd been pooling onto the ground turned to ash and solidified. He'd been beaten! But more importantly..the bags under its eyes faded.

Uriel shook Shakira awake and she said,"Y-you beat it? Thanks, Uriel!"

Uriel smiled,"No Problem, master Shakira. Let's just say we beat him together, as far as I'm concerned."

The enemy lava monkey yawned and said,"The light speers you sent at me..I feel like I've awoken from a long sleep. I...i don't know what came over me. It was like a dark magic had hit me..so long ago. And I've seen the light."

Shakira smiled,"Dark World has that affect on people. I guess even you ancients didn't all realize what had happened to this land! Uriel and I are happy to have shown you the light!"

The monkey nodded,"I'm...sorry for all the trouble I've caused the people of Jigoku..and I'm glad to have had this issue resolved."

****

Max and the others had heard about the battle Shakira had gone through merely days ago..and it was crazy to believe..but they all decided to believe her. Also, word had reached Raiterra of Freyala and Jigoku forming an alliance to hopefully prepare for the threat of the Dragons and phoenixes. A message is relayed of this fact to Raiterra, which makes them realize they couldn't fight both Jigoku and Freyala at once..so Raiterra states they agree to the alliance as well and had sent out a messenger to confirm it. Hearing this relieved Max, as he was glad to know things were going so well.

The dragons and phoenixes are fighting in Aine, so that would be the place of the battlefield, when the time comes. The thing was..could they win? What were they going to do? He'd been training with Heliopolis..and Jericho with Goron, as well as Leon with Lucian. But would that be enough?

As Max pondered on this, two men entered his room.

Max smiled. "Brokk...Cael. Man is it good to see you two again. How was your fights with Harding and Nrath?"

Brokk looked at the ground and said,"...let's just say we won."

Cael smirked,"Yeah. We'll tell the details another time."

Max replied,"the two of you came at a perfect time actually. You've probably heard..the Country of Aine has a war between Phoenixes and Dragons happening in the middle of it..and you two have been slaying dragons like crazy. Sure could use your help. Especially with this Abraxas figure."

Brokk looked very serious,"Did you say...Abraxas?"

Max nodded,"Yeah...why?"

Brokk replied,"Abraxas is where our power to slay dragons largely comes from. He gave such powers to Cael and I....I'm not sure if we even can beat him ourselves...or if we even should. We..sort of owe him our lives, considering."

Max frowned,"Considering the people who are dying out there in Aine right now..that's not very assuring. So what..are you just going to leave it to us then while you sit on the sidelines? You've been killing dragons all this time anyways, what's the difference? Just because he's bigger?!"

Brokk frowned,"No...he's more than just bigger. He's a totally different level of power."

Cael responded,"There are Phoenixes out there too, though...and other dragons aside from him. I'm sure we can find some way to be of use out there Brokk."

Brokk sighed,"Perhaps. This just makes me very..uncomfortable."

Cael laughed,"If it makes you uncomfortable, then I like it. But that might just be because I like messing with you."

Max sighed. These two hadn't changed..but this wasn't the time for jokes as far as he was concerned. Still...they needed any help that they could get, and he was glad this meant these two would still be helping out. Max thought about it...it was possible maybe, for Heliopolis and Goron to win right?

There'd be a great risk involved, however. Max just got an idea. If Max poured enough magic into his summon..he could summon Heliopolis at his true size. He'd discovered this while training with Raven. Heliopolis was far bigger than before..truly a huge summon but what if Max pushed it even further?

What if he used the majority of his own magic..and stored some extra of his own magic in some way..therefore doubling the power of his summoning spell? In theory...Heliopolis would be bigger and stronger..perhaps even the size and strength of Mangrielle! And of course..if this idea worked..Jericho could do the same with Goron to try to fight Abraxas! Maybe..it might work. It'd probably take the runological knowledge of Shakira..mixed with the potions knowledge of Knoll..but perhaps..it was possible.

Max went into the next room and told Jericho of his idea. Jericho and Max were currently sharing a bedroom to sleep in while using two separate bunk beds. Jericho had top bunk, because Max preferred bottom bunk and Jericho didn't really have a preference. Such things reminded Max of when Leon was his old roommate. In any case, as expected he found Jericho sitting on a chair in their room. Max immediately blurted out his idea to Jericho.

Jericho immediately smiled and said,"Fuck yeah! That sounds awesome!" He gave Max a nooggie and said,"That's a very smart idea! Let's do it!"

Max pushed Jericho off of him and said,"Yeah, just let me tell Shakira next."

Jericho nodded,"No problem! I'll be right here when you need me!"

Max then left the bedroom and headed for Shakira and Leon's room. He knocked and saw Shakira was in the room alone.

He said,"Got a moment?"

Shakira nodded,"Sure thing!"

Max said,"Shakira..you're good with carving runes into our weapons and equipement..I was wondering..could your runes be used to amplify our summoning spells?"

Shakira thought for a moment and said,"...Yes, I think it could. But it kind of depends on what you use it for. Why?"

Max said,"I have an idea. You know those Phoenixes and Dragons out there?"

Shakira nodded,"Mhm!"

Max replied,"Well, I have a phoenix and Jericho has a dragon. If we could in some way use the same technique we used to summon them at their true sizes..but with even MORE magic..we could probably give them more size and more power..making them on par with the Golden Dragon Abraxas and Mangrielle..at least, in theory."

Shakira nodded,"My runes could help with that, but it wouldn't be enough for THAT. You'd need some sort of po- you're going to ask Knoll for help too, aren't you?"

Max nodded,"You've always been pretty sharp, Shakira. Yes...next I'm going to be asking Knoll to help with our plan. Leon's your roommate, so feel free to pass the message along to him if you see him, okay?"

Shakira smiled,"Sure thing! I'll need some time to figure out what I should carve for the runes part of this plan anyways!"

Max nodded,"No problem! Hey I just thought about something..you got to defeat that ancient lava monkey..and next Jericho is going to try to defeat the leader of the Dragons and I'm going to try to beat the leader of the Phoenixes..it's like we're all having trials of sorts!"

Shakira laughed,"Yep, it's pretty much just like that! But that means Leon, Knoll, and Zack should have trails of some sort too! It's only fair, right?"

Max nodded,"That reminds me...so long ago, it wasn't just the six of us..well plus Brokk and Cael and for a time Raven. I really hope Connor, Jared, Tim..and the others. I really hope they are okay. Camp 2, as Mortas called them. They were said to be in almost as much danger as us. Middle of a scorching hot desert and all. It's been so long since

I've seen any of them. I assume Camp 3, as Mortas
called it are okay...but even them I have no way to
be sure. I just..I kind of miss all of our old friends-"

Shakira looked down at the ground.

Max went wide-eyed and said,"I'm so sorry!
I...I made you think about Joey didn't I?"

Shakira sighed,"It's-It's okay, Max. That's in
the past..and I know we have to be strong and move
forward for now. We all have each other..and we
gotta make the most of that for now."

Max offered Shakira a hug with his arms
outstretched and she accepted it as they both
hugged.

Max responded,"On a different subject..I'm
glad Freyala, Jigoku, and Raiterra formed that
alliance. We could probably use the extra help with
the Dragons and Phoenixes fighting out there. OH!
And Brokk and Cael are back too!"

Shakira half smiled,"No sign of Raven yet,
though, huh?"

Max shook his head,"He's still long gone,
sadly. But that's okay. I think we can still do this!"

Max waved goodbye for now and headed for
Zack and Knoll's room. Zack was in there, but no
sign of Knoll.

Max remarked,"Where's Knoll at?"

Zack sighed,"I tried to stop him..but he went
off on his own. He said he needed time to clear his
head. He headed for a nearby forest and insisted
nobody follow him. I don't know what he's thinking.

He made me swear not to tell anyone..which I only sort of half promised. I agreed that I wouldn't tell anyone until they asked. You asked, so I'm telling."

Max sighed,"Brilliant. It's dangerous out there and it's not like we have any way of knowing for sure if we can find him. Come on Zack. You and I are going to go looking for him. You decided to half keep it secret..so you should be the one to help me go find him. I'll write a letter and leave it in this room, in case anyone wonders where he went."

****

Knoll had to clear his head. There was too much going on at once, at too rapid of a pace. It was overwhelming his emotions. He was angry, scared, and any number of things all at once. Not that he was willing to admit it to everyone. Besides..it's not like himself and Zack had any summons to help bail them out of trouble!

Max had his Phoenix, Jericho his Dragon and so on. What did they have? Nothing but the magic of their own and HOPING they'd survive. That fact also made him angry...especially with the massive attack that happened in Aine. It was insane and almost as crazy was hearing Shakira tell of how she and Uriel defeated the lava monkey. It was all just insane!

Maybe that was the problem.. dark world was still affecting Knoll. But that's illogical..his parents had always raised him to think of things intellectually, and it just wasn't smart to let your emotions cloud your judgment..dark world or not. So here he was, going for a walk. He felt like the fresh air might do him some good...at least, that's what he'd thought before. But now..he was lost in the middle of a Freyalan forest, with no idea how to get back!

Knoll was disappointed in himself. He was better than this! Then he saw something in the distance..at first it appeared to be a lion. But it had multiple heads..the head of a goat and the head of a dragon were beside its head..and it's tail..was a snake. Dragon-like wings protruding from its back.

'A chimera!', thought Knoll.

The Chimera turned and noticed him and a spell circle formed under it. Suddenly a gust of wind was sent at Knoll! He easily blocked it with his own wind magic! The Chimera then had it's dragon head breath flames at him! Knoll again, easily deflected it with his own fire magic!

The Chimera spoke as it said,"It would seem we are evenly matched, young sorcerer."

Knoll responded,"Sure looks that way."

The Chimera said,"I have 3 riddles for you. To pass the time..won't you answer them?"

Knoll shrugged,"...sure. Say them."

The Chimera nodded,"First Riddle- The man who invented it doesn't want it. The man who bought it doesn't need it. The man who needs it doesn't know it. What is it?"

Knoll paused and thought for a moment. Doesn't want it. Bought it doesn't need it. Needs it doesn't know it. He then answered,"a coffin."

The Chimera smiled,"Correct! Second riddle- Number 8549176320 is unique. Why is it unique?"

Knoll paused and thought it over. He then replied,"All numbers 0-9 appear in alphabetical order and once."

The Chimera replied,"Correct! My Third and final riddle-I turn polar bears white and I will make you cry. I will make men have urinated and girls comb their hair. I make the famous look stupid and normal people look famous. I turn pancakes brown and make your whine bubble. If you squeeze me, I'll pop. If you look at me, you'll pop. Can you guess the riddle?"

Knoll thought for a long, long time. This one wasn't like the other two..there was some kind of trick to it sure..but a different one. But the problem was..the riddle made no sense! He sighed and responded,"No."

The Chimera smiled and said,"Correct!"

Knoll looked at the Chimera dumbfounded..thought about it..and figured it out.

He remarked,"The end of the riddle was asking if I could solve it..and the correct answer was no. A paradox. Very strange."

The Chimera responded,"Thank you for heeding my riddles..now resign yourself to oblivion."

Knoll saw that a circle was under him that was meant to force him in place, however, another circle had formed, preventing it as he used wind magic to levitate off of the ground.

Knoll responded,"I noticed you were preparing a trap spell on me while you were asking your riddles..a clever distraction, but one I saw coming. I was preparing a counter spell of my own at the same time, that would cancel out yours. More than just that, though..I had cast an additional spell you hadn't noticed while we were doing our riddles."

The Chimera began choking,"Y-you turned the rocks around me from a solid to a gas! You have matter transfiguration spells!" he continued coughing,"I-I give up. Spare me and I will declare myself your familiar!"

Knoll snapped his fingers and the gas turned into a puddle of liquid. He'd outsmarted the Chimera..and now it was his.

The Chimera nodded,"I will honor my word...I am now your familiar and I will obey your every command."

Knoll smiled but then suddenly collapsed to the ground. He saw visions...first of...himself? No..not himself..but he saw it as if it was himself! He had long flowing red hair and he was slicing down phoenixes..then a blur and he was..having sex with Syanne? Strange...then a blur and he was fighting alongside Allanon! Then a blur and he was slaughtering wizards! Then suddenly information overloaded into his brain..spell knowledge from generations and generations of wizards..it was over-whelming!

The Chimera approached him and placed its paw on his chest and suddenly his brain returned to normal. He got up and asked the Chimera,"What happened?"

The Chimera responded,"Your mind..it was being flooded with information. Had I not stopped it, you would have gone brain-dead. It would appear you have someone else's memories. Someone that is not your own. I've heard of such a spell before..it killed a man, but his memories live on in the mind of a friend of his. It was like two minds occupying one body. You have the memories of someone called Alexander..any idea who that might be?"

Knoll went wide eyed," Sort of. My friends Max, Jericho, Shakira and Leon...and our nurse, Anna...they were all Alexander in a past life! Does that mean..I am too?"

The Chimera shook his head,"No.That does explain a lot however...its not normal for one to simply reincarnate without some sort of extreme circumstances..let alone reincarnate into multiple people at once. The memories must have also been removed..but such memories don't just disappear..they either live on in the same person..or as seems to be the case with your mind...they had to go somewhere.

"So they went into your mind..or more likely, the mind of one of your ancestors. It was passed down, from generation to generation, until they could someday be unlocked. And you were the unlucky one for them to unlock into. I can seal off Alexander's mind from your own..but I can also allow you access to his memories..but only small bits at a time, and it will cause great stress to your mind so I don't ever recommend it. You are lucky I am your familiar, human. I will be able to keep your mind safe."

Knoll sighed,"That's reliving and all...but I'm also lost in this forest."

The Chimera smiled,"I can help with that. I looked into your mind when I touched your chest. I know the way back from whence you came and can lead you there."

Upon reaching the front of the forest, there was Max and Zack, who had begun looking for him. He quickly told them the story of what had happened with the Chimera..as he didn't want them to try to attack it. They accepted his story quickly..and Max, in turn, told him of the plan he had for powering up his summon of Heliopolis and for Jericho when he'd next summon Goron. Knoll nodded.

Knoll replied,"The plan may work, but you'll definitely need a buffer from one of my potions..and some sort of rune from Shakira."

Max responded,"I know. I told Jericho first, and I told Shakira before I told you."

Knoll nodded,"I'm prepared to attempt the potion, but it'll take time. Almost makes me miss the idea of Wands. I often wish I'd had one."

Max sighed,"Take the time you need, but please don't take too long..I've heard word that people in Aine are dying due to all of this."

Knoll nodded,"I'll try Max, I'll try."

Chapter 25- the Wolf

It was time for the joint meeting of armies. At the forefront, were the foreigners. That's what everyone was calling them anyways, and Leon didn't see a reason to correct them. Leon just figured it was a good name as any, considering that even now they hadn't fully explained where they came from..and it honestly didn't matter yet. For now, it was still about building allies and potential friends.

Apparently, from what Leon and the others had been hearing..the locals were shocked at how well these "foreigners" had done against the Raiterran armies. You see, Freyala was one of the most powerful armies sure..but even they couldn't fight the Raiterran armies with only six people.

Raiterrans were known for priding themselves on their great power..that's what made it ironic that the most powerful Raiterran family was the Okami's...originally a family from Freyala that had simply had a cousin move to Raiterra and start his own branch generations ago. Worst of all, the Freyalan branch had been nearly wiped out..with only Akemi as the sole survivor..and the Raiterran branch had surrendered to the North Capital's troops.

Akemi walked forward. He no longer had to hide..he was now the pride of the Freyalan armies for having "Found" the foreigners. He was the head general of the Freyalan armies in this alliance. He was their representative, in other words. It was time to meet whom Jigoku had chosen for theirs, and whom Raiterra had chosen for theirs.

Gratho entered the room. Jericho had briefly fought Gratho. Leon nodded. Gratho Okami...and Akemi Okami. He wondered what seeing these two meet would be like..and now he'd find out.

Gratho nodded,"Akemi. I don't care what they say about you among Freyala. You have my respect. You defeated Makoto, and are the only survivor the 3 warriors who beat him. When the Northern Capital attacked...you fought. My branch of the family did not. I've been fighting each day so that our branch of Okami could restore our honor..and be half the man you are."

Well...Leon hadn't expected that to be his response to meeting Akemi.

Akemi smiled,"Thanks.I guess. That was so many years ago..people feared me. I represent a resistance to the Northern Capital..if the King of the North finds out I live..he may bring his armies upon us all."

Gratho growled,"Let him. I'm sick of my fellow Raiterrans cowering in fear of him..and I think they are growing tired of it too."

The next person to enter was Han...representing Jigoku.

Akemi nodded,"That explains a lot. Good to see you have gained favor back with your people, old friend."

Han laughed,"It feels good to no longer be called a traitor...though I know this alliance between our three countries might or might not last."

Gratho smiled,"Han..is it true you are a descendant of Alger, the legend?"

Han laughed even more than previous. "Yes..he's my ancestor. But enough about all these formalities..we're here to come up with a plan. That's why we have one of the foreigners here in the room with us..isn't it?"

Leon the noticed people were staring at him. Guess it was his time to speak up.

Leon cleared his throat and spoke,"Yes. Currently...I'm the only one available right now because everyone else is preparing for the battle ahead."

Gratho frowned,"I'd hoped to see the man called Jericho. He fought valiantly against me. I respect that."

Leon replied,"Well, sorry but I'm not him. But I still am here to represent my friends so you'll have to respect me all the same."

Han replied,"But by the sounds of it..you foreigners DO have a plan of some kind, correct?"

Akemi nodded in agreement,"I would assume you all do..I saw two of your friends enter..I hear rumors of them everywhere...Brokk and Cael..the dragonslayers."

Gratho's eyes widened as he said,"...DRAGON....SLAYERS?! Dear God!"

Akemi laughed,"Which one?"

Gratho growled,"Don't change the subject."

Han responded,"Speaking of not changing the subject...Sir Leon..what plan do your friends have?"

Leon nodded as he paused to think of the right words to use. Should he tell them what he'd heard? They needed some kind of hope to cling onto..so he might as well.

Leon replied,"We may have a way to kill both Abraxas and Mangrielle."

Gratho laughed,"Absurd! No human has ever killed a Golden Dragon nor a Zizix..it simply cannot be done! Not either one..let alone both at the same time!"

Leon nodded slowly and said,"Max can summon a phoenix named Heliopolis. Jericho can summon a red dragon named Goron. With the help of Knoll and Shakira...they might have a way to increase the power and size of their summons..to match that of Abraxas and Mangrielle."

Gratho huffed,"Might. There's the keyword, isn't there? Even if I humor you and say there really COULD be a possibility of this happening..which I'll add there isn't...you yourselves aren't completely sure of that! We can't base our entire battle strategies over something that MIGHT happen."

Leon replied,"then don't. That's what we'll be doing. If it succeeds, Jericho will deal with Abraxas, and Max will deal with Mangrielle. Thier summons will help them do so. The rest of us will deal with the Phoenix and Dragons that remain..with Brokk and Cael there to back us up. You all can do whatever you please during that..you don't have to base any of your battle strategies off of us at all..just do whatever you want during the battle."

Akemi smirked,"He's got a good point Gratho. We really don't have anything better..no strategy we could possibly come up with can account for ever having a chance of killing Abraxas or Mangrielle. So we might as well just do what we can to fight everything else and hope Max and Jericho can cover it. If not..we'll all be dead anyways. And that's true even if we were doing this on our own...because I doubt any of our people are willing to leave their homelands behind."

Gratho shook his head,"No...there's one thing you all haven't considered. There is one other option."

Han gasped and said,"...NO. You don't mean..."

Gratho replied,"Why not? Do you really think him just a legend? This lady Shakira has proven that the Monkey isn't just a myth..so then surely the Wolf is real too!"

Leon inquired,"Akemi..what does he mean?"

Akemi paused and after several moments he spoke up. "The tale is hard to remember as its been retold with many different versions over the years..but they say that those of us from the lands of Shogun learned our elemental magic from creatures..for a few examples, in Jigoku it was a monkey who taught the original swordsmen their lava.
    "In Freyala, it was a raven who taught their original swordsman wind...and in Aine, it was Abraxas himself who taught their original swordsmen fire..when he was far younger. But the tale goes that these creatures themselves, aside from Abraxas at least, were artificially created...born from one creature..a male Wolf who cast a spell that created

each of them. This Wolf could manipulate every element and was more powerful than all of the creatures he created. They say he went into hiding in fear of Abraxas..others say he left because he didn't want to become involved in human affairs any further..who knows?

"The point Gratho is making..is that we now know the Monkey is indeed real...so the Wolf probably is as well...and if we turned to him in some way...we could use him to try to defeat Abraxas and Mangrielle. But even if that were true..how do we know he could? One version of the story even believes he was too scared to fight Abraxas!"

Gratho laughed,"I doubt that. The Wolf..itself a creature powerful enough to create life itself..including the Dragon/Tiger Hybrid..the Driger..the creature that is the source of Raiterra's lightning...why would something so powerful ever fear a single dragon?"

Han sighed,"Chasing some legend sounds foolish at a time like this."

Gratho growled,"Again, the Monkey is real, so the Wolf must be too! The Wolf helped the people of Shogun before..he can help us again, now that we really need him!"

Leon interrupted,"Max and Jericho and the others will be taking awhile to prepare anyways. If Zack and I go searching for this Wolf...and our quest in some way fails...we go with the plan to use Max and Jericho. If we succeed, we use the Wolf. Sound fair? All in favor?"

Gratho smiled,"Aye."

Akemi and Han looked to each other and had a long pause before both also saying,"aye."

****

Jared smiled. Himself, Connor, Ikuto and Simon had taken out 5 major settlements of Orcs so far. Things were going quite well. His smile turned to a half-frown however. This was too easy. Something was going to go wrong..he knew it. It just how things are..just their luck. Something was going to go wrong, and he was just kind of waiting for it.

Connor did the usual, as he shouted,"Ugly Orc bastards! Come out and fight us!"

As he did so, the hill above them showed a few Orcs coming down...then a few more. Then over 200 more...then another 200..then they seemed to number more than a thousand. There were way more Orcs at this outpost than they'd expected, and among them were some riding Jackaloves ...

Jared sighed,"Yep... I was right. I knew it."

Ikuto replied,"No use bitching about it, let's just fight."

Jared shrugged. Ikuto had a point. Jared then shouted as he grew to his 30-foot tall version of himself and began sending torrents of lava at the Orcs as they started falling.

Ikuto formed a flame sword and began using his newfound abilities to slice through waves and waves of Orcs. Simon was using his abilities to tank through objects, but he sometimes was getting hit by maces. That was his biggest thing..he could handle cut damage just fine.he was essentially immune to it, but blunt force attacks was a different story. Soon enough, his brother Ikuto was half defending him in between fighting for himself.

Connor did his usual of forming a flame sword in one hand and a lightning sword in the other hand and was slicing through Orcs as they'd catch on fire or become electrocuted with each swing he swung. But the Orcs continued coming and coming!

It didn't matter however..it was kill or be killed and though they were greatly outnumbered..more and more Orcs were still coming!

Jared shouted as he sent massive pools of lava at the Orcs, defeating entire rows of Orcs at once, only for more to take their place and attack him as well, they sliced at his legs, which caused cuts and he fell onto one knee from the blood. He then formed a bit of fire into his hand and cauterized the wound to seal it from bleeding. He then formed an earth pillar and sent it at some of the Orcs. That's one thing he'd learned.

Lava element was simply a mix of Earth and Fire. Once you know that..you realize one key thing- Jared could also use Earth Element and Fire Element attacks. He then stuck his hands at the dirt and formed armor made of the earth around him. It wasn't much, but it could provide some protection for his skin to prevent some of the damage. He was immune to his own lava anyways..though his friends weren't so he still had to be somewhat careful.

Connor dissipated his swords and created a bow made of lightning and began shooting arrows of lightning at Orcs, taking them down in waves. Seemed Connor was going more for ranged moves now.

Jared, who was still 30 feet tall, formed a giant stone axe and made the blades of it created from lava itself. He then used the gigantic axe to swing at Orcs and defeat them in massive waves. In between swings of his axe, he'd send small bits of lava to take out a few rows of Orcs at time, but like usual it seemed like anything he'd beaten would be replaced by even more Orcs!

Connor was suddenly about to get swung at from behind. Jared shouted,"Connor! Behind you!"

Connor changed his lightning bow back into a lightning sword and deflected the very tall black Orc's swing but the Orc seemed to be especially tolerant to the strikes!

Connor replied,"So this is the great black Orc I've heard rumors about."

Jared hadn't heard any rumors, but Connor could be telling the truth for all he knew.

The two began swinging back and forth. Jared realized that he would be causing Connor to have his full attention to be on that Black Orc. Jared needs to watch Connor's back while he was fighting. So Jared shrunk back down to normal size, as he didn't want to accidentally hit Connor. Jared still created a smaller version of the Axe he'd been using and began attacking any Orcs who looked like they were going to attack Connor while Connor was busy.

Jared shouted,"You focus on the Black Orc Connor, I got your back!"

Connor nodded as he continued his attack on the Black Orc, as they continued colliding blades, but eventually Connor got in a lucky swing and sliced the Orc's head clean off, with a violent electrocution shock due to Connor's sword being made of pure lightning.

Meanwhile, Ikuto and Simon were still picking off what was left of the Orcs, striking them down and using flame attacks and their unique attack styles they'd recently learned from Argos and Yuji respectively until eventually, the Orcs were all beaten for now.

Jared sighed,"I don't know about you guys...but I could use a break before we head for any other Orc settlements.

Connor laughed,"I'm with you, Jared. Let's go back to the Southern Kingdom and give them a progress report."

****

Leon and Zack continued their hike. They were headed for Fin'eowyn. Fin'eowyn normally would've been cautious of foreigners..but they stated they wished to remain on good terms with Freyala and thus would accept any "non-hostile expeditions lead by archaeologist-adventurers."..and basically said that as long as they stayed private and secretive and didn't attract much attention.

They could use that as their excuse for why they were there. It was a case that if caught doing anything suspicious the royal family of Fin'eowyn would use plausible deniability and deny any involvement.

Not the best way to enter a country, but it's what Leon and Zack had to work with.

Zack sighed as grabbed his jug of water and drank from it and then refilled it with his own Water element magic. "Guess I'll have to be careful with what I use when we get there. I here theirs many pools of water throughout Fin'eowyn, but most of it isn't drinkable due to the dark magic pollution."

Leon nodded,"Funny thing, I heard that even when the people of Shogun fought the south in the great war..they were the only armies among the North that didn't use Dark Magic."

Zack sighed,"So why do they say the Wolf would be in Fin'eowyn anyways?"

Leon shrugged,"I still don't know. That's just what the books we found in the Freyalan Libraries all pointed to. Mostly folklore and mythology so who knows if it's even true? It also suggested he might be in Auron, but it's best to look here first since Auron closed off its borders and won't interact with us. Guess we'll start with Aquaria. It's the first city we hit while here in Fin'eowyn and-"

Leon suddenly heard a voice in his mind. *I'm not there, but you are quite close.*

Leon replied,"...I think the Wolf is speaking to me telepathically."

Jee, what gave you that idea? Of course, I am, dunderhead.

Leon, "...band... he just called me a dunderhead...."

Do you wish to face me or not? Head 3 miles due east and head for the cave at the end of the fork of the road on the left. Can't miss it. Come alone. If you bring this 'Zack' with you, I will kill everyone you hold dear...understood?

Leon replied,"sheesh. Awfully harsh. Alright..I got it. Sorry, Zack, I'll have to go this alone. I'll meet you later in Aquaria I guess."

Zack paused and then replied,"Well alright, I guess. I'll try to maintain a low profile while I'm there."

Leon enters the cave and hears loud stomping as he sees a 150 foot tall Wolf appear in front of him, and that was on all fours.

Leon remarks,"Okay...guess I should summon Lucian then."

He does so.

Lucian says,"What did I miss?" He then looks at the Wolf in front of him and says,"Ohholyshitdeargod."

Leon says,"Let's do this, partner."

Lucian says,"uh...eh, what the hell. You only live once."

Leon responds with sarcasm by saying,"Technically.. in my case.."

Lucian says,"Oh shut up that doesn't count!"

While they are arguing, the Wolf is simply standing on all fours watching them.

Leon turns to the Wolf and sends a magic missile straight at the head of the Wolf. Followed immediately by Leon forming flames and water in his hands to create steam to cover their tracks as they retreat in opposite directions.

The Wolf opens it's mouth and exhales using a wind-based magic shield deflects the magic missile somewhere harmless off to the side. The Wolf then follows up by stomping and causing a fissure in the center of where Leon and Lucian were previously. Luckily, he didn't know they'd already dodged.

Leon then casts a spell which performs one of the gothic rock songs his band used to play, but as a bardic magic spell that plays during the fight. Leon remarks,"Time for my theme music."

Leon continued firing magic missiles at the Wolf while using the steam to hide himself, while meanwhile Lucian is flanking him and trying to get in close.

The Wolf responds by spitting out lava at the area the magic missiles are coming from.

Leon responds,"well, shit." and formed a wall of water as he jumped out of the way as much as he could.

The Lava went through but sort of dissolved. While Leon was dodging, Lucian jumped at the left side of the Wolf and was about to doing an extreme scratch attack at it, however upon attempting to do so, he hits a wall of lightning and was briefly electrocuted. Lucian fell to the ground but got back up as he spat a bit of blood and said,"That tickled." though one can tell he was simply playing tough.

Leon caused a water spout to come outwards from under the Wolf's chin, almost like an uppercut. It connected against the wolf and caused it to briefly fall on it's back. Lucian sliced through its belly,

which left a deep scar in the wolve's stomach
however it got back up and knocked Lucian with its
paw covered in flames and the flaming Lucian was
knocked towards Leon.

Leon made a big wall of water, with two
layers. One that was slightly warm to cool off without
causing steam, Lucian..and the other layer to catch
Lucian. The first layer was bubbling also so it would
be less solid and more able to catch Lucian than
harm him, not missing a beat, Leon then retaliated
with a flurry of flame attacks straight towards the
Wolve's eyes. The Wolf turned into a gigantic bolt of
lightning and dodged the attack before then
solidifying and then sent a gust of wind full of cutting
strikes straight at Leon and Lucian.

Leon formed a wall of water to block it,
followed by flames to push it away, as he did so, the
Wolf sent bolts of lightning at the water wall. Leon
wasn't technically touching the water, so luckily this
didn't harm him, but it did evaporate the water over
time. Lucian seems to be alright, he's just got
burned fur.

Leon smirks,"You have seen better days."

Lucian responds,"Very funny. Let's focus on
the fight, shall we?"

Lucian ran forward as a cloud of steam was
used by Leon to cover his movements. However, the
wolf seems to be predicting this, and sends a gust of
wind at Lucian, hoping to both harm him and clear
the steam, however the wind is blocked by a water
wall which was quickly formed by Leon who then in
the moment of confusion sent an enormous amount
of arcane magic at the Wolf who was directly hit by
the strike. The Wolf took a lot of damage but seemed
to be still getting back up again!

Lucian however, was still running forward and using his special extreme scratching attack to slice at the Wolf, which caused it a ton of damage, which showed that Lucian had grown greatly in strength compared to the old days. But the Wolf, staggered but still got back up again and this time decided to attempt to send Wind, Water, some rocks, and fire all at Leon at once, while it sent a lightning attack that hit Lucian, electrocuting him.

Leon shot a high-powered bunch of water into the ground and dived into a hole, dodging the whole attack. He then used the water to push himself back out of the whole once the attack had passed however upon doing so, he saw himself face to face with the wolf who sent a lightning attack straight at Leon, who is hit by the lightning, and is electrocuted. But, Leon after being sent far backwards, managed to still get back up, and spat a little blood.

Leon remarked calmly with the word,"Ow."

The Wolf growled,"that was supposed to kill you!"

Leon used a huge pillar of fire heading straight down from the ceiling, plus a water gaizer from below heads for him and smashed the Wolf in between the fire and water elements. Leon didn't skip a beat as he sent many magic missiles all at the Wolf at once on top of that, causing the wolf to be paralyzed as it fell to the ground and barely able to speak said,"......You win."

Leon noded,"I'm glad. Let's talk. Would you be willing to help us to fight Abraxas and Mangrielle?"

The Wolf allowed a weak laugh as it said,"I've met Abraxas before....there was a time I could have beaten him. He was younger...but so was I. I'm far too old now..as he got older, he continued to get stronger. As I got older...I've been fighting just to stay as strong as I was in my prime. All things considered, I think I maintained my youth quite well..but alas, I'm not as strong as Abraxas. I could never defeat him. I know not about this Zizix...but I refuse to partake in worldly battles. In truth..the very idea that you sought me out brought out my primordial instincts...I blame the dark magic flooding this world...it made me hostile towards you. Though I guess I shouldn't make excuses...even to little shits like you. Just some little upstart who beat big old me...figures."

Leon sighed,"So...you can't help us?"

The Wolf shook its head slowly,"I cannot. But if ever I do decide to some day return to the world of mortals..I will tell them of the only human to have ever beaten me. Still..it's unlikely I'll ever show myself again. I prefer to be left alone. It's better this way. Mortals are better off without my influence giving them, even more, power to kill each other with...now if that's all you came for...which I'm sure it is...could you please leave me alone?"

Leon said,"Wait. I don't get any kind of reward out of this?"

The Wolf looked at him,"You get the reward of having beat someone as powerful as me."

Leon frowned,"I can't come back completely empty handed. You gave the people of Shogun elemental magic back in the day..so you surely can give me something. I've beaten you."

The Wolf sighed,"Fine. Lucian, wolf of Leon. Come forward."

Lucian did as told and the huge Wolf breathed onto him.

The Wolf replied,"Lucian, you now have some magic spells of your own. You can cast the elements of Wind, Water, Earth, Fire and Lightning...that's all I'm willing to offer. Now, will you both please leave me alone?"

Leon nodded and bowed respectfully as he said,"Alright, I'll take my leave."

He then headed for Aquaria, to break the bad news to Zack.

Upon arriving in Aquaria he saw beautiful castles off in the distance and many small buildings of various marble and concrete designs. Had the sky not been covered in darkness, this town would have been a very beautiful place to behold. He entered a tavern and saw Zack. He was surrounded by beautiful women had to be at least ten of them... who all were listening to him telling a tale.

Zack replied,"And that..is the story of based on the world where the mystic and the real merged, creating an imbalance in space-time in which the heroes were the only ones able restore the worlds back to their original forms. I had the book published back in my homeland..and though it is a work of fiction, I knew it would appeal to someone here."

Leon grinned as he said,"Come on, lover boy. We got to go back home."

Zack grinned as he said,"I can't help it. I tried to maintain a low profile but I needed something to pass the time, and I figured just telling a story or two wouldn't hurt. How as I supposed to know it'd be popular?"

Leon smiled,"I think you knew, but it's all good. I just don't want us to get into trouble."

Zack replied,"Speaking of which..how did it go?"

As they walked outside into the streets, Leon frowned. "I defeated it. But, he told me that he cannot help us. He says he isn't strong enough and that he doesn't like doing things for mortals anyways. He seems to blame himself for the people of Shogun using elemental magic against each other."

Zack nodded,"Who could blame him? In a way, he's the origin of it all."

Leon nodded,"Either way..it's pretty clear to me now. We'll have to hope Max and Jericho can come through for us..."

Chapter 26- Heliopolis and Goron's Fight /Jared's Dilemma

The time had come. Knoll had prepared a potion that would increase the magic capacity of Max and Jericho, albeit for a brief time. Shakira and Knoll jointly created a device. With Shakira's rune carvings placed into it, it could store all of the magic that Max and Jericho could place into one each of them. Max placed all of the magic he could into it, which with the potion he drank, was greater in amount than usual. Then it was sealed, and he needed a single day's rest to restore his magic. Jericho did the exact same thing with his copy of the device and his portion of the potion.

That had been yesterday..and now Max had hoped, that would be enough. The amount put into his summoning spell would be nearly three times its usual amount that he used to simply summon the full sized Heliopolis. If that didn't do it, nothing will.

As they went onto the battlefield, in a land about 100 miles outside of the City of Kratus, which was still inside the Country of Aine. It was east of the border where Freyala, Jigoku, and Aine meet. Which was Aine's western border.

A funny fact people hadn't often thought about: Phoenix and Dragons were considered equals who had fought each other for centuries..but why? The Dragons had roughly 6 different races, maybe more. They were equal in every way to the phoenixes...except they were physically a lot stronger, and their hides were physically a lot tougher, making it harder to kill them. But that's just it..such toughness and strength made them mostly slower than a phoenix...which often was a lot faster. But Phoenixes were also much more clever a lot of the time..meaning Phoenixs could outsmart them at times.

It was an age old battle of Brains vs Brawn, though not all the time as Phoenixes had different races and it could vary with them as well. Regardless..this battle was a return to form for the Phoenixes and Dragons...they were once again at war with each other, and the people of Shogun, or as it was currently called, people of Mu... knew it.

In the middle of the battlefield was a massive river, with Abraxas and Mangrielle still fighting each other above it. For some, it might be hard to see, due to the eternal night of Dark World..but to the Northeast, the grass was burned and charred, from all the fighting of the Phoenixes and Dragons that had been attacking one another.

The majority of the Dragons and Phoenixes were on that side of the large river, a river that went from this land, all the way down into the Sea, Southeast of all of Aine itself. For now, though, it was simply the dividing line between the lands that were burned by the fighting, and the lands that weren't yet. To the southwest of the river, was the part of the land that wasn't burned yet, and hardly any Dragons nor Phoenixes had crossed that line..likely out of respect for their leaders fighting over the river.

The River was wide enough that it would take a long time to go from one side to the other for humans..but was also narrow enough to be like a serpent like shape, cutting through the valley. The river was hence called, "Great Snake River". The water was crystal clear and flowed through it peacefully. The lands themselves were a valley surrounded by mountains.

Akemi was leading the Freyalan armies, Gratho was leading the Raiterran Armies, and Han was leading the Jigoku armies. They were Southwest of the River, all their joint armies standing side by side. They sent volleys of arrows enhanced by their own magic into the sky, it was hitting the dragons and phoenixes.. the sheer number of them made it very unclear how much damage was being done.

They could not stop, however, as lightning arrows, fire arrows and arrows with lava on them were being sent into the sky at the numerous phoenixes and dragons. The joint armies then had some of the dragons and phoenixes descend down upon them, attacking the humans while they fought each other.

Akemi saw before him as a phoenix that was several stories tall was fighting a red dragon, they clawed and growled at each other. Akemi formed wind across his blade and began attacking them both! As did the people of Freyala nearest to Akemi! The sheer chaos of the battlefield was to where it made it difficult to keep track of it all, but here now Akemi's focus was on that Dragon and Phoenix.

The Phoenix sent flames at Akemi, who dodge rolled and sliced upwards, only to need to dodge again due to the fire breath of the Dragon, but his dodge this time was timed just right to cause the flames to hit the Phoenix!

It screeched in fury and began clawing at the dragon further, but Akemi wasn't about to be ignored as he sent wind cuts through them both, slicing scars into the phoenix and the dragon, though the dragon's hide was much tougher than the Phoenix's feathers..meaning it was good his wind magic could compensate some. The Phoenix seemed to be slightly faster than the Dragon, though, and

Akemi was constantly having to use wind magic to amplify his speed..as he had many near misses where he could have been killed with a single swipe of the Phoenix or the Dragon both near him.

Cael had that new pet dragon he'd mentioned he wanted to get..he named it Epnir..this one a green dragon that was slender in build and moved very quickly. Brokk and Cael were already out there, fighting any Phoenixes and Dragons they could, fighting well into the burned side of the battlefield, as they were much bolder than the joint armies were being.

Cael slashed one dragon in two as he moved in perfect unison with Brokk who was also in the air slashing them down, with Brokk apparently using Wind Magic to keep up with Cael whom was riding his dragon.

Brokk shouted as he sliced through a Cryonix..the ice equivalent of a phoenix. Oh yes, there were those on this battlefield too..plenty of them. Brokk shouted using his dragonslayer magic that could be cast through his mouth and it took the Cryonix's head clean off!

Leon, Shakira, Zack and Knoll were fighting near the River, but on the burnt side. This put them as bolder than the joint armies, but not as deep into the battle as Brokk and Cael were.

Leon summoned Lucian and together they both began sending magical strikes towards the phoenixes and dragons. Leon smirked,"Glad that Wolf gave you some elements, Lucian."

Lucian nodded,"feeling's mutual." He began sending wind cutting strikes high into the air via his claws mixing with wind elemental magic.

Shakira summoned Uriel and said,"Ready to show the others what you learned recently?"

Uriel nodded,"Ready!" and he began shooting lava, in the same way the lava monkey they'd beaten had!

Knoll was riding his Chimera as lightning bolts came from his Chimera at the nearby foes, as apparently, the Chimera had lightning magic.

Zack began casting illusions everywhere that was causing Phoenixes to attack their own allies nearby and a wave of confusion was causing issues for them.

As the battle raged on, the joint armies were slowly advancing forward. They were still not yet at the river itself, as the Dragons and Phoenixes were starting to get bolder themselves and go towards the joint armies, even whilst there was the chaos of them fighting each other at the same time.

Abraxas and Mangrielle were too busy fighting each other to stop the humans, but both seemed angry at all that was transpiring!

Max had a green glowing energy around him as he activated the device.

Jericho too, had the same glowing energy around himself as he too activated his copy of the device.

It would take time to prepare their summons, so, for now, they would simply have to wait, hidden behind the joint armies of Raiterra, Freyala and Jigoku.

As they sat and meditated their magic was been further and further prepared for the great summons that would soon come. Meanwhile, the battle continued!

Leon formed a sword of arcane magic and Lucian formed a sword of lightning. They began sending spells at the dragons around them as they continued casting and swiping through dragon after dragon and phoenix after phoenix.

Shakira formed fire around her fists, as her muscles on her arms and legs temporarily grew in size... and she began punching through the feathers of the phoenixes, her strength so great it was taking them down! Shakria had come a long way since her old days of being afraid and weak..today she was a warrior!

She moved at alarming superhuman speeds as she punched and kicked through dragons and phoenixes, knocking them down with her massive strength, as she smirked,"I learned that spell just for such an occasion." One of the Cryonixes and one of the phoenixes..both massive creatures in their own right that were several stories tall each..both attacked Shakira at once! She dodged one strike from one and then sent her flaming fists to hit the beast, but it had no effect!

She used the fists on the Cryonix and it only helped some! However, the phoenix let down a tear and threw it at the cryonix..it had healing tears and could cry to heal the Cyronix's wounds! The Cryonix then let out a tear and had it send for Shakira, who instinctively dodged it as it landed on a nearby tree and the tree melted away!

The Cryonix clearly had poison tears instead of healing tears! She then formed a sword made of lightning and began swinging it at the phoenix in a way to get it to back off, as she used her free hand to send a massive gust of wind with cuts in the air at the Cryonix and it cut the beast into pieces as it screeched and died. She then sent flames at the ashes, burning them so it wouldn't ressurect! She'd been doing so throughout the battle thus far, knowing that having an enemy come back would be too costly...she hadn't a choice but to do things this way today.

Leon grabbed his sword and went toe to toe with one of the bigger dragons. It growled at him, and breathed fire. He doged rolled to the side and sliced at one of it's legs, but it growled and swiped its claws at him, yet again he rolled and sliced through another leg.

It breathed fire at him and this time he blocked it with a pillar of water as he sent it at dragon immediately after! The Dragon growled and flew into the skies, but he sent arcane magic at it in massive amounts and the dragon was hit by the attack and weakened...but not yet beaten! He then formed the pillar of water under his feet to take to the skies as he sent magic missiles at the beast, firing many of them at the dragon, while he stayed mobile via the pillar of water under his feet, moving quickly so the dragon couldn't hit him!

The Dragon contineud breathing bits of fire in various directions but he kept dodging! Then, the dragon breathed lightning at him but he descended a bit so that it went over his head as he then went for the underbelly of the dragon and sliced it down the middle, splitting the dragon in two!

Lucian growled, "Be sure to leave some for me, Leon!"

Leon sighed,"There's plenty more around..I'm sure that won't be a problem."

Indeed their were many more Phoenixes and Dragons..and by now the Joint armies were starting to be well into the thick of it!

Zack meanwhile, had a phoenix and a dragon fighting around him as well! He sent a pillar of earth at the dragon, knocking it off it's feet as he used his free hand to send a torrent of water at the Phoenix.

"Cool it!" he said as he hit the phoenix.

He'd gotten their attention, as they both ran for him, but he pulled out a sword made of water as he mixed it with lightning element and he sliced the dragon in two quickly, using it's weak underbelly to do so! He then cast an illusion spell that made it look like the Phoenix was surrounded by Dragons attacking it!

They weren't real however and this gave Zack an opening as he used his lightning sword to cut the Phoenix, but it quickly recovered and ignored the dragons this time as it sends gigantic burning flames at Zack!

He dodged and sent bolts of lightning that were covered in water at the beast, greatly hurting it! He then formed a gigantic illusion of a dragon, but the beast ignored it and went for him..big mistake as Zack himself was the illusion and the fake dragon was actually Zack himself, hiding within THAT illusion as it sent bolts of lightning, mixed with water, and bits of flame, and even a gigantic bunch of rocks..all at the Phoenix at once killing it! He then zapped the ashes, preventing it from coming back!

Zack calmly said,"Rest in peace...I'm sorry I had to end your life. But I must continue forward."

Knoll readied his bow and arrows made from wind and fire element mixed as he began firing them into the crowd of Phoenixes and dragons. Hopefully, the Wind Element could compensate for the Phoenixes and Dragons being very tolerant to flame attacks. Besides..Knoll, much like the other people of Camp 1..had much stronger flames than say the people of Aine did...suddenly he saw some people of Aine hiding.

Knoll shouted,"People of Aine! Do not be afraid! Fight with us, to protect your own homelands!"

Some of the Aine people nodded, and he saw there were more in the cave than he thought, as hundreds of people of Aine ran outwards and joined him in the battle!

Knoll began taking charge as he said,"You 50 men over there, head due east! You 50 men on the other side, head due west! The rest, cut through the center! Spread out and we can win this!"

They followed his orders as he continued directing where they went as he sent his attacks at the beasts. Before anyone could make heads or tails. Knoll was now leader of the Aine armies that were present at the battlefield!

The Chimera laughed as he said,"I knew you had it in yeah, Knoll."

Knoll continued,"watch out! Don't let them get behind you! Try to focus on using more physical attacks, since the Phoenixes and Dragons both have partial immunity to fire! I also have some potions I can wip up to help you damage them! So take a few!"

He started tossing them to nearby soldiers as they said things like,"yes sir! Right away sir!"

Knoll saw a dragon head straight for him, this one of the bigger ones. He sent his arrows of wind mixed with flame at them, with a potion he'd whipped up enhancing his damage even further! He struck it and the dragon growled and swiped its claws at him, but he jumped over it and began climbing up the dragon's arm as he sent a fire/wind arrow straight into the dragon's eyeball!

The Dragon growled in pain as it breathed fire but he easily dodged and jumped back down to pierce it straight through the chest, going straight to where it's heart was located, killing the massive dragon instantly!

Suddenly a yellow dragon headed for Knoll and began casting lightning at him! He threw a potion that formed together with his wind spell to redirect the lightning as it hit a nearby purple dragon! They both screamed and flew towards Knoll but he dodged as they both ran into each other! He then smirked as he formed a sword made of wind that could grown and shrink at will as he began slicing through and leaving many cuts on each of them! The yellow dragon sent more lightning at him but he jumped out of the way as the Purple Dragon then spat poison at him!

The Purple dragon growled,"You stupid Yellow Dragons always getting in my way! I want that human!"

The Yellow dragon growled back,"shut up you Purple Dragon, he's mine!"

They began fighting each other as Knoll realized now was the time to strike as he cast a massive tornado filled with cuts and it ripped the two dragons into pieces, killing them as their bits of flesh fell onto the battlefield!

The Armies of Freyala and Raiterra were using team up powers as they'd sent bolts of lightning from the Raiterran's and mixed it with the massive waves of wind from the Freyalans as it headed for about 100 Dragons flying straight at the joint armies!

Akemi turned to Gratho,"See? I told you it was a good idea."

Gratho nodded,"Alright, alright you're right after all. It feels good to have the Okami families of our two countries fighting together..thematically anyways. Let us continue forward!"

Akemi nodded,"YES!"

Green energy filled the skies as the dark battlefield suddenly shined brightly. The sun briefly uncovered from the skies...and everyone and everything was slightly distracted by the sun being shown for the first time in years..as magical energy flowed down onto the battlefield as from the skies..they appeared.

Heliopolis and Goron. The estimated height of them each was roughly 600 feet tall, each. Putting them roughly at the same size as Abraxas and Mangrielle. To say that they towered over everything else on the battlefield would be such a huge understatement, that people would laugh at you in between crying.

Heliopolis screeched as Mangrielle took notice.

"Who are you? My child, you are larger than expected! Help me to beat Abraxas!"

Heliopolis spoke,"My name is Heliopolis. I am not your child. I serve the human Maxwell Schneider. I'm here to defeat you!"

Mangrielle frowned,"I've beaten plenty of Golden Dragons in my time, and other Zizix, when I had to. What makes you think you have the RIGHT to even challenge me? Your arrogance is blinding you, pup."

Heliopolis screeched,"I am no dog! I serve the human of my own free will! And today, I shall kill you!"

Goron growled at Abraxas and said,"On behalf of one whom has EARNED the right to be my master, I shall kill you Abraxas! My master, Jericho Wallrick..has deemed it so, and with one as powerful as myself, the great and powerful Goron, on his side..it WILL happen!"

Abraxas laughed,"I'm far older than some upstart such as you, Goron! It is YOU who will die today!"

Max shouted,"enough talk! Today..it is YOU who will die! Prepare yourself, Zizix!"

Mangrielle ignored Max, for it felt Max was beneath him and not even worth acknowledging. He only wished to address Heliopolis..whom as far as he was concerned, was an upstart phoenix who had somehow grown to be the size of a Zizix.

Jericho shouted,"Goron! Forward!" Goron did as told as breathed fire at Abraxas who dodged and laughed at the idea of a HUMAN telling a dragon what to do.

Jericho road his dragon as it growled and breathed fire again at Abraxas who matched it with a flame equally as strong!

Abraxas pulled his hand out and began chanting in dragonic as he cast a massive torrent of lightning from the sky at Jericho and Goron!

Jericho shouted as he cast a gigantic lava spell above Goron to deflect the lightning, as the lava absorbed it, he then sent the lava straight for Abraxas, who easily dodged and breathed fire as it sent its massive claws at Goron!

Goron tanked the scratch as he struck his own claws right back at Abraxas as they sent deep scratches into the hides of each other! Abraxas and Goron both growled in pain but neither backed down as they continued scratching each other and then both backed off at the same time as they flew higher into the air! Their massive wings sent shockwaves to the people and other phoenixes and dragons below!

Akemi looked up as he saw the 600 foot tall Goron and the 600 Foot tall Abraxas fight each other. Abraxas cast a spell that sent more lightning at Goron as he breathed fire at the same time!

Goron matched the flames with his own flame breath as there was a struggle of sorts as both converged continuously! Meanwhile, Jericho sent lava at the lightning strikes as the lightning continued to pour down, and the lava continuously kept blocking it! They seemed to be evenly matched!

Han saw the 600 foot tall Heliopolis fighting the 600-foot tall Zizix!

Max road his phoenix as it ran forward and sent flames at the enemy Zizix. Its wings beated as it sent massive waves of lightning at Max and Heliopolis! Heliopolis sent massive flames at Mangrielle while Max mixed his own wind spells into it to send at Mangrielle to deflect the lightning and redirect it!

They then clashed with each other, as Mangrielle and Heliopolis collided in the air, and Max barely held onto his phoenix. They separated and collided again with their talons thrashing at one another!

The massive wings of Heliopolis and Mangrielle were giving off heat as flames were on Heliopolis and lightning on the wings of Mangrielle..though Max was immune to being burned by his own summon.

Max and Heliopolis sent massive flames together as they mixed their two flame attacks at Mangrielle! Max also used mage hand, a spell that allowed him to move objects with his hand, and used said spell to send massive rocks that had been created by one of his friends of Camp 1 earlier, to send them at Mangrielle, whom easily blocked them with lightning but the flames had hidden lava in them from one of Jericho's strikes causing them to greatly burn the Zizix as it screeched but continued sending lightning so as to hit Heliopolis! He dodged the attack!

Max began forming arcane magic as he fired magic missiles at Mangrielle, these being mixed with actual lightning element! They headed for Mangrielle whom though they were simply lightning attacks and acted accordingly, but even then it almost succeeded but Max's attack overcame and damaged Mangrielle who screeched and flew toward them using lightning in her talons to cut through Heliopolis, but he put flames in his talons and attacked right back! Shockwaves happened as the two scratched at each other, causing massive quakes in the ground beneath them as fissures formed from the sheer magnitude of their size!

Suddenly Max had an idea and thought really hard about his plan. Heliopolis, being his summon, heard it telepathically. They both agreed. Max and Heliopolis formed their raw magical energy together as a massive blast roughly the size of Heliopolis himself was sent straight for Mangrielle! It was overcome as the Zizix was reduced to ashes! As this occurred, Max went unconscious. The ashes of Mangrielle would take many years to resurrect but Heliopolis before disappearing, wanted to make sure and shouted.

Heliopolis shouted,"Leon! Destroy the Ashes of Mangrielle! I never want her coming back!"

Leon did as told as he sent massive arcane magic attack at the ashes, ending Mangrielle once and for all.

Meanwhile, Goron and Abraxas were still colliding attacks! Abraxas sent massive waves of its own lava and lightning at Goron and Jericho! Jericho responded by sending Lava from himself and more flames at Goron, while they dodged the strikes at the same time that Abraxas was attempting with his claws during the distraction that the elemental attacks had apparently been.

Suddenly Goron flew forward quickly and got a hold of Abraxas's neck by biting into it with his massive jaws. Jericho telepathically sent an idea to Goron who agreed back telepathically.

Goron plummeted to the ground, and landed by using Abraxas as the shield for the landing. He still had a hold of Abraxas's neck and did a death roll, rolling around while still holding onto the neck, he snapped Abraxas's neck..killing him instantly.

Many Phoenixes, Dragons and sadly, humans...were killed during the death roll....but most of all..at least Abraxas was now slain. With that however, Jericho was low on magic and he had to send Goron away, as he barely held onto what strength he had left, and was caught in mid-air by Knoll whom flew up using wind magic and caught the falling Jericho.

With Abraxas and Mangrielle both dead..the few Phoenixes and Dragons left quickly retreated from the battlefield..and the battle had been won, for now.

****

It was Jared's birthday..happy birthday to him though, right?

Terragon was angry. Apparently, they'd been too flashy with their attacks the other day when they fought the extra bigger army of Orcs. Reports said that the Northern Capital would likley now know that the Southern Capital was alive and well..and send armies to wipe out what was left of the Southern Kingdom in due time.

Anna smiled. "Ah knew this would happen..and in fact, Ah planned for it."

Terragon growled,"Excuse me, bitch? My people have survived all this time by hiding! And you're telling me this attack on the Orcs was part of your plan to jeopardize us?"

Jared couldn't argue with that logic...but he just stood as he heard Anna and Terragon argue. They bickered and bickered. It annoyed him. He had to speak up.

"ENOUGH!" Everyone went silent. Jared was the quiet type..he had never yelled at any of them..but now...now he was.

"LISTEN! I know that both of you have your differences. I know that you haven't ever liked us, Terragon. But hiding for the rest of your life in these ruins is no way to live! Your people are sad, defeated even. But now you have a choice to make..you can attempt to regain what you have lost and fight the North with all of your strength..or you can sit here, and wait for them to come to you and most likely leave the civilians that are here, to wait to die.

"I suggest the first one! We send what armies you can gather, and us foreigners will even go with you...and we can go give them hell in the North! Then, if we fail..the South people here will die regardless..so wouldn't it be better if we tried to prevent that!"

Terragon sighed,"Fine. Not like I have a choice...we leave tomorrow. I'll gather what armies I can..and we will attack..the northern capital!"

****

Gratho growled,"You're kidding, right?"

Max shook his head. "Not at all. Look at what we achieved today. Do you think the Northern Capital is going to ignore the sheer power that your armies, as well as us foreigners who helped you..has done today? I'm willing to bet the North will find out very quickly..and come here to kill as much as they can..lower our moral.

They are afraid of what will happen if they rebel. I'm also willing to bet they'll hear about the fact the one who fought against the North before, Akemi..was fighting with us. I propose we attack the Northern Capital! Raiterra, Jigoku, Freyala, and whoever will join us! Leon has already asked Fin'eowyn..and they said they will join us!"

Gratho sighed,"I'll talk to my King and see what he says..but I cannot promise anything."

Akemi laughed,"This was inevitable. Everything always leads from one thing to another. I'm sure my King will agree to this battle."

Han nods,"I'm thinking the King of Jigoku will agree to it as long as Freyala does. So if Freyala agrees to it. Jigoku will likely answer the call too."

Max nodded,"Jericho is always itching for a good fight. The others want to go home..you see. We come from another universe..one that cannot be found on this world. If we go there, and help defeat the Northern Capital..maybe, just maybe. We can try to find a way home. They sent us here from our world..perhaps they can send us back."

Akemi sighed,"Sounds complicated..but if that means we all have a common goal, it works for me."

Max nodded,"Great. So..most likely..you'll all agree...we head for it tomm-"

Suddenly a distant message came into his mind.

'This is the Wolf of Shogan..I have a message. A message I'm sending telepathically to both of you..Maxwell of Camp 1...and Jared of Camp 2. Tomorrow you will both meet in the Northern Capital. You both want to do this. I have sensed this desire within both of you two...so I implore you to both arrive at the same time. Separately, you wouldn't have a chance. But together..you can defeat them. I will send you an exact time into your minds and a way to know it...so both arrive at that time. Good luck'

Max at Camp 1 said,"Guys.I have good news. We'll have much bigger armies."

He explained to them what had transpired in his mind. Meanwhile, Jared at Camp 2 was doing the same.

Max responded,"We have to do everything we can to make this happen...tomorrow...we fight the Northern Capital!"

Jared meanwhile, had revealed what was being said and replied,"We gotta make this work...tomorrow..we fight the Northern Capital!"

472

End of Arc V

Arc VI

Chapter 27- fight the Northern Capital

Note:

Camp 1 - Max, Jericho, Leon, Shakira, Zack and Knoll plus "The DWD (Dark World Duo)" Brokk and Cael

Camp 2 - Anna, Simon, Ikuto, Connor, Rally, Jared, and Tim.

Camp 3 - Anyone else who isn't dead.

For now, it was time to sleep. Tomorrow, they'd be headed for the Northern Capital to begin their big push..to bring hope to the people of Shogun AND the Southern Kingdom. A different outcome from what happened in the great war. But first...they drifted further to sleep. And the dreams began.

Brokk was first. The King sat on his thrown, worried. Much had happened. His knights were to return soon, and for some reason this time Brokk was seeing from out of body, looking down at the king, instead of from the perspective of his ancestor, and like before... he could hear thoughts. This time he could hear the thoughts of the king.

King Reynard had a lot on his mind. First, someone had executed his court jester. This was a tough position. He'd been thinking about firing the jester because he was more annoying than funny, and had angered many people. So while he couldn't blame whoever had done it, he couldn't allow murder of someone close to him to go unpunished.

Furthermore, some people had left Gallindor and moved to other kingdoms. He didn't blame them, they feared the Paraians. Most had stayed due to loyalty and nostalgia for their home, though he often worried that it could lead to their own downfall. However, now they couldn't if they wanted to, as the last few people to leave were ambushed by Paraians and executed. What's more, at some point back when the previous King was in power, the Goblins had been nearly whipped out.

They say God himself sent lightning from the heavens throughout the land and nearly exterminated them. What other explanation could there be for it, as no other creature was harmed? Furthermore, humanity had taken a hit as well, as it'd lost access to their magic.

Even today no one from Gallindor nor Paria could wield magic anymore. What started this sudden loss of magic were the "Years of Heresy" as they are often called, as during those days humans were largely either atheist or desiring to overthrow god (it varied on the person). So surely it made sense that such things had occurred. Gallindor and Paraians became highly devoted to god since those days, even if mostly out of fear. However, on top of that Goblins have now begun to re-surface.

They'd paid them no bother as they were too small in numbers to worry about with the threat of the Phoenixs, Dragons who often were in the mountains to their west, and the Griffins and Hippogriffs to the SouthWest all sometimes came down and stole cattle or caused disturbances...nothing coordinated, but still a gigantic hassle.

They still had houses that were never fixed due to the damages that seemed to often occur in the same places of the Kingdom. Not to mention bandits who loved to attack the roads, bandits that were too organized and mobile to ever completely wipe out... but now the Goblins were starting to strike at random times, then disappearing and hiding just as quickly. Roads weren't safe anymore.

It was almost deceiving really. The natural beauty of the open sky, the lake to their east that was great for fishing. Honestly, the plants and vegetation right outside Gallindor was often a sight to behold. And yet now few could go see it anymore for fear of their own lives.

And all of that was BEFORE the last battles with the Paraians had truly begun.

Since the battle had begun, they'd lost men left and right. The Paraian's troops were vastly superior to Gallindor's. What's more, his knights were few in number and while very skilled, could only do so much. It made the King long for the days that humanity still had magic, as that used to be the backbone of Gallindor's troops back in the day. Gallindor had amazing magical users in the past. To top all of his worries off... a dark and ominous cloud had begun to form far off in the north.

It wouldn't be so noticeable if it wasn't so large. Whatever it was, it never disappeared, and the kingdom below this cloud had closed its doors to any outsiders. Perhaps they were lucky however. Who knows what side the kingdom would take in the war between Paraia and Gallindor, and whichever side it took, would've surely won. So perhaps it was better they weren't involved, just in case it had taken Paraia's side.

A few men in armor with swords and shields walked in and kneeled. "Sir, we've got bad news I'm afraid. We made contact at the waypoint with the Freyalan Ambasadors. They say they cannot give us the aid they'd initially promised."

The King stood up from his throne and shouted,"Freyala is several times our size! We are merely but one kingdom, they are the size of enough to call themselves a country! Surely it would be child's play to send us aid! Why can they not?! Speak up!"

The guard who'd spoken was noticeably uneasy,"I-I'm sorry sir. They report a massive war between Freyala and its neighboring countries."

The King went wide eyed,"which ones?!"

The Guard gulped,"All five of them sir. There's more bad news I'm afraid."

The King dropped down into his throne, afraid of what might be said next,"...yes? Out with it!"
The Guard nodded,"A new Golden Dragon started it. It calls itself Abraxas and reports say the dragon has multiple dragons on its side working in a coordinated attack against Freyala and its neighboring countries... and unfortunately Aine and Fin'eowyn have discovered a way to harness dragonic energy as a weapon, and that's what started the whole war!"

King Reynard went wide eyed. "I...I understand Freyala's dilemma....that will be all. I am not in a good mood, so please leave me for now."

The guards got up and left the throne room.

Then a passage of time passed, and Gallindor lay in ruins.. Brokk felt this little insight into Freyala and the other Kingdom's history would have been more useful earlier.. but perhaps visions didn't always happen in order? Brokk wasn't sure what to make of it. But that's where the dream ended..for now.

Zack had a dream as well! This one was of his evil self again, but this time the man was being slain... a man with blue-green eyes and long red hair. Zack himself once again wore black and red armor. The man struck Zack down. Again, Zack saw it from the point of view as if it was himself.

Then he saw himself being killed..and then re-animated. The Red-haired man spoke,"I am Bahrik. I am your new master now. Zack, the butcher of millions. You will do nicely in my armies."

That's where the dream shifted to something else. Zack saw himself walking among others, and saw that he wasn't the only person who had been re-animated. He saw a man who stood about 5 foot 10, with short brown hair and was built rather tough but scruffy. He wore a pirate captains hat.

The man spoke,"Well, if it not be Zack, the butcher! Don't think ye be special! There be quite a few of us who were re-animated before ye! Such as myself, Aiden. Surely you've heard the name?"

Zack heard himself speak, and indeed he had the same voice as he said,"Yes, you were King of the Pirates Once. But you mysteriously died..even though people thought you were immortal."

The man shrugged,"Still am King of the Pirates. Anyways, I was killed by Bahrik. He stole me immortality. But that be in the past, as he resurrected me the same as you. Word of advice..I've tried killing Bahrik many times. Can't. I know that look, you want to. But your body won't let you, right? Same here. Part of bein resurrected by him."

That's where Zack's dream ended...but why was he still getting such visions of the past? And more importantly- what did it mean?

****

In the past few months, Camp 3 was coping with its situation. Nero had found Allanon's old journal, and was obsessively reading from it..but keeping it secret from everyone else and to himself. Nero had learned of many, many spells. He didn't necessarily know how to cast them all himself, but none the less he memorized everything he could from Allanon's Journal. He was determined to prove himself a better person than the coward he'd been before.

Today would be that day! The half-animal people had been attacking the barrier on and off for months! It scared people at first, but after awhile it became normal. Sometimes fellow students would even mock them and Sho would have to have them removed from the area just to be extra careful...and he'd often warn them that if they kept taunting them like that, he couldn't guarantee he wouldn't just shove them outside the barrier..though hopefully he was kidding.

Nero approached Miles, whom was at his work station as usual. The various puppets were creepy..especially since rumor had it, many of them were made from dead bodies of human beings. Nero approached Miles and Miles turned and said,"..yes?"

Shivers went down Nero's spine but he continued,"What do you think of Dark World?"

Miles calmly, and plainly said,"I don't like it here. I miss home."

Nero responded,"Want to go out and fight those intruders that keep attacking the barrier? Maybe they know a way to get us out of here."

Miles nodded and shrugged,"Sure."

Nero breathed a sigh of relief. That was a lot easier than he feared it would be. Nero added,"I'm going to have one more person join us...Christian."

Sure enough, it didn't take much convincing and Christian was on board for the idea as well.

Outside of the force-field was a were-tiger, were-bunny and a were-mole. Nero decided now was the time for him to prove his worth. He noticed some students were watching them attack the force-field. Perfect. An audience.

Nero, Christian, and Miles exited the force field from the side and the attackers took noticed and began attacking back!
The Weretiger smiled,"I've been looking for a good fight from you lot! YES!"

The Werebunny had her spear ready,"That's not the point, though, the point is YOU are intruders!" she looked to Nero and the others.

The Weremole didn't even bother to speak, he simply seemingly teleported to where Miles was and tried to slash at him with its claws. Miles easily dodged and blocked with one of his puppets, which grew a sword out of its arm and collided with the claws.

Nero formed a pillar of earth magic and then sent magic missiles at the weretiger, the weretiger grinned and dodged it and slashed at Nero but Nero formed a stone wall to block it and fired more magic missiles, shocking the weretiger!

Christian turned into his werewolf form, which apparently the students still didn't know about..and he began attacking the werebunny as she tried punching him but he slashed at her chest, but the armor blocked it as she tried to spear at him but he dodged that.

Nero formed armor made of Earth and formed a sword made of earth element and began fighting the weretiger toe to toe.

Suddenly, a lasso of divine magic formed around Nero, Miles, and Christian as they were pulled back into the force field. It was Sho.

Sho sighed,"this is counter productive. I'm not going to allow it to continue. If any of you have a problem with that, you will have to fight me."

Nero took notice," According to Allaon's journal, he's one of the few Wizards in the world to have ever had Divine Magic! How did you gain it?!"

Sho turned to him and said,"Allaon's journal? Didn't know he had one. We'll have to talk about that one later."

Sho approached the force field but didn't move through it as he said. "We did not mean to be here, we ourselves were brought here against our will. We don't know how long we will be here.. but I have faith our friends will find a way for us to leave..until then, you will have to live with us being here. I'm sorry for the inconvenience."

The weretiger growled,"I'm not interested in apologies! I WANT A FIGHT!"

Sho sighed,"The three of you clearly can't get through the forcefield, so 'want' to fight all you like. Won't really matter."

And with that, the fight ended rather anticlimactically for Nero. Still..he was starting to get looks..some of them even looked impressed...maybe things would be looking up in due time?

The next day, Nero had a lot to think over. He was probably going to receive a stern lecture from Sho at some point that day. Luckily, he had woken up in a good mood, inspired even. Today was going to be his day! As he walked through the halls, most of the students were in their dreary moods as usual. He saw a student weeping and admittedly, he felt sympathy for them. He was so distracted by this, he bumped right into Syanne!

Syanne exclaimed,"OOF!"

She then looked at him with a blank stare and acted as if nothing had happened. This puzzled Nero...she didn't even reply after he had collided with her! Nero had heard once before that Syanne was known for being a bitch, but mysteriously, ever since they entered Dark World, few ever even mentioned her. It was as if she had faded to the background. He hadn't even thought about it until now. Nero decided to initiate conversation with her and that his plan could wait a moment.

Nero responded,"Nobody has heard from you in a long time..where have you been?"

Syanne seemed distant and did not reply.

Nero inquired,"Did something happen to you when the school was attacked? It did for all of us, but were you-what I mean to say is... did you receive a magical gift?"

Syanne continued to remain quiet at first, but briefly looked up and said,"Yes, I did. But I don't want to talk about it."

Nero nodded and decided to probe further,"Was it an elemental ability?"

Syanne simply stated,"No."

Nero smiled,"Would you like to have one?"

Syanne slowly replied,"...yes."

Nero decided this would suit his own needs, and hopefully cheer her up as well. He nodded and said,"Follow me and I will do just that." He had been reading Allanon's journal, and this would benefit him.

As he continued down the hall, he found Christian. This was perfect. The student he had been looking for. It didn't take long after to find Miles as well. Once he had gathered the three students, they went into a secret tunnel. As they did so, Nero sang a song he had made for it. Nero had discovered the tunnel from old notes. This was likely the place that Allanon sometimes trained the summoners in.

As they entered, he found it was vacant. Again, this was perfect. They wouldn't be disturbed.

Nero turned to see that Syanne looked distant, yet slightly nervous. Christian appeared to be on his guard, and Miles was unreadable.

Nero smiled,"I'm not going to kill you guys or something. I'm genuinely going to teach you magic. Here, take this piece of paper."

He handed a piece of paper to Syanne, Miles, and Christian.

Syanne's paper froze, burned and turned to ash.

Nero replied,"Interesting. Ice and Fire."

Mile's turned wet and damp.

Nero added,"Water."

Christian's paper wrinkled.

Nero nodded,"Lightning. Okay perfect. I have memorized the lessons I can teach each of you, in order to bring out these elements. Today, I'm going to be your Sensei, as it were. I will teach you how to use elemental magic."

Nero smile widened. He would become useful to everyone at last. Teaching this group would be a good start.

****

Max, Jericho Leon, Shakira, Zack, Knoll and the others waited patiently at the rock shaped like a wolf. This was the meeting place, now they just waited to meet up. The dark sky and being out in the open made Max feel somewhat uncomfortable. Even with the joint armies of Shogun there beside him. Sure enough, here came Jared, Anna, Simon, Ikuto, Connor, Rally, and Tim. Behind them were the Southern Kingdom's armies.

Max approached Jared and gave him a hug. Jared hugged him back. Max said,"bro! It's been long since I've seen you!"

Jared responded,"Same dude, same."

Max said,"You're my bro, bro!"

Jared responded,"Don't make this weird."

Max laughed,"I'm teasing. We could all use a bit of a laughter around here.. anyways, so what have you guys been up to?"

Jared smiled,"You have no idea. Let's just say Orcs..lots of them."

Max smiled,"I defeated a 600 foot tall blue lightning bird while fighting in a war between Dragons, Phoenixes and a bunch of swordsmen. The ones right behind me over there in fact. Top that."

Jared said,"Okay..I admit, you fought something much...bigger. Probably more powerful too. But what did you sleep in? We spent every night either sleeping wherever we could find, or in a bunch of ruins of the Southern Kingdom."

Max responded,"...touche. The place we slept in was typically really nice. Sometimes a bit of a small room, but a really nice one. In Freyala, the wind swordsmen country."

Jared nodded,"Yesterday was my birthday by the way."

Max laughed,"Happy belated birthday then! A bit of a late gift..but Camp 1 and Camp 2 are united at long last!"

Tim came up from behind Jared and responded,"this is nice and all, but shouldn't we start getting ready and discussing battle plans or somethin'?"

Jericho did the same, coming up from behind Max and said,"Agreed. I feel the same way."

Tim smirked,"well if it ain't dark eyed and angry!"

Jericho smirked back and said,"good to see you too, Tim."

Suddenly they heard a voice say,"It's good for me to finally meet your Camp 2, Max."

They turned and it was Raven!

Max said,"Raven..where have you been? You trained us so much, and then you just disappeared!"

Raven replied,"I was searching for my younger brother, Connor. I wasn't able to find him. When I learned from rumors of seeing your armies moving..I figured you'd be attacking the Northern Capital and would need my help. You also don't have long..since if I heard about it, they probably did as well. You'll need all you can to defeat King Bahrik."

Zack approached them all and spoke up,"Did you say Bahrik?"

Raven turned and said,"...yes? Why?"

Zack told him of his dream. Raven's face turned very serious.

"...I didn't even know my brother was dead."

Max said,"I thought you said your younger brother was Connor."

Raven replied,"I did...Aiden is my twin brother. This evil counterpart to Zack also worries me, of course. But....forgive me. I- I need some time to myself."

'Poor Raven, thought Max. He just found out his brother was resurrected from the dead and now serving the douchebag we are going to be fighting. Can barely imagine how he feels. I have my younger brother back home..but that's about all I can use as a reference.'

Max shivered,"have I mentioned it's friggin cold up here! Even with us all wearing what we can to keep warm, I much prefer the temperature of the battlefield in Aine where we fought the dragons and phoenixes!"

Jared shrugged and laughed,"this is warm compared to the South Pole..where we've been this whole time, I'll add."

Akemi spoke up,"In any case. We need a plan for the joint armies here. We have Freyala, Jigoku, Raiterra, Fin'ewoyn, and some of Aine. We have the Southern Kingdom. What shall we do? They will no doubt soon meet us with an army before we can reach the cities."

Knoll nodded,"I have some ideas, if anyone is interested."

Meanwhile, at the Northern Capital.

Bahrik sat on his throne, with Clifton and Percival...the former 6th Knight of Gallindor.

Bahrik said,"Clifton, Percival. Prepare the armies...they will be here shortly. Kill them. I will remain here, off of the chess board. I will not face them myself unless you fail. If you are to fail, return to the city. Do not fail. Clifton, as my General..you are in charge of the armies. Percival, you are to go as well, regardless."

Clifton was a somewhat shorter man, five foot three with blonde hair and blue eyes. He wore brown cloth shirt and pants that had nothing special or regal to them, because he wasn't much for dressing fancy unless the occasion called for it. He had skin that was scarred on his arms.

Clifton nodded,"I have strategies in mind that should be more than adequate."

Percival was a tall man, standing at six foot four. He had short black hair and green-red eyes, and wore black colored plate armor. He was built like a what a knight should be. But he had veins on his neck and arms in certain areas, no doubt due to being one whom had brought himself back from the dead before.

Percival growled,"I hate being told what to do...but it IS you, so I shall."

And with that..soon enough the first battle would begin.

Skipping ahead to the battle...the Armies of the Northern Capital moved forward towards the armies of Shogun and the Southern Kingdom. There were hundreds of them, mostly clad in black armor done in a more viking-light manner due to the cold temperatures of the Northern Capital and holding magical guns.

488

It was a stark contrast to the armies of Shogun whom were all only swordsmen, with some archers mixed in, or the Southern Kingdom whom didn't even have any magic. The Northern Kingdom were hitting drums, basically announcing that they were moving forward.

Knoll nodded to the people of Freyala as a cold front went over the front of them. The air went through the enemy army and began knocking people into the air and the enemy armies shouted as they charged forward towards the allied armies.

Some of them ran for trenches where Jigoku people were shooting at them with lava arrows! It only slowed the enemy down, it didn't stop their progress..it didn't need to as once some of them entered the trenches, lava filled them and began killing off enemy troops! It was also difficult for the enemy to see due to the wind currents the Freyalan's were doing with the snow in the air.

Suddenly Knoll shouted,"FIRE!" and the armies of Aine began firing flaming magic missiles at the enemy armies! It was insanity as the enemy armies began attempting to return fire! Suddenly a wave from behind brought up specialized shields and began blocking the magic missiles Aine was using that had been initially so successful

Some of the Northern Capital's armies began climbing up a hill, however at the top were some Fin'eowyn troops. It then revealed a massive mudslide making it hard to
climb the hill.

Then the Freyalan's used the cold wind to freeze the wet mud and then rolled logs and rocks to finish off all those trapped. It was effective at taking out some of the soldiers, at least. But some behind them used spikes in their boots and began climbing the surface. This was their homeland, afterall. They began shooting at the enemies.

So far Knoll's plan wasn't quite working the way they wanted, it seemed to only be slowing the enemy down and eliminating little bits a time.

Suddenly, in the distance a bald man with a goatee and was holding twin swords began swinging his blades at Rally, Ikuto and Simon whom were backing up the Fin'eowyn troops!

They were just narrowly dodging.

Ikuto growled,"it was a distraction. You think we're the weakest link, so they sent one of their strongest soldiers to take us out!"

Suddenly Jericho blocked the bald man's swords and said,"Mind if I help you guys out?"

The bald man grinned,"Good! A worthy challenge! Clifton's plan for me to attack the weak didn't please me at all! I've heard about you, Jericho! You took out the Golden Dragon Abraxas! Now you will face the me...the God of War- Gronok!"

They collided blades as Jericho dodged and asked,"Really? How is it that the god of war is serving mere mortals?"

Gronok frowned,"I was killed by my son, Bahrik. He then brought me back from the dead. It's fitting since I killed most of the gods myself in the past, including my own father. Now..ENOUGH TALK! FIGHT ME!"

As this was happening, another person was targeting the weaker foes..as per Clifton's plan.

A woman with long flowing red hair, and a brown attire. She had chain blades all too simliar to the ones used by Gronok. She was swinging them at Connor and Jared!

Jared used a pillar of earth to block it.

The Red haired woman spoke,"I'd heard the two of you killed Orcs in the South. A very powerful feat, and warranting needing someone such as myself..a former Queen..the great warrior Alyiana!"

Connor replied,"what makes you think we are weak? Jared and I were the leaders among those of use fighting the Orcs!"

Ayliana laughed,"In truth, there are two that are considered slightly more of a threat than you two. That's already being dealt with shortly! Focus on fighting me for now!"

Connor deflected her attacks with his sword of lightning and his sword of fire, but he could hardly keep up with this womans fast attacks!

Jared tried to form his earth armor, but her blades cut straight through it and shattered it! He tried to form lava and her blades went through the lava like it wasn't affecting them at all!

She swung her blade about to cut straight through Jared, but Max deflected it and said,"perhaps I can help you guys out?"

Jared nodded quickly and said,"Yes! Yes please!"

Connor smirked,"what he said. With you helping us, now we have a chance!"

Aiden began swiping his sword back and forth. It hadn't taken long for him to be noticed and the armies weren't letting him through! Ann and Tim had been his targets, but he wasn't doing masterfully at subtlty.

Raven ran forward and pulled out his own sword and they collided as the sky seemingly shook.

Aiden grinned,"Good to see ye, me friend."

Raven smiled,"You don't have to maintain the voice with me..I know you better than anyone, my brother."

Aiden grinned,"regardless, old habits and all that. It's funny, really. Gronok, the god of war is out here on this battlefield somewhere..but you and I know better don't we? We're the real gods in all but name you and I. Lived for thousands of years, fought many battles. We just never called ourselves that, did we?"

Raven swung his sword to try to kill Aiden, but he easily blocked as the battlefield began to release hail. They swung their blades at one another but kept blocking each others attacks as the earth around them shook.

Raven frowned,"I don't want to do this, but it looks like I will have to burry someone dear to me again."

Aiden smirked,"I already died. At this point, I'm just a husk fighting some idiot upstart kid who stole my immortality. But he's a lich now..and he commands me whether I like it or not."

Their blades collided again as the ground shook.

But all of this was only the start of this battle..and more would come soon enough...

Chapter 28-Ayliana and Gronok

The battlefield had been treacherous but the fight was far from lost! Gradually, Knoll watched as his strategies didn't go quite as well as he'd hoped. But then noticed a change in the tide..some of the enemy soldiers were no longer using guns and pulling out swords, and spears and the like. He formed a hypothesis- the guns, being powered by magic..worked kind of like the devices he'd helped Shakira make... they could store magic.

It's likely that a lot of the enemies in the armies weren't magic users themselves! This meant they had a limited ammo capacity since they couldn't replenish the magic themselves. This mean if he could gather his armies and try to get them to last long enough, it would force the opponents into close range more!

Yuji, Ryo, Argos, and Zimri were backing up the forces of the Southern Kingdom.

Yuji was crowd control, as he detached limbs and sliced people to pieces with his sword and his magic that allowed him to remove arms and legs and heads, etc with clean cuts!

Ryo was fighting with him using his two-sword style and fire magic on his blades to cut through the armies like flies! He was easily a one man army.... today he'd make sure people remembered the Southern Kingdom! He also found it kind of funny to see his former homeland of Aine was fighting on the battlefield as well, but he hadn't gotten the chance to speak to any of them thus far and at the moment he didn't intend to just yet.

Zimri swung his ice blade through opponents as he laughed to himself happily. This was almost like a joke to him.

Argos growled as he said,"Oi! Zimri! Leave some of them for me too!"

Zimri laughed,"Sorry my friend, guess you're just too slow!"

Argos growled more as he said,"I'll show YOU who's too slow.."

As he began throwing knives much quicker into opponents and he himself began laughing as well.

Zimri,"that's 28 I've killed so far..what about yourself?"

Argos growled,"29!"

Zimri laughed,"You killed 15, I've counted for you as well."

Argos huffed,"well if you were counting mine too, you shouldn't have asked!"

The four continued their assault.

Meanwhile, Gronok swung his blades into the air and began slashing towards Rally. She leaped backward and began shooting magic missiles at Gronok, mixed with lightning elemental magic!

Rally smirked,"Ice isn't the only thing I have anymore!"

She then continued sending the lightning and magic missiles at Gronok but he blocked it with his blades and yet could still block the blade strike from Jericho at the same time!

Ikuto formed a sword made of flames and then pointed out Gronok to try to detach his limbs! Gronok growled as he had his body tighten and then he forced his arms outward and he warded off the magic! Ikuto did it again, but this time it didn't manage to have any affect at all, as meanwhile Ikuto had to dodge roll out of the way as Jericho blocked the strike, meant for Ikuto, that Gronok tried to do with his blades. It was like Gronok was immune to Ikuto's newest magic ability completely!

Jericho sweated as he said,"This guy's fucking hard to fight!"

Ikuto looked to Rally and Simon and shouted to them,"Keep your distance and used ranged attacks on him! We'll let Jericho deal with him at close range! I could tell just by looking, he's a better fighter than any of the three of us! The rest of us can't afford to fight this guy head on! "

Simon and Rally both nodded and said,"Roger!"

Gronok tore his cloth shirt off and revealed he had various tattoos. One was of a pirate ship on his shoulder-blades/back area, but there were various different ones on his shoulders, arms, chest, and everywhere all over his upper body that his shirt had been covering. One shaped like a snake glowed on his arm and he suddenly summoned a giant snake, probably no less than 14 feet tall!

Ikuto smirked as he formed a blade of flames and sliced the giant snake in two like it was nothing! However it split into two more snakes, so Ikuto and

Simon coordinated together and stabbed them both instead of slicing..killing them both easily!

Ikuto replied,"Don't let his attacks distract you Jericho, we got that covered."

Gronok swung his blades at Jericho who narrowly dodged them, then Gronok swung again before Jericho knew what hit him and it left a scar across his arm as it bled.

Jericho replied,"Good cuz this guy is fucking scary!"

Next Gronok's tattoos glowed again and suddenly blue flames formed over Gronok's blades!

Jericho heard Goron tell him telepathically,'watch out for those. They are hotter than regular fire.'

Jericho telepathically responded,'I got ya.' Jericho put his hand to his arm and healed the cut with his own healing magic.

Rally exclaimed,"That's kind of funny that Jericho of all people, got healing magic."

Jericho replied,"I got other surprises too!" He formed pools of water magic, but the amount of water magic was like forming a gigantic lake all around the part of the battlefield they were at! The enemy soldiers were being knocked over, but allies as well!

Jericho replied,"Sorry friends, this fucker needs to die."

Gronok blocked the waves and continued moving forward. Jericho took advantage of the situation to swing his blade at Gronok but Gronok's tattoos glowed again and a wind based force-field went over himself and knocked Jericho backwards as the water started to dissipate. He then threw his blades outward while the chains were still attached to his arms as he sliced a cut, deep into Jericho's arm!

Jericho had to jump backward as he attempted to quickly heal the wound before he bled to death from the really deep cut!

Ikuto thought to himself, *'Jericho need's my help. Gotta figure this out...got it.'*

Meanwhile, Max was dealing with Ayliana! She too had blades with chains attached, much like Gronok did.

Ayliana's blades weren't just swinging at Max however, they were taking out nearby allies and enemy alike as they extended outwards along with her blades and were cutting off the heads, arms and legs of anyone near to her, meaning that getting in close as not just a bad idea, it would prove fatal.

Jared and Connor seemed to get the memo, as they were keeping their distance. Max on the other hand, was being targeted by her now and was simply on the defensive, using his blade to block any of her strikes that were coming his way! This wasn't a fun time for him..he hated being stuck on the defensive.. but what choice did he have? He couldn't find any openings on her what so ever!

Suddenly she stopped for a moment and sent a torrent of flames his way! He blocked and advanced slowly forward but she then began using her blades in tandem at the same time and he saw himself blocking and not advancing once again! It frustrated Max so greatly, being stuck on the defensive like this!

Jared and Connor looked to each other and got an idea however. Jared began sending lava at her and the same time that Connor was sending lightning at her! She jumped into the air and dodged it entirely however and then dived straight for Jared!

Jared sighed,"Oh fuck!" He formed armor made of earth but her blades cut straight through it like Paper and he found himself backing away as fast as he could. Max got in between then to block the strike!

Max growled, "Dammit! This bitch is too tough!"

Connor sent lightning at her back but she jumped out of the way and Max and Jared had to both dodge the lightning bolts now!

Max shouted,"watch out Connor! You could've hit us!"

Connor shouted at them,"sorry!"

Ayliana then sent more flames at Max as she swung her blades outwards and Max found himself blocking once more. More of this crap! He HATED being stuck on the defense so much! What else could he do however?! There were no openings!

Max only hoped Jericho was doing better at this point..

Back at the fight with Gronok, Ikuto pointed to nearby enemy soldiers who were still regaining their footing alongside the allies. He detached arms and legs off of random enemies, and with their weapons still attached such as swords, speers, and even magical guns! He caused the arms to float in mid-air so he could use them to attack and distract Gronok while Jericho was healing himself!

Gronok seemed to not be distracted for too long as he sliced through and cut anything that was attacking him as he continued running towards Jericho! Rally launched a bunch of ice and lightning attacks at Gronok as he charged forward, but Gronok deflected those as well, and it was only slowing him down slightly more! Simon joined in and sent a bunch of flames at Gronok and it stopped him long enough for Jericho to finish healing!

Jericho then ran forward and swung his claymore at Gronok but Gronok easily blocked as he said. "Only Cowards can't fight me one on one!"

Jericho smirked,"they're my friends. Besides, all is fair in love and war."

Gronok smiled as he said,"So true!" And chanted in an unknown tongue as he threw one of his blades straight at Simon, and it skewered Simon as it went straight through his chest!

Ikuto screamed,"Nooo!"

Simon coughed blood as he said,"I-I'm sorry Ikuto."

Ikuto sent massive flames straight at Gronok! Jericho formed flames onto his sword as well as cut forward at Gronok!

Ikuto's flames turned Blue! Ikuto cried heavy tears as he continued shouting!

Gronok seemed to be distracted by the Blue flames, but they weren't hurting as much as one would hope.

Jericho took the opportunity and sliced Gronok's arm off!

Gronok growled as he sent a blade and it narrowly missed Ikuto as the blunt side merely knocked him unconscious! Rally grabbed Ikuto and began defending him from random soldiers whom were attacking them both now! Her lightning and ice attacks froze some foes and took out other random opponents as she continued defending the knocked out Ikuto!

Jericho swung his blade at Gronok who blocked the strike. Gronok kicked Jericho off of him but as Jericho flew into the air, he sent lava at Gronok who was tanking the strike!

Jericho swung his blade outwards as he sent flames through the air at Gronok and continued slashing forward at him and ran up close to Gronok, the last place Jericho wanted to be, but he was going for pure agression...perhaps that would win the day today. He swung his blade down at Gronok and Gronok blocked, but Jericho used his free hand to send flames straight into Gronok in the face, Gronok was blinded by it, but not harmed!

That was all it took however as Jericho sliced Gronok straight down the middle, through his head, through his chest and torso all the way down his midsection! Gronok was killed!

Jericho shouted into the air victoriously! He'd killed Dark World's supposed "God of War"!

Back with Alyiana, Max was still stock blocking and dodging any strikes Alyiana lay before him, yet again! Max wasn't a patient person..but he had little choice in the matter with this. One fuck up would cost him an arm and a leg..literally!

While she was doing so however, people were dropping like flies! However, some of the Southern Kingdom soldiers started using sheilds to block her strikes! Connor tried to use the distraction to send lightning but she'd jump over it and it'd hit the allied troop instead! Connor found himself frustrated with how good she was at that, and he felt himself powerless against her!

She went through the shielded Southern Kingdom troops, she jumped over one strike and sliced the arms of one soldier, then she jumped upwards and decapitated another man. She then sliced another man in half along his waist, all the while having to dodge around the shields, which were making it difficult for her to hit them.

Jared sent a bit of flames, carefully so it'd hit her but she still jumped over it! It was like she had eyes on the back of her head at all times! She easily dispatched the soldiers, though it did take her time to do so thus far.

Suddenly. Gratho sent lightning Bolts at her to catch her off guard as he swung his blade at her! Ayliana blocked his strike easily and sent her blades at him! He dodged each time she threw them and sent them back as he got closer and closer to her. He swung his blade at her however she dodged and managed to pull out a smaller blade from behind her back and stabbed Gratho in the gut! He bled profusely!

She jumped backwards and held a blade in each hand as she decapitated him! Gratho was now dead! She didn't miss a beat however and was already headed straight for Max again!

Max got an idea and sent a gust of wind, causing a shield that knocked her blades back at herself! She easily dodged but this definitely threw her off guard as Jared and Connor sent lava at her. She jumped over the attack however but Max sent Fire, Lightning, and used cuts in the air and sent all three at once at her, while Connor did the same with fire and lightning, and Jared sent earth element, fire element and lava element all at her as well! The strikes overcame her and she was killed!

A woman with long green hair attacked Tim. Tim jumped out of the way and said,"Gabriel. Looks like we got another girl who needs a little spank."

Gabriel appeared before him and nodded as he turned into a shovel.

The Green haired woman screamed,"I'm so jealous! My Sister got to go to your world!"

Tim became curious,"Your sister eh?" he said as he dodged a bunch of fire magic and lightning magic that she sent at him as he dodged the attacks.

The Green haired woman replied,"Yes...why does scum like you wanna know?"

Tim grinned,"She had purple hair, didn't she?"

The Green haired woman replied,"Yes..yes she did. I taught her everything she knew. I'm greater than her."

Tim had Gabrield appear. Tim replied,"Show her what ol' purple hair looked like."

Gabriel sighed but hesitantly shape shifted to look like her.

Green Haired screeched,"You killed my little sister, didn't you?!"

Tim Mason dodged a massive lightning strike from the Green haired woman as he replied,"Guilty as charged."

The Green haired woman sent, Fire, lightning and Ice elemental strikes of pure elemental energy at Tim, but he dodged rolled the strikes as she continued screaming at him and sending more and more at him, but he kept dodging it, but it was getting more and more difficult for him to dodge.

The Green haired woman said,"You're not the only one who can call upon spirits of the dead, you know."

She then shouted into the sky,"Old Great Spirit of the Goddess of the Hunt! I know that long ago, the God of War Gronok took you down..but you are mine to command now! Come forward! So that we may become one!"

Suddenly a massive wind came down and a giant female spirit clad in cloth armor appeared wielding a bow and arrows. She was beautiful. She then entered into the Green haired woman's body as she said,"My name, is Morgana by the way."

Morgana glowed as a faint ghost like image of the goddess of the hunt appeared around Morgana as she sent torrents of water at Tim, who jumped out of the way as he said,"Well, two can play that game, lady!"

Tim looked to Gabriel and said,"Now!" Tim joined together with Gabriels Spirit, as Gabriel entered into Tim's body... and a faint ghost like image of Gabriel appeared around Tim.

Morgana took on a very serious face as spiritual armor formed around her and a bow and arrow made of spiritual energy formed onto her back. A long sword made of a spirit-like water formed in her hand as well.

Tim nodded, as he prepared a similar spell. A Ghost like knight armor appeared around Tim and a large two handed Warhammer engulfed in flames of rage and a large tower shield appeared. A large sword made of spiritual energy was also created and was on Tim's back.

Tim shouted as he swung his warhammer at Morgana but she blocked it with her blade as if the hammer was nothing! Tim smirked as he sent spiritual flames at her, but she dodged it and sent spiritual water at him but he rolled out of the way of that!

She then jumped backward and sent spiritual arrows at him but he blocked it with his tower shield as he sent spiritual flames back at her straight from his warhammer! She jumped out of the way of that and sent more arrows at him, which he in turn blocked with his tower shield some more!

He then swung his hammer at her some more but she in turn blocked it with her blade. She sent spiritual water at him but he canceled it out with his spiritual flames. Nothing seemed to be working!

He then ran forward and swung his hammer with full force, long enough to knock her blade out of the way, he then shouted as a nearby ghost grabbed a hold of Morgana!

Morgana, "W-who is this spirit?!"

Tim replied,"Her? She's just Hanna. She told me all about how you killed her. She's happy to help me take your sorry ass out!"

He then swung his hammer down upon Morgana's head and her head splattered into a pool of blood and brains!

Meanwhile, the gunfire had gotten much less at Knoll noticed that the battle was shifting more to close range! He shouted,"NOW! DO IT MORE!"

And suddenly the magic missiles mixed with flames were laying onto the enemy forces and doing magor damage to them! The attacks came on and on, and for the first time..Knoll felt like they might have the advantage again!

Then he saw it, as a massive army of the undead ran forward and made the numbers even greater! They were undead..but much different than say Aiden or Gronok...all in all, they were glorified Zombies, except they seemed to know the different between ally and foe. The moral started to drop as the allied armies started panicking.

Knoll shouted,"Hold the lines! They are weak to fire, use that to our advantage! Light them up the same way you've been attacking the enemy armies!"

They did as told and sure enough, it continued to do well as the undead hoard were being set ablaze, even amongst the harsh cold winter-like winds of the battlefield. Considering the eternal night they were under, the flames made quite the spectacle.

Meanwhile, Brokk's blade clash into his opponent whom blocked. It was Percival!

He smirked,"You look familiar, Kid. Are you any relation to Josh of Gallindor?"

Brokk nodded,"He's my ancestor. Why?"

Percival smirked,"Didn't know the brat had any descendants! Thought I killed him and his entire family line. Guess I was wrong."

Brokk smirked,"I didn't need the motivation to fight you before, but you certainly gave me some!"

The two collided blades as the began fighting. Brokk shouted as it took down a wave of the enemy behind Percival who had dodged the shout himself.

Percival smirked,"Funny thing really. I taught Bahrik a lot of the undead spells he uses. Did it myself. It's how I cheated death, ya know."

Brokk smirked,"You talk too much." He swung at Percival but he dodged the strike.

Percival smirked right back as he said,"Good effort at least!"

The metal clashed as they continued fighting.

Rally and Ikuto were mixed up in the thick of the fight, when suddenly Rally realized among all the chaos, she had been split up from everyone else! Rally was fighting her way through enemies with all the magic missiles she could muster. She was at this point unarmed somehow, but she still had her magic on her side!

Suddenly an enemy stood before her who stood at 7 feet tall with a massive blade, and on it read the words "Kingsglaive". The man wore plate armor and his face wasn't visible.

The man smirked,"This is a cursed blade of Saitoryu Mountain. You will FALL today, stupid stupid little girl!"

Rally frowned. She wasn't ready to unleash it now. But-she had no choice. It would take up a lot of her magic, but in the time she had been training, she had obtained a spell from Dark World. No one else even knew she had it, but her- and she feared summoning it might even kill her. But this man seemed far out of her league, and she couldn't find where her friends were on the battlefield. She had no choice, she had to use it.

Rally allowed a small grin on her face. She had wanted to do this anyways. Rally began chanting the words she'd overheard her friends say anytime they performed their summons and ended it with,"I Beseech thee as my summon: Archeia!"

And with that, a female white dragon with cold-light blue eyes appeared. It stood at 200 feet tall, with a massive wingspan and its skin had icicles dangling from it.

The Dragon responded,"Why have you summoned me?!"

Rally gulped as she replied,"Archeia, you agreed to help me in my greatest times of need, did you not?"

The Dragon, clearly named Archeia, responded,"Yes. You rescued me and I owe you my life. But remember that I only agreed to be summoned in your times of greatest need."

Archeia remembered the moment vividly. She had been injured in a previous battle, and while her foe had long been defeated, she was vulnerable to future attack. Then, a group of humans began bombarding her. They were skilled swordsmen, but wouldn't pose a threat to Archeia if she had been at her full strength. Rally defeated the swordsmen by freezing them into solid blocks of ice. Archeia swore an allegiance to Rally ever since, in exchange for Rally not killing Archeia, herself.

Rally replied,"I'm on a battlefield and my life is in danger! This is such a time!"

Archiea nodded but sighed in annoyance,"So be it. I will help you, human Rally."
She lowered her neck and allowed Rally to get onto her back. Rally quickly formed an ice pillar to bring her up to Archiea and got onto her back.

The plate armor knight grinned,"You've earned the right to my name. My name, is Burke!"

Burke ran forward with the sword and Rally sent the ice pillar she had used to get on Archeia and threw it at Burke, who then sliced it in half. Rally noticed and after he has sliced it, she sent a bolt of lightning at him, hoping it will render him unconscious. His massive strength, most likely from the cursed blade, lead to him wielding it rather fast. Burke formed a shield out of dark magic and deflected the lightning bolt.

Burke laughed,"You'll have to do better than that against a man who's bloodthirst is never Quenched!"

Rally continued firing lightning bolts at him. Each time the lightning bolt was fired at him, Burke deflected it by making the shield appear again. Rally realized this must mean he can't keep the shield up continuously.

Archeia breathed ice to try to get the electrical current from Rally's lightning to go down the ice, to help amplify her attack. Burke's shield was lowered and he was knocked backward and he fell against the icicle he had previous cut in half. As he did so, Rally and Archeia approached him, and Burke swung his blade at the Dragon who deflected it with her talons on her front leg, however, was knocked backwards by Burke's physical strength alone!

Burke jumped into the air to slash Archeia in the face, Rally liked the idea from her dragon and used her ice, melted into water form, and as it hit Burke, she then fired her lightning at Burke! This time Burke didn't wish to go on the defensive and decided to counter by firing raw dark magic at the attack, causing the lightning magic to be overpowered and the dark magic to head for Rally! Suddenly a powerful shield of ice deflected the dark magic.

Rally was surprised,"That wasn't me- my ice isn't strong enough!"

Archeia responded,"It would be a blow to my pride if you were to die while in my charge. It was my work."

As Burke continued to plummet towards Rally he slices his sword across the air, sending a dark magical cut towards Rally, however, the ice from Archeia deflects it and breathes ice onto him, freezing him and then she swallows him whole!

Rally grinned,"Chill."

Archeia managed a small grin at the pun, but then spoke up. The female dragon known as Archeia said,"I must now take my leave. If I stay here for too long, the amount of magic it takes you to summon me would kill you. I can carry you to the one known as Ikuto that I hear from within your mind, but then I really must take my leave."

Rally sighed,"I understand."

Meanwhile, Zack stood as he saw before him was the other Zack! Their faces, hair, hairstyle..and general build were nearly identical.

Zack looked to his evil counterpart and said,"I knew it would come to this, sooner or later."

Evil Zack smirked,"I had not. Never thought I'd see my own reflection, staring back at me as an enemy."

Zack cast an illusion but Evil Zack simply casually sidestepped and tripped the real Zack as he said,"I knew all along I was speaking to your illusion. You'll have to do better than that."

Evil Zack then slung his chain-attached blades at Zack who dodged as he sighed,"I noticed in the distance there are two other people with this type of weapon on the battlefield. Jeez, you guys could use some variety."

Evil Zack swung his blades at Zack, whom casually dodged them as he said,"Perhaps the two of us should start taking this fight more seriously?"

Evil Zack smiled as he said,"indeed." before letting out a massive force field as a massive amount of magic missiles rained down from the sky, as they'd been pre-casted by regular Zack himself, but Evil Zack had seen it coming.

Evil Zack swung his blades at the regular one, who dodged the strikes. He continued dodging and staying on the defensive, formulating a plan.

Meanwhile, Brokk and Percival continued their duel. Percival used mage hand to send pillars of rubble at Brokk, who simply sliced through them with a flaming blade.

Brokk ran forward and their blades met. Percival parried and tried to regain footing but Brokk parried that and their blades then twirled and collided.

Percival replied,"It would seem we are more evenly matched than I anticipated. No matter, you will fall in time."

Brokk head butted Percival who backed off and jumped backward at the act. He then touched the ground and caused several undead to surrounded Brokk. Brokk sliced them down in between having to block strikes from Percival whom was still on the attack!

In the background, Evil Zack had been still attacking this whole time. Evil Zack swung his blade at Zack who dodged it quickly and blocked each strike from Zack. Swing. Clang. Block. Another strike, block, clang. Repeat. Evil Zack was panting.

Zack's plan was working. Evil Zack was getting tired.

Back at the fight with Brokk, the undead had been beaten by Brokk, as Brokk and Percival collided blades, but Percival punched Brokk, and Brokk staggered. Percival grabbed Brokk by the collar and kicked him the gut and began punching him a few more times! Brokk knocked the grip away from Percival and tried to swing his blade at him, but Percival blocked! He swung his blade at Perival again, who blocked again! This time Percival tried to swing at Brokk but he was the one to block this time! Then Brokk moved his blade upward and knocked Percival in the chin and stabbed him straight through the chest.

Brokk said,"come back from that." and spat on Percival's face as Brokk took the blade back out of him.

Percival fell to the ground, lifeless.

Evil Zack began sending flaming arrows he'd formed out of pure magic in the air and began sending them at Zack! Zack blocked the strikes and sent some flaming arrows of his own right back!

Zack ran forward and swung his blade yet again at Zack, whom blocked and dodged as usual. Evil Zack swung again, only to miss. Swung again, was blocked. Evil Zack was still getting tired as regular Zack then quickly changed his speed, no longer matching Evil Zacks as she quickly sliced him in half, and defeated his evil counterpart at long last.

In the distance, a voice could be heard. It was Clifton,"Retreat! We have plan b with us!"

As Max, Shakira, Knoll and some of the other people looked towards Clifton, they saw in his arms he was holding an unconscious Rally and someone besides him was holding a knocked out Ikuto!

Clifton smirked as he shouted,"I'll leave them both alive, for now! Come to fight us soon, if you dare!"

Aiden swung down his blade, sending Raven flying backward, as Aiden fled with the other retreating troops. While some soldiers continued fighting, the enemies gradually retreated and for now..the battle was over.

Chapter 29- the 5 Paladins of the North

Max closed the eyes as they burned Simon over a funeral Pire. He held Shakira closely as she wept. Another of their dear friends had died today. And who knows for how long Ikuto and Rally would live either. The dark sky was haunting. How many more had to die?

A mass funeral was being held for everyone who had died at the battle merely one hour ago. Max cursed under his breath.

'Why? Why did so many people have to die? Will I be next?', Max didn't want to die! Max felt the fear of his own death creep up on him, as these questions circled in his mind.

Max began to sweat heavily as he began panting and hyperventilating. Shakira held him closer, hugging him as she kissed his cheek and said,"Shhh....it's going to be alright."

Max sighed,*I feel like a coward. Just now she was crying and I was comforting her. I'm supposed to be the strong one right now..she knew Simon better than I did even... but now she's comforting ME.'*

Shakira said,"Do you want to talk about it Max? I'm listening if you want to."

Max slowly nodded,"I-it's not just that Simon died. It's not just that all these people died yesterday. I mean..don't get me wrong.. one of the biggest things scaring me right now is..that could have been me on the pire right now. Any one of us could die at any moment..and I've never been more afraid of death than I am now. But it's also one more thing... Ikuto. I hugged and interacted with Jared.

"He and I are old friends. But I used to know Ikuto at one point in the past two. He and I are old friends, just like Jared and I are. But I never once even spoke to Ikuto before the battle. I didn't even say hi to him..and now.. well I'm not sure if he's even still alive.

"Clifton SAYS he's keeping him alive, but I don't know why he would do that when killing him would be easier...what if he's doing some sort of experiments on him or something? What if right now. Ikuto is screaming in pain, begging for the very death that I'm not terrified of? I should've been there, making sure he was okay!"

Shakira replied,"It's not your fault... you were fighting your fight and he was fighting his. There's nothing you could have done."

Max nodded slowly and turned and kissed Shakira on the lips.

Shakira kissed him back and they held closely together in an embrace.

After they finished, Shakira asked,"Does this mean we are back together?"

Max thought for a moment and said,"I'm not sure yet. I think we might be." He paused for a moment then continued," Going through all of this has made me realize what's really important to me, and one of those things is you. So yeah, I guess we are back together."

Then Jericho appeared beside them. He bowed and seemed to be silently honoring Simon.

Max grew angry at seeing Jericho and walked over and punched him in the face, right afterwards, Jericho instinctively flipped Max onto his back and held him against the ground.

Jericho held Max down as Max shouted,"YOU WERE WITH HIM! WHY DIDN'T YOU MAKE SURE NOTHING BAD HAPPENED TO HIM?! BECAUSE OF YOU, IKUTO AND RALLY BOTH WERE TAKEN AWAY BY CLIFTON!"

Jericho responded calmly,"...I'm sorry... Max." but continued to hold Max down until Max stopped trying to fight him. Then Jericho let go and backed off as Max got up. Jericho sounded Genuine, but it was hard for Max to tell as Jericho's face was expressionless.

Zack shouted at both of them,"ENOUGH. Fighting amongst ourselves isn't going to solve anything, so both of you just knock it off!"

Jericho looked like he was about to say something, but decided against it.

'Good', thought Max,*'Say nothing.'*

Zack sighed,"I recommend a small team go inside the city, rescue Ikuto and Rally...and maybe even attack them from within. They'll expect us to still be recovering, and indeed we still are. By the time you are within the city itself, we'll resume our attack. While they are busy fighting us from the outside, this team will go within, rescuing the kidnapped people and then attack them where it hurts. Knoll will remain outside here to lead our forces out here. Max will lead the inside team."

Akemi nodded,"I don't mind that. Knoll has proven to be quite the strategist, even if not everything he thought of worked initially."

Knoll walked forward having overheard the whole thing as he said,"Do you have someone in mind to go with Max?"

Zack nodded,"Yes, I do. It'll be a 5 person team, as any bigger will draw too much attention. Shakira, Connor, Jared and Anna. Shakira can be there to help Max with leading the team. Connor and Jared have proven to be good at working with Max as a team when they fought that woman, so they'll be perfect for it. Anna can be the team's medic and help repair any wounds they endure..and she's a strong fighter in her own right as well.

"Jericho won't be going..it'll draw too much attention after he defeated the God of War. Same goes for Tim and I. Besides, when the enemies see the 3 of us fighting out here on the battlefield, it'll draw their attention towards us. Which is exactly what we need right now."

Knoll nodded in approval of the plan, as did most of the other people present. Zack said,"I'm glad you're all on board. Because you leave right now, to get a head start. Bring any food you need to eat with you."

Max flinched a little. Was a tad bit soon to be going out there, but he understood that time was of the essence so he simply agreed to it.

It took them five hours to reach the outside of the city. They'd have to find the entrance, somehow.

Max quietly said,"So..how do we find a way in?"

Anna quietly responded,"Leave that to me." she chanted to herself quietly, repeating the same phrase 3 times in a row as she said,"Alapagua Dasonfa." each time. Suddenly a blue energy appeared and drizzled into a smokey path leading to the backside of the fence they were near. She motioned for them to follow. They walked for several minutes until they reached an area of the wall. It appeared to be leading into the wall.

Max said,"So...this leads to a friggin wall. I'm going to guess there's some kind of hidden door?"

Anna smiled,"Yep. Right about...here." She pushed the wall a certain way and a small portion of it formed a 4-foot tall door. She giggled,"We'll have to crawl in though."

Connor smirked as he sarcastically said,"Oh goody."
Jared replied,"Hey, I don't see you coming up with ideas."

Connor nodded, "Touché."

They each entered, with Connor and Jared bringing up the rear part of the group as they walked through a tunnel. It went on for awhile. They hear commotion above them.

"They're attacking our outer wall! Sound the alarms! Ready the troops, they enemy has come!"

Max quietly motioned to the others what he'd heard. They all nodded. Knoll's troops were here. Guess the five of them had taken longer to get inside than expected. They were in for now, none the less, as they continued until they entered a dark cave, apparently underneath the city.

There were five stone pillars. Each one had a color. One was purple, one was orange, one was blue, one was red, and one was black.

Max touched the blue one. It did nothing. Max sighed,"Ahh.I always liked the color blue. Wait..Connor. Your lightning is blue. Touch the blue one! Jared, you got lava.. touch the orange one!"

They did as told and the pillars glowed the corresponding color. Max touched the black one and it glowed. Shakira touched the purple one and it glowed. Anna touched the red one and it glowed.

Suddenly ancient words formed onto the wall. Anna remarked,"I..can read it. It's an old language but my father taught it to me. It say...the five paladins of the Northern Kingdom would use this entrance in the old days to enter the city. The Pillars only respond to whom the magic cast over it deems as worthy of being the five paladins.

"I guess it thinks we are worthy of such titles. Each Pillar has a corresponding color that chooses it's paladin. Max has been chosen as the Black Paladin, myself as the Red Paladin, Shakira as the Purple Paladin, Connor as the Blue Paladin and Jared as the Orange Paladin!"

A telepathic voice spoke to them. "*I am the Wolf of the North. My brother, the one known as the 'Wolf of Shogan' sent you here. I call upon you five for an ability that I shall awaken in each of you. Some of you already have this gift...the ones whom re-incarnated from Alexander inherited it from him..though none of them have realized it...and the ones with the dream visions have the potential to unlock it as well... as do the five you. The gift..of foresight.*

"This land use to belong to me and it's former people..before it was conquered by the people of Bretonyama. They were in civil war with each other, but once that was resolved, they took over the people of Shogan..and they also took my lands. To do so, they killed the five paladins charged with protecting it. You five have been deemed worthy..I shall forcefully unlock all doors that lead to the gift of foresight for you. For now, it shall give you the ability to predict opponents movements seconds before they do so. It can grant you many other things, with time."

A light briefly filled the room, one was orange and hit Jared. The next was blue and hit Connor. The next was purple and hit Shakira. The next was Red and hit Anna and the last one was Black and Hit Max. One by one, it hit each of them and the gift of foresight was unlocked within them, as far as Max was guessing.

Max said,"I'm grateful for this and all..but you said that those from Alexander all could regain it because he had it..so what about giving it to Leon and Jericho?"

The Wolf spoke telepathically further: 'I'm only able to help unlock it within the five paladins...those two and any others who have the potential to do so..will have to unlock it on their own.'

Connor shrugged,"Hey, I'm not complaining. If this is true, it'll be a lot of help."

Jared nodded,"Indeed."

Shakira quietly threw her fist into the air as she said excitedly but in a hushed voice,"Alright! I can't wait to try it out!"

Another doorway opened and they entered a maze. It separated each of them as walls came up! Max shouted,"let's just meet at the end guys!"

Everyone else hopefully got the message. As Max continued through the maze, he saw an image on one of the walls.

It was of Ikuto, but was wavy. Beside him was Simon and Roger. "Turn back...it's too late to save any of us now..just turn back and save yourself."

Max shook his head and continued. Another wall shown an image..this time of the grim reaper.

It spoke,"..it's me you fear most...isn't it Max? One day, someone will kill you. You've been fighting so hard..but sooner or later, all it'll take is one little mistake and you will be with me forever!"

Max shivered. It was true. Hell...he didn't even have time to fear dying of old age..like he used to when he worried he wasn't doing anything with his life. Now he also had to fear the fact that all it took..would be one little mistake in a battle..and he'd be gone forever! His world, his entire universe would be over..he would simply cease to even BE! At this point..who knew if there was an afterlife even? It could just be all over. Just like that. He continued walking, but each step he found more and more difficult.

Maybe he should turn back? I mean...sure he'd be a coward..but at least he wouldn't be dead. He could live to see another day. But what kind of existence would that be? He'd live knowing he was a coward..who abandoned all of his friends. It's not like there was any guarantee they'd even find a way home anyways!

No. He could never do that. Too much was at stake. He HAD to do this..not for himself..but so that hopefully..after all of this was over..SOMEONE would survive it all. Whether it was him or not. Fight so that maybe..just maybe they'd find a way home. He continued forward!

In the next part of the Maze was Shakira. She saw on a wall images of Joey and Simon. She huffed,"Really wall, you'll HAVE to do better than that. All this does is make me angry enough that I want to knock the head off of whomever's idea it was!"

And with that, she continued forward.

Next was Jared's wall. As he continued forward he saw images of his parents. His mother and his father. His cousin. His sister.

"You miss us...don't you? You'll never see us again. You're an entire world apart! You will never get to see us again..you'll never be home again. Just give up, and accept your fate!"

Jared tried to ignore it, though he must admit, it was getting to him. He continued forward. Next to appear on the screen was Nero.

"I got Earth..what's your lava now? It kept you alive..but for all you know, I might be dead! It's all your fault! You brag about your lava, but how much good did it do you now? You should just give up while you're ahead! Because you won't survive much longer!"

Jared spat at it and said,"You aren't Nero. Fuck off." and continued forward.

Next was Connor. First, he saw the images of Jermaine, Joey, and the other sparks.

"You taught us Lightning magic..just like yours..but what good did it do us? We all died because of you!"

Connor stuttered,"N-no! It's not like that! I did my best, I really did! I'm fighting forward for you! All of you!"

"How can you fight for us..we're already dead."

Connor replied,"I-it's in your honor! You would want me to live.....wait. Why am I arguing with you? You aren't real! The real Sparks wouldn't be discouraging me right now!" and with that, he continued forward!

Next was Anna. She saw images of her father on the wall. "Why are you helping these people? I raised you to kill Allanon, yet you help his pupils?"

Anna replied,"My Pa was his pupil too once. And my Pa was wrong. Allanon was a great man, and Ah'm proud to have served with him. Be gone from my sight, foul illusion!"

It disappeared and she continued forward. They all reached the end of the Maze...

Shakira said,"alright! We made it! I still didn't get to use my foresight yet, though, I hope I will soon."

A voice nearby said,"Good, because you'll get to find out if it's going to help you any right now."

A man appeared. He had black short hair and dark brown tanned skin with dark brown eyes. His tanned skin was notable considering the eternal night thing. He wore a black and grey striped sleeveless shirt, with a black tricorne hat with skull pins on it and black pants with very long black boots that almost came up to his knees but not quite.

"Name's Blackjack. Captain is out fighting his brother Raven. Means us other pirates are sitting in here getting all restless. But Captain knows best and he said we'd find a fight within the city! Boy, he was right!"

Suddenly, as if sucked like a vacuum, Max was separated from the others and went flying in another room!

Before him stood a man whom was five foot 3. It was Clifton!

"I knew you'd be sending scouts to try to recover your friends. I allowed it to happen. I figured you'd send some of your strongest people in to do so, and I could widdle down some of you by separating you from everyone else. You didn't disappoint me, coming yourself.

"I can have the honor of assisting in killing the one who defeated the Zizix. That's right Max, I know who you are. My intel is good for that. You'll also find this room won't allow you to summon your Phoenix, so don't bother trying. Same goes for any of your friends with summons that are within this city."

Max frowned, "Fuck you!" He ran forward at Clifton but was blocked..by Ikuto!

Clifton said,"Now, now. That's impolite. After I went through all the trouble of reuniting you with your friends! Ikuto..Rally...say hello to Max for me."

Max jumped backward as a bunch of fire and Ice were sent at him!

He looked and saw, standing before him was Ikuto and Rally..but their eyes..they were darker. Some sort of spell..controlling them.

"Shit! So that's why you took them.", said Max.

"Bingo.", said Clifton. He added,"I must be going now. I have to make sure my strategy is working on the battlefield. Two fronts, one here and one there, you know. Tah-tah for now."

Max tried to run at Clifton but was cut off as Ikuto formed a sword of flames and swung at Max, Max blocked but had to jump back as more Ice was sent his way. He dodged it. But now what? He was afraid Ikuto and Rally would have faced a fate worse than death..torture. But he hadn't been prepared for this!

Meanwhile, in the other room, Jared formed an axe made of earth. If he formed lava it might cut off their oxygen in the caves, so he couldn't do that. Not that the fire was that much better either, so he was stuck with Earth element!

BlackJack had his own battle axe ready, and he had a pouch beside him that he patted. "I can't wait to add your scalp to my collection."

Jared gulped and said,"Fuck you! You're not getting mine!"

At the same time, Connor was going toe to toe with a man clad in green leather armor. Connor kept sending lightning at the man but he kept tanking it. The man smirked,"It will take more than that to take down the crew of the King of the Pirates, lad!"

Anna was being fired at with a flintlock by a female pirate! Anna said,"Fight me up close, you bitch!"

The woman smirked,"It's not my fault you and I must be opposites! Blame it on fate that I was told you have the same name I do! Daddy is Captain of this crew and he wants his dear old little Anne to take the head of the one called Anna!"

Shakira was trying to figure out how to open the area that had taken Max..eventually, she managed it, but as she opend it, the door closed behind her! Instead of being sucked into the area like before, she was simply in the room beside the previous one. Sitting a fireplace was a woman with brown hair. She turned and stood up out of the chair as she said.

"Kaitlyn. And you must be Shakira."

Shakira replied,"I didn't ask for your name, but ok."

"It's only polite. My brother is the King so I guess that makes me the dutchess...I died many years ago..but dear old brother wouldn't let me stay dead..and now he has me doing dirty work like fighting you, apparently. Nothing personal...I'd rather still be dead."

She swung her sword at Shakira who sidestepped quickly out of the way and parried it. The battlefield outside where the bigger battle was happening could be heard in the distance. Jared's axe collided with that of BlackJack. Jared changed swing and BlackJack blocked that. BlackJack attempted a swing of his own only for Jared to block it.

BlackJack said,"You're quite good, what was your name again?"

Jared responded,"Jared."

BlackJack nodded,"I'll remember it."

Jared thought to himself. *'This guy is actually far better with an axe than I am. If I wasn't predicting his moves right before he did them, he would've killed me a long time ago. Gotta thank that Wolf sometime.'*

Anna sent magic missiles at Anne but Anne pulled out her cutlass and was deflecting each strike! Anna sent a magical flame at Anne, who pulled out a magical gun and deflected it with magic energy from her own gun!

Anna screamed as she said,"I've had enough of you!"

Anne said,"it be mutual!"

As they both ran forward and knocked each other unconscious!

Connor meanwhile kept sending magic missiles at the man who kept being strong against it. However, then he got a feeling. He sent a magic missile and predicted the man would dodge it, and he DID! He did so again and predicted where the man would dodge next, but he tanked that one as well. Connor got an idea. If he could predict what this man would do next..maybe just maybe..this would work. He formed a sword of lightning and slashed at him but the man blocked it with this cutlass..big mistake as it electrocuted him, defeating him!

Back with Max, he was dodging their strikes. Shit! He'd have to take them alive...there's no way he could bear the thought of killing his friends! But how was he going to do this without killing them? The thought was aching at him as he continued dodging the shots of flame and ice. He noticed himself gradually predicting when they'd strike next. That didn't mean much, however, as he was barely keeping up with Ikuto as he swung his flaming blade at Max. Max then realized something.

He formed wind magic into his hands as he continued dodging. That flaming sword and the fire of Ikuto....it was slowly cutting off all of the oxygen in the room. But what was Max's favorite element to use? Wind! He used to train with it many times in fact. He thought back on when he was with Raven. Raven used to always tell him to stop flying around in the air and goofing off. In fact, Max loved using wind element so much. Raven had to make him practice with other elements as well just so he could have more variety! Since doing so, Max had learned all kind of things. He could form tornadoes, he could send wind cuts in the air..but most of all...everyone breathes Oxygen. He could cut THAT to a low.

He sent a vacuum around Ikuto. It was difficult to pinpoint while dodging Ikuto and Rally's attacks..especially because they didn't stay still and he had to focus on getting them into the vacuum and not himself. But it worked! The air around Ikuto and Rally went so low, they couldn't breathe and they gradually got slower as he continued dodging..until they then both fell over.

Max said,"Out cold... No pun intended, considering the weather outside."

Then a man entered with long black hair and a scythe. Max had his guard up ready but the man put his hand up,"Hold on there. I'm not here to fight you. On the contrary..I don't like that my Captain, Aiden, is serving someone else. Hardly being free, is it? We're Pirates..and what we value most is our freedom. I'll give you a map..should lead you right to your friends here, and then also straight to Bahrik himself. I'm doing this because I want you to let me grab my friends that have been fighting yours.

"Then, we're all going to go out and help your mentor, Raven... we won't serve that fool Bahrik any longer! We follow our Captain's orders..but I've been thinking about it for awhile now..they weren't his orders being given, he was merely a puppet! Thing is..we weren't strong enough to take down Bahrik ourselves. Who could be? Then Aiden fought you all. If anyone can..you can. You're welcome to not believe me of course..I'm known for being deceitful anyways. The choice is yours."

Meanwhile, Shakira and Kaitlyn clashed swords. Shakira had found one and was using it to her advantage! The swords clashed repeatedly, however as the fight went on, she found herself predicting what Kaitlyn would do next. She noticed a pattern. Downward thrust, she dodged. Sideways thrust. Dodge. Then a stab. Dodge. Repeat, with occasional mix-ups with other moves..just to make it seem random and less like a pattern, but she saw it. Then her prediction abilities saw that she was going to intentionally change the pattern, to throw off Shakira further.

A fire attack came followed by an erratic bunch of different strikes and parries that normally would have been entirely too fast for Shakira to react. But her abilities meant she saw it coming. She dodged all 10 strikes right at perfect timing and then instinctively stabbed her through the heart.

Shakira apologized,"I'm sorry I had to end your life...though you told me you were already dead. So perhaps I'm simply ending your suffering."

Kaitlyn cried as she said,"Thank you. My brother should never have brought me back. I want to rest in peace....please...stop my brother. He's no longer the great man he once was. He's killing this world...it's life force itself is waning...please stop him before he leads to the death of the very little of life that's left..."

Somehow, perhaps by magic itself..she was able to say that much...even with a blade through her heart.

Shakira nodded,"I will. Max and I both will, I promise."

Back with Max, he was still thinking about the offer. Max paused and thought for a moment more and said,"what choice do I have? I got no idea where else I could go. Gimme the map, and I'll do it!"

Max took the map, finding Shakira along the way...and in due time he found his friends.

Max asked,"Connor, Jared, Anna..how are you guys doing?"

Jared sighed,"why's that guy behind you?"

Max replied,"We don't have to fight these pirates any further! We're on the same side!"

Max explained what had happened and the group nodded.

Connor replied,"that's actually kind of a relief. We can continue forward."

Jared agreed,"Yeah. I'm not sure how much more of fighting BlackJack I could take."

BlackJack smirked,"You weren't too bad yourself Jared, lad! Sorry I didn't stop sooner..just didn't know what Mazin and Captain were up to..just following orders, ya see. Captain tells me to kill ye..and well, I was gonna kill ye!"

Black Jack laughed as if it was the funniest thing in the world. Jared simply laughed nervously.

Max sighed,"I wonder how everyone's doing on the battlefield outside all this time, though..the fighting has gotten quieter."

Heliopolois told him telepathically: *'The battle is going well. A lot of the stronger enemy troops have been beaten, but the battle isn't over yet. Knoll is gradually pushing them back, but Clifton's strategies are mostly leaving them at a stale mate. I'm linked to Lucian and he's telling me. Knoll is feeling confident in this though and is sending Leon and Jericho to meet us here.'*

Max nodded as he relayed the message to the others..soon enough, it'd be time to continue forward...to attack the king himself! Of course, they may still have more opponents along the way...

Chapter 30- The end...for now.

Anna was awoken by Max as he said, "You were brought to be the healer, so I have one request of you. Could you please heal us? We need our strength, stamina, magic... all of that replenished to full if we are going to go after the King himself!"

Anna nodded, "Damn y'all, right to the point! I just woke up, gimme a minute!"

Max replied, "Sorry, we just are short on time, I figure."

Anna sighed, "Here it goes", then cast a spell on all of those present to restore to each of them their being. "Normally a simple thing me, though we've all been through a lot, so I'm a little out of it. Still, the job is done. Let get this finished."

Max nodded as he offered a fist bump to everyone. Shakira, Leon, and Jericho quickly did the same, putting theirs forward as they looked at each other.

Anna then sighed, "Sure, why not?" and put her fist in.

Ikuto nodded, "Looks dorky, but I'm in", and put his fist in.

Rally said, "This might be totally awesome to do anyways!"

Connor smiled, "I'd be happy to", and put his fist in.

Jared smiled, "Well, I don't wanna be the jackass who is the only one who didn't so...", he put his fist in, allowing a small half-smile.

They all fist bumped as Max said, "Let's go kick King Bahrik's ass!", completing the fist bump together with a collective nod.

They headed up a long staircase as they went throughout the castle, taking out guards along the way. None of them were much to worry about, so they didn't even bother with magic, relying on physical combat to get through them all. They then entered a long hallway, continuing to defeat more guards as the battle raged on for everyone else.

They reached a doorway labeled so as to signify it as a throne room. It was a massive entrance, no less than one hundred feet tall and perhaps even more. Pushing with their collective might, it finally opened;
Max, Shakira, Leon, Jericho and Anna entered in as it slammed shut behind them.

On the other side, they could hear a massive ambush as what sounded like a very real struggle was happening! Immediately, Max and Leon were the first to attempt opening the doors but they wouldn't budge. Shakira, Jericho, and Anna joined in to no avail, when a voice behind them said, "Welcome, my honored guests. Please, sit down for a while. Have some dinner."

They turned and saw tables off to the side with foods of various kinds, many resembling foods from their own world and banners with their names on them. King
Bahrik wore a brown leather jacket and white button-up shirt, tan cloth pants and a sword sheathed to his side, as well as black leather boots. He had blue eyes that sometimes changed to a slight greener tint, as well as long red hair.

Over his regular clothes he was wearing black metal plate armor, with a long white cape with golden trim. He also wore a crown upon his head made of pure gold with various gems and diamonds in it.

Max was caught off guard by his appearance, but heard Jericho speak first. He said, "What kind of game are you playing? You've been trying to kill us and fought many battles... and now you offer us food?"

Bahrik calmly smiled,"You've proven yourself worthy. Besides..you are foreigners..helping them fight me. My beef was never with you."

Max spoke up,"Bullshit. You sent Mortas, and Vorkalth and various others to attack our homeworld! Don't pretend you aren't our enemy! You killed my friends, you killed our mentor..don't act like you're our friend now!"

Bahrik frowned,"That's unfortunate. But you can see around you what's happening to this world. It's dying..what choice did I have? We have to find a new home for all of us to live on."

Shakira replied,"But you are killing this world with all of your dark magic! This is your own fault!"

Bahrik said,"this isn't black and white you know. My mother was killed in front of me. My sister as well. I HAD to become king. No matter the cost. So that there would be peace all over my world. Wars could stop, people would stop dying. I had no way of knowing the outcome..especially not this one."

Leon said,"It sounds like to me, you aren't taking enough responsibility for your own actions."

Bahrik replied,"Enough about that..I have an offer to you. I can take you all back home. It was never my intention for any of you to come here to this world. My greatest pupil did that. Mortas. That's him. His pupils were Aldos and Vorkalth. I taught him, and he taught them. Of course, some of my other pupils went with them. Whom better to send but the very best of my pupils? I had no way of knowing they'd rebel from me and try to take your world for themselves, in their own way.

"Nor did I know they'd send all of you here, unwillingly. So it's in my best interest as well as yours, to send you all back home. I mean, that's what you want, right? To go home and see your friends and your families again. To maybe even take revenge for the way my pupils have wronged you? I can make that happen. It'll take time however..so you'll have to be patient.

"And I can't do any of that if your friends outside keep attacking me..so we'll have to do something about that. I don't want to have to kill them..so maybe you can help me? Talk some reason into them..or whatever it comes to. I'm sure they'll listen to you more than they'd listen to me."
Max and the others were taken aback by all of this. Could it really be this simple?

"They'd never expected to hear something like THIS from the King of Dark World. Would it really be that easy to just simply, end this war now..and peacefully head back home? The thought had never occurred to him that it would be this simple. No...something about this just didn't feel right.

Max replied,"No..I don't think we will be doing that. When we leave..what assurances do we have that you won't simply kill everyone else here? I don't trust you, and I don't know what kind of schemes you might try to pull if we did try to trust you."

Shakira nodded in agreement,"Your sister spoke to me, Bahrik-"

Bahrik responded,"KING BAHRIK....but continue."

Shakira rolled her eyes and continued,"Regardless.. your sister spoke to me. She said you are still killing this world with all of the dark magic you and your armies are using. Even now, this world itself is slowly dying. You need to be dethroned and this needs to be fixed. What you are doing clearly isn't working..and your insistence to your title shows signs of arrogance."

Jericho nodded in agreement as he said," Your reign is at an end, Bahrik." he emphasized in his tone of voice the fact he called him by name, without the use of his title. Max could tell Jericho was trying to passively insult the king of dark world.

Bahrik frowned,"It's treason then." Green energy filled the room as he summoned and a 200 foot tall undead dragon. The dragon looked like it was a skeleton of what was a dragon, with bits of flesh still remaining on it throughout.

Max summoned Heliopolis at his normal full size, putting him at roughly the same height as the undead dragon.

Jericho summoned Goron at his normal full size, which was about the same height too.

Shakira, Leon, and Anna summoned their respective summons as well, though none of them

537

were quite as large as the before-mentioned summons.

Bahrik pulled out his sword and swung it at Max and Jericho in one swift swing as his sword extended in length!

They both blocked but only narrowly! Anna sent magic missiles at Bahrik, whom simply tanked them and seemingly felt NOTHING.

Shakira sent lightning, Leon sent arcane magic at him, but he simply endured the attack and seemed to be unharmed as he swung and cut off Jericho's arm! Jericho screamed!

He swung at Shakira and managed to lay a deep cut into her side as he continued his swing and nearly took off Leon's head!

Meanwhile, the summons were fighting the Dragon! It breathed blue flames at the summons who scattered and each sent elemental magic right back at the dragon but it had no effect as they began scratching and biting at each other!
Anna says,"this isn't working guys..forgive me for doing this..but it's the only way. You'll thank me later."

She began chanting a large chant as she floated in mid-air and tried to avoid all of the fighting.

Bahrik was attacking them all but they were trying greatly to keep their distance as they were continuously being attacked by a man who's raw strength and speed seemed to be out doing them! If they didn't come up with a solution fast, they WOULD be killed by this man simply out of his natural strength, toughness, and speed alone, and he was not even using any magic at them!

As Anna's chant finished she shouted,"By the power my father taught me..I now commence the re-unification spell! It will only be temporary and have a time limit of which I'm unsure of..but it must be done! Today..we become Alexander once again!"

Suddenly each of them began glowing...Shakira, Max, Jericho, and Leon immediately flew towards Anna with rapid speed and their bodies collided as a blinding red light formed! Sparks filled the room and then immediately after bright red flames!

From the flames, a figure stepped forward in their place. His flowing long red hair was glowing deeply, no doubt an after effect of the fusion spell, but none the less the glowing was continuous..as if the glowing would never stop and indeed it might not... as his almost cold-looking green eyes hid an inner fire that many whom had known him in the past were very familiar with. He was clad in brown leather armor and he had a ten-foot long sword with a small miniature skull at the bottom of the hilt. It was Alexander!

Alexander spoke,"My memories have not returned...instead I remember...I remember it all. I remember the fear of death, yet the continued determination to continue to fight... I felt as Maxwell Schneider. I remember the rage and anger I felt towards anyone who underestimated me..as Jericho Wallrick. I remember the joy of my friends..the sheer energy I had to keep going..yet the sadness of the death of my friends...as Shakira Nomura.

"I remember my continued loyalty I felt..as Leon Mcknight. I remember the hope I could give others..as Anna Smith. I remember all of the many things I felt as each of them. I may look like the Alexander of old..but I have no memory of being him. Instead..I am the five of them..all in one...and in honor of all of that I am..and all of my friends who have been fighting, some of which have now since passed on...I will KILL you, Bahrik!"

As he said all of this of course. The summons were still fighting the Undead Dragon Bahrik had summoned earlier.

Alexander cast a spell that sent many arrows made of flames at Bahrik continuously on auto-pilot. It was a spell Anna had heard was a famous one the real Alexander used to use. Having that in the background the whole time could be of use to whittle down the will of their opponent, especially since the spell itself would be stronger than usual now that it was being used as Alexander.

While that was doing so, Bahrik smiled and cast Ice, Fire, Water, lightning, lava, wind, earth, Sand and many other elemental attacks that were all hard to keep track of..but he cast them all at once!

Alexander put his sword in front of him to block the strikes! Bahrik's first spell of the fight, and it was a fitting one, all things considered!

As Alexander was blocking, Bahrik ran forward and attempted to swing at Alexander from the side, but Alexander jumped out of the way and then attempted a swing but Bahrik jumped out of the way of that!

It became a battle of speed as they kept attempting to swing at one another but the other kept dodging! Then their blades met and hit one another and the room shook as a shockwave filled the room! Bahrik swung his blade upwards and then back down again. Alexander blocked the strike and swung his blade for a sideways slash, but Bahrik obstructed his strike right back! This process continued twice more, but both times they blocked each others attempts!

Bahrik smiled,"It would seem we are evenly matched. For now."

Alexander shouted as he jumped into the air and did a downwards attack, but Bahrik simply dodged. He then swung his blade straight at Alexander's face but Alexander managed to parry that! Each time their blades hit, the air itself seemed to tremble!

Bahrik grinned as he shouted,"Curse of the Putrid Husk!"

Suddenly an illusion filled the eyes of Alexander! This illusion made it appear his flesh was rotting and falling off his body, and that his internal organs were spilling out! Alexander shouted as he clenched his fists and put his arms close to himself, and then outward, dispelling it! Alexander smiled grimly as he said,"Jericho learned that move from fighting Gronok!"

The arrows continued being sent at Bahrik, but it wasn't even slowing him down, making it hard to tell if it was even damaging him!

Alexander remembered another of Anna's known spells as he cast and shouted,"TRAP THE SOUL!"

He pulled out a gem and attempted to grab onto Bahrik's soul and imprison him in it!

Bahrik shouted as he held strong to the ground! It gradually began pull him in but then he cast a spell, as he shouted,"GRATHNORGARNOK!" and the spell dispelled, but suddenly Alexander felt an intense pain as he threw up blood and he felt dizzy. Alexander used healing magic to undo the effects, but was quickly back in battle as the swords collided! They swung at each other as their swords clashed! Despite all that was going on, and all the vast sword knowledge of the people within him, he found himself on the defensive! Bahrik swung, Alexander blocked. Bahrik swung again, and he continued to block!

Then his Leon part of his brain had an idea..perhaps he could tire Bahrik out. That would take quite some time however..but maybe while the arrows continued to hit Bahrik in the back, it would assist in gradually doing so! Alexander swung his blade into a saber lock, and Bahrik punched Alexander backward and attempted another swing, but Alexander managed to block this one.

Meanwhile, the battle of the summons was still happening as Gronok attempted to grab the undead by the neck, but it seemed unharmed as it scratched at Goron, leaving some scars on his stomach! Heliopolis used healing tears to heal Goron, while Lucian was firing lightning magic and Uriel was fireing lava magic both at the undead dragon, being careful not to hit Alexander. The Undead seemed unharmed by it, but it was at least slowed down for now and then continued firing said magic at it, as it at least was slowing its movements.

Meanwhile, Alexander still found him blocking strikes and on the defensive against Bahrik. Bahrik growled,"Stop defending so much and fight me like a man! You coward!"

Alexander didn't let it get to him and continued to strike and block the attacks, Bahrik managed to land a kick and send Alexander back though

Suddenly, he cast Dark arcane magic at Alexander, who responded by casting the regular arcane spell and their blasts continued to hold against each other! The spells continued and continued..but Alexander remembered that this was all to similar to what had killed Allanon...this would surely overpower him with time. At the last second, as his spell began to lose to Bahrik, he dodged out of the way and allowed it to hit a nearby wall instead.

Alexander's fire arrows still continued to hit Bahrik during all of this, in the back...of course. But the affects were still hard to say. He immediately swung his blade at Alexander again however, whom blocked it further, and allowed a small parry to catch Bahrik off guard, though it did little good...it at least might allow Bahrik to not notice too much of his plan.

Alexander swung his blade to appear offensive, though of course as he knew..Bahrik blocked it and swung his own blade at Alexander whom blocked it. Then Bahrik swung his blade again and Alexander blocked that as well, but managed a punch that he put mage hand into, so it'd send Bahrik flying backward..which it indeed did.

Then Alexander cast wind element to attempt to cut off the oxygen of Bahrik. It was a technique he'd used as Max to defeat Ikuto and Rally before..maybe he could take Bahrik down alive.

Bahrik sent a massive burst of lightning, as the massive strike shined through the room with a massive electrical power at Alexander! Alexander had no choice but to dodged out of the way, breaking his concentration and freeing Bahrik of the attack! Alexander sent his own lightning bolts of equal size right at Bahrik immediately after however, but Bahrik dodge rolled out of the way of that strike himself and sent a burst of flames at Alexander, whom in turn sent an equal measure of flames to cancel each other out, literally fighting the fire with fire!

Out of the flames, Bahrik blind-sighted Alexander and managed a swing that cut Alexander in the chest some as he was attempting to dodge.

Bahrik then did a gripping motion as he used mage hand to choke Alexander, whom was now suffocating!

Bahrik smirked,"You fool! I could have made you great, you know. Under my tutelage, you could have surpassed my greatest pupil, and together we could have killed him..we'd be like brothers! But instead, you are forcing me to kill you!"

Alexander choked and choked, but managed to reach out his hand and grab some of the earth beneath Bahrik's feet and knock him over with it. As he did so Alexander swung his blade, pouring arcane magic over the blade while doing so, to try to finish Bahrik off, but Bahrik blocked!

Alexander used his free hand to attempt to cast lightning in Bahrik's face, but Bahrik used a spell that caused the lightning to dissipate into nothing! Alexander changed his spell to mage hand, but so did Bahrik as their mage hand spells hit each other and they both went flying in opposite directions from each other! Bahrik then cast a lightning spell, but this one was faster than Alexander was ready for and he was electrocuted! He felt the shocks hit his body as he felt great pain course throughout his body! He very barely moved out of the way as Bahrik attempted to slash him in half during the spell!

Alexander jumped several feet back as he thought to himself. This was it..it was now or nothing. Alexander couldn't afford to continue to try to tire Bahrik out..it wasn't working. He had to do an even greater gamble..he'd have to cast Wish. It was a spell that by simply speaking aloud, you can alter reality to better suit you. The risk? If you failed the spell, it would kill you. Even if you succeeded, it would cost you nearly all of your magic to use. But what choice was there? This was it..if he didn't do it..sooner or later, Bahrik was going to kill him.

Alexander spoke the word..the word that in his memories as Anna, he never thought he'd have to resort to using. He said," Wish."

As he did so, Alexander focused his thoughts on killing Bahrik. He had trouble thinking of how, or what he'd want...but Wish seemed to be deciding it for him as the room twisted and turned..then Alexander went unconscious and all went black.

As a person awoke, he saw Bahrik was long gone, and before him was his friends..except he wasn't Alexander anymore..he was Max. And beside him, he saw Jericho and the other pieces of Alexander were awakening at the same time. Jericho had his arm back, good as new.

Sitting beside Max as he lay there, was Ikuto. Ikuto said,"You alright, dude?"

Max said,"Yeah.I uh..feel like my head got smashed in a vice, but yeah I'm fine. What happened?"

Ikuto smiled,"You guys killed Bahrik. We don't know how, but you did it! Then, Connor and Jared and all of us, got the door open and saw you all laying on the ground! Shortly after, we heard Knoll coming inside. He told us that Aiden had somehow turned good again and Raven didn't have to kill him or something... it was all confusing for me... but the point is..Clifton surrendered to us and they didn't even have to kill him! Knoll had managed to be winning towards the end anyways, so that helped. Now we're just waking you guys up as best we can."

Max gradually stood up as Ikuto helped him up. He leaned on Ikuto as he saw Jared was helping Leon stand up. Connor was helping Jericho stand up, and so on.

Max said,"So now what?"

Jericho said,"Well...Bahrik had said he had a way to send us back home..do you think he was bluffing?"

Leon shrugged,"Hard to say, but I think it's worth looking into."

Shakira smiled,"Definitely."

Anna sighed,"Did y'all even stop to realize somethin? Guys...we won!"

Max smiled,"Good point..that is nice-"

Jericho replied,"No DERRR!!!"

Seemingly everyone laughed at Jericho's sarcasm, though the 5 whom had just been Alexander all groaned after they laughed, still very sore from the fighting.

Max said,"I guess there'd have to be a book or something of some sort that Bahrik could have. It'd tell us how to do it.."

Knoll nodded and said,"Guess we better start searching. It might be awhile."

Zack agreed as he nodded and said,"In the meantime, we should probably help everyone figure out what the future of Dark World is going to be like while we are here. We can't just leave everyone behind without helping with that much."

As a time passed, things did eventually settle down. Max smiled as walked into the throne room. On the thrown sat Akemi who smiled and waved at him.

Max said,"Good to see you again your majesty!" He then bowed.

Akemi smiled,"My dear friend...none of you ever have to bow to me. You're the real heroes, not I!"

Max stood back up as he smiled. Akemi was crowned King of the North, though he made their system of government a looser..essentially he only was truly King of Bretoyama and the Northern Capital. Anything else was lead by their own kings, and mostly independent, only ever reporting to Akemi if they needed his help with anything. There was an immortal council that served under him, made up of Aiden and Raven..and apparently their brother Connor too, over time.

That had been quite some time ago now, though.

Max smiled,"Things really have changed...my birthday is coming up you know. I'll be 26..jeez, I feel like an old man." He laughed as Akemi laughed with him.

Akemi said,"what does that make an elderly man like me? Extinct?"

They both laughed even further as Max said,"Ever figured out who's next in line when you pass on?"

Akemi smirked,"Nah! This old geezer has plenty of time to think about that! Don't you worry about me! Besides..you and your friends finally get to go home today!"

Max smiled,"True, true. It'll be good to finally see the sun again...speaking of which..do you think this world will ever get over its air pollution issues and see it again yourselves?"

Akemi frowned,"Who knows? I'll do everything in my power to make that happen...but who can say anymore? It's really just hard to judge after all the damage Bahrik has done over the years..."

Max shrugged,"I guess I'll see you later. This is getting awkwardly gloomy!" He waved and smiled as he let out a nervous chuckle.

Akemi waved as well as Max walked into the preparation room. There he saw Shakira, Jericho, and Leon.

Shakira smiled,"It'll be interesting not fighting this restless feeling dark world always leaves us in. I'll be able to breathe a sigh of relief and finally feel comfortable."

Leon laughed,"I agree. I'll bet Jericho feels it most of all..he hasn't had a good fight in a while!"

Jericho smirked,"I'm sure we can arrange something when we get back. Speaking of which..what do you guys all wanna do when we get back? Visit family sure..but what about after that?"

Max shrugged,"What about starting Allanon's School for the Gifted back up in some way?"

Leon was intrigued. "Really? That IS an interesting idea. We could have the six of us from Camp 1 as it's founders too!"

Jericho nodded,"I like the idea."

Max smiled,"I'm not sure if we'll be able to reveal the magic to the public, so it might end up being lie the old one..I guess we'll figure that all out when we get there, though."

Leon shrugged,"Who knows? I've been so busy helping this new system of government from here in the Northern Capital that I hadn't really thought about things like that as much as I'd like. Mainly just been thinking how happy I'll be to see my friends and family again."

Max nodded,"And don't forget Camp 3! I've visited there only once recently, Nero is teaching them all magic of all things! But we don't go there much, as it's really far! I think as far as I remember, only Jericho and a few of us from Camp 1 have been there!"

Jared walked in as he laughed,"Did you say, Nero? I remember that guy. I really missed teasing him about my lava all the time. At this point, I'd be willing to help him learn how to use it himself if he wants. But if he's teaching our old school all that stuff, he might already know how!"

Ikuto entered next and did a fist bump with Max.

Max grabbed both Jared and Ikuto and hugged them. "I'm comfortable with myself enough to hug you guys!"

Jared hugged him back, Ikuto just said,"Oh brother" but managed a small laugh.

Max said to Ikuto,"Are you as ready to go home as the rest of us?"

Ikuto said,"Yeah...though I wish my brother could go with us."

Max said,"..sorry dude."

Ikuto shook his head,"Nah it's fine dude. That's the past, you know? Just gotta move on with your life, that's how it is for all of us."

Max said,"true, true." he looked at Shakira while she was off to the side talking to Rally.

Shakira was excited," we're finally going home!"

Rally said,"awww yeaaah!" and fist bumped Shakira who did the same.

Shakira said,"What are you gonna do when we go?"

Rally said,"Probably go out and do some singing, try to record a new album. I'm not sure anyone will believe what we went through so I'll have to say the subject of the songs is entirely fictional, just to be safe!"

Shakira nodded as she said,"I guess that makes sense."

The talking continued for awhile, as people continue entered and exiting the room over time, but eventuall, it all settled down as each of them entered.

Knoll and Zack started a chant, as Anna joined in. It was finally time for them all to go home.

Eventually, a purple portal appeared.

Zack said,"Well guys..this is it. We're finally going home."

Knoll nodded,"indeed. Let's just get on with it!"

Everyone shouted,"YEAH!" as they all threw their fists in the air, excitedly. Not out of any kind of rudeness..but on the contrary..everyone was just so happy this would all finally be over with and they could go home! And so..they all entered the portal. The portal itself was an iridescent, purple, distortion in the fabric of space and time. It opened it's mouth wide, but it was hard to see what was on the other side..it was a haze that made it difficult to see. Everyone of Camp 1 and everyone of Camp 2 entered it...a sister portal was being formed by Sho and Nero back in Camp 3 so they could head back at hopefully the same exact place, or as close to it as they could.
Sho said,"I hope this thing works like Max said it would. Hard to be sure."

Nero smiled,"You'll tell everyone of how I taught a lot of people in the school magic, right?"
Sho smirked,"I talk about a lot of things, but usually, your personal business is not one of them."
Necro sighed,"I guess you are right. I will admit, I was going to keep Allanon's Journal for myself until you caught me with it."
Sho replied matter of factly,"case in point."

Nero sighed, "Alright, already. Anyways..should we go ahead and tell everyone that the portal is ready for them to go home?"

Sho replied back,"The sooner, the better, but do it quietly."

It was hard to be sure if this would all work the way it was intended, since the spell wasn't their own but everyone seemed confident enough to try it. So without further ado, Camp 1, Camp 2 and Camp 3 were all headed...home.

Epilogue

As each left the portal they felt a little dizzy. It seemed that only Camps 1 and 2 were there, just inside the town nearby the school. On the distant hill though, they saw Camp 3 and the school was also over there.

They'd just landed outside the portal and were in the town near where their school and it's students had just appeared. They'd be sure to visit the school and the others later, instead taking notice that everything about the town had changed. Various stores had come and gone, with new ones in their place. This didn't add up, Max grabbing a newspaper out of the top of a trash bin.

Max went pale," This... it says June 8th, 2024! That means it's been... One. Two. Three..."

Shakira, "About twelve years... and it's thirteen days until your birthday!"

Max replied, "Jericho, too. He and I were born on the exact same day, month and year... That means even though for me, I'm twenty-five years old... plus twelve, that's... Thirty-seven! If I'd still been here I'd be thirty-seven years old!"

Leon sighed, "Thirty-eight for me... but that's the thing, we're not. It's been much shorter than twelve years for us, and that's a fact."

Max nodded, "Sure felt like twelve years, all the hell we went through... we have all grown so much, and been through utter hell. Fought in all those wars. I was excited to be home, but I didn't even begin to expect this! I mean..."

Jericho interrupted, asking, "Are we going to stand around all day or are we going to figure out what to do next?"

Max responded, "That's not all... it says there is a ceasefire... it says one year ago there was a World War III!" And with that our heroes are left bewildered and unsure of what to do next!

To be continued...

Made in the USA
San Bernardino, CA
03 July 2017